⊰ THE INCREDIBLE ⊱
CHARLOTTE SYCAMORE

Kate Maddison

Holiday House / New York

Library of Congress Cataloging-in-Publication Data
Maddison, Kate.
The incredible Charlotte Sycamore / by Kate Maddison. — 1st ed.
p. cm.
Summary: Preferring adventure to an arranged marriage, the sixteen-year-old daughter of
Queen Victoria's royal surgeon sneaks out to sword fight with two friends when the three are
mauled by what looks like rabid dogs.
ISBN 978-0-8234-2737-6 (hardcover)
[1. Rabies—Fiction. 2. Conspiracies—Fiction. 3. Victoria, Queen of Great Britain,
1819-1901—Fiction. 4. London (England)—History—19th century—Fiction. 5. Great
Britain—History—Victoria, 1837-1901—Fiction.] I. Title.
PZ7.M2557In 2013
[Fic]—dc23
2012019564

*Dedicated with much love to my teenage daughter, Samantha,
who was the inspiration for Charlotte, and to my husband, Greg, for his
thoughtfulness and for always listening to my plot problems.*

ACKNOWLEDGMENTS

I owe many thanks to my wonderful agent, Erica Spellman Silverman, for encouraging me to write this book when I pitched it to her over a lovely lunch in New York. I feel very fortunate and honored to be represented by such a dedicated person, and appreciate all the hard work by the rest of my agency team at the Trident Media Group.

I would also like to thank my enthusiastic editors at Holiday House: Pamela Glauber for being a champion of the story and helping me to make it shine, and Julie Amper for her talented guidance and for taking such good care with the final details. I'd also like to thank my publisher, John Briggs, and editor-in-chief, Mary Cash, and the rest of the team at Holiday House for being so all-around amazing and devoted.

Thank you to illustrator Antonio Javier Caparo for helping Charlotte come to life in such an extraordinary way.

Thank you to author Kelley Armstrong who so graciously took the time to read the early manuscript, and gave me such a thrill with her generous quote.

None of my writing would ever be possible without the loving support of my husband, daughter, family, and friends. Hugs forever.

CHAPTER ONE

London, early June 1876

FATHERS don't need to know everything. Sometimes it's even necessary to tell them a fib or two, to keep them from worrying too much or jumping to the wrong conclusions. Especially my father, Dr. James Sycamore. He worried about every detail.

And there were exactly three details I omitted to tell him this evening:

I wasn't going straight to bed.

I snuck out of the Palace without permission.

I was sword fighting again.

If my father knew what I was doing at this moment, he would send me to my chambers for a month. He'd get that crushed look of disappointment on his handsome face, which the female servants keenly watched when he was unaware. He'd bow his head in shame and, without so much as requesting an explanation, give me a nod of dismissal.

That look. That nod.

In my defense, I was only being myself. Isn't that what he'd always taught me?

Charlotte, you must always be truthful to yourself and your beliefs.

But I wasn't allowed to be myself. Fathers are like that. They tell you to do one thing, but expect another.

So here I was, standing beneath the yellow haze of a gaslight well past midnight with my two closest friends, brother and sister Jillian and Peter Moreley. Twins, with the same friendly brown eyes. I brushed away my long black hair (at the Palace I was never allowed to wear it down) and adjusted the fencing mask to my forehead. I was testing one of my latest gadgets. Inventions were a hobby of mine, something else my father was only vaguely aware of. This invention, a lightweight sword whose blade tip rotated, ran on batteries that were charged by steam. It was meant for smaller persons who couldn't bear the weight of a larger blade but still wished for its power and might.

Me.

I buckled my leather padded vest and stepped into the deserted warehouse district of London. We stood somewhere between the flowing waters of the Thames and the slums where my friends lived. We were miles away from my embarrassingly luxurious residence in Westminster. (I mean, how many clocks can Buckingham Palace hold? Two hundred and twenty-three was surely enough, now wasn't it? They had two full-time servants who looked after the clocks alone.)

Dressed in a worn-out skirt and blouse loaned to me by Jillian, I faced Peter with my sword held high.

"On guard," I called beneath a cool sky about to burst with rain.

It wasn't truly fun sneaking out of the household unless I could share the adventure with someone. I'd missed Peter for the year he'd been gone, fighting pirates in the Royal Navy. Much had changed in him. His shoulders now filled his shirts and there was a new awareness about him, as though he looked at the world through a different lens. I wanted to stare at him longer to note these fascinating changes, but I didn't want to give him the wrong impression.

"On guard yourself. What in the name of God is that skinny thing?" Peter tilted his head and peered at my slender blade. His dark brown hair fell against his fencing mask—in a very attractive way, I might add. He looked at the clumsy metal hilt where the batteries were stored.

"Never mind," I said. "You'll be surprised what it can do."

He smacked my sword with his own. The strength of his blow vibrated up to my shoulder. The game was on.

"Nab him, Charlotte!" Jillian shouted with delight.

"Do your worst," he added with a laugh.

Jillian darted among the deserted buildings, a blur of reddish-brown hair and swirling skirts. My hems brushed the cobblestone street, sunken from centuries of footsteps and rolling wagons. My nostrils flared at the sharp smell of burning coal, horses, and sewage in the Thames.

Yet I loved my freedom away from Buckingham Palace. I snuck out once or twice a month, whenever my father was busy with his scientific meetings and we weren't traveling with the Queen to her other castles. Jillian was able to keep a secret better than anyone I had ever known. She'd never breathe a word to her mother, a carriage cleaner in the Queen's stables, that I was hiding in their wagon, leaving the Palace gates for the evening beneath a pile of horse blankets and straw.

"Still as dangerous as always, I see," Peter said with humor. He swung around a light post and lunged with his weapon.

I jumped out of reach and bounded onto a row of wooden boxes. "Did you catch any pirates while you were away?"

"Three. But none female."

"Pity. We make the most interesting prisoners."

"Charlotte!" Jillian scolded, but Peter only laughed.

We continued clanging and banging. A light rain misted my face. Jillian shouted, "Did you know Peter is staying home for good?"

My sword stopped in midair. "He is?"

Peter leaped at me. His blade came within an inch of my mask. I squealed in good fun, ducked, and rushed him with my weapon. I pushed the metal button near my thumb, hoping it would work this time. In response, the tip of my sword rotated and shredded a patch of his vest. He looked wonderfully shocked.

"What kind of weapon . . ."

"Yes, for good," Jillian continued. "Now that he—*we*—are seventeen, Mother says he's old enough to start training for a position with the Metropolitan Police. They hire as young as eighteen, you know."

Scotland Yard? How remarkable. I backed away to allow him to regroup, then wondered what it might be like to have a mother. The only thing I had to remember my mother by was the blue sapphire ring I wore. She was wearing it on the fatal night of labor and hemorrhage, when we'd met for a brief five hours and thirty-two minutes, according to my father.

"A bobby?" I smiled at Peter, calling him by the police nickname. "You'll have to better your game, then."

"Huh-ho. Really?"

We weaved round the corner, testing each other's blades in the dim light of a courtyard. We dodged bare wagons and empty barrels. A minute passed, perhaps two. All was quiet beyond the clicking of metal.

Too quiet.

"Jillian?" Trying to keep one eye on the game, I nervously glanced at the path from which we'd come. "Jillian?"

I lowered my sword. Peter followed with his. A faint growling noise echoed against the far stone walls. My pulse thumped against my windpipe. Something was wrong.

"Jillian!" Peter raced toward the foggy street and we sprang past the warehouse into another empty courtyard.

I careened to a stop beside him, my shoes slipping on wet cobblestones. We spotted Jillian, as frozen as a statue in Hyde Park, surrounded by a pack of six dogs. Teeth bared, they snarled at her. Black flesh rippled on their jaws. Their mouths frothed as though spitting dirty water, their demented eyes riveted on their prey. They looked diseased. There was a quiet whimpering. I realized with a gut-twisting wrench that it was coming from Jillian.

My thighs shook with terror. Jillian was fifty feet away, well beyond our reach.

"Easy," whispered Peter to the closest dog, "easy, boy, easy." He inched closer, sword poised. The other dogs swiveled their black eyes, as though in some machine-like unison, to settle on Peter.

Then the canine leader howled as if giving a signal and they swung back at Jillian. With a grotesque leap, the big beast sank its tainted teeth into her shoulder. It whipped her about like an onion by its stalk.

"No!" Peter shrieked, and lunged forward. He cut off the head of one that tried to attack him, then a second as he rushed to his bleeding sister, held unconscious by the beast.

"Stop!" I raced toward the dogs, pushing the button of my blade over and over in outrage, but it jammed.

Two of the dogs noticed my weakness. I watched in horror as they slowly circled. I followed the crazed eyeballs of one as it paced to my right. I was well aware that another was pacing to my left, looking for an opening. When the delirious eyes flashed, I made my move. I thrust my blade through the heart of the leaping giant, at the same time kicking out my left foot at the other dog.

My blade did its work. The giant fell.

However, the other dog had sunk its teeth into the top of my leather boot. I kicked my foot repeatedly, but it held on. I tried to scrunch my toes inside my boot to protect myself, hoping the little stab of pain was coming from the twisted leather and not the gruesome teeth.

There was no cure for rabies, once the symptoms appeared in a victim. I'd heard my father say it. Rabid dogs plagued London and all of Europe. When a person was bitten, the disease made its way to the brain and spinal cord, causing swelling and infection. Then came swollen jaws, frothy saliva, incredible pain, a lunatic madness, and death.

I gripped my blade, holding steady. I maintained eye contact with the sickly beast in the rainy darkness while it twisted my foot as though calculating the best angle to lunge at my throat. My inner thigh muscles stretched and burned as I tried to keep my balance, swiveling on one leg.

In the background, Peter bravely continued to hack limbs and fur and frothing jaws, and scream curses at the monsters.

The dog on my foot finally let go and leaped at my head. I screamed, lifted my sword and allowed it to impale itself. With a shudder, I withdrew my weapon and looked up at the wreckage.

The growling had stopped, all six dogs dead. But I was horrified to see that Peter lay crumpled, unconscious, by Jillian's side. He'd managed to cut off the head of the dog that had attacked her. Leaping forward to reach my friends, I slid through pools of black blood draining from the animals. Jillian lay pale and motionless—barely breathing. Part of her shoulder was gone. Her bleeding was massive.

My heart pumped madly. I clawed off the petticoat Queen Victoria had given me for my sixteenth birthday last week. She and I shared the same birthday, the twenty-fourth of May, but no one ever fired any cannons for me. I bunched up the cloth and put pressure on Jillian's wound. I tried to remember the medical things I'd seen my father do in the numerous cities we'd lived in over the years while he tended patients and I worked as his scrubbing girl, cleaning his equipment. I couldn't think of anything useful here.

Jillian's blood seeped into the fabric, then stopped as I tied it around her shoulder joint. I prayed for her life as I glanced quickly about.

My sword and padded vest were splattered with the dark blood of the dogs, but there was nothing on my hands. I removed my mask and pivoted on the balls of my feet.

"Peter? Peter, can you hear me?"

He lay still. I shook.

He'd just come back from a year away, and now this? I'd spent hardly any time with him. *No,* I refused to imagine such a loss.

My eyes blurred with tears, but I checked his injuries. Had he broken something? I ran my hands up and down his pant legs, as I'd once seen my father do for a fellow who'd fallen off a horse. I checked his shirtsleeves. All the bones seemed solid. The hem of his pant leg was shredded where a dog had chewed it, but Peter didn't appear to have any bites. I noticed a trickle of blood on his temple, and slid off his fencing mask. The skin was scuffed and bleeding. Had he fallen and knocked his head? Or was it a dog scratch?

What about my foot? Were all three of us tainted with rabies? Were we all doomed to die in madness?

How I wished my father were near.

"Help!" I shouted into the night rain.

Nothing but the distant sound of trains at the nearest rail station, the bray of a mule somewhere, the rustling of rain on spring trees. Then I heard the slow hum of voices very far away. Perhaps a tavern somewhere. There would be people there to help.

First I had to get my friends to safety. I turned toward the courtyard and spotted a barn. I dragged Jillian first, silently pleading that no more dogs were coming to attack. I laid her inside on a pile of clean straw and headed for Peter. That's when I noticed that the narrow street wasn't covered in blood.

It was covered in slippery black oil.

These weren't dogs. Their hacked steel limbs glistened in the rain, silhouetted by the glow of the gaslights. I'd never seen or heard of anything like them. They weren't made of bones and muscles and natural fur. They were made of metal bolts, screws, and artificial fur. These were some sort of mechanical monsters.

⚜

"Sir, wake up. There's an emergency! Wake up, sir! The Queen has a toothache!"

The heavy knocking on the doctor's wing of Buckingham Palace roused Dr. James Sycamore, Royal Surgeon to Queen Victoria. He was one of several on the team of royal physicians, but as their prominent head, and trained as both a physician and a surgeon, he was the one who currently lived and traveled with her.

"Thank you, Russett," James called through the door. He sprang to attention. His bare feet hit the cool wooden boards.

"Do you need assistance dressing, sir?" Panic rattled the man's voice.

"I'm fine."

The Queen favored protocol and would expect James to look proper, even at this hour. He slid into waiting clothes he always had ready—pressed shirt, cravat, and jacket.

The servants invariably reacted to the slightest ailment of the royal family as though it were a life-threatening event. However, an infected molar—which James had been watching for weeks—could never be as harrowing as some of their other medical conditions he'd treated in the past two years. A scalded wrist from too-hot tea. Foot surgery. Several high fevers in visiting grandchildren. An unexpected inverted birth. A miscarriage. Mental illness that still no one would acknowledge. Near-fatal malaria from a tour in India. An infected bladder because of which the Queen had to cancel all appointments until her discomfort had left. James, who always took great care not to breach the privacy of these situations, never explained the details to the servants.

He ran a comb through his black hair and turned toward the golden clock on the fireplace. Twenty minutes past two.

Grabbing his general medical bag off the desk beside the velvet drapes, he opened the door to his private sitting room. The manservant stood waiting to help, looking up at James. Russett, in his sixties, was the shape of an apple. The vest buttons of his dark uniform strained over his girth.

They dashed to the restricted medical rooms across the hall. Russett was breathing like a bear. His lantern lit up the walls of the great medical library, then row upon row of cupboards overflowing with medicines, tools, splints, and the best surgical equipment that money and power could provide.

How much should James take for a toothache?

Too much, as always.

He passed Russett his surgical bag, plus a bag of dental instruments. He added a drug and opium bag. Including the medical bag he'd taken from his bedside, that made four bags in total. Yet they were leaving behind so many—the pediatric ones, the obstetrical, and the traveling saddlebags he took to Windsor Castle and the summer castle in Balmoral, Scotland. He would toss those over his horse whenever he accompanied the Royals on a hunt, in case of falls or accidental shootings.

At this moment, James and Russett were so overloaded they had to leave the lantern behind.

By God, wouldn't it be easier if the Queen came to him?

But it wasn't his place to say. James strode down the hall at a good clip, the sound of his footsteps dampened by the Persian carpet. Russett waddled behind under the weight of equipment. Wall candelabras lit their way.

Something glittered on the burgundy damask wallpaper.

A Golden Butterfly.

James smiled as he rushed by, always amused to see an invention created by the Royal Gadget Engineer. This one was a large mechanical butterfly whose fluttering wings were painted with twenty-four-karat gold. It collected mosquitoes, spiders, flies, and bugs from the Palace walls and floors and delivered their carcasses to hidden trays emptied by the maids every morning. Two dozen Golden Butterflies roamed the Palace this time of year. In the winter months, when the bugs were fewer, the engineers released half as many.

They passed the hallway that led to Charlotte's chambers. James tilted his head instinctively to listen for signs of trouble, as any parent would; hearing only silence, he exhaled, content that his daughter was warm and safe.

Royal Surgeon to the Queen, yet you couldn't save your own wife in childbirth.

James tried to shake the thought out of his head. But along with the pleasure and pride he took in his esteemed position in the Queen's court, and in the culture and luxury he was able to provide for his young daughter, the guilt was always there.

His marriage to Beatrice had been arranged by his father. James had liked his wife on the day of their wedding, but on the day of her death he had loved her. What was all that sentiment good for, then? Marriage was for having children, and at thirty-eight he was no longer interested in marriage.

He was, however, interested in arranging Charlotte's.

Two more steps and they were there. His wing of rooms was positioned near the Queen's, for obvious reasons. He passed two whispering royal advisors, three servants milling about the Queen's doors, and finally two guards who surveyed him and his bags. All relaxed at the sight of James.

"How long?" he asked Russett.

The footman slid out his pocket watch. "Only three minutes this time, sir."

"Better than my last."

"Quickest surgeon we've ever had."

In a true emergency, such as an assassination attempt, he would've been here within seconds. There had been several attempts on her life so far, scattered throughout the years before he'd taken this post.

One of the guards gave a light rap on the door and announced, "Dr. Sycamore."

James entered the plush chambers. Thirty feet away, beside a massive four-poster canopied bed, the Queen's personal maids and one of her confidantes, a lady-in-waiting, hovered over her. Two magnificent black-and-white greyhounds lay quietly beside the roaring fireplace. Another dog, a sandy Pekingese, nestled in the bed against a royal leg.

"James," the Queen mumbled through a swollen jaw.

Dressed in a billowing black cotton nightshift buttoned high to the collar, she sank her rounded shoulders into the pillows behind her.

Her gray braid, usually pinned up, fell across her ample bosom. Furrowed lines of pain marred her forehead. One fussing attendant held a cloth to her left lower jaw. The Queen took it from her and shooed the woman to the foot of the bed.

He bowed his head toward the Queen in the proper protocol. Now that she'd spoken to him first, he was allowed to address her.

"Your Majesty. I'm sorry to hear you're in pain."

She spoke as if cotton wadding were stuck in her jowls. "You'd think we were giving birth, from how many attendants we have."

In her public duties, and if she wanted to maintain a distance between herself and others in the room, the Queen often referred to herself as "we" and not "I." She was speaking on behalf of a nation—some even believed she was speaking on behalf of herself and God, as in her God-given right to rule. When she was speaking privately with her family or friends, and usually with James, she used the singular "I."

In any case, given that the Queen was fifty-seven years old and widowed for fourteen years from her beloved Prince Albert, her comment was rather humorous. Indeed, what would the world think if she were again with child? James was the only one in the room, though, who dared to chuckle at her joke.

He placed his bags on her nightstand, motioned for Russett to do the same, then carried on with the Queen. "They say, Ma'am, that dental pain is worse than childbirth."

"That was probably said by a man with a toothache."

She was again making light of the situation. He always enjoyed her quick wit, but having been through nine deliveries herself, the woman was an expert on pain. He bowed his head to acknowledge her suffering, then walked backward to the basin in the corner to wash his hands. This ensured his back was never turned toward the Queen, giving proper respect to the woman who ruled one-quarter of the world's population.

He returned to her side, lowered himself into a brocaded chair, and gently removed the damp silk cloth from her jaw to have a look.

"Anyone not expressly needed here may leave," he said.

There was a shuffling around him as staff and servants curtsied and bowed while they backed out of the room. Soon only he, Russett, and one personal maid—Henrietta with the thick blond plait and gentle hands—remained.

"Russett, please remove the dogs." James turned to his patient. "Ma'am, I can best control the situation without the animals." *And some animals spread disease*, he thought, but saying this aloud might insult Her Majesty.

"As you wish," she murmured.

While Russett took care of the pets, James was very much aware that the door behind him remained slightly open for the guards to protect their Queen. However, he'd come a long way from two years ago, when they insisted upon remaining in the room while he did his examinations. The Queen could stand this annoyance for only two months until she gained full trust in James, and had since banished the guards to the halls.

"It's that molar I suspected would give you problems, Your Majesty. It's finally grown rotten. I'm afraid it needs to be extracted."

She sighed. "Take it out, then."

"Opium, Ma'am? Or would you prefer chloroform to allow you to sleep?"

"No question. I'd prefer chloroform."

There it was—the singular "I." It meant she felt safe and comfortable in his care.

And so he searched through his four wondrous medical bags, rifling through the exquisite instruments, the most expensive and rarest potions and medications that could be bought on any continent, and rendered the monarch of the greatest empire in the world unconscious.

CHAPTER TWO

I had nothing.

No bandages. No tonic to cleanse Jillian's shoulder or Peter's head wound as I'd seen my father do. No stethoscope to listen to any heartbeats—and whatever else those hollow tubes were used for. No one to take charge.

Terrified, I crouched in the straw beside my two unconscious friends. Thank God they were both still breathing. My heart pounded as loud as a meat clever on a butcher's block. Could I leave them here, bleeding and alone? Would more dogs come to tear them apart?

If I ran to the streets, would any monsters come after me?

Think.

My tutors consistently told me I had the ability to think clearly with a logical mind. They said it was why I scored perfect percentages on my science and mathematics exams. If it were up to me, I would've preferred to go further in my education, but last year my father stopped my studies to pursue what he called more "wifely skills." Embroidery, etiquette, and how to be a perfect hostess, a perfect wife.

Fat good it did here.

"Jillian." I shook her gently and pleaded. "Open your eyes, Jillie. If you could just open your eyes, I promise to curl your hair again just the way you like."

No reaction. Only the whoosh of my own panicked breathing. I turned to Peter and rocked his arm. "Peter, please. You've got to help me get her up. She's lost a lot of blood. Peter," I begged, "you promised me a game of dominoes."

He remained still.

My mind raced for options. Their house was too far away to reach. The Palace was ten times farther. What I had to do was find that tavern and secure help. *Now.*

I jumped up in the dimly lit barn, hearing for the first time how hard the rain was beating on the lopsided roof. It leaked in around the edges and splattered the straw in big blobs.

There were no blankets to cover my friends, but they'd be warm enough. I dragged a sawhorse over to partially block the view of their bodies, on the chance someone evil walked in. I hid our swords and fencing gear in the floorboards, then spotted a jacket hanging on the wall. It looked like a fisherman's raincoat, old and tattered, with a hood. I shoved my arms through the sleeves and rushed to the barn doors. I bolted two from the inside, but left a side door unlocked so I could get back in.

Running into the downpour, I realized I still hadn't removed my punctured left boot to inspect my own foot.

My big toe hurt, but I was too scared to inspect it.

The mechanical dogs had rabies symptoms, I believed, but I couldn't be sure of anything. Could fake dogs with rabies cause the same infection as real ones?

And who on earth could be responsible for constructing such monsters?

Around me, the hacked limbs of the dogs gleamed in the gaslight, their bodies shiny with rain, like glossy icing on a black cake. I hated those dogs. Black oil ran in rivulets down the streets to a nearby grate, into the newly completed sewer system of London. I turned away from it, ran past a warehouse and several blocks to the main street. I saw no one.

Whenever I had snuck out before, we usually stayed in Jillian's barn, playing card games and dominoes and talking well into the night, stopping now and again to pat her cow and feed her horse. We practiced dancing and sword fighting there. Last year, Peter had occasionally accompanied us to the Thames to watch the night boats pass by, but I wasn't used to the streets. Now I wondered if my two friends hadn't allowed me to see this side of London to shield me from potential danger. Tonight, *I* had pleaded that we go farther from home, to celebrate Peter's return. This was entirely my fault.

To my supreme happiness, I spotted two men in rags reeling out from a corner. One turned in my direction.

"Sir! Please stop!"

He tilted away, swaying as if his boots had come unglued from the ground, as I'd done so many times playing as a child, holding hands with another and spinning and spinning till we both fell over laughing. The other man stumbled to all fours on the curb.

I was breathless from running as I reached their side. "My friends are hurt. They've been wounded."

"How?" asked the man on his feet. He was older, with a long, untrimmed beard that trapped the rain. His front tooth overlapped his lower lip and wobbled, as if a good bite into a carrot might snap it.

"Dogs. Not real dogs. Man-made ones," I panted. "With rabies. I think."

The man on the ground sneered. He smelled of peat moss and stale beer.

"Please help me." I spun, arms wide, ready to show them where, but they didn't budge. "Please, there's no time to spare."

The man with the jutting tooth wavered, trying to focus on my face. The other hiccupped. I'd never seen poor drunkards before. Rich ones, yes, but not those needing a bath. Their behavior didn't look so different.

"Please," I begged. "You'll be amply rewarded. My father is the Royal Surgeon to Queen Victoria. I live in Buckingham Palace!"

They looked me up and down and blinked at my ragged clothes.

"Aye," the one with the loose tooth finally replied. "And my father was Abraham Lincoln." He patted his pockets as if looking for something. "Now where did I put me keys to the White House?"

His friend howled with laughter.

I wilted. They weren't going to help.

"Where are your doctors?" I shouted, looking frantically at the stone factories and shacks. "Which doors? Which houses?"

This produced more laughter. Why? My father held many meetings of physicians and surgeons—I knew because I organized tea and biscuits at every one—so I was well aware London had a great many doctors.

"Are you daft?" one asked.

"Such rubbish," said the other.

With a gasp of disgust, I left the laughing jackals. I ran round the corner in the direction from which they'd come. Perhaps the tavern was there.

I spotted two young women in capes entering an alley. Finally, kind-hearted women! I chased after them. One turned my way.

"Miss?" I asked, breathless.

She was oddly made up with cosmetics, rouge and lip color. Her eyes were rimmed with kohl, but due to the rain, dark lines were weeping down her pale and bony cheeks.

"Are you ill?" I turned to her plumper friend. "Are you taking her to seek help?" I thanked my lucky stars I'd run into them. We could go together.

"Mind your business," snapped the plumper one. "Get off our corner!"

Then the pale one started coughing and hacking so hard her cape shook.

"But you're obviously unwell."

"You stupid cow!" The weak one snarled at me and I jumped, hurrying down the street, confused as to why they'd be so angry and why they weren't seeking help. There were free clinics here. I'd heard my father and his colleagues talk of it only yesterday.

When I looked up again, a red sign with painted black letters announced THE BULL AND TALE. The hum of voices and banging of a piano filled my ears. I rushed inside. Heat from the fireplace and from the bodies of drinking men warmed me. That's when I realized what those two women were.

Streetwalkers.

I'd once overheard the Palace maids gossiping about those types.

Women who sold themselves for . . . for all sorts of vulgar acts with men they didn't know.

Had I actually spoken to a prostitute? *Get off our corner!*

They thought that I . . . I closed my eyes for a moment and swayed.

"Miss? Are you all right? I say, miss, what can I 'elp you with?"

Blinking, I looked into the round, clean face of a heavyset young lady. She had long, curly brown hair and wore a barmaid's tunic over her blouse and floor-length skirt. Had she been speaking to me for long?

"I need assistance," I mumbled.

"With what?" She was Irish. "Do you wanna drink?"

"No, please no."

"Matilda!" A customer, a man dressed in working clothes and with a bulbous red nose, flagged her from the other end of the long, winding bar. She turned to look, but the bartender got to him first and refilled his mug of ale.

Matilda turned to me once more. "You speak different."

"Do I?" I didn't want to sound too high-and-mighty again by declaring who my father was and where I lived. Why should anyone believe me? And any mention of mechanical dogs might have her laughing in my face, in similar fashion to those two men in the street.

"What can I fetch you?"

"I need a physician."

"You're hurt?" She looked me over, holding up a tray of empty beer glasses.

I shook my head.

"You seem a bit stunned. You're not from around 'ere, are you, miss?"

I shook my head again.

She scoffed. "There's no physicians in this place."

"My friends need help." My eyes stung from the bright wall lantern. "They've been injured—"

She held up a hand to stop me. "I don't wish to know."

Oh. I was momentarily startled. "Is there a hospital?" The rich didn't go to hospitals. Doctors came to the rich. But for the poor . . .

"Far away. But it's a true place of misery. You're forced to stay for weeks and sometimes leave sicker than arrivin'. Even so, to be admitted you have to prove you are worthy of the charity."

With a sinking feeling, I scanned the drinking men. "Is there anyone nearby with medical knowledge? Apothecary? Nurse? Midwife?"

Matilda studied me for a moment. "No one nearby. No one this time of night." Crackling light from the fireplace spilled over her tunic. For the first time, I noticed she had a bump underneath her clothing. Was she with child? She had a full bosom, too, and looked matronly, despite her youth.

She noticed me watching her and said softly, "I delivered three days ago."

I thought she was joking. I thought surely a woman doesn't deliver a baby and come back to work three days later, if not sooner. Where was her child? Who was looking after it? The confusion must've registered on my face.

"I'm tellin' you the truth because you look like you've been through a war."

Yes, my skirts were sopping wet and stained with black oil, and Lord only knew what my face and hair looked like. "Who helped you?" I pleaded. "Who helped you deliver your baby?"

"My sister was my midwife. She's lookin' after Sara now."

Relief flooded through me. Finally, someone older with experience who could help me bandage Jillian and know what to do with rabies.

"She's twelve," Matilda added.

"Twelve years of age?"

Matilda nodded. "Five years younger than me. She doesn't know anything. She can't help you."

I swallowed hard. That made Matilda seventeen. One year older than me. Yet she had a newborn baby. "There . . . there are free clinics in this area somewhere. I've heard of them. Where?" I swiveled my shoulders toward the windows. "Could you point me?"

"Free clinics?" Her eyes narrowed. "Yea, there was a free clinic 'ere last week. Everyone was excited. Line was three days deep. Slept in the streets, we did."

"What happened?"

"It was open for six hours. Said that's all they could do that day, but they'd be back in another two months."

"But how do you cope with illness here?" My voice crackled with frustration.

"We cross our fingers."

I stared at her, and at the faces of the men who were starting to bob around her, leering at me with interest.

My mission was useless, but perhaps I could still manage something from it. I lowered my voice to a whisper. "Could you please give me some towels to mop the blood? A tablecloth? Anything."

"You can pay?"

"No." I had no money in my pockets. I hadn't needed it with Jillian and Peter.

"If I did that," she said, "I'd lose my employment. Me and my baby and sister would be out on the street come mornin'. You see the man behind the bar? He owns this place, and I've done enough talkin'."

"Matilda!" A big man with muttonchop whiskers snapped at her from behind the bar. Matilda went racing back to work, but when her boss looked away, she stepped toward me again.

Her dark eyes glistened with sympathy. She tossed me the towel from her shoulder, then spun back to her tables.

I grabbed the cloth and ran out the door. I escaped the leering men, running and running and running through the rain until I was back at the barn. I recalled the large elm on the corner and the low fieldstone wall beside the barn, so I knew I was in the right spot. But the remains of the dogs were gone.

I looked about. Who could have taken them? The black oil had drained into the sewer and the rain had washed away our tracks. Then I panicked that Jillian and Peter would be gone, too.

I dashed in the side door. They were lying on the straw, still unconscious.

Whoever had removed the dogs didn't realize my friends were here. Otherwise, wouldn't they have tried to question them? Or . . . or perhaps tried to do them in for good? But then who could guess what went on in the minds of such criminals. I was only grateful that Jillian's bleeding had stopped and that both she and Peter were breathing steadily. I looped Matilda's towel across Jillian's shoulder for extra support.

Shivering to my boots, I removed the raincoat and hung it on a nail. It was dripping wet and only made me colder. I crouched on the straw beside Peter to warm up, feeling comforted by his nearness if only for a moment till I could think of a new plan. My bones dragged heavy with exhaustion. I'd come back to my friends as empty-handed as I'd left. How useless was I? I couldn't picture Peter ever coming back empty-handed. He always took care of everyone.

There was no choice; I had to go to their mother. Their house was far away, perhaps a mile, but it was the only option left. I could try to contact the police. I'd read in my father's newspapers that bobbies patrolled these neighborhoods, though I hadn't come across any. How was I to find one?

I should've asked Matilda. I should've done so much more.

Leaning against the stall boards with my knees pulled up to my face, I tried to remember the path we'd taken from Peter and Jillian's small barn to get here. My head slumped with weariness. Was it the right or left alley from the main street?

⊰⊱

A shouting voice startled me. Light seeped into the barn. Oh, no, I'd fallen asleep!

"Jillian!" boomed the deep male voice again. "Peter!"

Someone was calling from outside. With a quick look at my unconscious friends, I seized the raincoat and ran into the street. My hood protected me from the cold, damp morning. It had stopped raining, and the sun broke through some spots in the clouds. The place had come alive in the couple of hours I'd slept. There were factory workers heading to work, children walking to school, a shopkeeper opening his door across the way, and two men with a cart selling fresh bread to a line of customers.

These were decent people. Hardworking people I could relate to.

In the middle of all the commotion stood a man dressed in woolen overalls and a big gray hat, shouting, "Jillian! Peter!"

I didn't recognize him. He was roughly ten years older than me, with large, callused hands. Jillian and Peter's father had passed away long ago, so this man was an uncle, perhaps, or an older cousin. How many others were looking for them?

I lurched forward and held up a hand to get his attention, but no words came. I lowered my arm. Something stopped me from telling the full story—I feared that Peter and Jillian's mother might lose her employment at the royal stables if it became known that I had snuck out last night in her wagon. That all this trouble we three had gotten into would rest on her.

So I walked by him as if I were marching to work, too, then turned about. "I saw a young couple enter that barn. You might want to have a look."

"That one, miss?" He had a square, friendly face.

I nodded.

"Could you show me?"

"I'll—I'll be late for the factory." I marched on as if I had purpose, adding, "You'll want to know, I heard of dogs in the area last night. Demented dogs with rabies."

His mouth lost its color. "The saints be still."

I could only hope that he'd do all he could for Jillian and Peter. I raced off toward the Palace, fully intending to seek the help of my father.

My stomach growled. My forehead pounded. My legs felt like heavy cement sacks. Dizziness overtook me and I stumbled against a young boy.

"Miss? You feelin' all right?"

He was ten or eleven, yawning and half asleep himself. He scratched at a red rash on his wrist. A younger brother tagged along beside him. Both were blond, with a boxful of freckles scattered on their cheeks.

I tried to focus. My toes were numb—I hoped only from the cold. I had to find a place to wash my injured foot soon. "I'll—I'll be fine. You go along to school."

"We're not on our way to school, miss."

"But all these children." A dozen in my view. "There must be a grammar school nearby."

He yawned again. "No, ma'am, we're headin' to the factories."

Factories? My lashes fluttered. Yes, right. I'd often skimmed my father's newspapers when he thought I was tossing them out—*The Times* and *The Morning Post*. I knew young children of the lower classes worked. They went to mills and shops and farms and factories rather than their studies. Laws had been passed that prevented children younger than nine from working. I'd also read of other things—horrible crimes, murders and robberies, slum landlords and diseases.

I knew all of this intellectually, but I had never seen it in person. I had never felt the blow to my heart as I did now.

His younger brother chased after a frog that hopped from the cobbles to the grass, then turned and smiled timidly at me. He had a terrible red rash on his jaw, similar to the one on his brother's wrist. The younger boy's handsome front teeth looked as though they'd only just grown in and hadn't quite reached their full potential yet. How could someone with such young teeth be headed to work? I watched the brothers enter the side door of the leather mill across the street, followed by two slightly older girls, an occasional adult, and more children.

I weaved a crooked path in the street. Dizzy again, I fell to one knee. I stumbled back up, weak and worried how on earth I would make it home.

What I was seeing was overwhelming, completely different from the life I knew.

The sobs came without control. My father hated it when that happened, so I didn't let it happen very often.

"Do grow up, Charlotte," he'd say gently. "Tears are for children."

But I couldn't stop myself. I sobbed and cried like the naive, stupid girl I was. I cried for the yawning boy and his frog-chasing younger brother who would never open the pages of a book. I cried that Matilda had thrown me a towel at the risk of losing everything. I cried that last year at the Christmas luncheon, the Queen had accidentally nicked her finger with a table knife and I had counted eleven people jumping to help her, including my father. I cried for the cruelty of the person who'd developed the mechanical dogs, and that Jillian and Peter and I might now have rabies.

What kind of world did I live in?

I cried for my London.

CHAPTER THREE

WHERE was Charlotte?

Benjamin Ford, a sixteen-year-old apprentice groom working in the Queen's stables, carried two buckets of water to the Thoroughbred racehorses. He kept a watchful eye on the doors open to the court-yard outside. Dozens of staff were arriving for their duties. Some came straightaway from their residence on the property, others entered through the gates near Lower Grosvenor Place, all of them milling about the stables and carriage houses collectively known as the Royal Mews. But no Charlotte.

"Where could you possibly be?" Benjamin whispered to himself. "Hurry, Charlotte. Let me know you're safe."

It had to be half past six already, more than an hour past sunrise, when Mrs. Moreley, a helper to the carriage cleaners, usually pulled in on her wagon with her daughter, Jillian.

But even they hadn't arrived yet.

Something was terribly wrong. How long should Benjamin wait before going to Dr. Sycamore and confessing he'd helped Charlotte sneak out last night?

He would lose his job. Charlotte would be banished from talking to him ever again.

Perhaps the answer was simple. Maybe she fell asleep at Jillian's house.

He nudged the stall door with his thigh, walked in and poured his buckets into the trough. Carrying full buckets two at a time was a lot easier now than when he'd first started in this position a year ago. Not only had his muscles gotten bulkier from the practice, but he'd grown a full six inches, and now at sixteen he towered over most men.

The Thoroughbred mare with a glossy black coat nuzzled him, but he quickly retreated. He would've liked to pat her soft nose, but he wasn't permitted to touch the racehorses. Nor the Cleveland Bays, the Windsor Greys, the Arabian stallions, the American quarter horses, the Clydesdales, nor any horse ridden by any member of the royal family.

The animals were considered too valuable, and he was considered too uneducated in the matter of fine horses.

It made no difference that he'd been in a saddle since before he could walk. This morning, though, he'd been apprenticing for exactly one year, and one of the senior liveried helpers had declared that as of today, he would be allowed to handle the everyday horses used for the upkeep of the Palace gardens: the powerful Suffolk draft horses.

Benjamin had wanted to share the splendid news with Charlotte, but now he only wished to see her walk through those doors, safe and well. He wanted to see her collect her clothing, hidden in his personal trunk where she'd put her things last night, give him a smile, and leave for breakfast, as she did whenever she returned from an overnight stay at Jillian's.

He backed out of the stall, empty buckets in hand, and foolishly didn't look where he was going. He crossed the path of several men walking by and gazed straight into the face of a stout man in his mid-thirties with dark, swept-back hair: the Queen's eldest son, His Royal Highness the Prince of Wales. The man slated to be the future King.

Benjamin dropped a bucket in surprise. It hit the ground with a smack and rolled toward their boots.

"Pardon me . . ." He shouldn't dare address the Prince when he hadn't been spoken to first. *Idiot.* Feeling his face grow red hot, he turned to look instead at the annoyed veterinary surgeon to finish his comment. " . . . sir."

Benjamin snatched his buckets, backed away, and fled into the overcast morning. The breeze ruffled his black hair. Silently cursing his clumsiness, he hoped his blunder wouldn't affect his promotion.

While the Prince and Princess of Wales preferred to live in London at Marlborough House, it was said the Queen preferred her country palaces, especially Windsor Castle. He'd heard through the gossip channels that parliament had just given the Queen the title of Empress of India, taking effect this coming January. So her official duties had brought her into the city this week.

Which meant he would see more of Charlotte.

Worried again for Charlotte's safety, he scanned the extensive grounds. The Royal Mews was like a village unto itself, with stables that could hold two hundred horses, a forge, residences, and a schoolhouse for children of the staff. He didn't spot her, so he headed to the well.

He slipped his buckets under the pump and worked the handle, listening to the slosh of water as wagon after wagon, filled with all sorts of meats and wines for this evening's celebration at the Palace, passed by.

He wondered what it might be like to go to one of these fancy parties. He wondered about this one in particular, since it was a private affair and had nothing to do with the Queen, and what the guest of honor might say if he appeared.

His buckets brimmed with water. He turned to hoist them and spotted a girl in a ragged raincoat and hood who looked like Charlotte, sitting on the rear of a supply wagon.

He caught his breath, hoping it was her. But this girl was wearing a filthy skirt. When she hopped off the back of the wagon, she was slow and had problems walking a straight line. She dodged a horse and picked up her pace.

Benjamin pretended he needed extra time to lift his buckets, waiting for her to draw nearer. She tilted her hood up.

He spotted the long, straight black hair and green eyes, and exhaled all the worry that he had pent up inside of him in one long breath.

Head down again, protected by her hood, Charlotte walked right by as though she didn't know him. Easily lifting the filled buckets, he followed her inside to the stalls. Two barnyard cats scampered past, chasing a bird out the doors.

They passed several workers who were so focused on their duties that they didn't notice Charlotte, who looked similar to every other member of the staff. She slipped inside a far room, a cramped, unoccupied locker that contained Benjamin's trunk. He lowered his buckets beside a water trough, then, making sure the coast was clear, slipped inside the room with her.

"What happened?" he whispered, trying to steady his low, deep voice.

"A terrible accident. Jillian and Peter were mauled by dogs."

Fear returned with a hot jab to his heart. His friends. "They're alive?"

"Yes," she said, staring up at him, "but I think the dogs had rabies."

The news jarred him. He swiped his mouth with the back of his hand.

"Did their mother come to work?" she asked.

"No," he said softly. "I haven't seen Mrs. Moreley."

Charlotte ran her fingers across her forehead. "Poor lady must be dealing with it now."

"How bad?"

"Jillian's shoulder is ripped apart."

Benjamin winced.

"Peter bumped his head. He's unconscious. I'm praying he wakes up."

"What about you, Charlotte?" he whispered. "Are you hurt?"

She took a moment to answer. "I—I don't think so. But I need to speak to my father."

"You're going to tell him you were out?"

"I'm not sure. There's no telling what he would do. But I need to seek his advice for our friends in such a way that he won't discover . . . oh, I don't know what I'm going to say to him." She rubbed her temples as though it was too much to think about. "Could you please bring in your bucket? And a cake of soap? I need to wash my feet."

Voices carried, and people were passing outside the door. It wasn't safe to speak here, especially with the Prince walking about.

Benjamin waited until the voices faded.

"Couldn't it wait till you get inside the Palace? If I'm caught helping you bathe—"

"Please, I wouldn't ask if it wasn't important. And please don't toss away these soiled clothes. I need to show the oil stains to someone."

He looked down at her hems and the rim of black stains. It was useless to fight her.

"Whatever you ask of me, I shall always say yes."

"You've been such a good friend, Benjamin. There's so much more to tell you, but not here."

He opened the door a crack, peered out, saw no one, then left and returned quickly with one of the filled buckets he'd left by the trough. He pointed to a cake of soap and towel on a shelf and left her.

He found another empty bucket, and did one more round of pumping and hauling before she was ready to appear.

When he saw the door open a crack, he held up a hand to indicate she should wait. When he saw it was clear, he whistled a signal.

She stepped out, fully clothed in the blue skirt and form-fitting jacket she'd worn the night before. She must've left a hairbrush in his trunk, too, for her black hair had the sheen of a newly brushed mare.

Now that Charlotte was out in the open and wearing her own clothes, it wouldn't matter if anyone saw her. She could say she was practicing her riding. This was where many of the royal children and grandchildren took their lessons, as well as children of the upper circle of the Palace.

He tried not to stare at her, but she seemed much paler now than she'd been, and quieter.

She took another step and nearly tumbled into the stall boards.

Just in time, he caught her by the shoulders before she fell.

"Charlotte," he called in alarm, knowing how improper it was for an apprentice groom to be touching the daughter of the Royal Surgeon. He felt awkward and foolish. He had nowhere near the experience and sophistication of the young men in her circle.

"I think I'll feel better when I eat."

He released her. "Let's hope so. You have a big event this evening."

She regained her balance and patted her skirts. "I may not go."

"You don't mean that."

"How can I, with Jillian and Peter hurt?"

"I'll send word if I hear anything. They'd want you to carry on." He pointed through the open doors to the line of wagons heading down the wooded path to be unloaded at the Palace kitchens. The

Palace dogs—several large and small breeds—nipped playfully at the turning wheels.

"The feast has arrived." Benjamin eyed the heavy wagons. "And I imagine the maids are pressing their uniforms as we speak."

"It's a ridiculous party," she insisted.

"But you're the guest of honor. It's not every day a girl gets engaged to be married."

CHAPTER FOUR

IMAGINE going to an engagement party in your honor when your fiancé won't be attending. Imagine he was five thousand miles away on some ship—by choice—studying beetles and bugs in the rain forest of South America. Imagine you had to represent both of you before three hundred guests, smiling and pretending it was the loveliest night of your life, and having to preserve the secret that you didn't particularly care for Mr. Nelson Abercrombie. That you wished his trip would be prolonged indefinitely.

Imagine being engaged to a man you'd never met.

This was my life.

My father's idea.

I listened to the tick-tock of the clock as I lay smothered in a feather bed. Not fully rested even though I had slept till noon, I stared up at the high, plastered ceiling with its fine touches of gilding. I hadn't wanted to fall asleep, but sleep had found me.

My father was in with the Queen and wouldn't be available until after luncheon, I was told. I couldn't very well barge in on the Queen; her guards would likely shoot me. So I prayed that Jillian and Peter were receiving the help they needed until something could be done from this end, and decided to order breakfast in my sitting room.

I shoved the covers aside and sat up with no dizziness this time. I inspected my left foot, as I had when I was washing it in the stables. Not an easy thing to look at. My big toe was swollen, and once again I counted six red puncture wounds on it and the adjoining two toes. Dog bites.

What was I to do?

Was I dying?

I wondered how Mr. Abercrombie would feel if he unexpectedly returned from his business trip to a bride frothing at the mouth. It would serve him bloody well right.

He wished to marry me? He should be here!

In his two letters to me thus far, he had asked me to call him Nelson, but I was having a hard time of it, even in my head. At thirty-four, he seemed older than Hadrian's Wall. He was more than twice my age, four years short of my father's.

What did it matter if he was an acclaimed naturalist, a student of Charles Darwin? If my father enjoyed him so much, he should marry the man.

But fathers were fathers, arranged marriages were common, and as much as I had pleaded, my father remained firm. He'd gone over it with Mr. Abercrombie, and Mr. Abercrombie had agreed to provide me with a London home, a country estate if I should want one, and a "genetic background" (a term scientists liked to use) which would likely produce strong, healthy babies.

Ugh.

I tried to slow my thumping pulse.

I wasn't ready to be married. I fancied my freedom just the way it was.

The good thing about being engaged to Mr. Abercrombie was that he was far away. He was slated to return in perhaps two months, I was told, but I was dreading the moment.

For the time being, I'd stick to my plan. It was a tad daring, but I had nothing to lose. My plan was to keep writing letters to Mr. Abercrombie that were uninteresting and childish. He would grow tired of me, move on to someone more suitable to his fossil-loving scientific mind, and I would be free to marry an exciting young man of my own choosing.

But for today, I had to uncover exactly how rabies was transmitted. If I touched someone, or drank from the same cup, or shook their hand at the engagement party, could they catch it, too? Benjamin had touched me unexpectedly, as had the working boy who'd helped me outside his factory, but both times it had been through fabric.

If my father didn't arrive soon, I would go to his medical library and search through his texts.

I glanced to my own bookshelf beneath the bright windows that overlooked the Palace greenery. There were no medical books, only shelves and shelves of my personal collection: *The Swiss Family Robinson*, *Tales of Robin Hood*, *Aesop's Fables* (I had loved those growing up), *Mother Goose Rhymes*, *'Twas the Night Before Christmas*, a row of etiquette books, *Pride and Prejudice*, and the complete works of William Shakespeare.

My current favorite was *Romeo and Juliet*. I would have liked to meet Romeo. I would have tried to reason with him. I mean, why buy poison over the word of only one messenger? If he hadn't bought the poison, he wouldn't have had it to drink upon seeing Juliet sleeping in the crypt. True, he could have killed himself with a dagger instead— but that was debatable. I should try to remember not to be as hotheaded as Romeo in deciding my own fate.

Perhaps the mechanical dogs couldn't carry the rabies germ because they were made of metal. If that was true, I was worried for nothing. I wondered if this question about mechanical creatures could be answered by the Royal Gadget Engineer.

I wished I had some friends here. I wished everyone didn't treat me like a stranger, which I suppose I was, bouncing from palace to palace behind my father without a life of my own. I wished I could make my own decisions about who I wanted to be.

A slash of sunlight fell across the well-worn traveling trunk pushed against the wall. A symbol of instability, it was the only stable thing in my life. How ironic.

A loud rap on my exterior door carried into my bedroom. I recognized the knock. My father's.

"Coming!" I raced to the hook behind the door, threw on my robe, and flew through my private sitting room to the hallway door.

My chambers consisted of three rooms—bedroom, sitting room, and dressing area combined with bathing room. Maids weren't allowed into my bedroom uninvited if they thought I was sleeping. And my father usually never went beyond my sitting room.

"Good day, Charlotte." He entered in his formal suit. I could tell he'd been up for some time, for his shaved cheeks were starting to grow in again with a fine, dark shadow. His hair, black like mine, had a swirl that fell against his forehead, also like mine. We both had green eyes, too.

"Father."

He looked for somewhere to sit, but the settee was draped with the extravagant ball gown I would wear tonight. The maid had also taken out jewelry and accessories she believed would make an attractive match.

Before I could close the door again, a "between maid" appeared. Polly was a pleasant new girl, fourteen years of age and roughly my size, who alternated between the kitchen and bedchambers, wherever she was needed. Even her hair, always pinned back beneath her cap, was *between* the colors of gold and peach. Her face glowed with newly scrubbed freckles. She smiled and handed me a note, not fully trained yet that she shouldn't maintain too much eye contact with those she served. I liked that about her. It broke the loneliness I felt living here.

"Miss, a message for you."

"Who's it from?"

"I don't know, miss. It was found on a platter in the kitchen. I was told it has your name on it." Which meant she apparently couldn't read it herself.

"Thank you." She left with a dutiful nod, and I thumbed it open. It was brief.

It read *Word*.

No signature, but it could be from only one person. Benjamin had gotten word about Jillian and Peter. My heart began to pound. As I tucked away the note, I wondered if Benjamin had written it. If he had, it meant he could read and write, of which I was unaware.

"What is it?" asked my father.

I turned back to see he'd found himself a chair. He looked rather uneasy, leaning forward, hands on his long legs.

"A message about the . . . the party." Another lie. But this one was important. I would in no way expose a friend who was trying to help me.

"Charlotte, have a seat, please. I've come to tell you some difficult news."

He looked serious. What more could there be today? I reached out with slippery palms to the upholstered chair across from his. I gripped the ties of my robe as I sat down.

"I'm aware you sometimes go riding with one of the girls who works with her mother in the carriage house. Jillian Moreley?"

Oh, God, please don't tell me she's dead. "Yes?" I said weakly.

"There's been a terrible accident. She and her twin brother— Peter, I don't know if you've ever met him—have been quarantined."

"Pardon?" What on earth did he mean by *quarantined*?

"They were attacked by vicious dogs. It was the second attack last night. The first happened a few blocks away. Killed a man right in the street. A witness said the dogs were rabid."

My mind was reeling. There'd been another attack before ours? "How is Jillian?"

"Weak and dizzy. She lost some blood. Unfortunately, she'll be disfigured for life. If she survives the rabies."

My stomach went rock-hard with terror. I was quiet for a moment, clenching my fists in my lap. "How do you know? You saw her?"

"No, I was with Her Majesty. But I'm informed of everything that goes on in the Palace and the grounds, in terms of illness and injury. I must know, in order to protect the Royals."

"And her brother?"

"Unconscious. He was bitten badly on his ankle."

I was startled that Peter was still unconscious. And that I'd overlooked his bite. I had seen the hem of his trousers torn from the dog's teeth, but I hadn't thought to lift the cloth. How could I have been so careless?

"Isn't quarantine reserved for things like measles and smallpox?" My voice was getting shaky, but I couldn't suppress my nervousness.

"They're being kept in a house under lock and key."

"You mean someone can catch rabies from them? Wouldn't they have to ... even though they're people, wouldn't they have to bite someone?"

"I've never read of a single instance where rabies was transmitted from human to human. Even from someone with full-blown symptoms. As far as we know, you can only contract rabies by being bitten by a rabid animal. Dogs, foxes, bats."

My father read a multitude of books. He subscribed to several medical journals. *The Lancet,* for one. *British Medical Journal* for another. He was a contributor, a writer himself. On two occasions, he'd asked me to double-check his spelling because his assistant wasn't available and there was a deadline to meet. I didn't completely understand all of the medical terms, but my written grammar was excellent. And I'd found no mistakes.

Yet I had to be sure I understood. "What if—if Jillian or Peter's saliva came in contact with someone?" I looked at the bone china on my breakfast tray. Should my dishes be destroyed?

"Saliva is not enough to transmit the germs."

"What if they touched someone's skin? Can that person catch rabies?"

He shook his head. "Impossible."

"What if someone came in contact with their blood?"

"You're asking a lot of specific questions, Charlotte. You needn't worry too much about this. And the answer there is no, too. Rabies cannot be transmitted simply from touching their blood. Theoretically, I suppose it could happen if the blood gets into another person's wound. But I've never heard of it happening, nor read of it."

Which meant no one could contract it from me, either. Such a relief. "Then why?" I pleaded. "Why on earth imprison them if they're not putting anyone else in danger?"

"It's hardly an imprisonment, Charlotte."

"It is. They're being jailed. Jillian and Peter would think so. Please, as a man of science, you can't agree with this."

"When you get into a mob mentality, Charlotte, sometimes it's better to lock up the people affected by an illness. You're too young to remember, but ten years ago there was a great epidemic of cholera in London. It killed thousands. People fear this sort of thing, even when their facts are wrong. They panic. Sadly, if Jillian and Peter were allowed to leave their confinement, they would likely get attacked by a mob and not survive. They are safer locked away."

They were being jailed for their own security. How sad. I gulped. "What are their chances of developing rabies?"

"Charlotte, I don't favor upsetting you—"

"*Please.*"

I didn't blink as he weighed his answer. I had to know.

He sighed. "Well, considering the extent of their injuries . . . that they were clearly bitten by the dogs . . . ninety-nine percent."

My head swam. I felt as though I would throw up. This also meant *I* had a ninety-nine percent chance of a death sentence.

If I lifted the edge of my robe and showed my father my injured toes, he would surely imprison me, too. Or if not he, then the advisors to the Queen. No one took any chances when it came to the Monarchy. I couldn't let my father know I'd been bitten.

"Come to think of it, sir, I was out in the stables this morning. Looking at the horses and preparing for my next riding lesson."

He pushed away the black hair at his temples. "Yes?"

"And I thought . . . I thought I heard someone talking about dogs. That there'd been an attack. I never pieced it together till just now." I had to let him know *somehow* that the dogs weren't natural but man-made, even if I had to make up an imaginary conversation. Perhaps then he'd change the ninety-nine percent death sentence to zero.

"So word had gotten out early. I was with the Queen and wasn't informed until minutes ago."

"And this may seem quite strange. But I thought I heard someone mention they thought the dogs were mechanical."

He shoved his wide shoulders back into the chair. "Mechanical?"

"Yes. You know, like our Golden Butterflies."

"Who said this?" His green eyes flickered.

"I—I don't remember. There was a crowd around me. In my etiquette classes Mrs. Burnhamthorpe is always instructing me not to eavesdrop, so I tried not to. But they—whoever it was—said they heard some dogs last night had black oil and metal parts and were vicious and they looked like they had rabies—"

"They're confused. There's no such thing as metal dogs. They must've been telling a story, Charlotte, and you didn't hear the full conversation. That's exactly why Mrs. Burnhamthorpe tells you not to eavesdrop."

"You're quite right, sir. But . . . do you think it's possible to construct a mechanical dog?"

He took his time answering. It was truly one of the things I admired and adored about my father, that he was open-minded when it came to science. Narrow-minded when it came to his daughter, but he had a great capacity and imagination for nature and mathematical calculations and possibilities mankind had never thought of before. Once, I had even heard him asking the Royal Gadget Engineer if there'd ever come a day when men could harness enough steam power to make a machine to fly to the planet Mars. Imagine, my father believing that possible.

"I suppose, if men could make a clockwork butterfly," he said, leaning back in his chair, making it creak, "others could make a clockwork dog."

It gave me some relief that he thought it possible. But what should I do with this now? I suddenly realized I was the only one who'd actually witnessed that the dogs were made of metal and springs. As soon as Jillian was bitten on the shoulder, she fell unconscious. Peter, too.

My robe slid beneath me as I shifted on the chair. "Who is the poor man who lost his life?"

"A street beggar, I'm told. Seems he was getting ready to participate in a robbery when he was attacked and killed by the dogs. His accomplices got away with stolen merchandise. Dozens of solid silver spoons."

Were they the same artificial dogs that had attacked us? I could barely focus on those details, so worried was I about my friends. I knew there was no cure for rabies once symptoms appeared, but was there something to prevent the disease in the early hours?

"Now that you're done with the Queen, are you heading off to see Jillian and Peter directly? Bring them medicine to stop the rabies?"

"There is no medicine to stop it, I'm afraid. Only a poultice to keep the wounds from festering. Perhaps an opiate for the pain."

Was there no hope of preventing the rabies? I lowered my head, struck by the devastating blow. "They'll appreciate whatever you give them."

"You misunderstand." He shook his head. "I'm not going to visit."

"Why not?"

"I'm the Royal Surgeon to the Queen."

"How does that make any difference—"

"Don't raise your voice, young lady—"

"They need your help—"

"Enough, I said!"

I was breathing hard. I lowered my voice, but the words still contained heat. "Since you take care of the Royals, where do the servants go when they need help?"

His features—straight nose, firm jaw—didn't budge as he stared at me. "Are you accusing me of casting them to the streets?"

"It's a simple question, sir, from your daughter."

He softened. "They have their own physician who is made available. Dr. Kenyon. He doesn't live here in the Palace, but he's assigned to check on the health of all the staff. Their skin, their teeth, their ailments, whatever they need. I've sent word for him to go."

He made it sound as if the servants were livestock. "But not you?"

"Charlotte, I have sworn allegiance to the Queen and the royal family. My hands cannot touch the bodies of other infected people while I'm in Her Majesty's service. And don't give me that face. It's to avoid the transmission of disease, not for any other slight. Imagine if I carried something to Queen Victoria and she fell ill. Imagine if she contracted diphtheria, or one of her grandchildren whooping cough. I dare say I would be sent to the gallows. And perhaps worse than losing my life, imagine the pain and chaos it would cause in the British Monarchy."

All hope drained out of me. He wouldn't help. I was alone.

My father rose to leave. Towering over me, he glanced at my ball gown on the settee and gave me a weary smile. "Try not to think about this, Charlotte. Dr. Kenyon will do what he can for your friend and her brother. All you can do is send a prayer. Then try to enjoy the pleasure of preparing for your special evening."

"But sir," I called out, "how long does rabies hibernate inside the body before symptoms arrive?

"Charlotte, you ask too many questions. You needn't worry about that. It's too gruesome. I'll see you at the reception."

He stepped out the door and closed it. When the latch clicked behind him and echoed against the walls, it punctuated how isolated I was in this battle.

There was so much I had to do before the party began.

CHAPTER FIVE

HE was there. My father's grumpy assistant, Mr. Bloomberg.

"Uh," I muttered under my breath when I dashed into my father's medical rooms and nearly bumped into him. I was terribly worried about Jillian and Peter and wasn't paying attention.

"What on earth?" Mr. Bloomberg, in his late twenties and ever so tall and wiry, looked down his pointed nose at me. He took a few steps forward between the massive cupboards, walking in his usual strange manner—knees first. His knees entered every room before the rest of him did, which gave him the air of a cantering horse. "Watch where you're going, child."

"I'm sorry." I despised it when he called me a child. It was his way of needling me. Especially since I was old enough to be having an engagement party in six hours. My temper sprang to my lips. "But perhaps you shouldn't be standing behind the door, Mr. Bloomberg." I tried to sound more respectful than I felt.

He clicked his tongue in annoyance—a sound I was used to hearing from him—and rudely turned his back. He searched the shelves of the huge medical library as I wondered how to reach for the textbook on animal diseases. I needed to discover all I could on rabies, for perhaps there was a morsel of information I could use to counter the effects of the mechanical dogs. A fireplace crackled and popped at the other end of the room, sixty feet away.

"Shouldn't you be fussing over your hair or something?"

"Plenty of time for that." There wasn't really. I had barely escaped my personal maid as she'd laid out lotions and body powders in preparation for my bath. I'd vowed to return in no more than an hour to dive into the tub and wash my hair. But I knew that an hour wouldn't be long enough, because I still had one more place to visit after this.

"I promised my father I'd wash his instruments," I said, fabricating an excuse to be here. "He was in with the Queen this morning, you know."

"Of course I know," he snapped.

I knew that he knew—it was my way of needling *him*.

I headed straight for the washing vats, worried because my left shoe now felt a lot snugger than my right.

Just as I suspected, the dental instruments used on the Queen were soaking in antiseptic solutions, and I could clean them as I tried to think how to reach the textbook. I slid into a large working apron and tied it across my front. I had changed out of my robe into a fashionable day dress, with its double skirt and long, buttoned bodice.

For some reason, Mr. Bloomberg had taken an instant dislike to me six months ago when he'd started training as an apprentice surgeon with my father. I had tried to be kind and welcoming, helpful even, showing him the library and the instruments, but the more helpful I became, the more his irritation grew. Finally I realized the man resented my proximity to my father and involvement in his work—as small as it was—and definitely did not wish to discuss anything of scientific value with a girl.

I wondered if he would respect the Queen's opinion, for she, too, was female, but my father would be mortified if I ever implied it about this man.

Unfortunately, Mr. Bloomberg was a distant cousin of Her Majesty's favorite footman, Russett, and this relationship had gotten the apprentice surgeon firmly rooted in the royal household. Mr. Bloomberg's family was quite wealthy from owning a fleet of ships, and proudly supported his training with the Queen's surgeon.

The man's snarly attitude and comments toward me never surfaced in front of my father, so it would always be my word against his.

I would never let him win.

I bent over the basins and reached for the instruments, trying to puzzle out how to gather the necessary supplies for Jillian and Peter without being seen by Mr. Bloomberg. Nervously, I hummed as I worked.

"Could you stop humming? I'm trying to read."

My throat clamped up. I knew he was preparing for one of his oral examinations next week. He was always in the worst mood when he was studying.

Perhaps his distraction could work to my advantage. I turned to the cupboard that held opiates and pain relievers. With a glance to ensure the bully was occupied, I walked toward it as though searching for more antiseptic solution, then opened the cupboard and spotted a dozen packets of morphine tablets. I scooped three into my pocket.

My hair stood on end in fear of being caught, but when I turned back, Mr. Bloomberg was bent over an anatomy book and thumbing through diagrams of the human stomach.

With another flash of confidence, I slid a jar of cleansing solution and powders for making poultices to a lower shelf, then a roll of gauze.

I threw a clean towel around all of the supplies to hide them. When the materials clattered together, I nervously cleared my throat to mask the noise.

"For God's sake," said Mr. Bloomberg. He looked up as I was bending over my cache of about-to-be-stolen goods, causing me to quake in my polished leather shoes. "Would you pipe down?"

"Frightfully sorry."

Swinging back to the tray of soaking dental instruments, I rinsed off the blood and dipped them into soapy water. Two barrels of clean water were positioned beneath the far window, along with a filled basin that was warming in the sunshine. The fireplace blazed at the far end, in case I needed it to boil more water.

I lifted an empty pail, pretending I was going to do just that, while I surveyed what else I could take that would assist my friends.

After filling the pail with water from a barrel, I took it to the special machine nicknamed "Fireworks" by my father. It was a copper and wood contraption three feet high, shaped like a tree trunk. It had been invented by the Royal Gadget Engineer to disinfect surgical instruments. It spun over the floor on rollers, and had three stacking segments with various spikes to hang pails and cauldrons over the heat. It was connected to the wall by three cables filled with steaming water, which supplied it with power.

After placing my pail on the Fireworks, I opened another cupboard that contained beautiful royal blankets. I ignored the silky big ones and reached for a lavender baby blanket made of long-staple cotton. The tag read *Gift from the King of Saudi Arabia.*

There were three others beneath it, different colors, with tags that said the same thing. There were no babies currently in the Palace, so the blankets weren't needed.

With a snap of the string, I removed the tag and tossed it into the fire. The flames flickered for a brief moment, then the tag was forever gone. Surely no one would miss the blanket among the dozens and dozens here. I clutched the softness to my chest—I would arrange for its delivery to the barmaid, Matilda, as an anonymous surprise. If only I could find a way to get it there.

On to the next article. A new invention from America.

My father had been very keen to show me the crate when it arrived not too long ago. It held over three dozen jars, with several gone because he had already distributed them to members of the royal household. I had heard that the Queen herself loved the invention.

I went straight to the jars, lifted one, and jammed it into my apron pocket. It was called Vaseline.

"Made of petroleum jelly," my father had told me. "A byproduct of oil drilling. You apply a thin layer onto the skin. It has wondrous healing properties for cuts and scrapes. Not to mention preventing rashes on the bottoms of infants."

It would be perfect, I thought, for Matilda's new baby.

Unfortunately, I would need help with the final item. I pictured the rash of the two boys who were working in the leather mill. I didn't know what sort of disease they had.

"Mr. Bloomberg, sorry to bother you, sir." I placed a tea towel on the bottom of a cauldron, then removed the dental instruments from the soapy water and placed them on top of the towel. I poured clean water onto it all, intending to boil the instruments for a good half hour for their final cleansing. "I know you covered skin diseases last month, and I was wondering if you might help me—well, not precisely me, but one of the maids. She's developed a skin rash on her wrist."

"Why don't you go to your father?"

"He's occupied with Her Majesty today."

Mr. Bloomberg grumbled something. "What's the rash look like, then?"

"Overall, pink. Tiny red spots thrown about."

"Are the red spots bleeding?"

I raised my head in alarm. "Bleeding?"

"Flea bites? Ticks? That sort of thing," he said with exasperation.

"No, no bites."

"Do the red spots have white heads? Or watery pustules?"

I shook my head. "Just a bumpy redness."

"Likely a skin reaction to something. A strong flower of some sort. Or perhaps she's been working with hay or wool."

Hay. Straw. *Straw mattresses*. That's what the boys had reacted to.

"I'll let her know. Thank you. Do we have any ointments that might help the itch?"

"Top shelf to your left. In the tin. It has an oatmeal base."

"Thank you." I reached for it, looking over my shoulder as I did. He'd flipped a page and was now studying a diagram of the chambers of the heart.

I was feeling generous. Perhaps Mr. Bloomberg and I could bury the hatchet.

"Would you like me to quiz you?" I asked with a timid smile. "I'll have lots of time tomorrow, if you'd like." Maybe I could make a friend out of him and he could in some way, unknowingly, help me with my rabies. "I could pretend to ask you questions like my father would—"

"Who on God's green earth do you think you are?" His voice rumbled. He stiffened. "A child asking *me* questions?"

My face flooded with a thousand degrees of heat.

I glanced at the open book in his hands: *Anatomy of the Human Organs*. I had read most of the book last summer out of boredom when I was trapped here helping my father clean, sanitize, and reorganize his cupboards. At first I was intrigued by the magnificent ink sketches, then found myself reading the captions, then finally whole sections.

I certainly knew enough to quiz anyone about it, and could prepare especially good questions if I had the text right in front of me.

"Mind your business, girl." He snapped his fingers repeatedly in front of my face. "Get that cauldron hung and be out of here. Don't bother me with anything else."

How dare you snap your fingers at me, you wretched beast! Why are you so miserable?

I bit the inside of my cheek to keep myself from saying it.

Humiliated, but not wishing to jeopardize my hidden supplies, I did as I was told. I wasn't able to acquire any books on rabies, but at least I had something. Straining beneath the weight of the cauldron, I huffed my way to the Fireworks and planted the handle on a sturdy spike. I dialed thirty minutes on the mechanical timer and listened to the sputtering steam cables, all the while trying not to sputter at Mr. Bloomberg.

However, my fury made me bolder. I snatched a pretty wicker basket with a lid, slid my treasures inside, and sailed out of the room, right beneath his arrogant nose.

This was a man never to be trusted.

⊰⊱

Peter's mind flashed in and out of consciousness.

Black sky . . . vicious dogs . . . snarling louder and louder. His eardrums beating blood.

He had to turn away . . . he tried to move but his body wouldn't budge. Jagged dog teeth floated closer. Their growling rumbled through him like a locomotive.

He tried and tried to push up against the heavy blackness. The jaws opened. His pulse thundered. His eyelids flew open. With a snap, he bolted up in bed.

Conscious.

Sweat drenched his clothing. He gobbled air.

Where was he?

He didn't recognize the place. He was in a small room in a dilapidated house, in a narrow bed with a scratchy brown wool blanket. A crooked window, slightly open, gasped in daylight and noise. The view looked onto a dirty brick wall, which meant he was on an upper floor.

His ankle throbbed with pain. A headache seared his temple. He held his head and tried to recall what had happened the night before.

Sword fighting by the warehouses. Jillian laughing that he'd come home.

Charlotte engaging him to fight.

Where were the girls now?

Panicked, he swung his legs over the edge of the bed. The movement came too fast and caused his head to swim. He closed his eyes for a moment to compose his brain.

Dogs. Big black dogs with dripping snouts.

He shuddered and opened his eyes again to erase the image. Then he remembered: rabies!

"Jillian! Charlotte!" He listened through his open bedroom door. Nothing.

He heard faint voices from the window—traffic of wagon wheels, the calls of men, everyday noise of pedestrians going about their business.

"Jillian!" he called again, remembering that she'd been savagely attacked. He rose from the bed. The pain in his ankle flared, reminding him he'd been bitten, too. He cursed the dogs under his breath.

Then he thought about Charlotte. What had happened to Charlotte?

He shuffled to the hallway. It was dim, the doorways small and cramped, wooden floors scuffed and stained from decades of wear. He peered down the narrow, two-foot-wide stairway. It led downward to a bolted door on the ground floor. He wondered what was beyond it. There were two more doors on this level, plus an open nook that served as both a sitting area and kitchen. Lopsided cupboards protruded above a standing dry sink that contained a chipped porcelain basin. Mice scurried about the filthy base. The fireplace was unlit and he realized how cool it was in the house.

Everything smelled stale, like mold and cobwebs.

Who'd brought him here and left him? He was in the same trousers he'd worn while sword fighting, but a different shirt. A clean one.

"Charlotte?" He took a step forward into the hall and opened the door beside his. No Charlotte. It was a small bathing room with a tin sitting tub, a few mismatched shelves, and a faded wall mirror.

"Jillian, where are you?" When he opened the next door, he found her lying still on a cot. "Oh, Jillie."

She was sleeping. Or still unconscious? He sat on the edge of her mattress, the straw crunching beneath him as he gently turned her toward him. Her left shoulder was wrapped in towels soaked through with dried blood. He winced at the mess.

He called her name again and patted her fingers. "Can you hear me?"

There was no response.

Should he try to shake her awake? Was it better that she sleep through her massive pain? Maybe someone had given her medicine to help ease it.

He scoffed at the thought. As if anyone of his kind would be able to afford medicine. Liquor, yes, but he couldn't smell any on her.

He left her to look for Charlotte, leaving the door open.

He soon realized Charlotte wasn't here. He hoped that meant she'd made it home safely. Had she been bitten, too? When he'd last seen her, he didn't think so, but then he'd blacked out. Did her father know what had occurred last night? Maybe she was in deep trouble now, confessing, but perhaps bringing help for his sister.

Peter couldn't be sure of anything.

He made his way down the narrow stairs, having to turn his wide shoulders slightly to make it through. When he reached the landing, he turned the doorknob. It was locked.

He gave the wooden door a good bang. "Let me out! Hey! Open up!"

A peephole, three inches by three inches, opened and a rotund red face appeared. The man had red whiskers. "What in bleedin' 'ell is all the ruckus? Keep it down, or we'll have to gag you as well as lock you up."

"Let me out."

"Not today."

"I demand you release us. We've done nothing wrong."

"Simmer down and accept what you got. At least you're not dead like the other one."

Peter's lungs stopped moving.

Charlotte?

His heart weakened. Oh, no, please. "What—what do you mean *dead*?"

"The other 'un attacked by the dogs. Was torn to shreds. Saw the face myself." He shook his head. "Ack. You wouldn't want to know. You're lucky you got put in there, before the crowds got to you. Dare say it was the work of your uncle and your mother."

Peter barely heard, so lost was he in the news he'd just been given. Charlotte was gone? Torn to shreds by the dogs?

He stumbled back against a cold stucco wall. Bile rose in his throat and he felt as though he would vomit. What a way to leave the earth. God, how she must've suffered. The torture . . . all alone. He hadn't even spent any time with her, not the kind he wanted to spend.

And he hadn't done one damn thing to help her. He cursed and slammed the wall.

The peephole cover creaked again. A big, dark human eye strained to look in.

"You, there," his jailer called. "Best simmer down and not make yourself a nuisance. People won't stand for it, you know. Some say— the kinder ones—that you should be put out of your misery *now*, your sister and you. Before the madness of rabies twists your brain. What say ye to that?"

Peter's pulse took a mad leap.

"If you'd like," the brute continued, "you can edge a little closer to the door. I'll rip a bullet through your chest. I don't mind, you know. I'd do it for me own brother."

Peter gasped and leaped away from the door. He clawed his way back up the stairs. He perspired in terror, wondering how he might protect his sister against the enemies outside the door, and his heart clenched at the desperate thought that he'd lost Charlotte.

⋇⋇⋇

"Polly, can you read this?" Ten minutes after I left Bloomberg in the medical library, I grabbed the young maid as she was stripping the sheets off my bed. I thrust the note and instructions I'd written for Benjamin beneath her nose.

"Would you deliver this basket to the person here?" I pointed to his name.

Polly's cheeks colored. "I'm sorry, Miss Sycamore. I don't read."

What a relief. I had suspected she couldn't, but had to be sure. It meant she'd be perfect to deliver the wicker basket and medical instructions to Benjamin. Since I didn't know her very well and wasn't sure if she'd betray me, the less she knew, the better.

I *was* hoping that Benjamin could read. Otherwise, he wouldn't understand what any of these medical supplies were for. I had already applied some of the poultice liniment to my own injured foot, hoping the swelling would subside and no infection would take place. But I was alarmed by how quickly my foot had already swollen up.

I looked again at Polly. Could I trust her?

Did I have a choice?

"Polly, you remember the cake of lavender soap I saw you touching last week?"

Her eyes widened and she swallowed hard. She slapped at a pillow to fluff it. "I'd like to apologize again. It ain't my place to be testin' anything. It's just such a pretty scent, and I never seen nor felt anything so delicate."

"I'd like to give it to you as a gift."

Her head snapped up in surprise.

"You seemed to enjoy it so much," I explained.

"Oh, no, I could never . . ." She shook her head. Her cap slid about on her light hair. "If the headmistress should ever find it in my bedroom, I'd lose my job."

She was right. How could a between maid justify having such a luxury in her tiny bedroom above the kitchens? They'd accuse her of stealing.

"Then I'll tell you what. I'll keep the soap on the small pewter dish in the bathing room. You know it?"

The maid nodded.

"I won't touch it, but we'll both know it's yours to use whenever you come inside my rooms."

"Miss Sycamore, that's awfully generous, but—"

"It would make me very happy. You remind me of a younger cousin. I don't get to see her very often. She lives in Scotland. And please call me Charlotte when we're alone."

Polly's face turned the color of strawberry jam again, but she smiled slightly, as though pleased. "I don't have any family, myself. Not anymore."

"Maybe in return, you could deliver this basket and note to Benjamin Ford in the Royal Mews. He's an apprentice—"

"Groom," Polly finished for me.

"You know him?"

Polly looked away as though embarrassed to reveal she'd noticed him. "Never spoken to him, myself, miss . . . I mean Charlotte . . . but some of the maids in the kitchen . . ." Polly didn't finish, and concentrated on folding a blanket. Obviously, some of the maids in the kitchen had noticed Benjamin.

Of course they had. He was handsome. Funny how I hadn't realized it till now. Last year when he'd first arrived at the royal stables, and I'd just returned from the Isle of Wight with the Queen, I was simply interested in making a friend. He was a boy who tagged along behind my father and me, awkward and self-conscious in his rubber boots and barely able to look me in the eye. Now here he was, taller and bigger and turning the heads of the kitchen maids.

Polly scooped up all the sheets. "I'll do it, don't you worry. I'll get the note to Benjamin."

"Without telling anyone?"

Polly nodded as if it was the most natural thing in the world I was asking.

I slid the note inside the wicker basket. Polly grabbed the handle and tucked the basket beneath her pile of sheets, totally hidden from view. She marched out of my rooms toward the laundry.

I hoped with all my heart I could trust her. I looked at my settee and all the clothing set out for my engagement party. It would have to wait. I grabbed my cloak and raced out the door. There was someone else I had to see, and it was urgent.

CHAPTER SIX

I loved this place. I loved everything about the Royal Gadget Engineering Hall—the stone architecture, the spires, the vaulted ceilings. Most of all, I loved that it was never boring here.

Fortunately, it was located on the grounds of the Palace, which was considered my home, so I was never required to visit with a lady's companion or chaperone. I came and went as I pleased.

Perhaps I'd find some answers here about the mechanical dogs from Mr. Harold Snow. He ran the department. He alone held the title of Royal Gadget Engineer. Everyone beneath him was a junior engineer.

I entered the front doors. The hiss and sizzle of the thirty-foot-tall steam machine in the foyer vibrated pleasantly through my body. The sound was soothing, although not soothing enough to distract me from the fear of losing Jillian and Peter. Mr. Snow, who'd created the steam machine, had nicknamed it his "Silver and Glass Spider" because of its eight legs. It had a round, silver body. Eight curved steam tubes made of glass stuck out from its sides. Hot water bubbling inside the tubes was tinted an amazing turquoise. The water raced up from the concrete fountain the machine sat on through the twisting tubes to the top, and gushed over into a waterfall. It looked as though the spider was giving itself a spray shower. Mesmerizing to watch. In the lower floor, beneath this massive structure, blast furnaces were fed by wagonloads of firewood. The furnaces heated the water in the fountain, and the resulting steam power provided all the energy needed for the gadgets being developed here.

"Afternoon, Miss Sycamore." A guard near the door nodded at me.

"Nice day," I replied, hurrying through the vaulted archways.

The building itself had been completed only a few months ago and sat beside the lake opposite the Palace. It, too, was protected by railings and guardsmen who circled the perimeter. The Engineering Hall was formerly located in a lower wing of Buckingham Palace, but due to the accident two years ago (an explosion during one of Mr. Snow's experiments gone wrong) the royal advisors had decided the Gadget Engineers would be moved out of the Palace for fear of further fire and destruction.

Fortunately, the explosion that had ripped open a hole behind the area that housed the laundry, heating, and water supply had occurred early on a Wednesday morning when the guards and staff were in full force and able to fight the flames. The blast had interrupted my etiquette class and we'd run into the hallway, smack into the middle of all the chaos and fun.

When the fire died down, it turned out that what had been singed worst was the pride of Mr. Snow. Since then, everyone avoided bringing up the accident while around him.

I didn't mind confessing that he intimidated me a bit. Well, not just a bit. A lot.

He was so incredibly intelligent, and so very impatient if I asked too many questions.

And God help anyone if they ever *ever* mentioned that famous Wednesday morning.

Mostly, I asked my questions of his kinder main assistant, Mr. Turnbull.

I quickened my pace in the direction of their back offices. It didn't take long before I reached the long rows of working tables in the hallway, laid out with exciting new gadgets they were working on. To most onlookers, there didn't seem to be any order to the mess. Wooden clamps sat screwed to the edges of tables. Boxes of bolts and nails lined the tops. Massive metal shelves overflowed with wires and casings and ball bearings. I passed a blacksmith who was holding a piece of pipe above a contained fireplace, another who was banging metal over an anvil. I inhaled the scent of sawn wood and soldered metals.

My eyes moved to the little nook in the corner where I spent several hours a week, whenever I was able to visit the Engineering Hall, to tinker with my own ideas. It was where I'd developed the rotating sword (still hidden in the floorboards of that barn). I wondered how and when I would get it back, then focused on the set of goggles tucked on the table's lower shelf.

I was attempting to invent special goggles for horseback riding that would protect me from oncoming bugs. I detested getting hit by a fly in the mouth or the eyes. I wanted to coat the lenses with something that would repel flying insects within a three-foot radius of my head, so they wouldn't come *anywhere* near my face.

"Stop right there!" someone shouted.

I shrieked in surprise.

Mr. Snow was bellowing at me, but I couldn't see him.

"Don't move another inch," he commanded in his familiar roar. "Sit down."

I looked at the stool tucked next to my working corner. "There?"

"Yes."

I did as I was told. He was odd that way. He never said hello. He simply started in with whatever he wanted to say. I glanced about to find him.

The doors to the science and engineering library were open, but there was no sign of him. I looked farther to my right, from where his voice had boomed. There. He sauntered out of his office, where he usually worked on his blueprints. Although in his late sixties with a thick head of solid white hair, he was easy to imagine as a young man. He was well over six feet tall with a straight posture, a bulk to his shoulders, and an energetic gait. He rarely smiled, though.

"Now let's see your shoes."

"My shoes?" I mumbled. Did he know something about my swollen left foot? I didn't think I had been limping. Good Lord, did he know something about my possible rabies?

I tried to suppress my nervousness. But he was a man of science.

He would definitely report me if he thought I would be a danger to the Queen or anyone else at the royal court.

"Come, come. Haven't got all day."

I remained frozen. What was this man intending?

Impatient, he whistled three times. Behind him, two automatons—self-operating machines—came whirling out. They were made of polished brass, each in the shape of half a sphere laid on its flat side, and moving on rollers.

They rushed toward my feet at the same time Mr. Snow shouted, "Don't fight them!"

I thrust my shoulders backward, I was so startled, which lifted the hems of my dress and petticoat, which in turn allowed each automaton to clamp itself onto a leather shoe.

The next thing I knew, metal hooks came out of their sides and they gently removed my slip-ons, rolled themselves backward, planted my shoes on their backs, and stopped two feet in front of me.

I giggled. "Shoe removers." Then I was flooded with guilt that Peter and his sister were injured somewhere, and I was being amused.

"My latest invention."

"How do they work with laces?"

"As long as the knot is simple, they can manage it."

"Amazing, Mr. Snow."

A whoosh of cool air passed over my stockinged feet. Could he see the outline of my bandage?

"How do I get my shoes back?"

"Whistle four times."

I pierced the air with the sound. I was a strong whistler. Always had been.

The robots returned, tucked on my shoes, then quickly rolled away and parked themselves next to the wall.

"What brings you here, today of all days? Aren't you busy?" Mr. Snow clapped and signaled the robots toward him. I got up and followed them into the Great Exhibition Room.

"I have a bit of time yet." Well over three hours until the party.

"What time is it starting, again?"

"Six o'clock. In the garden tent."

Mr. Snow was a puzzle. As a scientist and engineer, he was meticulous in timing everything he did down to the last second, whether working with instruments, experiments, or steam power, yet in his personal life he didn't follow the time. He was constantly late for dinners and celebrations and special events.

We entered the Great Exhibition Room. The robots parked themselves in a spot by the door.

It was a magnificent space, with high cathedral ceilings and wide plank flooring. The windows were tall and large and let in lots of sunshine. Mr. Snow's inventions hung from ropes and wires at all angles. Two fireplaces at opposite ends of the room kept it warm on chilly days. One was presently lit.

There was something new on the wall, a metal gizmo attached to a window and flowing downward as though it were a drapery. Then there was a massive glass ball hanging from a twenty-foot chain directly above me that was swaying to and fro, half-filled with water. We walked by an open-seated horse carriage, then a saddle with wires attached to metal stirrups, a broken umbrella, a walking cane with a floating metal handle, and a metal birdcage with a note inside.

A wall painting caught my eye, and I twirled around to look closer. It hung crookedly, and the landscape wasn't painted very well, as if someone had smeared too much paint with every stroke. What sort of invention would that become?

"I was wondering, Mr. Snow, what other new gadgets you've been working on." It was a weak attempt to start the conversation in the direction I wanted, but I couldn't very well come right out and ask if he knew anything about mechanical dogs and rabies, in case he suspected I was somehow involved.

He stopped at a wooden bench and picked up an experimental leather shoe in a large male size that had a steam cylinder strapped to each side. He found a screwdriver and tightened a screw near the heel. "That's why you came?"

"I'm—I'm rather nervous about this evening, and thought a visit here might be helpful to calm me. Familiar things and all that."

"Ah, I understand." He held up the shoe toward me. "See, another failure."

"Still can't get it to work?" He was trying to make steam-powered shoes that would help a man outrun a horse.

"Never mind faster than a horse. The weight of the attached cylinders makes a man run even slower than he usually does."

I was struck by the irony, and rubbed my nose to hide my curious expression.

"But this failure led me to think of the shoe removers. One failure often sparks another success."

I took a deep breath and blurted out the question I'd come for. "Is there anyone else in London, Mr. Snow, who is working on gadgets as you are? As advanced as yourself and your staff?"

"Of course not. Don't be ridiculous." He seemed insulted by the question. "I'm funded by the Queen to outwork and outsmart every engineering society in the world. Have been for seven years. We are the best at what we do not only in London, but in the entire Commonwealth. Including all those upstarts in America." He muttered something about some young Thomas Edison.

"Right, right," I said, trying not to upset him. "Sorry. The silly question popped into my head." Then before I could stop myself, I added, "Did you hear that one of the girls from the Mews was bitten by a rabid dog last night?"

He tightened a bolt on the shoe. His head snapped in my direction. "Awful news, isn't it?"

So he'd heard.

"The dogs . . . did you hear how exactly it happened?"

"She and her brother were attacked." Then his voice cut like the edge of a sharp knife. "Can't say they aren't blameless, sneaking out in the middle of the night like they did. What can anyone expect?"

My skin prickled with anger at his unfair assessment. We weren't to blame that we were attacked by vicious dogs. I pulled away from him. "I heard the dogs got hold of another man, a street beggar, and killed him."

He muttered something I couldn't quite catch.

"Did you hear it, too?"

"Wrong time. Wrong place."

I waited, hoping he'd say something to indicate he'd heard they were clockwork dogs, but he said nothing more.

He turned his head my way and gave me a strange look. I had an odd feeling he knew something else. I couldn't think how to extract it from him, without disclosing that I had been there myself and had witnessed the dogs.

My soiled skirt was still in Benjamin's trunk. I had initially wanted to show it to Mr. Snow and ask his opinion on the black oil, where it might have come from and whether he recognized it, but now I was relieved that I hadn't had a chance to bring it. My stomach rippled as I looked at his stern face. I wasn't so sure I could trust him.

"Mr. Snow, who created the Golden Butterflies for the Palace?"

"Everything here is my creation," he grumbled.

Well, not precisely. Everything was labeled as his creation, much the same as a fashionable garment was labeled with the name of the fashion house, but there were sometimes dozens of people assigned to the task. Mr. Snow scowled at the question and I knew I was irritating him.

He lost himself in his task, tinkering and turning and squeezing, and I had to leave. What had I learned from coming here? Nothing, really. I turned away in disappointment.

"Good-bye, Mr. Snow."

Entranced in his work, he didn't respond. He never said hellos or good-byes, but everyone always overlooked his bad manners.

⊰⊱

I tried to ignore my pounding foot as I dashed past the displays at the other end of the Great Exhibition Room. I zoomed by the miniature windmills, waterwheels, specimens of butterflies under glass, displays of poisonous snakes and frogs, and various darts and arrows made by African tribesmen. When I raced out to the hallway, Mr. Turnbull, the main assistant of Mr. Snow, and another junior engineer walked by. They were both in frock coats.

"Miss Sycamore, enjoy your celebrations this evening."

I whirled in their direction, skirts in hand, to see Mr. Turnbull's friendly face. I sighed in comfort. He had much more patience with me and my questions than Mr. Snow.

"Thank you," I responded.

Mr. Turnbull wasn't nearly as intimidating or ill-humored. Whenever I was in his presence, he listened carefully and made me feel grown-up, as if I had a voice. In his mid-thirties, he had dark hair and an average build. He looked similar to his younger brother Aiden who worked down below in the furnace room.

The other engineer present, a quieter man—whose name escaped me because he'd only recently started here—was dark-haired as well, but he had a trim beard and wide jaw. It seemed that everyone here in this elite field of science knew my fiancé. However, my father hadn't invited either of these two men to my engagement party, given how junior they were in this department.

Mr. Turnbull nodded toward me and rested a hand in his pocket. "Mr. Abercrombie is undoubtedly sorry he's missing the festivities this evening."

"As am I."

"And I'm terribly sorry to hear about your riding friend from the stables."

"Oh," I said, somewhat surprised that he was aware Jillian and I rode together.

"I add my sympathy," said the other engineer, sunlight catching the short hairs of his beard. "You often ride right past our windows."

That's how they knew. "Very kind of you both. Did you hear exactly—exactly what happened to her?"

Mr. Turnbull shook his head. I had hoped to get more of an answer.

However, the other man added, "I imagine the police surgeon will examine the other body—that beggar man who was attacked. Perhaps they'll discover a clue as to what occurred."

Police surgeon?

My mind flashed. Yes! Scotland Yard would be investigating the circumstances of the unfortunate other victim who'd been killed by the dogs. The police surgeon might perform an autopsy, as gruesome as that was to think about, to examine the bite marks. Perhaps he'd discover traces of mechanical oil or unusual fur, or *something* to show I hadn't imagined the whole thing.

Perhaps Mr. Turnbull wanted to steer my thoughts to something more cheerful, for he changed the topic. "Annabelle delivered."

I smiled instantly. "She did? When?"

Clean-shaven and polite, he grinned at my reaction. "Early this morning. Five pups."

"Five?" I gushed. Annabelle was a lost cocker spaniel who had found her way to the Palace gates two weeks ago, her belly swollen with the coming pups. She'd been adopted by the men in the Engineering Hall. Why hadn't Mr. Snow told me about her delivery?

"Three females. Two males."

"How are they doing?"

"Quite well."

"I'd like to see them," I said.

"Do you have time?"

I was torn. I looked to the wide, curved stairwell beyond the Silver and Glass Spider, wishing to go down to Annabelle's favorite nook beside the warm furnaces. But my maid was waiting to help me prepare for this evening's events.

"There'll be time tomorrow, miss," said the other man. "We don't wish to delay you." He seemed a bit impatient to move on. I was keeping them from their work.

"You're quite right. I'll return as soon as I can." I lifted my skirts ever so slightly, about to leave. "Oh, Mr. Turnbull, I was wondering if you could tell me about the Golden Butterflies. How did they come to be invented?"

Mr. Turnbull blinked as he thought about it. "Mr. Snow's patent."

"I wanted to congratulate you, too, for surely you helped in their development. They are truly amazing. If only you knew how much I dislike spiders in my bedroom."

"All Mr. Snow. You'll have to thank him."

So Mr. Snow had been telling me the truth. He was the genius behind the clockwork butterflies. Was it a stretch to think he might be the mastermind behind the dogs, too? But what about the Silver and Glass Spider? Who exactly had worked on that? One question only led to a dozen others.

"Good-bye, then." I made a hasty exit into the afternoon sunshine.

I hadn't left empty-handed, after all, for I'd discovered there was a police surgeon investigating last night's death.

It was crucial that I get the results of the autopsy. I hoped the results would help me uncover who'd developed the clockwork dogs, and how to reverse their poison. My father would never discuss those gory autopsy details with me, so I would need to find another way. If only I didn't have to waste my time preparing for the silly evening ahead. I hurried along the path and wondered with every step how my two closest friends were doing.

CHAPTER SEVEN

"WHERE on earth have you been, Miss Sycamore? Mrs. Burn-hamthorpe is counting on me to get you properly prepared and dressed." Jolene, trained as a lady's maid, sounded frustrated as I brushed past her in my chambers. I headed for my private bath.

Jolene was only ten years older than me, but sometimes it seemed like decades. Whenever she suffered stress, she grew bossy. Her dark hair was pulled back tightly into its usual knot. The uniform that covered her tiny frame was pressed and spotless. I felt like a sloppy giant beside her. She'd been hired as my personal maid because she spoke impeccable French and German, and could teach me. She was usually fairly pleasant and helpful, but always feared getting yelled at by the headmistress of the royal household, Mrs. Burnhamthorpe, who had a military grip on her staff.

"My apologies. I didn't intend to take so long. I needed a breath of fresh air."

"You were gone long enough to walk to London Bridge and back!"

I looked to the clock by my nightstand. "It's only three o'clock. I don't have to be in the gardens till six."

"Your father was just here and said he'd like you there by five. The Queen sends her regrets, for she won't be attending due to her toothache. However, as a gift in lieu of her presence, she's arranged for the royal photographer to take your portrait. At *five*."

I groaned. What girl would want her engagement photo taken without her fiancé?

The Queen's absence was more of a relief than a disappointment. There was too much tension at these affairs if the Queen was present. Everyone tried to behave perfectly around Her Majesty, including me.

"Two hours to wash and curl and dry your hair! Two hours, miss! And we've had to top your bath with steaming water three times already."

"Again, Jolene, I . . . I apolo . . ." My head swam, as though I were falling underwater. I attempted to turn at the doorway to the bath, but stumbled. My shoulder hit the wall.

"Miss," Jolene lunged and grabbed my elbow. She shrieked, "Polly!"

Polly was arranging rose petals in the porcelain bathtub and looked up in alarm. She turned away from the tub with its gilded claw feet and raced to support me on my other side. She was equal to me in height and stature. They sat me down on a cushioned chair.

Polly got a cool cloth for my forehead. It revived me. While I rubbed my head, I caught sight of the cake of lavender soap in the pewter dish. It was wet. Which meant Polly had recently used it, as we'd agreed. It also meant she'd delivered the basket to Benjamin. I glanced at her. She discreetly nodded at me to confirm it. Thank heaven.

I waited for a moment to recover, and for an opportunity for Polly to slip me another note from Benjamin, but she didn't. I assumed this signified he knew nothing more than what my father did about our wounded friends.

"Polly," snapped Jolene, "fetch some dried apricots from the kitchen. Scones and strong tea."

"Yes, ma'am."

Polly flew out the door.

Jolene softened her voice. "No need to worry. We'll help you prepare quickly. I'll work on your hair while Polly does your pedicure—"

"No pedicure." God help me if they should see the bite marks on my foot. Jolene was ever loyal to Mrs. Burnhamthorpe and would turn against me as quickly as the west wind changed directions. "And I'd prefer a private bath, please."

"But we could do so much more if we worked at the same time—"

"I'll be speedy," I insisted.

Jolene drew an impatient breath. On most occasions I allowed her to direct me, since she was so well trained in the ways of the Royals. She did, however, recognize the tone in my voice when I wished to make my own decisions. Such as now.

She lowered her lashes. "Very well, miss. Are you feeling any better?"

I nodded. "Could you please show me the clothes you've readied?"

With a pleased smile, Jolene sprang to her feet and stepped into the adjoining walk-in wardrobe. She brought out article after article of undergarments, corset, an intricate silver necklace with sapphire and pearl inlay, matching sapphire drop earrings, and bejeweled slippers.

"I think I'd prefer the burgundy shoes."

"Well . . . I suppose the color does match better with your gown."

The color wasn't the reason for my selection. The burgundy shoes would be looser on my swollen foot.

Polly returned quickly, carrying a tray and platter covered with a silver lid. The food and drink renewed me. In privacy, I worked with haste in the tub, lathering and rinsing my hair. I carefully washed my injured foot. The toes didn't look too horrible—more swollen than before, with a tinge more redness around each tooth mark, but I had just been on my feet for more than two hours. When I arrived at the party, I would try to sit through most of it.

I toweled my wet skin and slipped my tender toes into leather slippers. When I reached for my bathrobe, I called for the maids.

Jolene must've had her face glued to the door, for she burst in immediately and took over toweling my hair. I sat in the chair as the two fussed over me. They tied the ends of my hair with rags to curl the strands as they dried. They filed my fingernails and massaged my hands with lotions.

My heart raced every time I thought about Jillian and Peter, and whether the staff doctor had been able to help them. I wondered if my supplies had reached the right hands. If Matilda enjoyed the anonymous delivery of the baby blanket. If the factory boys would understand what to do with the skin ointment.

My thoughts turned to the evening ahead. I had no choice but to pretend all was well. I wished I was going to all this trouble for a future husband of my own choosing. I tried to imagine how it would feel if I were in love and preparing for this night. Would I feel any different physically? Would my stomach twist and turn, my hands sweat, my heart beat rapidly?

Did all love come with great passion? Would I ever feel the giddiness of it?

I was so inexperienced with boys; I'd never been kissed. How would it feel if a boy pressed his lips to mine? I'd never even had a suitor. My fiancé didn't count, for I'd never met him. What I longed for in courtship was romantic time together—carriage races in the country and summer strolls in Hyde Park. I was going straight from reading *Aesop's Fables* to marriage.

Why couldn't I be preparing for someone younger, more thrilling? Someone who would show me how it felt to be kissed. Someone like . . . someone dangerous and dashing like Peter, or loyal and handsome like Benjamin.

They were decent and friendly and amusing.

Sadly, my father wouldn't approve of either boy. One was training to become a bobby, the other was an apprentice groom. My father would prefer I spend my time with someone of a higher social standing. Well, I thought impatiently, that would be out of his hands, too, once I had a say about things. Unfortunately, tonight I wasn't preparing for anyone special. Only a crowd filled with my father's friends and a handful of people from Mr. Abercrombie's side.

While the maids tidied the bathing room, I went to my bedchamber. I slipped into my silk stockings, silk drawers, and heavily boned new corset.

Jolene entered and attempted to give the ties a good yank, but she was too small to tug as firmly as she'd like. "Polly, give us a hand please."

Polly took the ties and pulled hard. I nearly choked at the stranglehold.

"Sorry, you all right?"

"Take a deep breath," Jolene instructed.

I did as I was told.

"Once more," Jolene commanded Polly. I couldn't believe they wanted it tighter.

Polly yanked again. My ribs felt as though they were being crushed by one of the metal vises in the Engineering Hall.

They gave me a moment to settle into the new shape, then laced me.

They sat me at my desk, with its standing silver mirror, hairbrushes, and fragrances. They applied lotions to my face. Polly added a layer of pink-tinted beeswax to each fingernail, which gave them a polish she then delighted over.

What a waste of time. I could be reading about rabies in my father's medical books!

Jolene opened one of my windows to allow the breeze to dry my hair. My bedroom was twenty feet above the ground, too high to jump when I wished to escape the Palace, but it did give me a pretty view of the gardens.

Jolene pinched my cheeks, which sent the blood rushing. Polly applied a layer of Vaseline to my lips for sheen. Jolene untied my hair, then pulled the strands to my crown.

"Still a bit damp, but it'll do."

After what felt like forever, she finally finished primping my hair.

"Don't you wish to look in the mirror?" Polly asked.

"I'll wait until you've finished."

The truth was, I wasn't enthused enough to look. Nelson Abercrombie wouldn't even be there.

At Jolene's prodding, I rose from the chair and approached the ball gown, a beautiful soft pink color, spread on my bed. I tried to get some pleasure from how lovely it was, designed by one of the royal dressmakers. He'd told me during one of my numerous fittings that he'd created it using princess seams—the latest rage in royal circles—which went straight from shoulder to floor. There would be no waistline seam; the bodice and skirt were cut as one, so the effect was to elongate the body.

I slipped into it. It was exceptionally form-fitting. The maids buttoned me up at the back—thirty-two pearl buttons, Polly reminded me. And a train six feet long.

"There." Jolene stepped back to have a look at me. "All you need are your shoes."

"Oh," gushed Polly, eyes glistening with wonder. "Oh," she repeated.

I headed for the dressing room, where I'd left my flat-soled shoes. As I passed the full-length mirror, I stopped in surprise. The dress was truly something. Set off the shoulder with narrow sleeve cuffs, the fabric swept low over my bosom, down the flatness of my stomach, over my hips, and pooled at my feet in a great ruffled hem.

From the front, the dress was a soft pink shade. It made the color of my skin come alive. When I turned to see my profile, I could see the bustle on my behind cascading in multi-colored fabrics layered upon each other. The fabrics had been dyed especially for me. The upper half of the bustle was done in pale pinks, the lower edge a rich burgundy. In between, there were three more tones of pinks and wines. One of the pink fabrics had a very thin pinstripe of sea-blue color, which gave it a subtle sheen.

The long train fell into a beautiful semicircle.

My hair was pulled up on my head, black curls upon curls. Pinned above my right ear was a soft white feather, inlaid with pearls and diamonds. The blue sapphire drop earrings dangled just above my bare shoulders. A silver necklace rested at my throat, its silver pendant adorned with another brilliant blue sapphire, as well as pearls and rubies from India—a gift from my father, who'd gotten it as a gift from a maharaja. The necklace matched my mother's sapphire ring, which I twirled on my finger nervously.

Looking into the mirror, I instantly wished Peter or Benjamin could see me in this. Then I felt guilty for being so selfish when my friends were in such danger, but I couldn't help my thoughts.

What a shame there'd be no young man to kiss me tonight.

O Romeo, Romeo.

Would my mother have approved of my father's choice of Nelson? Perhaps she'd be more reasonable. Weren't mothers softer, more understanding of the nature of love? I wished she were here. *Well, I* thought, *she isn't, and I have to make the best of this situation.* Peter and

Jillian and I could be infected with rabies, and I was the only one with access to calculate a way out of this horrid mess.

I entered my dressing room and slid my feet into the burgundy shoes.

I gasped. A week ago these shoes had been loose and almost floppy. Now they pinched my left toes so tightly that they barely fit.

What was happening to my foot?

CHAPTER EIGHT

"NO smiling, please," said the royal photographer.

He perched his box camera atop a tripod and pointed it at me and my father. The man bent over, disappeared behind the curtain attached to the camera, then slid out a large, hairy hand and adjusted the lens.

I sat up straighter on the chair. Early morning rain had cleared to full sunshine. In long, white evening gloves that reached to my elbows, I clutched my lacy parasol against the blazing sun and wiped all trace of emotion from my face. It was said that smiling would ruin a photograph. Twisting your mouth and face wouldn't give a true sense of what you looked like. Older people said smiling in a photograph made you look foolish and simple-minded. Why did older people always take things so seriously?

Standing beside my chair, my father drew back his shoulders.

Click-snap went the camera.

"Just one more, please." The photographer slid out a thin rectangular plate from behind his curtain and replaced it with another. His long black beard glistened in the late afternoon rays, as did his formal dark tailcoat.

"Turn to the right, please, miss."

I swiveled, trying to take a deep breath in my corset but unable to. I tried twice more before the air went down with satisfaction. How much longer for this torture?

If Peter were here, he'd say something to make me laugh.

Click-snap.

My father, dressed in a black tailcoat and top hat, came to speak to me.

"According to Dr. Kenyon, both of your friends have regained consciousness."

At the wonderful news, I lost my ability to breathe again. I slid a hand over my corset. "They're awake? They're fine?"

"Well, I wouldn't say fine, but they're no worse."

Thank you, I said in silent prayer. While my father joined the photographer, I tried to compose myself. Jillie was awake. She was awake! And Peter . . . my body flushed with an unexplained feeling of warmth and excitement. Was I simply joyful at the great news that he was conscious? Or was there more meaning to my joy?

I would sneak out of the palace again at the first opportunity to see them both.

For now, I'd continue my charade.

I looked about. It was well past five, and no guests had arrived yet. Maids, footmen, and the head butler fussed over the banquet tables filled with wine, drink, canapés and other hors d'oeuvres, set beneath several large, white tents. We'd start here, then go into the Palace for the formal dinner. Thank goodness there'd be no dancing this evening. It was the one thing my father had easily agreed upon. Since the engaged couple couldn't dance together, it was not unreasonable for *all* dancing to be eliminated.

Two maids at the tea trolley glanced in my father's direction. They whispered to each other. He didn't seem to notice the looks of admiration. I wondered how anyone could be interested in my father in that way. He was just so . . . old and fatherly.

I rose from my seat, ever conscious of my aching left foot. I looked past the weeping willow tree that had formed the backdrop of the photographs. On a lush hill in the direction of the Royal Mews, a small crowd of workers had gathered. They appeared to be watching me.

Me? I raised a white glove to my necklace, uncomfortable with the attention.

Thirty feet to my right, Benjamin appeared from behind some shrubbery, leading a horse and wagon. He didn't look my way and seemed oblivious that I was here. I was dying to tell him that Jillian and Peter were awake.

Scooping up fallen branches and logs, Benjamin tossed them into his cart. He had two other stablelads assisting him, and I gathered they were heading to the Engineering Hall. Firewood was always needed for the Silver and Glass Spider. But what was Benjamin doing, walking alongside the great draft horse and giving her a pat? Since when was he allowed to touch the horses?

If anyone saw him, he'd face a reprimand. I watched with anxious curiosity as he loaded his arms with twigs. When he stepped nearer to me, he happened to look over. I smiled. Benjamin's gaze lowered from my face to my neckline to my hips, then he stumbled. Firewood toppled out of his hands. His companions saw the tumble and laughed, while my cheeks heated in confusion.

Had he been that surprised to see me?

He gathered his fallen twigs and never looked at me again. I wasn't sure how I felt at the slight. It wasn't my fault he'd dropped his wood. He was always dropping things.

Or was he thinking of the basket of secret supplies I'd sent him? Had something gone wrong with the delivery?

My throat twisted with worry.

Whatever the problem was, Benjamin collected his firewood with his back turned in a cool stance, as though he was angry at something. He continued as if I wasn't even here. What on earth was wrong with him?

What on earth was wrong with boys? Why couldn't they just let you know what was troubling them as it happened, and why did they have to make everything a big mystery?

❧❧

The trouble came when I had to stand.

My injured foot wouldn't stop pounding.

When my father introduced me to Nelson's parents, Mr. and Mrs. Joseph Abercrombie, I rose to greet them. I'd been told they would be representing Nelson at the party, standing on one side of me in the receiving line. My father would be on the other.

"Sir. Ma'am," I said upon our first meeting. "How do you do?"

"Very well," said Mr. Abercrombie as he took my hand.

Unfortunately, he reminded me of one of my favorite characters from the Mother Goose rhymes—Humpty Dumpty. Pale, short, and round. In contrast, his wife was stunningly beautiful. Her glossy brown hair was swept into a chignon. She was poised and sophisticated, with lovely skin. I wondered which one of them their son resembled.

Both of them had ready smiles, which I returned.

Mr. Abercrombie was a gentleman farmer, an egg farmer who owned a great deal of property in Dover. How ironic about the eggs, considering he looked like Humpty. My father had told me this gentleman had acquired so many tenants on his estate, all of them egg farmers, that they provided his income and he no longer needed to work himself.

"How wonderful to meet you, my dear." Mrs. Abercrombie gave me a kiss on the cheek. Her citrus perfume soaked the air. "Nelson has written such wonderful letters about you. Hopefully you'll be moving closer to Dover, near us, when you settle down."

"That . . . that would be lovely."

Not that lovely. I didn't wish to leave London and the few friends I had. Was this something else that'd been discussed behind my back, by my so-called future husband? When would *I* get to choose some details of my own life?

"Will any of your relatives be joining us today?" Mr. Abercrombie leaned in with a pleasant smile. His collar protruded awkwardly.

Oh, I thought. They didn't know my family history.

"My father's side . . . well, you know there's no one left on that side . . ."

The couple nodded with sympathy.

"And my mother's side from Scotland . . . well, they . . . they are unable to make such a long trip."

Should I tell them the reason?

My maternal grandparents blame my father for the death of my mother and haven't spoken to him since a few days after I was born.

It had been a terrible falling-out, I'd heard from one of my early governesses. My grandparents had argued that they should raise me, declaring he was helpless without a wife. My father insisted I belonged by his side. I was grateful that he hadn't let me go. Yet I wondered what it might be like to have a large family where I could always depend on someone to be available when I needed them.

The next time I looked up, hordes of people were forming a receiving line. I curtsied deeply as the Prince and Princess of Wales walked to their position at the head of the line. The Princess was wearing a lovely shade of canary yellow.

"Congratulations on your engagement, Charlotte," she said to me.

"Thank you, Your Royal Highness."

Standing beside my father, I dutifully welcomed his friends, many of them titled aristocracy—dukes and duchesses, earls, viscounts, lords and ladies. I was glad my father was beside me to say their proper titles, because I couldn't keep them straight. I suspect they all knew who had to follow whom in line. People of title were sticky in that way. They became annoyed if they were overlooked in favor of someone beneath them. The poor staff were always reprimanded when that happened.

"You!" the Earl of Kennington snapped at a footman half an hour later, when we were chatting near the banquet tables. "More champagne. Can't you see our glasses are empty?" This occurred after a viscount asked for oysters and caviar before Lord Kennington was served. The footman jumped to attention and scuttled to make it up to the man.

I was happy for the distraction. It provided me the opportunity to hobble behind the trays of tropical fruits, pineapples, bananas, and slivers of oranges to sit on a chair and slide off my shoes. If Jolene knew that I'd removed my stockings entirely before I'd left my chambers, she'd have a fainting spell. But it relieved some of the ache. I shoved my left foot out from below my hems, where I could see it better in the light, then was sorry I had.

My skin was streaked with red lines that followed along the veins of my foot, from the toes where I'd been bitten, up my ankle in the direction of my heart.

Alarmed, I retrieved my shoe.

What had I just witnessed? Why was the skin so red above my veins?

"Why the glum face?" An older man with long, white sideburns and white beard, dressed in an all-white tailcoat and top hat, leaned against a shiny silver cane as he stepped toward the tables.

I blinked, trying to remember his name.

He stopped at the array of pineapple slices. He slid some onto a platter and sampled. "Not quite as ripe as in the South Pacific, but then nothing is."

He must've noticed me squinting at him, for he reintroduced himself.

"Charles Darwin."

Ah, yes, the great Mr. Darwin. I'd never met him before this evening, but I was well aware of how enthralled my father and the rest of the scientific community were with his theory of survival of the fittest.

I wondered if he thought *I* would survive, if he knew about my rabies. Of course, I couldn't tell him.

"If it's Nelson Abercrombie you're concerned about, don't be. He's a fine man. He'll take jolly good care of you."

"Thank you," I murmured.

"Say, have you seen where Joseph Lister went? I've got a quibble with that last piece he wrote for the *Journal*."

Joseph Lister was a surgical pioneer, another friend of my father's. He'd developed the process for sterilizing surgical equipment and cleaning wounds to prevent infections. He'd discovered the very tonic I'd cleansed my foot with—carbolic acid.

I pointed to the sweets table, where two men stood in heated discussion. "That's him, debating with Mr. Snow." Scientists and doctors were always arguing about something. Every little detail seemed to them like the end of the world. Many were alarmed by Mr. Darwin's theory of evolution, as well, saying it went against the Church.

Mr. Darwin chewed his pineapple and studied the men. "So that's Mr. Snow."

"The Royal Gadget Engineer."

"Indeed, the famous gadget-maker."

"Yes, sir."

"What sort of chap is he?"

Unfriendly was the only word that came to mind. Mr. Snow had been late arriving, and never made it to the receiving line. Why hadn't he come to say hello to me privately, to wish me luck on my engagement?

"Brilliant engineer, I'm told," was my more courteous reply.

"Yes, yes. Must go say hello." Mr. Darwin handed his empty platter to a passing footman and tipped his hat to me. "All the best in your upcoming nuptials."

"Thank you."

Mr. Darwin strode off toward the men, leaning on his cane.

As he lifted it from the ground, it made a slight pop and sizzle, then a stream of orange flames burst from the bottom of the silver cane. It spit fire!

Actual fire!

The walking stick was splendid and caught the eyes of the crowd as Mr. Darwin made his way to his colleagues. How did it work? I wondered if he pressed a button, or was it the mere release of pressure from being lifted that created the fireball? Mr. Darwin seemed amused that the cane was causing people to point and stare and laugh.

Surrounded by a swell of people at my own party, I realized I still didn't fit in. Even after two years, no one my age had befriended me in any meaningful way. They were polite, usually said the right things, but never invited me into their private conversations. To the Royals— the granddaughters and cousins who might be my friends—my untitled father was considered paid help. It would be awkward for them to stoop to my level.

Yet to the working staff of the Palace and the Mews, the maids, footmen, sentries, and gardeners, my father was considered too high on the social ladder for any of their children to befriend me.

Except for Peter, Jillian, and Benjamin. They didn't mind being my friends.

Mostly, I was stuck in the middle of nowhere.

"Charlotte, hello," called a feminine voice behind me. "Sorry we're late!"

Then there was the Hill family.

Fiona and Theodora Hill. They were the daughters of the veterinary surgeon who looked after the horses in the royal stables.

I mustered a smile at Fiona, who was calling my name. She and her sister, both tall, with mounds of curly blond hair that never seemed to stay pinned in place, waddled toward me in satin dresses with silk bustles. From a distance, the sisters were pretty. They would be pretty close-up, too, except for the nastiness that spilled out when they opened their mouths.

Their gleaming skin was scrubbed ten times over, their faces pinched into half-smiles. (A proper lady never smiled too widely, Fiona was always reminding me.) Fiona was my age, and Theodora two years younger. They ruled the social scene at the Palace for the daughters and sons of the higher staff, such as my father and theirs. They tended to leave me out of their plans because of my disjointed traveling schedule with my father and the Queen. That's what I told myself when I was trying to be generous.

"Our father had a private meeting with the Prince," bragged Fiona, "about the new stallion, and the hour simply got away from us."

Yes, I wanted to say, *but the Prince himself was able to make it on time.*

"Wonderful of you to be here," I said politely.

For a moment, I envied Fiona's position. She'd just had a coming-out ball, sponsored by one of her father's aristocratic friends. Girls of our station—with untitled fathers—didn't normally have them, unless sponsored, for it was a formal event where the girl was presented to Her Majesty. Fiona was looking forward to the season and having her pick of many eligible young men. Within the next two years, it would be Theodora's time. I didn't need a coming-out ball, my father had told me. I already had Nelson.

"That's an interesting choice of gown." Fiona's cheeks tightened as she looked me over. I braced for an insult. "Are you sure Mr. Abercrombie would approve of you wearing something like that, without him here?"

"Exactly," Theodora agreed. Her teeth were always a shade of pale yellow. "Why, there's not one seam that runs across your waist. It follows your curves as though you're wearing nothing at all."

I felt my face flush, although my parasol was still shading me. Perturbed, I rolled my tongue to the roof of my dry mouth. "It's not that daring. All my parts are covered."

"Still, I should think a lady might prefer more discretion." Fiona's eyes were narrowed like a cat's.

"Well," I said with a hopeful smile, "I see you've found it in your gown." I hadn't meant it as an insult, but Fiona's mouth dropped open as I glanced at the mounds of fabric and all the fussy bows and ribbons on her bodice. She was ever so conscious of her looks.

"Well, if that's how you're going to be . . ." Fiona turned on her heel and stomped away, leaving me and her younger sister staring uneasily at each other.

"Congratulations on your engagement," said Theodora clumsily. "It must be awful with Mr. Abercrombie an ocean away. I would never stand for it myself."

I sighed as sister number two trudged off to the food tables. If only she knew how painful her arrow was to my heart.

⊰⊱

The Palace Ballroom looked as stiff and formal as I felt, from the high, arched ceiling inlaid with golden crowns and emblems, to the marble columns and hanging tapestries. Chandelier lighting made everything sparkle. Queen Victoria rarely used the Ballroom anymore. Since the passing of her husband, she'd retreated from hosting social gatherings.

The Ballroom was the largest public room in the Palace; it could seat at least three hundred dinner guests. Twenty tables, with sixteen chairs apiece, were set and waiting. The most magnificent things (I'd been told to look for them by Mrs. Burnhamthorpe in my etiquette classes) were the priceless paintings: Rubens', Rembrandt's, and Canaletto's beautiful landscapes of Venice.

I sat with my father, several of his colleagues, and the Abercrombies.

Rising to speak, my father thanked everyone for their presence. The Abercrombies thanked everyone on behalf of Nelson, and the Prince raised his glass in a toast.

A pianist and several musicians serenaded us as we ate. Dinner, six courses, took three hours. Honestly, I could have gulped down my portions in five minutes and been done with it. As it was, I had very little appetite. Underneath the tablecloth that draped down to the floor, I removed my left shoe and allowed my foot to throb.

Footmen brought in wine, julienne soup, and fillets of several fishes, followed by roast mutton and venison served with an array of vegetables. There were grilled grouse and bread sauce, roasted potatoes, raspberry jelly, custards and puddings, and finally platters of cheeses with fresh strawberries and grapes. My favorite was the wine, although I was fearful of drinking too much due to my sore foot. So I sipped.

When the men withdrew to a smoking salon, the women retreated to a drawing room, then strolled the Picture Gallery to admire the hanging art. I mingled and chatted. I listened to stories of where Mr. Abercrombie and I should live, where I might shop for my wedding gown, how many children we should have, and how they should be schooled.

It was exhausting to think up creative replies.

"You don't say?"

"I shall take that under advisement."

"If ever I need help deciding on the color of our draperies, I will call upon you."

Finally, near the midnight hour, the evening came to an end. The Prince and Princess made their exit first, per protocol, then others followed. I noticed a swarm of women, titled and not, bedazzled by my father and eager to place their hands in his to bid good night.

I said good-bye to the Abercrombies with mixed emotions. I felt sorry for them. Wouldn't they be more pleased if their son found someone of his own choosing, too? Someone who had much more in common with him than I did. Someone who perhaps loved him.

"Wonderful evening, my dear," said Mrs. Abercrombie, bending to brush my cheek with her own. "Perhaps the next time we see each other, Nelson will be with us. The end of July, I expect. A mere eight weeks."

"Oh," I gasped, more from shock that it was coming so quickly than from pleasure.

"I hope you enjoyed the meal," said my father, shaking the other man's hand.

"Much too much food." Mr. Abercrombie patted his stomach with satisfaction and I could see how proud my father was that he'd been able to provide such a celebration. I felt somewhat guilty for my plans to persuade Nelson to call off the wedding. But not that guilty. In time, Nelson would see he'd be happier with someone else.

Someday when I brought another young man home to meet my father, I hoped my father would shake his hand and be as welcoming as he'd been to Nelson's family.

Mrs. Abercrombie spoke to me. "Nelson insisted we give you something, as a gesture of all he feels. He asked his father to pick it out, here on the Strand." She motioned to one of the footmen, who brought over a large parcel wrapped in red velvet and bows. It was a cube, one foot square.

I wriggled with discomfort. A gift from Nelson on our official engagement night? I wished he hadn't. "That was very thoughtful of him."

"Open it later, at your leisure."

We said good-bye. The heavy package shifted in my arms as my father and I made our way down the Grand Hall and ushered his friends into their various coaches. My left foot felt as close to bursting as a ripe tomato.

It was an hour later, when I was finally in the solitude of my bedroom, that I was able to open the package.

Nelson had written earlier that he didn't wish to send an engagement ring until his ship came in and he was able to buy one in person, in London. So what did the package hold?

Part of me hoped he was an incredible romantic. Was it a beautiful hair comb? A silver hairbrush inscribed with our initials? A bolt of precious fabric whose colors reminded him of me? Something wistful and terribly personal? Perhaps some wild grasses from South America that he'd knotted together with his own hands. Maybe he'd made them into a bracelet and had asked his father to buy a clasp from a jeweler.

I took a deep breath, untied the plush ribbons, and removed the lid.

I peered inside. It looked like an ornate bronze statue of nothing in particular. Just lines and curves. I lifted it from the box; it was as heavy and cold as an anchor.

Like our relationship.

Nothing personal at all. Not a lover's gift, but something his father had selected. Something anyone's father could select. There was no inscription. No entwined initials. It was not a leather sash made with adoring hands. It was not a sketch of a lover's face. Just an icy lump of metal from a stranger.

Sighing, I wished Nelson Abercrombie the best. I truly did.

CHAPTER NINE

IT was early the next morning, Sunday, after services in the Royal Chapel, that I was finally able to read *Diseases Transmitted by Animals*. I had made my way to my father's library, tired from the late evening before and unable to eat much breakfast. My toes were still swollen, the veins still red. A headache torched my temples. My sore throat felt like a burning rope every time I swallowed. I was alone in the room, and hurried to read the words before I was caught.

Rabies usually develops within two to eight weeks of being bitten. On rare occasions, it may take only days. The nearer the bite occurs to the head and brain, the quicker the progression of the disease.

Good news for me and Peter; we'd both been bitten on the feet. Bad news for Jillian with her injured shoulder.

I read on.

The disease develops faster in children and those with a large wound.

A tingling shot through my left calf. I rubbed it as I continued along the page.

Ah, here was the part I was looking for—symptoms.

Symptoms advance through several stages. At the onset, there may be a heating sensation or tingling near the wound.

My eyes widened. I'd just felt that.

Initial symptoms are much the same as influenza. Fever. Fatigue. Sore throat. Lack of appetite. Headache.

I winced. I had some of those symptoms, too.

How could this be? It was too early to be suffering from early stages.

I was feeling tired only because I hadn't slept well. I didn't have an appetite, but who could at a time like this? As for my headache, it was likely due to not eating, that's all.

I swallowed to test my throat. It didn't truly hurt. Not truly. I just hadn't had my morning tea yet. It was a bit sore from having to speak so much at the party last night.

Pain in the abdomen. Nausea. Vomiting.

See? I didn't have it.

Quick temper. Hallucinations.

What did that word mean? I reached for my father's dictionary.

Seeing or hearing things that are imaginary.

How awful. I put the dictionary back on the shelf and returned to the diseases book.

A person may exhibit only some of these symptoms, not all. The most violent symptoms may occur quite abruptly when the disease has damaged the brain, just prior to death.

Oh, how suddenly that word came. I shuddered, unsure whether I could read on. I forced myself to.

The early symptoms may progress to "furious rabies," which may include the following strange and frightening behaviors . . .

Footsteps creaked outside the door. I plunked the book onto the bookshelf. I didn't have time to close it and place it upright between the other ones where I'd found it, so there it lay in full view.

The door opened. Mr. Bloomberg cantered in, yawning and rubbing his cheek. I reached for the rag I'd stuffed into my apron pocket, and dusted the tabletops.

"You?" His footsteps faltered. "Since when do you start so early?"

"Good morning, Mr. Bloomberg. Fine day, isn't it?"

Even he seemed to realize his rudeness. "Yes, yes, fine. Did you enjoy your evening?"

"Lovely, thank you." Last night in the Ballroom, he hadn't once come to say congratulations on my engagement. I'd overheard him and his wife asking my father about Nelson and the upcoming marriage, but they hadn't directed one single query at me.

Whose wedding was it? Why did everyone always congratulate my father? It was true I didn't want the marriage, but Mr. Bloomberg didn't know that.

Staring at the bridge of his pale, thin nose, I thought of something trivial to say. "I especially enjoyed the pianist."

"My wife, as well."

"Very good." I dipped my cloth into lemon oil and ran it over a mahogany desktop.

From the corner of my eye, I saw Mr. Bloomberg walking past the bookshelf. He stopped and looked at the book I'd been reading.

Oh, God, it was even open to the page about rabies.

My pulse rushed throughout my fingertips as I pressed them deeper into the dusting cloth. When he picked up the book, my breathing stopped. I'd been discovered.

I waited and waited for the coming interrogation. *Why are you reading about rabies? What do you know about the Moreley brother and sister? What are you hiding?*

But he simply closed the book and tucked it back where it belonged.

In a minute or two, when my breathing returned to normal and I could see he wasn't budging, I removed my apron, set down the cloth, and left the room.

I wondered when I would get the chance to finish reading what strange and frightening behaviors the author was trying to warn me about. Was it possible the rabies symptoms might develop faster in the three of us because they'd been implanted by artificial means?

<hr />

"But I've never worn a disguise. I don't know if I can pull it off," I whispered to Benjamin in the privacy of the stables.

It was several hours later, Sunday evening after ten o'clock, and we were standing in the dark, deserted room that held his trunk. I was finally heading out to see Peter and Jillian after a long day of watching clocks and waiting for night to fall. The light of the moon shone through a small window. We heard the occasional footsteps of late workers from beyond the door. It had been difficult to sneak out of the Palace, but I'd bade my father an early good-night and Polly had helped me out through the kitchens. After I had forced myself to eat some dinner, my energy returned. Although my foot was mildly throbbing, my head wasn't. Perhaps the symptoms I'd thought I had earlier were something I'd imagined.

Benjamin held out a blond wig that would conceal my black hair. It was puffy on top, piled with curls, and bundled into a tail behind the neck. "Charlotte, if anyone asks when we're outside the Palace," he whispered, "you're my older sister."

I tugged the wig from his hands. "How much older?"

"Maybe thirty. I'll mark some lines around your eyes with this charcoal. They'll look like wrinkles. Maybe a mole or two on your forehead."

"Why can't I pretend to be something else?"

"Like what? A boy? Your skin's too smooth. Maybe if we had some whiskers to glue to your face, but we don't."

"I suppose you're right. If I wear my long cloak along with the wig, I'll be fairly concealed. Go ahead, then, mark my face." I had to be careful never to be seen or recognized outside the Palace, walking the streets without a proper chaperone, or God forbid alone, or I would be severely reprimanded by my father. The rules of upper society were very strict.

Benjamin stepped in front of me and lowered his head to have a look. He was so close I could hear his breathing. I recalled how he'd dropped his firewood last night, but for some reason I was too shy to mention it in his presence. Funny how he hadn't mentioned last night, either—nothing at all about my engagement party. Didn't he care?

I wondered what Peter would have said if he'd seen me in my gown.

Benjamin squiggled the charcoal beneath my eyes and on my forehead.

"You're sure the supplies were delivered to Peter and Jillian? What about the two factory boys?" I asked. "And that girl at the tavern?"

"By a messenger I trust like a brother. His name's Adam. He's a stable lad, a little younger than me. Last month, he nearly lost his job when two horses got out from an unlocked paddock. I saved his skin. He's forever grateful."

"And he doesn't know who the supplies are from, correct?"

"I wrapped them in brown paper and didn't include any notes. Just told him who to deliver to. He wouldn't peek. Even if he did, he wouldn't make any sense of the supplies."

"That makes me feel more assured."

When Benjamin was done with my face, I put on the wig.

"How do I look?"

"Older, definitely. In the dark, no one will be able to tell."

I slung the cloak over my shoulders and tied it round my throat. It reached all the way to the ground. It covered my simple day dress and the flat-soled boots that protected my swollen toes. He was wearing all black, too. Black shirt, trousers, and vest crisscrossed with leather straps.

"Benjamin, I have to tell you something more about the night of the attack." He didn't yet know that I'd been bitten two days ago as well.

Running footsteps outside our door startled us.

"Can it wait till we get out of the gates?" he whispered.

I nodded. "What's happening out there?"

Benjamin opened the door a crack. We peered through it. Several experienced horsemen were leading two Windsor Greys from their stalls. A man I recognized as one of the Queen's favorite coachmen rushed by, out of uniform.

"Only the royal family can use the Windsor Greys," said Benjamin. "The Queen must be planning one of her midnight coach rides."

"I forgot—it is Sunday. She must be going to the Albert Memorial."

It was an open-book secret among the staff that the Queen stole away from the Palace whenever she could to visit the monument she had built to honor her late husband. It often happened on Sunday. My father had gone with her once, he'd told me. He watched her get out of the coach, sit on the steps at the foot of the bronze statue of Prince Albert (unveiled only last year), and speak to him as if he were there, as if he could hear her every word. The Queen had once called herself a "broken-hearted widow." Even though he'd passed away fourteen years ago, she was still mourning his death, still dressing in black and limiting her social outings.

For security reasons she used an unmarked coach, and her

coachmen and guards dressed in unmarked uniforms. She was superstitious, though, that Albert wouldn't recognize her from afar, and so insisted her Windsor Greys draw the coach. It was sleek and appeared to belong to an aristocrat, but unless someone had a trained eye, the horses wouldn't necessarily hold any significance.

If the Queen visited the Memorial in the daytime, she would be unable to leave the coach for fear of being mobbed.

Benjamin and I waited, motionless, until the clamor died down. After a solid ten minutes, the horses and men disappeared, likely into the carriage house to connect the team to the coach.

"Ready?" Benjamin looked at me and I nodded.

"All set."

I pulled up the hood to conceal part of my face. We moved swiftly through the dark. My heart beat a wild rhythm, fearful we'd be caught. We followed two milkmaids out of the stables, and a dozen more workers toward the western gates. It was remarkably easy to slip past the sentries. They didn't pay much attention to people who were leaving the Palace grounds; there was much more scrutiny of faces coming in, which is why the easiest time to sneak back in was at the beginning of the work shifts—with the staff of the Mews at about five, or with the gardeners by six. I wondered, as we passed the low stone residences, which room Benjamin bunked in.

Once out of the gates, we walked quietly along Birdcage Walk. The Albert Memorial was in the opposite direction, so we'd be safe from being noticed by the Queen and her men. But Benjamin's stride was much longer than mine, and soon my leg hurt.

"Please slow down."

"Sorry."

The sun had already set beyond St. James's Park. The trees swayed in silhouette. Gaslights shimmered along the street. A man on horseback rode by, followed by a private coach, a couple in an open hansom cab, and two men on bicycles. We passed a crowded public bus pulled by a team of horses. It was a double-deck bus, called by that name because it had another "deck" of passengers on the open-air roof. Those were the cheapest seats. A long wooden bench ran lengthwise along the top, where a row of men were squeezed shoulder-to-shoulder. The double-decker turned right as we went straight.

"Benjamin, I can't walk all the way to the East End." My foot was sore, and I had to slow my pace.

"What is it? It's safe enough to talk now." He indicated a park bench, but I shook my head. I wanted to keep walking. I wanted to see my friends.

"I've been bitten by the dogs."

He immediately stopped. "By the rabid dogs?" His voice was too loud; fortunately, no one was nearby to hear.

I closed my eyes to stop the welling emotions, then opened them again and simply nodded.

"God, Charlotte, why didn't you tell me?"

"This is the first chance I've had."

"Where?"

"The toes on my left foot."

His voice softened. "Is it painful?"

"Not so much. I put ointment on it and wrapped it with gauze. But it is swollen, and getting worse."

He rubbed the back of his neck. "Did you tell your father? Can he help?"

"No, he'd be forced to lock me up to protect the Queen."

"She could catch it from you?"

He obviously wasn't worried about himself.

"No, you can only catch it by being bitten by an infected animal."

He gulped, and I could see he was trying not to panic. "God, Charlotte, that's awful. It's unfair and just awful. There's got to be something I can do."

"For now, please just find us a horse or carriage to get to Peter and Jillian."

He thought for a moment. "There's a transport depot across the river. It has livery stables on one side with horses for rent, bicycles and carriages on the other. It's massive and always busy. We shouldn't be noticed. I have coins in my pocket; enough to pay."

He steadied me as we weaved among dozens of people along the Thames.

"Benjamin, there's more to the story. You might think I'm mad, but just listen."

He pulled me aside, and this time forced me to rest on a low stone wall at the end of the bridge. Water rippled in the evening light.

"Peter and Jillian didn't see what I saw; they were unconscious. But the dogs weren't real."

"Not real?" He shrugged. "How is that?"

"They were mechanical. Someone constructed them."

He tilted his head in the sliver of orange light, as if doubtful. "Good enough to fool Peter and Jillian?"

I nodded emphatically. "Glued-on fur. Real teeth. Even the dripping saliva and the growling."

"If they looked so real, how do you know they were clockwork?"

"Peter and I hacked them to bits with our swords. I saw the bones. Well, not bones, but metal sticks. Springs and bolts. Black oil instead of blood."

"The black oil on your skirts." He stared at me but I couldn't see his eyes directly, just the shimmer of his dark hair and the shape of his shoulders. "But that's good, then," he said, suddenly cheerful. "If the dogs were mechanical, they couldn't have rabies."

I moved my feet, and my cloak stirred around me. A young couple walked by, and I lowered my voice. "They were frothing at the mouth and aggressive. Snarling as though demented. Someone had definitely created them with . . . with this horrible illness in mind."

"Someone sick," Benjamin said with disgust. "But you can't be sure it's rabies," he insisted. "You can't give in to such thoughts."

"I'm trying not to, but I may be showing signs of—"

"No!" He snatched me by the elbow and led me among more people, past the rumble of the trains at Waterloo Bridge Station and over the tracks to a saggy brick building. I spotted horses and carriages in a courtyard. It had to be the transport depot.

When we were alone again, Benjamin continued the conversation. "What do you make of the news this morning?"

"What news?"

"I thought you'd heard it from your father. There was another mauling last night."

"Dogs?"

"Yes."

"Rabies?"

"Witnesses think so. Two men were killed. There was a robbery of a jeweler's across the street, and—"

"A robbery?" I said. "Another one, at the same time as the mauling?"

"Yes."

"Did anyone mention mechanical dogs?"

"The dogs got away, apparently. So no one saw them up close."

"But another robbery at the same time as the attack? That's how it happened on *our* night."

"Cab!" Benjamin flagged down a driver.

The man wore a scruffy jacket and an old wool cap. Expertly, he pulled the hansom cab to the side of the street. The rickety two-wheeled carriage, drawn by one horse, came to a creaking stop in front of us. Scratches and scuffs from years of use became visible in the glow of a nearby gaslight.

"How much to the Tower of London?" Benjamin asked.

The Tower was a wise choice. It was close enough to where we were going, and no one would notice us if we were dropped in such a public area. After the driver and Benjamin settled on a price, I climbed into the seat. My stomach clenched at the thought of what the night might bring.

CHAPTER TEN

WITHIN ten minutes, we had crossed the river on busy London Bridge. We made our way to the Tower on the north bank. Benjamin seemed to know all the dark corners of the city, for he asked our driver to stop at a bend in the Thames.

"Very good," said the driver upon payment.

We climbed out. I tried to suppress a cough. I had taken some tea and lemon before I'd left the Palace, and it had soothed the scratchiness, but now my throat felt as though something was stuck in it.

Benjamin tugged on his cap to hide his face, and escorted me across the cobbles toward the Tower on the hill. The grass, the trees—everything on the grounds was in full bloom and smelled like spring.

The Tower of London, with its imposing stone castle and columns set behind stone walls, had served as palace, fortress, and prison over the centuries. It no longer had those uses, but was known as the place where the Queen securely stored her Crown Jewels. During the day, people paid admission to see the display. As we marched toward it in the darkness, the Tower sat in relative silence as pedestrians and carriages hurried by on the bank of the Thames. I recalled my father taking me once, when I was little. He had lifted me high onto his shoulders so I could peer into the cases, laughing as we ducked from the guards. We used to get on so well; I missed that.

We passed the dry moat that circled the Tower and the dozens of sentries who stood guarding the bridge and main entrance.

"How are you on this hill?" Benjamin whispered.

"I'll be fine. My foot's not too sore." It was tender, but not as bad as it had been last night. I wondered why it had improved so much. Perhaps it was the meal I'd taken.

"It's a good fifteen-minute walk," he said with concern.

"I'll keep up."

The streets got narrower and the houses more crooked. Smells changed from fresh to stagnant: coal fires, damp brick walls, an occasional flash of sewage. Shop owners had drawn bars over their windows and bolted their doors. It was getting late, gaining on eleven, and we were passing fewer and fewer people. Some looked as though they were coming home from work, others from a tavern or eatery. Gaslights lit our path, and the surroundings began to resemble the warehouse district from two nights ago.

Benjamin wasn't saying much, and my thoughts turned to last night's garden party.

"Did you get your wood collected?" I asked.

"What wood?"

"The firewood you dropped."

He spun toward me in surprise, but didn't answer directly. "Did you enjoy the festivities?"

"It was boring."

"Boring? How can you say that about your own party?"

"Because it was."

I couldn't read his expression; it was masked in darkness. He indicated we should turn left.

I tried not to let my voice carry as we walked on. "I saw you handling the draft horses last night."

"They're now allowing me to handle the ones that serve the Palace grounds."

I stopped. My cloak swirled round my boots. "Benjamin, that's wonderful. A promotion?"

He nodded.

"Why didn't you tell me?"

He kept walking, leading us down another darkened alley. "I could hardly celebrate, with all that's happened."

"Well . . . when this is all over, we'll have a drink together, won't we? You and me and Jillian and Peter."

"Yes," he said firmly. I caught sight of his hopeful expression. "When this is all over, you must all chip in to buy me one very large drink."

We laughed at that, and I wished with all my heart this horrible situation would be over soon. "Your choice of tavern. Somewhere not too close to the Palace, of course."

"Of course. Provided Mr. Abercrombie's ship doesn't come in before then."

"Now, why would you bring that up?"

"Why wouldn't I? He's your intended."

"His ship is nowhere near—"

"If it was me, I wouldn't like it if you shared a drink with another—"

"Well, it's not you, is it? It's *my* decision!"

"There's no need to boil over."

"I'm not boiling over," I snapped, knowing full well I was. Could I not even suggest a drink with my friends without someone advising me about it?

And why was he so irritated by Nelson Abercrombie?

"I'm not even sure I'm going to marry him."

"*What?*"

"The engagement wasn't my choice."

His features were resolute. "I gather it wasn't meant to be your choice. Maybe . . . maybe your father knows best on certain things."

"Humph," I said in frustration. "You have no idea what it's like to be a girl. Fathers are always telling us what to do."

I shouldn't have to explain myself. In the year Benjamin and I had known each other, we'd never spoken about anything this personal. We usually talked about horses, or our favorite types of saddles, or how the stables at Windsor Castle compared to those at the Palace.

"Charlotte, you're not well. I don't want to argue. We have to find Peter and Jillian and decide what to do."

We didn't talk anymore as we wound through the maze. The streets weren't marked with names, and I was lost. The brick and stone walls all looked the same—the grime, the narrow entries, and not a shrub or tree in sight.

"Here we are," said Benjamin, coming through a gap between two buildings where a road opened up. "The place they're keeping Jillian and Peter."

He nodded at the brick row house across the way. A brawny man sat on the crooked front stoop. Was he a guard? Benjamin pulled me back by my cloak so we couldn't be seen. We took a moment to get a good look at the two-story building. On the left side it was attached to another row house, but on the right there was an alley. On the alley side, the house had two windows on each floor. Perhaps there was another entry round the back.

"There's likely a guard at the rear, too," Benjamin whispered, thinking along the same lines.

He peered down the sidewalk at the shops. One looked like a grocer's, another a dusty café. A handful of people walked by.

"Come with me." Benjamin led me to the grocer's door. "Wait here a few minutes. Pretend you're browsing. I'll see how much they charge for ale."

"Ale? How can you drink at a time like this?"

"Not for me. For the guards, to distract them."

"Oh, good idea. Then take this. You paid for the cab." I slid some coins from my small satchel.

He hesitated, as though he didn't wish to take it.

"Please, I'd like to contribute."

He pocketed the coins, went into the shop, and two minutes later returned with a small crate of bottles.

"Now what?" I asked, rubbing my hands to keep them warm.

"Now I deliver them. Wait here."

"But what shall I . . ."

He was already walking across the street. I turned and pretended to browse at the grocer's smudged window: several dried sausages were hanging to one side; there was a crate of eggs on the other, and a slew of used books. I strained to read the titles. In no time, Benjamin was back at my side. His crate was gone.

"Well?" I said.

He led me round the corner of the grocery shop to the darkened alley. Windows on the stores above us were lit, and shadows of people crossed the panes.

I looked up at his dark profile. "What happened?"

"He took the ale and thanked me. Said he'd share it with the guard at the back door."

"How'd you get him to take it so quickly? Wasn't he suspicious?"

"I told him Mrs. Moreley sent it as a thank-you for looking after her children."

"Wise thinking."

"He told me she'd been here an hour earlier."

"How is she?"

"I couldn't ask, or it *would* seem suspicious that I didn't know."

"What do we do now?"

"Wait a few minutes. Hope they get preoccupied so we can slip inside."

"But surely you didn't manage to get the key from him, too?"

Benjamin shook his head. "No, but I can fit through the bottom window. All I need is two minutes uninterrupted."

"I'm coming with you."

"It's not safe. And you've got a sore foot."

"It's fine. It was my idea to visit them tonight, and I need to know they're all right. I need to tell them that the dogs were mechanical." I prayed for Jillian's strength; the dogs had been so vicious. And Peter, how brave he was to have fought so hard for his sister. I couldn't wait to see him again, too.

"But it's not as easy to get in—or out—as I'd hoped."

"If you get in," I insisted, "I'm following."

"Then you have to promise that if we get caught, you'll do and say whatever it takes to get yourself free. Never mind me. I can handle myself."

"I can't promise that."

"Then I'm going back to the Palace."

I sighed. So stubborn. I crossed my fingers behind my back. "All right. I promise."

"It's not so hard to be agreeable, is it?"

We inched slowly round the corner to look at the lopsided row house again. The man on the stoop was gone. I imagine he thought he and his partner would be less visible drinking at the back door than the front. Neighbors then couldn't complain that he wasn't fully focused on his job.

By the same reasoning, I bet the guards would finish the ale quickly to get back to their posts.

"Wait here till you see me slide the bottom pane upward," said Benjamin. "Then be hasty."

"I will. Be careful."

Benjamin sauntered across the way and slid into the dark alley adjacent to the house, while I waited and held my breath.

⧈

Peter thought he heard a thud downstairs. He shifted in the chair he'd planted next to Jillian's bed. The gaslight outside her window lit the dingy room.

"What was that?" Jillian opened her eyes and turned her good shoulder toward him.

"Probably nothing. A cat or some animal outside."

He strained to listen, but couldn't hear anything beyond the usual street noises.

He didn't wish to worry his sister. He certainly didn't want to tell her the gut-wrenching news that Charlotte was dead, mauled by dogs. He was still reeling from it himself, nauseated by what her last few minutes on earth must've been like and outraged at himself for not being able to stop it. Mostly, he was angry that in the two years he'd known Charlotte, he'd never once approached her or made his feelings known.

Jillian had finally woken up yesterday afternoon, when Dr. Kenyon from the Palace had arrived to clean her wound. She must've been roused by all the prodding and moving. Unfortunately, the doctor had muttered the whole time about how bad the wound looked. He'd given her an injection of morphine for the pain, then applied a poultice to fight off festering of the torn skin—if it wasn't too late already, he'd said.

He'd done the same for Peter's ankle. Peter had grimaced and watched the whole thing. It had been bloody awful—burned like mad.

It still did, with red lines streaking up his veins in the direction of his heart.

The doctor had been speechless when he'd seen the streaking, and had declined to explain what it was. Which meant it was even worse than Peter suspected.

He'd allowed the doctor to give Jillian a needle of morphine, but refused it for himself. Morphine caused drowsiness, the man of medicine had said, and Peter needed his mind clear. He needed to defend himself and sister in the event that the guards, or the crowds, came after them. As soon as Jillian regained a bit of strength, he vowed they'd break out of this prison.

Jillian closed her eyes, resting again.

Late last night, an anonymous basket of medical supplies had been delivered to his mother, who'd brought it here. Peter assumed Dr. Kenyon had sent it. It contained morphine tablets, which Jillian was able to take on her own when she required, instead of getting needles from a physician.

Thump.

Peter heard the sound again. There was something—or someone—down there.

He slid out of the room, silent as a fox. On the way out, he picked up a long hunk of wood he'd stripped off a cupboard and placed in the corner in case of emergency.

It was hard to take the stairs without creaking.

He slowed, hiding in the dark shadows by the walls.

The thumping sounds were coming from the side window. He wondered if the guard was still positioned in his usual spot outside the front door, and why he didn't seem to be reacting. Peter took another step down. He moved into the parlor, face and body craned toward the sash window, wood cocked above his head and ready for assault.

There were no furnishings on the ground floor. He could've moved himself and his sister here but decided they were safer upstairs, away from their jailers and other lunatics who might want to see them dead.

It was dark outside and the alley was poorly lit. He made out the cap and shoulders of a tall man at the window.

Hell.

Peter's heart raced.

The bottom portion of the window moved slightly, then got stuck on the lock. The bumping sound of wood pushing against wood turned his muscles to rock. He'd inspected the sliding lock earlier and thought it quite sound. Now he realized a strong brute could easily snap it away from the rotting wood.

The person outside did just that.

Peter clung to the wall beside the window, not daring to breathe.

The man at the window slowly raised it. Nothing happened for a moment. Peter imagined that eyes were peering in, casing the place, wondering where Peter and his sister were positioned.

The intruder would damn well soon find out.

The window was up. Noises from the street carried in: horses' hooves and faint voices.

The figure leaped in onto the floor. Peter raised the wood and came down hard on the man's shoulders and cap.

Thwack.

"Uh," the man muttered, falling face-first onto the planks. His cap fell to the ground.

Peter raised the wood again, about to give another blow to make sure the man wouldn't wake up anytime soon, but another figure slid through the window.

How many were there?

"Stop," the female figure called in a hoarse whisper. "Stop!"

Dressed in a black cloak, blond hair bobbing over her shoulders, she landed on her feet. How could a young woman be involved in such a horrible crime?

While the man on the floor was out cold, Peter raised his make-shift weapon at the woman. He caught sight of her face and stopped in horror.

"Gawd blimey! I can't believe . . . you look just like her. What . . . are you a ghost?"

CHAPTER ELEVEN

"WHAT have you done?" I demanded of Peter. He was talking nonsense. I pushed the window closed so our voices wouldn't be heard, and dropped to Benjamin's side.

He was groaning facedown on the floor, regaining consciousness. He turned his head and labored for air. His cap lay beside him. I ran my hand over the back of his head. I didn't see or feel any blood, but there was a good-sized lump. He raised his arm to rub his skull, still dazed.

"Who are you?" Peter asked, waving the wood above us.

"It's *me*. Help me turn him over."

I grabbed hold of Benjamin's left arm to hoist him, but Peter stood there, wood in hand, staring at me. I couldn't make out the details of his face in the dark, but he was rooted solidly to the ground, not moving a muscle. "What is it?" I asked. "*What?*"

"*Who are you?*" he insisted.

"For mercy's sake, it's me! Charlotte!" Exasperated, I grabbed hold of my wig and chucked it at his feet.

He didn't move.

"I thought you were dead," he whispered gruffly.

"Why on earth would you think that?" I gave Benjamin's arm a good yank, frustrated that Peter still wasn't helping. "Hurry," I begged Peter, "before the guard returns."

That set him in motion. He kneeled beside our fallen friend and asked me, "Who did you come with?" We rolled Benjamin over. "Benjamin," he said in surprise. He sat back on his heels, stunned. "Why didn't you announce—"

That was as far as Peter got. Benjamin made a fist, turned over, and punched Peter in the stomach.

I yelped. They rolled.

Peter punched back.

Benjamin walloped the side of his ribs.

With a curse, Peter rammed Benjamin, trying to pin him to the floor. Benjamin was a couple of inches taller, but Peter was thicker and more muscled.

"Stop it," I rasped. "The guards will hear, stop!"

But Benjamin kept pounding.

Peter punched Benjamin's jaw. I heard a crunch.

Madmen! They were gasping now, hitting and punching and rolling out of control. I made my way to the chunk of wood Peter had dropped. I wasn't sure what I was going to do with it, but as my fingers clawed the splintered wood, another voice rang out.

It was weak and female and coming from the stairs. "Peter?"

Jillian appeared as a stumbling shadow near the top of the stairs. Rolling on the floor, both boys stopped instantly. The three of us stared up at her. She was bandaged, and struggled to hold herself upright at the railing.

I lowered my chunk of wood in relief. Jillian was alive and walking!

Benjamin was the first to get to his feet. He scowled at Peter for attacking him, but when Jillian stumbled at the railing again, Benjamin bounded up the stairs to help her.

"I'll be fine," she told us. "Good to see you both."

I smiled. "Oh, Jillian."

"Were you just fighting?" she asked Benjamin with disbelief.

"Let's get you to a chair." He looked embarrassed that she'd caught him and Peter brawling, and helped her turn on the tread. They made their way back up the stairway.

This left me and Peter alone.

Peter sprang to his feet, rubbing his sore jaw. He wore a different shirt than when I'd last seen him. This one was clean and white.

"Are you hurt?" I whispered.

He turned toward me, took the hunk of wood from my hand, and let it slide to the floor with a soft thud. Then he took my wrist, pulled me close, and embraced me. He squeezed so hard my lungs could barely expand.

No boy had hugged me before. Ever. And this wasn't the sort of hug I'd ever witnessed, not between relatives, not between friends. This one felt rock-solid, as though he thought he might never see me again. Had he been that concerned about me?

After a moment, his arms loosened. I thought he was going to release me, but he still held on. And this time, his touch was different.

It was a full-body embrace. I felt every part of him, first from his warm cheek on mine, and then to where he buried it on my neck, to where our chests met, to where his hips were nestled against my body, his knees, his legs, everything.

I'd be in so much trouble for this hug if one of my chaperones saw me!

I didn't know boys could smell so good.

I didn't know boys could feel so good.

I didn't know boys could make *me* feel so good.

Suddenly I was confused. What did this embrace mean?

Surely it meant more than a simple hello.

My skin rippled with excitement, from my toes to my fingers to my lips. I flushed with warmth, as though I were standing in a blazing summer sun.

When he finally pulled free (for I seemed to have no control over the situation) he stood mere inches away in the dark. I tilted my head way back to look up into his face. Light coming through the window flickered over his wavy black hair, the sharp lines of his cheek, the dried bloody scratches on his temple, and his glistening brown eyes.

I stopped breathing, because I thought he was going to kiss me.

He hesitated, and I waited and waited and waited. Then we heard the shuffling of footsteps at the top of the stairs.

"Is everything all right down there?" Benjamin took a few steps closer, breaking the spell. He still looked irritated with Peter. "Need a hand, Charlotte?"

⋇

Catching our breath, the four of us sat in the dark in the upstairs parlor, on ratty furniture that smelled like old shoes. We didn't wish to light a lantern, in case we'd be visible from the outside.

So much had happened in the last half hour. So many feelings, so much emotion among all of us.

Peter rinsed a cloth in a basin of cool water and handed it to me, and I passed it to Benjamin. I asked him, "What happened to the quiet, restrained boy I met last year when he came to work in the royal stables?"

Benjamin put the cloth to the back of his head on his egg-sized lump. "He no longer exists."

"But I liked him," I said.

Benjamin shrugged. "He grew up."

"To beat up your friend?"

"Why are you blaming me? He's the one who whacked me with a brick."

Peter flew off his chair. "It wasn't a—"

Jillian scowled at her brother, and Peter didn't bother to finish his sentence. Enough was enough. Why were these two going after each other like boxers? Then I wondered how much Benjamin had witnessed downstairs. Did he think Peter had kissed me, and for some reason that had upset him?

Well, he needn't worry. I was still an unkissed girl.

Oh, lucky me.

I shifted on the ripped settee next to Jillian. Her long, reddish-brown hair fell across her blouse. It was a fresh one. Her mother must've brought her a change of clothing. Her collar was open, bandages exposed at her collar bone.

"It's good to see you awake. How's your shoulder?"

"It was painful, but I barely feel it now."

"Dr. Kenyon gave her something for the ache." Peter leaned forward on his chair, dark hair falling about his ears. "And my mother delivered a basket of medicine last night." He pointed to the wicker basket that I had sent, then my role in it dawned on him. "You arranged that, didn't you?"

"I wanted to help."

"I don't know why I didn't guess, when she said it was left anonymously. Thank you." The words were right, but his expression was not. He was avoiding my gaze.

Benjamin, a big dark shadow sitting in the corner, rearranged the cloth on his head and turned grudgingly to Peter. "Why did you think Charlotte was dead?"

"One of the guards told me the third person who was mauled by the dogs had died."

It took a moment to understand the mix-up. "The third person," I said. "The beggar in the streets. You thought that was me, because when you woke up I wasn't there."

Peter nodded in the dark.

"You didn't tell me that." Alarmed, Jillian pulled back on the settee to glare at Peter.

"I didn't want to upset you."

Jillian's temper flared. "That's mean of you to keep things from me!"

"*Mean?*" Peter raised his voice.

"You treat me like a child! What's the point of working together if you keep things from me?"

"You call this working together?" Benjamin interjected. "He almost killed me!" He tried to adjust the compress on his head, but accidentally dropped it on the floor.

"I'll get it." I rushed forward, eager to do something useful. I took the compress and the basin to the pitcher of water by the window. As I poured, Peter walked up beside me. I flinched.

"Look, I'm terribly sorry," he murmured.

"What on earth for?" I snapped, hurt that he was apologizing for hugging me.

"I shouldn't be coming anywhere near you. " He dropped his voice again. "Because you are engaged."

And there it was. The awful truth.

"Well, look at the bright side," I said, lifting my refilled basin and slopping water. "At least when we argue, I forget about my other troubles."

"Let me know when you need some more relief," he said sarcastically as I stomped away, trying not to limp.

"What's going on?" Jillian sat up as I returned. "Now you two are fighting?"

I placed the water on the side table and gave Benjamin a fresh compress.

"Let's stop, right this minute," said Jillian.

Peter sighed. Dark-haired, broad-shouldered and oh so proud, he glanced at all of us. "You're right. I'm sorry to everyone here. Sorry, Jillian, for keeping things from you. Sorry, Benjamin, for the whack on the head. Sorry, Charlotte, for . . . for what happened back there."

For the embrace, or the cross words?

The embrace, I felt in my heart. I tried to calm myself, but my feelings were horribly bruised. He was trying to wipe away the hug as though it meant nothing.

Benjamin shrugged at Peter. "I didn't mean to hit you back."

Peter seemed to take it as an apology. "If I'd known it was you, I would sooner have whacked my own head with a hunk of wood."

"I might like to see that," said Jillian.

Benjamin grinned. Jillian smiled. Tension eased.

"I'll be all right," said Benjamin. He dabbed at his head, then took the cloth off and leaned forward in his chair toward me. "You need to tell them about the mechanical dogs."

"What mechanical dogs?" asked Jillian.

I felt badly that I was the bearer of more worrisome news. "Remember when you fell unconscious? I dragged you to the barn. When I came back out, that's when I saw their bodies." I explained everything about the dogs. Everything except that I'd been bitten, too. Benjamin peered at me intently, as if waiting, but I doubted Jillian was strong enough to hear the entire story all in one sitting.

"Who could do such a thing?" asked Peter. "Who has the capacity? The knowledge? Access to materials? The ability to keep it secret?"

The depth and straightforward nature of his questions reminded me that he wanted to be a police officer. Maybe I was being too sensitive about the hug. Since he had thought I was dead, seeing me must've been a shock to his system. The hug was a first reaction.

"Thank you for not questioning what I saw," I told them. "For believing me."

Jillian swung her knees toward me on the tattered cushion. "Of course we believe you, Charlotte. You're the most logical and honest person I've ever met."

"I don't know about honest . . . I think my father would have something different to say about that."

"Honest with us."

"In any case, they're some sort of engineers," I guessed. "Could be any kind. Engineers who develop iron bridges. Or gas clocks or patented machinery."

"Absolutely," Peter agreed. "Someone brilliant but diabolical."

"There's the Engineering Hall on the Palace grounds," said Jillian. "The Royal Gadget Engineers."

"I asked Mr. Snow if he knew of anyone who's developed anything like the Golden Butterflies. He insists they're at the forefront of development. That no one else is ahead of Her Majesty's engineers when it comes to inventions."

"He doesn't know that for sure," said Benjamin. "Whoever developed mechanical dogs is certainly not going to announce it."

"Maybe it's *them*," said Peter.

"The Gadget Engineers?" I asked. "Mr. Snow does behave rather oddly. I do believe he's worth watching, but I can't understand what his purpose might be. Or anyone else's."

No one seemed to have an answer.

"There's the mechanical engineering society," I said. "And the geological one."

"What about a lone engineer, working by himself? No member of any society?" asked Benjamin.

"Or someone with no engineering background—simply a mad brilliance for tools and machinery," Peter added.

"Tool and die makers number in the dozens," groaned Benjamin. "In London alone."

It seemed impossible to track down all these potential clues.

Peter bolted upright in his seat. "There was another dog attack this morning! My mother brought us fish and chips for dinner, and she wrapped it in today's paper. . . ." His voice trailed off as he sprang out of his seat and headed to the unlit fireplace.

"I was telling Charlotte the same news story on the ride here," said Benjamin.

"How is your mother?" I asked softly of Jillian.

"Terribly upset. She does nothing but cry. She believes she's going to lose us both."

I sighed. "You mustn't focus on that. Focus on getting well. No matter what anyone else says about the rabies."

"Where is that paper?" Peter crouched beside a pile of kindling and newsprint. "I was saving it to start a fire . . . awfully cold in here. Ah-ha!" He unwrapped a torn ball, walked to the bare window, and read to us.

"Two men near the Tower Bridge were mauled to death by rabid dogs. They were in the process of robbing a banker who was walking in the area."

"Did they get away with anything valuable?" I asked. An idea was formulating in my mind. "My father told me the other man who'd been mauled on the night of our attack was in the middle of a robbery, too. That his accomplices—unseen by anyone as far as I know—had gotten away with dozens of silver spoons when they smashed into a shop."

Peter held the sheet of newsprint to the light of the window again, silently reading. "Yes, it says the two men knocked the banker unconscious, and when he woke up a block away from their mauled bodies, his wallet and gold pocket watch were gone. But the valuables weren't found at the scene of his crime, or on the dead men."

"Well, that doesn't make sense," said Jillian. "If the dead victims robbed the banker, and the stolen property wasn't found, where did it go?"

"Another person came upon the scene of the two bodies and took it," suggested Peter.

"A fourth man," said Benjamin. "There was the banker, the two robbers who got mauled by the dogs, and then the thief who robbed them."

"It's possible," I said. "But it still doesn't fall into place. . . ."

Silence fell around us as we continued thinking.

"Tell them"—Benjamin tapped my right boot with his own and prodded—"or I will."

"Tell us what?" asked Jillian.

"You're not the only ones who were bitten that night," said Benjamin glumly.

Peter swore. He reacted so strongly at the news that his broad shoulders heaved back on his chair. His head moved in the dark across from me, as though he were examining my body for signs of injury.

"Her left foot," Benjamin indicated.

Jillian looked aghast. She went pale.

"There's a way out of this. I know it," I said. "We have to find the monster who created the dogs. Discover what he implanted. We need to know if we're dealing with rabies or something else. If it's a stronger dose than normal, or a weaker one."

Peter was still withdrawn.

"Maybe you should go to your father," Jillian whispered. "Maybe he could help you."

I was about to tell her that I had tried and failed, when a noise from the lower floor startled us into a deep, frozen silence.

Someone was banging on the door.

CHAPTER TWELVE

PETER reacted first. He leaped out of his chair and motioned us to be silent. As the banging continued, Benjamin rose slowly to his feet, muscles clenched, ready to fight. Jillian and I shot forward on the settee, bracing ourselves. My lips went dry and my scalp rippled.

More pounding rattled the front door.

I reached for the blond wig lying on the cushion beside me and slapped it onto my head. My black cloak was draped about my arms. Jillian pulled her shawl around herself, but she could barely move her injured shoulder and arm.

"What're you doing in there?" A man growled from down below, through the front door. He shouted something unintelligible, blasphemies of some sort.

"Guard," Peter whispered to us.

"Drunk," Benjamin warned softly.

Feeling cornered, I wondered if we'd done the right thing in giving the men alcohol. Perhaps they'd turn into horrid drunkards and try to harm us in some way. But it had been only three bottles apiece. How much did a man need to get intoxicated?

Perhaps we'd given them only enough to turn them nasty, while still leaving them strong enough to chase us.

From the look of terror in Jillian's posture, I suspected the banging and cursing had happened before. None of this was fair. My friends being locked up in this shack, having to protect themselves from ignorant people who wouldn't believe that rabies wasn't contagious, then being terrorized by the very guards stationed to protect them.

I rose quietly to my feet.

Benjamin shook his head at me in the darkness, indicating I shouldn't move, but I wanted to be ready for anything.

"Let me handle them," Peter whispered. "They know my voice."

"I know you're up there!" the guard shouted. "Answer me!"

Peter walked to the stairwell and yelled down. "What do you want?"

"Wondering how that sis—sister of yours is doing!" His words were slurred.

All eyes turned to poor Jillian.

"I'd—I'd like to come and talk—talk to 'er!"

The good-for-nothing brute.

Peter shifted at the stairs. "We're both tired. Maybe in the morning!"

The guard wasn't content with that. He beat on the door so loudly that I wondered how long it would take before the frame collapsed. Where was the other guard? Had he gone back to his station at the rear of the house?

I waved my hand at Peter, silently asking if there was a window that overlooked the back alley.

He shook his head no.

A jangling of keys at the door made us all stiffen.

Peter whispered in dread, "He carries a pistol."

Benjamin grabbed a hunk of wood and circled close to Peter. Peter grabbed another piece of wood by the stairs. A long nail protruded from it.

Taking Jillian's good arm, I motioned that we should go to the nearest room by the landing. I wanted to avoid her bedroom, for if the guard burst in, it might be the first place he would look. We made it into the small room—it contained another washstand and basin. I pulled the door almost shut, keeping it open a crack to see what was happening.

"Breathe," I whispered to Jillian. "Don't move unless I do."

The front door fell through with a thundering crack of splintered wood. Jillian shuddered. Air trapped in my throat as though I'd swallowed a frog. I peeked through the opening of my door to see both guards fall onto the lower landing along with the door they'd been pushing. They cursed, then rose to their feet, reaching for their pistols. They were coming for us.

Peter and Benjamin stepped away from the line of fire and hid in the shadows at the top of the stairs.

The bigger man with red whiskers, who'd been on the front stoop, took the stairs first. "Pretty girl," he hollered. "How about you and me and Burt have us a little talk? Without your brother."

Jillian cupped her hand over her mouth, disgusted, while I stood horrified.

Footsteps boomed up the narrow stairs.

When they reached the top landing, not two feet from us, they swiveled in the direction of Jillian's bedroom.

Peter leaped out from the shadows and used his piece of wood to clobber the first man's pistol. Bones cracked.

"Ahhh!" The guard shouted in pain as the pistol dropped from his broken hand.

The second man, shorter, thinner, and darker, seemed stunned—perhaps from the liquor. He stumbled forward so slowly that Benjamin had enough time to whack him over the head. The man's gun fired, and the bullet hit the wall.

With a loud jolt, a foot suddenly kicked my door. I gasped and pushed it closed. Jillian moaned and helped, pressing her good shoulder against it.

I heard clattering and thudding and cursing as the men fought. They moved away from our door. When the sounds traveled from the top landing to the parlor, I took a deep breath and pulled at the latch to have a look.

"Don't," whispered Jillian, putting out a hand to stop me.

"Get ready to run."

She clung to the wall, shaking her head. "I can't."

"I'll help you."

I prayed for Peter and Benjamin's safety. The crack in the door revealed one man now on the floor of the parlor, apparently knocked out. He was the bigger of the two, the one from the front stoop with the broken hand. Nearby, Benjamin leaned over to get the man's fallen gun from the floor. That's when the second thug kicked Peter in the back of his knees, and Peter fell.

I winced.

"Now," I said to Jillian. I whipped open the door, supported her good side, and dashed toward the stairs.

Jillian stumbled to a stop. "Peter," she called out.

"We need to move," I told her.

"Not without them!"

"They'll follow!"

She stood there, frozen at the sight. Benjamin jumped on top of the back-alley guard who had attacked Peter, and wrestled him. Peter was still on the floor, unable to catch his breath.

"Go!" Looking up, Benjamin shouted at us. "Run!"

I pulled on Jillian. "We have to believe they'll make it! Come!" Finally, she followed. I slipped onto the next step with her, wrapped my arm round her waist, and nearly lifted her off the stairs. My fear doubled my strength.

We stepped over the front door and onto the stoop as I struggled to keep Jillian upright.

"I can't walk as fast as you," she said, breathless.

"You *must*. And we can't walk, we have to *run*."

"I'll try."

The street immediately in front of the house was empty. A few pedestrians crossed the alleyways on both sides of us, moving toward a nearby tavern. Gaslights shone intermittently through the narrow streets. I adjusted Jillian's shawl about her shoulders.

"We'll head toward the people," I suggested.

"Away from the people."

"We can hide among them," I insisted.

Catching my breath on the front stoop, I waited as two laborers walked by in high rubber boots and overalls. They didn't notice us in the dark. More thudding from upstairs made me bolt.

"Now," I said to Jillian.

I took the two steps quickly, firmly anchoring my arm beneath hers. She stumbled beside me, then we fell into a steady rhythm.

What was happening with Peter and Benjamin? I met the crowd coming toward me, and swiveled to look over my shoulder. The boys weren't there.

"Where are we going?" Jillian asked between loud gulps of air.

My heart ached for the friends we were leaving behind. "I don't know."

⁂

"Who on earth would send me somethin' so heavenly beautiful?" Matilda had been staring at the baby blanket for several minutes. She had just slipped home from the tavern for a midnight interval to feed her little peanut, but Sara was still sleeping. Matilda nestled her own face against the softness of the knit.

Thank you very much indeed.

A burning candle flickered on the table of her one-room tin shack. There were no windows, so it was forever dark inside. Her sister, Eveleen, lay on the cot by the door. Baby Sara was sleeping peacefully between them in a drawer from a broken armoire they'd found in the alley. The three-foot-long drawer was the perfect size. It wasn't a proper crib, but now Sara had a proper blanket.

Matilda lowered herself to a bench at the plank table. She didn't know anyone in the position to afford such a pretty gift. Some of the patrons in the bar might, she imagined, but they had their own wives to go home to, and why would any man to whom she served liquor send her tyke presents? If they wanted to woo Matilda, or roll her in the sack, wouldn't they send her a lacy handkerchief, or perfume?

Eveleen had said she'd found the parcel, wrapped in brown paper, by the back door. It had Matilda's name printed on it.

Matilda looked at the second gift—a glass jar sitting on the table. What could that be? Raised lettering in the glass spelled out "Vaseline." She didn't know how to pronounce it, let alone use it. She opened the lid and sniffed the whitish jelly. A pleasant fragrance. Was it edible? Some sort of lard?

She glanced at the brown paper for clues, but there was no note.

She was about to toss the paper into the crackling stove in the middle of the room when she noticed pencil scribbling on the inside.

It read: *Vaseline for baby's skin.*

She dipped her finger into the jelly and smeared a thin layer on her dry knuckles. It took a moment to absorb.

"How nice."

Sara squawked from her makeshift bed. Eveleen's hand shot out instinctively from her cot to comfort the infant, and Matilda thanked the blessed saints she had such a tender sister.

Matilda pivoted from the bench and lifted the squeaky bundle. "I've got 'er, Eveleen." She kissed the downy head. "Are you hungry, sweetheart?"

Matilda put the baby to breast. Sara was a ravenous feeder. Thankfully, Matilda's employer, Mr. Donahue, let her take fifteen minutes every four or five hours when she desperately asked. She usually pretended she needed to use the outhouse, but came instead to feed Sara. Although Mr. Donahue knew she had a baby, he wouldn't stand for too many motherly duties coming between her and the bar.

Heaven help her when she actually did need to use the outhouse, for then she had to make up another excuse such as getting more ale from the stone storage house, or fresh towels from the back room.

Luckily, it was only a few steps from the tavern to this shack, which was a former smokehouse. It still smelled of cured meats, and Matilda suspected her clothing was also tinged with the scent. Things could be worse. They could be homeless. Mr. Donahue had been intending to tear down the smokehouse when Matilda and her sister and baby had showed up on his doorstep, a day after Edward had passed away from pneumonia—a nasty inflammation of the lungs. Now they lived here, but only until Matilda was able to save some shillings to rent a flat. Something with windows.

"Look what Mama has for you." Matilda wrapped the soft, lavender knit around Sara. It was the first bit of brightness that had come into the household since the passing of her husband, six days earlier.

She looked over at her slender sister. People often mistook Eveleen for Matilda's child, too, since she was so thin and looked closer in age to nine than twelve.

But did Matilda truly look old enough to be her mother?

Matilda urged her sister, "Try some of this here on your knuckles."

Eveleen yawned and sat up. Her brown waves tumbled over her shoulders. "Did you figure out what it might be?"

"Aye, indeed. Something pretty, for a pretty sister."

Eveleen rubbed a tiny blob of jelly onto her hand, lifted it to her nose, and inhaled. Then she smiled.

It was the first smile since they'd lost Edward. The three of them together—Eveleen, Matilda, and Edward—had slept overnight in the line for the clinic. They had waited for thirty hours to be seen by a doctor who never came, Matilda nearly ready to give birth, Edward about to die.

"Shouldn't you be gettin' back to your work?" her sister asked.

"What time is it?"

Eveleen lifted the latch of the tin door and peered outside. Matilda knew she was looking between the buildings, past the bar, at the clock that swung over the corner store.

"Five minutes beyond twelve."

"Almost done feedin' Sara. Hurry up, sweet girl. Mama has to go."

CHAPTER THIRTEEN

I clutched Jillian's arm as we headed round the corner, glancing back between the strangers at the thin, dark-haired guard, who was gaining on us. He'd caught sight of us four blocks earlier. We'd lost him when we cut through a courtyard, but he picked up our trail again at a crumbling brick wall.

"Faster, Jillian, please."

She staggered in exhaustion.

I tugged her along. I wasn't feeling well myself. It had been twenty minutes since we'd fled the house. My left boot squeezed my sore toes. My throat pounded with every raw breath, and my muscles seemed too heavy to move.

I couldn't very well shout for help, or I'd be putting Jillian in danger; the guard would surely expose her as infected with rabies. People would snatch her, perhaps send her right back to him. Twice he'd bellowed at us, but we'd disappeared into doorways before anyone else had turned to see who was causing the commotion. He'd be in trouble for allowing Jillian to escape from a house he'd been guarding, that much was certain.

We were fortunate he'd been drinking, for his weaving slowed him down. I wondered what had happened to the other guard and how seriously he was injured, but I was more concerned about Peter and Benjamin.

Where were they? Were they all right?

Where on earth were we going?

I was lost.

We wound through a maze of narrow, dirty streets crammed with shops, inns, men calling out vulgar things, and painted women hanging over balcony railings.

Swinging round again, I bobbed up and down, trying to get a good look at where the guard might be. I wasn't looking where I was going, and knocked straight into a chimney sweep. His brooms and brushes and bucket flew to the ground.

"You little imp!" he shouted. He grabbed for his runaway bucket with soot-covered hands.

"I'm sorry." I scurried to help him.

The cold, familiar voice of the guard roared ten feet behind me. "Stop those girls!"

Slowly I rose and turned toward him. Jillian panted beside me.

A handful of people, including the chimney sweep, halted and stared.

The guard stood beneath a lamppost, its light illuminating the scratches on his face, likely from the wood and nail Peter had hit him with. A trickle of blood oozed from his ear. His bottom lip was swollen and bright red.

Here was my chance.

I raised my arm and pointed. "That man has bubonic plague! Look at him! He bleeds from his ears and mouth!"

Heads turned in fright.

His eyes bulged with alarm. "That's not true!"

"He sleeps with rats, and they've been nibbling on him!"

"She lies! The girl she's with has rabies!"

"He only says that because I revealed that he has the Black Death. Look at the blood on his face, how he wobbles when he stands!"

People screamed. Guns and knives appeared from beneath men's jackets as they cornered him in the street.

I grabbed Jillian and we flew from the alley. We ran and ran till my heart nearly burst. When we turned another corner and I heard no footsteps behind us, I loosened my hold on Jillian's waist. Finally we stopped. I bent over to catch my breath, while Jillian collapsed against a short brick wall to catch hers. Her shawl clung to her back.

"How"—Jillian wheezed—"how'd you know what the plague looks like?"

"I don't," I panted. "I made it up. I thought no one else would be sure either."

She groaned, then started gasping and couldn't seem to get enough air.

Frightened for her, I patted her back. My cloak brushed against the ragged bricks. She leaned over at the waist, anchored her arms on her knees, and sucked in the cool night air. When I heard footsteps racing round the corner, I flinched and turned to look, this time knowing it was too late.

I stuck out my foot to trip one of the men, but he sidestepped it and muttered an exclamation.

"Bloody hell, Charlotte! You trying to kill me?"

"Benjamin?" I tried to make out their faces in the darkness. "Peter?"

Jillian let out a sob of relief. Her breathing subsided.

Peter, moving stiffly on his injured ankle, helped her to her feet. "Are you all right?"

She hugged him in reply.

"What happened to you?" I asked the boys.

Jillian pulled away from her brother. Peter, in dark jacket and clothing similar to Benjamin's, made an impressive, looming figure. I felt protected by their sheer size. If they were carrying weapons themselves, knives or firearms, I wouldn't object.

Benjamin pulled us to a shadowy alcove where we couldn't be overheard. "We lost you." He pointed through the alleyway where we'd come. The straps crisscrossing his chest puckered the fabric of his black shirt. "We kept backtracking and ducking into every alley and street, but they all looked the same." He took a deep breath. "The big guard is out cold. He kicked me and kept kicking me, and I reacted. I punched him in the gut—"

"Then the brute grabbed his pistol and fired," said Peter, "so I hit him with my club. I told him to stop, but he fired, so what else could I do but defend us?"

"You mean you took his gun again and shot back at him?"

"No. His bullet ricocheted off the fireplace and nicked him in the leg. We had nothing to do with the gun."

"You'll be blamed," I said.

We fell silent. A man was wounded because of us. Not a very good man, nor a kind man, but a senseless injury nonetheless.

And now Peter, who wanted to be a bobby, was implicated in a crime. We all were.

Hushed, we rubbed our faces and thought things through.

"We better move," said Peter, "before we're noticed."

"Where to?" asked Jillian, having recovered her breath. Her long, auburn hair shifted against her shawl.

"The main street."

Walking slowly, we passed some stables. Mules and horses could be heard inside, shifting their hooves and whinnying to each other. A few more steps along the deserted street brought us to a shop with a sign reading TOOL AND DIE MAKER.

We all noted its significance and came to a halt.

The shop's front window displayed a number of tools. Jigs, gauges, clamps, metal things I knew nothing about. The machinery, though, looked similar to some of the machines used in the Royal Gadget Engineering Hall.

This shop's location bothered me. It was here, very close to where the mechanical dogs had attacked us. Was that a coincidence?

"Who owns this place?" asked Jillian. The shop wasn't marked.

Peter tried the door. It was locked, which was no surprise as it was well past midnight. He cupped his hands and peered through the darkened glass panes. "We'll have to come back another time and speak to the owner."

"What do we do with you two?" Benjamin looked at Peter. "You and Jillian?"

I was thinking the same thing, but was too frightened to say I had no idea where they might hide. I had no friends outside the Palace, no one I could trust who could harbor my wounded friends.

"You can't go back to your mother's house," said Benjamin. "They'll be waiting for you."

"We'll get pulled away again and jailed," agreed Peter.

Jillian nodded. "And now they'll accuse us of wounding that guard." Her brow furrowed and she swayed on her feet.

"Jillian!" Peter swooped in to steady her. Benjamin took her other side, and they helped her sit on a curb hidden in the shadows.

"Sorry," she mumbled. "It's just I'm so hungry. . . ."

I suddenly remembered the coins in my pocket. There had to be someplace nearby to use them. I looked to the left and noticed a large clock swinging above a store. The area looked familiar, but that was impossible, since I never frequented these streets. I glanced to the right. A red sign with painted black letters hanging above a tavern caught my eye. THE BULL AND TALE.

Matilda.

"I'll see if I can buy us some food," I told my friends. "I'll be quick to return."

⊰⊱

Matilda mopped a wine spill from the gleaming bar top and dropped her cloth into a pan of soapy water behind the counter. With speed and precision, she yanked the cork from a bottle of Guinness and poured the brew into two glasses. She smacked them down in front of two working lads, and moved to the next customer.

"Shot of Irish whisky."

She reached for a bottle and filled a shot glass.

"I'll have a pickled egg," said another patron, squeezing in.

Matilda removed the lid of the huge glass jar with its floating hard-boiled eggs, set one in a bowl, and slid it to the customer. Then more rounds of ale, a bottle of port, cigars for the men in the far corner, and vodka for the Russian immigrants near the window. She was just wiping down the tables at the fireplace and thinking how comfortable Sara must be in her new blanket, when the bells above the front door jingled.

A blond girl in a cloak entered slowly.

Matilda nodded that she'd be right over to find her a seat.

Heading for the bar with a tray of dirty glasses, Matilda passed two rude blokes, one of whom reached out and grabbed her for the third time that night. Exasperated, she leaned over to the man, who was missing a tooth and telling bawdy jokes. "Sir, you might like to know that I've spoken with the owner. If you grab my behind one

115

more time tonight, he's kindly given me 'is permission to stab your bloody hand."

Flustered, he sat up straight and put his dirty hands in his lap.

Satisfied, Matilda continued on to the bar. Her Edward, God rest his soul, had taught her a few things about defending herself. She set the tray of dirty glasses behind the counter, then returned to the front door for the blond girl.

"Welcome to The Bull and Tale. Will you be 'avin' a bite to eat, or just a drink, miss?"

Dirt streaked the girl's chin. She had a mole beneath her eye, and one on her forehead. The lines about her eyes made her look weary. But when she glanced at Matilda, the light from the wall lantern skimmed her face. The mole on her forehead was smeared. Matilda squinted. Was it drawn on?

Matilda looked into the familiar green eyes, up at what she suspected was a blond wig or dyed blond hair, and suddenly she knew where her lavender baby blanket had come from. Instead of feeling warm and grateful, she was shaken by a bolt of fear, like a premonition that trouble was coming. She reeled backward, her curly brown hair swaying against her tunic. "You sent the Vasi—Vasi—"

The young lady pronounced it for her. "Vaseline."

"It was kind of you. But I think you had better go."

"Please, I only came for food. Something quick." She hovered by Matilda's shoulder. "You have pickled eggs on the counter."

"Yes. . . ." Matilda saw coins in her hands this time. "How many would you like?"

"Umm . . . say eight."

They went to the side of the bar, where Matilda removed the eggs one by one and placed them in a dish. The blond girl stood in the shadows and turned away from men's inquisitive eyes.

"You're in trouble?" Matilda whispered. "Again?"

"Not so much me. My two friends."

"Same ones from before?"

The stranger nodded slightly. "Only worse this time."

An image of Eveleen shot through Matilda's mind. Her sister was rocking the baby in the shack at this very moment, hungry herself but not wanting to raise a fuss.

Matilda was obligated to protect that bond. There wasn't anything she could do to assist this stranger—although the girl wasn't asking. "Thank you for your gifts, but there's nothin' I can do for you or your friends. Would you be wantin' the gifts back?"

She seemed startled at the question. "No," she mumbled. "You keep them. I only came for food." She glanced nervously over her shoulder at the front window, as if checking for someone, though no one was outside.

At a loss for what to say, and conflicted about what to do for this quiet girl who had sent her such a bonny blanket, Matilda handed her the eggs. "You'll have to return the bowl."

The girl nodded and paid for the eggs. "Thank you, I'll . . . I'll return in a few minutes with the empty dish."

Matilda walked to the door and opened it for her. "Who are they? These friends of yours?"

The blond girl blinked in the moonlight, as though wondering how much to tell. "They're our age, brother and sister, both injured. They need a safe place to stay for a few days." She tilted her face and looked as if she had the weight of the world on her shoulders. "To be fully honest, perhaps a couple of weeks. I'm not sure."

"Did they do something bad?"

She shook her head. "They're good people."

"Are they rich like you?"

Her lips twitched in surprise. "No, they're working people."

Somehow Matilda felt comforted by that. She'd be embarrassed to show what little she had to someone rich. Working-class people she understood. And perhaps there would be no harm. She sighed. "I don't fancy owing anyone a favor, so please, if I do this one thing for you, we're even for the blanket," she said firmly. "All right?"

Taken aback at the offer, the girl nodded.

"I know someplace quiet. You'll 'ave to come back when I finish my shift. Actually twenty minutes after that, so I can feed the baby first. Meet me in the alley behind the tavern at twenty minutes past two."

"Thank you ever so much. My name is Charlotte."

Then the mysterious rich girl in the dark cloak and golden wig slipped away.

CHAPTER FOURTEEN

"FOLLOW me." Matilda led us through the dark alley behind The Bull and Tale.

We'd eaten the eggs during the two-hour interval, but they hadn't been enough to satisfy us. We'd walked to the Thames, where Benjamin spotted a pub and bought us sausages, buns, and much-needed water. Then we'd watched the freight barges float by in the eerie quiet while we regained our strength.

I couldn't control my limp anymore. Nor could Peter. Jillian could walk a straight line because her feet were solid, but the strain on her face indicated the pain she was in. Her injection had lost its effect. The morphine tablets I'd taken from my father's supplies were back at the prison house. I could try to get her more in the days to come, but that wouldn't help her now.

Matilda pulled her shawl tight over her dark tunic. She didn't carry a lantern for fear we might be spotted on the narrow, crooked paths. I'd been shocked when I saw her slide out of a tin shack behind the tavern. Was that where she and her sister and baby made their home?

Was it possible that someone could live in a tin shanty?

It had smelled like good salt beef. So did she.

"Here." Matilda stopped one street down from the tavern, at the back of the livery stable we'd seen earlier this evening, close to the tool and die shop. A fenced paddock sat across from the stable on the other side of the alley, along with a small, crumbling stone barn. A warehouse and slaughterhouse ringed the back and sides of the grassy area.

"We can't stay here." We heard the movement of animals inside in the stable. "It's a business. People work here during the day."

"Just one." Matilda crossed her arms in the chill. She remained at a distance and kept her voice low. "Old Ivan Isaacs. He has a son who normally helps run the place, but he left earlier this week for Scotland. Gone to be married and bring back 'is new wife."

"What time does Mr. Isaacs arrive in the morning?" I pressed my shoulder close to Jillian's in the dark.

"He works five o'clock in the mornin' till five in the afternoon. Goes away for dinner. Returns once more, briefly, round nine in the evenin' to check on the animals. I know because he's been comin' into the tavern for his supper and likes to talk about his news."

Benjamin circled nervously, gauging the other quiet shops and businesses to the left and right of the stable. "If he's in there with the animals for most of the day, then it's impossible for us to hide inside."

"That's not what I had in mind." Matilda turned and pointed to the decaying stone barn nestled in the paddock. Stone steps a yard wide led half a story underground to a double-door entry. "You could stay there."

"What does he keep there?"

"Goats usually. But they've moved the goats into the main livery while 'is son's away. The small barn will be empty till 'is son returns."

"I don't follow." Benjamin loomed tall in the darkness. "What's to keep old Mr. Isaacs away from the empty goat barn?"

"The man's in his seventies. Painful rheumatism in both knees, he told me. Couldn't take those stairs if 'is life depended on it. It was Harold's job. The son," she explained.

"So," said Peter, warming up to the idea, "Jillian and I would be safe till the younger Mr. Isaacs returns."

Matilda nodded. "I'm not sure when that'll be. Could be gone two weeks. Maybe a month or more. You have to promise you won't damage the barn in any way."

I nodded. "We'll be careful."

Jillian leaned against her brother in exhaustion. We could all see she desperately needed to rest. Matilda frowned at her with sympathy. "The place is clean." Matilda's long, curly hair caught glimmers of light in the black shadows. "Mr. Isaacs told me Harold scraped it out before he left. Added fresh straw. I see a window at the side, there. Maybe you can open it for fresh air. It's 'idden behind the bushes, see? It'll give you some light, too, if you don't want to show yourselves during the day," she added with a hesitant pause. "If you don't want your faces recognized."

"It's not that, Matilda," Peter whispered, as if suddenly wanting to explain things to this girl who was risking so much to help us. "We fought with two men who were trying to attack my sister. They were hurt, and it's our word against theirs."

Matilda stiffened. Her demeanor changed instantly. "I don't wish to know." She backed away in the darkness. "Don't come near The Bull and Tale again. Please . . . I have a baby."

She rushed away down the alley we'd come from. Night bugs chirped. An owl hooted. The four of us looked at each other and, without another word, headed to the goat barn.

⋇

It was hard to turn my thoughts away from my friends and their troubles, but I had to focus on the pages in front of me. Back at the Palace two hours after leaving Peter and Jillian, I moved my lantern closer to the book I was reading. I sat alone in my father's library, cloaked in the silence and darkness of five o'clock in the morning, just before the royal household would come to life and I would escape to bed. My eyelids stung from being awake too long.

I found the spot where I had left off.

After the initial stage of rabies, I read, *more severe symptoms may follow.*

I blinked at the page, my lids so dry they hurt. The black lettering blurred. I took a moment before I resumed.

The early symptoms may progress to "furious rabies," which may include the following strange and frightening behaviors: fits, convulsions, biting other people . . .

Oh, God, I would turn into an animal.

I read on.

. . . violent delusions, and seeing and hearing things that aren't there.

The line blurred again and I pulled back an inch to focus.

During furious rabies, the patient usually has an uncontrollable fear of . . .

A loud bang in the outer corridor made me slam the book closed.

I listened.

Someone was walking in the carpeted hall. Footsteps were getting closer. I snuffed out my lantern, leaped up to the bookshelf, and shoved the textbook crookedly back where it belonged. I ducked to the floor behind my father's desk.

Uncontrollable fear of what? *Fear of what?*

Was I having an uncontrollable fear now? Of being caught? Was I hallucinating the sounds in the corridor?

I listened.

The door swung open. Light from the wall sconce in the corridor bathed a dark figure in a suit. Mr. Bloomberg.

He was an hour early. Likely here to study for his exams.

He stopped. "Anyone here?" He sniffed the air. Did he smell the lantern I had just put out?

"Hello?" he called.

I clenched my arms around my legs, praying for a miracle. Perhaps he'd disappear into smoke. Perhaps I would.

I barely felt the throbbing of my injured foot. I ignored the heavy weight in all my muscles and the hunger pangs in my stomach.

He trotted in his awkward gait to the lantern by the far wall. When he lit it, light poured over his side of the room but barely reached mine.

Would I be trapped here all day? How was I to get out of this?

I heard him make his way to the door again and open it. He must've forgotten something. Here was my chance. I scuttled across the floor, set my lantern on the counter where it belonged, and hurried to the other door at the far end of the room. The pockets of my cape were stuffed with the pain tablets I'd taken for Jillian and cleansing supplies for my foot. In the shadows, I paused to listen for Mr. Bloomberg.

I heard him heaving and sputtering and dragging something heavy—like a sack of cement—toward the front door. Precisely when

I heard him turn the doorknob, I twisted mine. When he stepped back inside the medical room, I stepped into the corridor.

Only when his door closed did I move. I tiptoed down the carpeted hall, half-limping to my chambers, wondering what he was up to and then what other horrors about my condition the textbook held.

⋇

At noon, after I'd had seven hours of solid sleep, Mr. Russett stared at me through the crack in my private sitting-room door and presented me with horrible news. "The Queen has requested your company this afternoon at four."

"Me?" My throat trembled. Since I was barely awake and still in my robe, I wasn't presentable. I hid behind the door. Polly had just delivered tea and breakfast, and I had given her a pillowcase stuffed with medical supplies to deliver to Benjamin in the stables.

Mr. Russett cleared his throat. His vest puckered over his heavy stomach. "The Queen requests your presence for a game of those checkers she enjoys so much."

"Magical Hong Kong checkers?" I tried to keep my voice from wavering.

"Yes, miss. At four sharp."

"Please th-thank Her Majesty for the invitation."

The Queen's favorite footman left and I closed the door. My head churned with dizziness, as though I'd been riding a weaving horse for hours.

How was I to handle this? I couldn't very well turn down the Queen, but I knew what she wanted. She would ask me questions about the garden party on Saturday night. Who arrived with whom, whom I had conversed with, and what they had said. What unscrupulous boys may have looked my way, and how I got on with Nelson's parents. At least I hoped she would contain her questions to those about the engagement party, and not ask about last night, or my friendship with Jillian, or why I had this limp.

I desperately hoped she hadn't heard of Jillian and Peter's escape, nor the wounding of the guards.

Groaning, I flung myself onto my bed. The soft feather covers dipped around my body. It wasn't possible to fib my way out of the game.

I wished one of my friends could save me, but no one could fight the magic of the checkers.

It was me she always settled upon, her favorite opponent. My father had mentioned my skill once two years ago, when we'd seen her competing with her barrister. My father told her that he'd taught me the game when I was young, and now he could never beat me.

So the Queen had summoned me to play.

I believed I knew why she enjoyed competing with me so much. Unlike all of her other opponents, I never allowed Her Majesty to win.

I didn't see the point. Why pretend to be less intelligent than you are?

At least, that's what I'd thought two years ago. Now that I was older, I understood why people gave in and pretended they couldn't match her. Then they wouldn't have to play with her anymore. They wouldn't bruise the Queen's pride. They wouldn't jeopardize their employment at the Palace. They wouldn't have to endure the endless round of questions they were forced to answer under the spell of magic.

Should I send word to the Queen that I couldn't accept because I wasn't feeling well?

No . . . she would only alert my father.

Was it too late to pretend I was dim-witted when it came to checkers?

Oh, Lord, yes. She knew I was magnificent at the game.

But I despised *those* checkers. They were invented by the Royal Gadget Engineer to amuse her. And now I would be Her Majesty's little mouse. It wasn't truly about the game of checkers at all; it was about whether I could resist the magic.

CHAPTER FIFTEEN

MONDAY afternoon was well under way at the Palace, but there were several obligations I had to face before my meeting with the Queen.

First, my foot. I soaked it in Epsom salts, trying not to panic at how swollen my toes had become and how the red streaks had progressed halfway up my calf. I dabbed the cleansing tonic on the wound again, wincing at the sting, and wondered if it was doing any good. The swelling had subsided from the night before, probably because my leg had been elevated in bed, which helped the circulation. I would try to keep it raised whenever I could. Tea with lemon was helping my throat, so I continued to sip. All I could do for Peter and Jillian was hope that the morphine tablets and bandages I had packed were en route.

Second, I had to write a letter to Nelson.

Wearing a loose-fitting white blouse and navy blue skirt, I slid behind my writing desk. I propped my left leg on a pillow-topped chair and found my silver dip pen and a sheet of parchment. The letter would be sent by a Royal Navy ship on its next trip to South America. Nelson would likely get it in four to five weeks, or perhaps in New York, before he crossed the Atlantic for home. Hopefully my letter would make him prolong his stay.

Even though it was too late to pretend I was a poor checker-player with the Queen, I had been wiser with Nelson right from the start. When I had learned of our engagement three months ago, I'd immediately sent an awkward response to his sticky-sweet letter, focusing on how incredibly young—and hopefully boring—I was. If he read between the lines, he would see we weren't suited to be husband and wife. If my father wouldn't accept my refusal of this marriage, then it would have to come from Nelson.

To my delight, the writing came easily.

I dipped the nib of my pen into the silver inkstand and began.

London, Buckingham Palace, June 5, 1876

Dear Esteemed Sir,

How splendid of you to present me with a sculpture as an engagement present. I have put it on my shelf right between my porcelain baby dolls and my favorite book, Mother Goose Rhymes.

It was lovely to meet your parents. They told me all about their egg farm. Have I ever mentioned how much I love eggs?

They are especially fine when they are soft-boiled. Sometimes the cooks who wait on me day and night prepare them lightly fried on one side. I prefer when they're not runny. Hard-boiled, on the other hand, can be a bit too hard. I've often wondered how many eggs a hen can lay in one day.

Well, I must be going. I rose rather early today, at noon, and am still awfully tired. I think I shall take a nap.

Respectful wishes,
Miss Charlotte Sycamore

Pleased with myself, I read it over. I added a squirt of ink to the bottom, as though I had clumsily spilled some. There. I slipped it into an envelope and put it in the basket for Jolene, ready to send.

Now on to my other obligations.

❧

Just past one o'clock, Peter sat on a small stool inside the goat barn and looked into the burlap potato sack he'd found hidden in the bushes.

Morphine tablets. Bandages and cleansing tonics.

God bless Charlotte.

Jillian had told him several days ago—before the night of sword fighting—that Charlotte's engagement party was approaching. He wondered if it had come and gone; he hadn't even asked about it.

He didn't feel like asking about it.

Nor did he wish to speak of it at all. Didn't even care to say the groom's bloody name. Peter had to push her engagement out of his thoughts in order to concentrate on more pressing goals. He also fought against the image of seeing her alive for the first time and how nice it had felt to hold her. There was no sense recalling any of it— how pretty she'd looked in the drab clothing, how warm and soft she was—it only reminded him of what he couldn't have.

It was ghastly awful that she'd been bitten, too.

Outrage hit him hard. They'd find a cure. They had to.

Only when he found the vile lunatic responsible for the mechanical dogs could Peter clear their names of the attack on the guards. He would collect and present all the facts to the police, like a true detective. It would be his chance to prove how smart and brave he was, that he belonged in Scotland Yard.

He rose and walked to the mound of straw where Jillian was resting, and gently held out two pills.

"What's this?" She sat up, shifting her weight, stiff with pain.

"Morphine from Charlotte."

Jillian visibly relaxed. She took the tablets and drank from a canteen of water he'd bought this morning while she'd been sleeping. He'd also bought roasted chicken and bread. He'd passed a second-hand clothing shop and haggled for a few necessities for himself and Jillian. His money was thin, though. They'd have to be careful.

"Why don't you rest awhile?" he asked his sister. "Give the medicine a chance to work. I need to scout the area. When I come back, you won't be in as much pain and I can re-bandage your shoulder."

She nodded and fell back on the straw.

Peter took a few minutes to cleanse and wrap his red, swollen ankle. The cloth gave the joint stability. It reduced his limp so it was barely noticeable.

Ensuring that the coast was clear, Peter slid out of the barn. He stepped into weak sunshine, happy to be free of stone walls.

He knew exactly where he was headed. He made his way through the shoppers and residents. Horses clomped in the street; rickety bicycles weaved past him. A man behind a hot grill shouted: "Roasted chestnuts! Get 'em here!"

Keeping his head lowered, Peter pulled his cap down. Most of the people he knew lived a mile away, so he didn't expect to see anyone familiar, but he didn't wish to risk the chance.

This time when he turned the handle of the tool and die shop, the door opened. A bell tinkled above his head.

"Hello?" His voice echoed in the long room.

No one answered. A fireplace and forge blazed along the far wall. On the other side of that wall, Peter calculated, was the alley that led to his and Jillian's hiding place.

Wooden shelves lined the room, crammed with boxes and trays of fittings and iron castings and metal parts and cardboard patterns.

Eight magnificent machines were arranged in the center of the space. Jig borers, grinders, lathes, milling machines. Peter guessed they were examples of the machines the tool and die maker made, awaiting delivery. Several other machines he didn't recognize sat close to the forge and appeared to need fire to run.

All of the equipment was sparkling clean. Whoever owned this shop was precise about his work.

He picked up a jagged sheet of metal in the shape of a small wheel.

"May I assist you?" a deep male voice two feet away from Peter asked.

Unflinching and not easily shaken—characteristics Peter was proud of, that would be helpful as a detective—he turned round to face the man.

"Good afternoon," Peter said firmly.

The man wore a leather apron over his heavyset frame. A mustache extended over his lips but was neatly cut into a straight line. Sandy hair was combed into a side part. A dot of blood speckled his smooth right cheek. Peter noticed the fine details, and deduced the man had just had a shave.

"You here to pick up the work for the cathedral?"

"No, sir. I'm here to enquire about your prices."

"On behalf o' who?"

127

"Myself."

The man snorted in amusement. He turned away when he'd done it, but Peter noticed nonetheless.

How could the man know how much or how little money Peter had? It was possible he had a vault full. Just because Peter was young didn't mean he couldn't afford this man, or that someone older hadn't sent him. Appearances weren't always what they seemed. Which was why Peter wasn't judging the man just yet.

The toolmaker lifted a set of pliers and squeezed them around a sheet of metal. He walked to the forge, placed the metal on the heated anvil by the fire, and hammered dents along the bottom.

Why wasn't he taking Peter seriously?

"I was wondering, sir, if you could make me a clock. Quite an intricate thing. Shaped like a face, I thought, with eyes and teeth—"

"Teeth?"

"Yes. They have to look true to life. Similar to a crazed animal's."

"What's this for?"

"A circus," said Peter, having worked out the details in his mind. He needed to request something similar to the mechanical dogs, to see if this man had the capacity to create them. "A traveling circus. It's to hang from wires above the clowns when they do their act in the center ring. A sort of comedic timepiece, I suppose. Like a cuckoo clock."

"Impossible."

"You can't do it?"

He shook his head and kept pounding.

"May I inquire why not?"

He stared at Peter, as if trying to assess who the young man was and what he wanted. "I don't work with clockwork details. Can't you see what I make?"

Peter looked about at the machines. Just because the toolmaker had made these didn't mean he couldn't make clockwork dogs. He wouldn't very well display those out in the open, now would he?

What was Peter to do? Shove his way past the man to see what else he had in his other rooms?

The man narrowed his eyes at Peter, squinting with suspicion.

Time to leave.

"Sorry to bother you." Peter sauntered to the door, lingering by some of the handiwork as if he'd honestly come in to price it. Just before he left, he turned back in one last attempt. "Do you by chance know of anyone who does specialize in details? A mechanical engineer? Or another tool and die maker who could fashion steam machines for a circus?"

"What's the name of the circus?"

"I, ah . . . the one that came in from Maidstone last week. Haven't you been?"

The man waited for the name. And waited. And waited. He was hard to read.

"Bally Brothers Big Top."

The man smirked. "I like clowns. What role do you play?"

"I'm one of the clown's sons," Peter said, making it up as he went.

"Do you let 'em dab all that white paint on your face? Put on those floppy shoes?"

Peter nodded very seriously, as though it was serious work. "My uncle is the head shoemaker."

The man's cheek lifted into a grin and Peter was confident he'd finally broken through.

"Only two men in London could handle clockwork like that. Justin Longfellow in Piccadilly. Thomas Cookstone by the wharf."

❧

My etiquette class today at two o'clock would focus on embroidery.

How delightful.

As though there was nothing better I had to do with my time!

But missing my lesson would only look suspicious. Leaning on my parasol to hide my limp, I rushed through the lower halls of Buckingham Palace. I swung into a sunny drawing room, panted hello to Fiona and Theodora, and nodded my respect to Mrs. Burnhamthorpe. "Good afternoon, ma'am."

I took a seat on a Louis XVI cushioned chair next to the sisters. It felt good to rest my pounding foot.

"Good afternoon, Charlotte." Mrs. Burnhamthorpe rarely smiled. I believe she thought of herself as a general on a battlefield; if she let her soft side show, her soldiers would run amok. True, she had a household of maids to run, but surely she could loosen her bun on occasion, powder her shiny nose, or dress in colors that weren't dreary. Why, her starched blouse could sit up on its own.

The headmistress turned away to rummage for our sewing pieces.

Fiona nudged me. Her blond lashes cast shadows on her wide cheeks as she whispered, "What's that for?" She indicated the parasol. "Expecting the sun to burst through our ceiling?"

Her sister chortled.

I ignored them.

"Now, Charlotte, here is yours." Squinting at the stitching that was partway done, Mrs. Burnhamthorpe gave me the folded blue table-cloth I'd been working on.

"Thank you."

"Fiona. Theodora." She handed them two linen runners that would be used for a dining table.

"Thank you, Mrs. Burnhamthorpe," cooed one sister.

"Very kind of you, ma'am, to supply such colorful threads," cooed the other.

For heaven's sake. Sometimes they went on about nothing.

"Charlotte, do tell about your engagement party. How was it?" The headmistress had worked behind the scenes in helping to prepare for the event.

"Lovely, Mrs. Burnhamthorpe. We were fortunate with the weather."

"What couples looked particularly impressive?"

"Well . . ." I began.

The Hill sisters beat me to it, but I was grateful. "The viscount and his wife," said Fiona, needling her runner. "She wore a flattering shade of apricot."

Theodora patted her curly blond hair, pinned back from her face. She'd done something odd to it, for at the back it looked like a haystack blowing in the wind. "My sister and I had our fabric ordered from Belgium."

Mrs. Burnhamthorpe listened keenly, asked many more idle questions, then asserted her opinion on the subject. "I hope you ladies watched your manners. Curtsied deeply enough to the Prince and Princess. Avoided chitchat about the others."

If you looked past Mrs. Burnhamthorpe's stern exterior—and some of the staff couldn't—she had good intentions and her questions were harmless. But it was rather humorous how much our etiquette teacher loved to gossip.

Ignoring my headache (when had that started?) I lowered my head and stitched for the next half hour. I worked as quickly as an ant recovering eggs from a broken nest. I had to leave soon in order to make it to the Engineering Hall before I met with the Queen for checkers. This time, I was determined to look deeper for clues about the making of the clockwork dogs.

"Why, Charlotte, you're not taking your time at all." Fiona smirked in my direction.

"Perhaps you'd find more pleasure in learning your wifely duties if you slowed your pace," Theodora added with a sniff. One of the buttons at the waistline of her dress was undone, and she didn't appear to know it. Should I tell her? It would be the polite thing to do. The gap puckered and her corset was visible. Discreetly, I pointed at her buttons. She frowned at me, not comprehending.

"Theodora, who dressed you this morning?" Mrs. Burnhamthorpe glowered at the girl.

Fiona looked at her younger sister and stifled a grin. Theodora turned a shade of splotchy pink. Then she glared at me, as if my pointing had somehow alerted Mrs. Burnhamthorpe to her sloppy dressing, but it hadn't. I had made sure the headmistress wasn't looking!

Theodora buttoned up. Mrs. Burnhamthorpe frowned in disapproval at the vulgarity of Theodora fixing herself here in front of us, instead of asking to be excused.

I truly didn't care. I turned back to my work and repeated my patterns along the bottom edges. The running stitch. Cross-stitch. Continuous locking stitch. There was a square knot on the corner, and more Italian cross-stitches.

I had so many more important things to do, yet I had to sit there!

I used the precious minutes to think of another letter I would send to Mr. Abercrombie tomorrow.

❈

Dear Esteemed Sir,

My father sat me down today and carefully explained—so that even I could understand—how important your research expeditions are. He told me that they often take many, many months, often years, to complete. Please rest assured, there is no need to cut short your South American journey on some false notion that I may need you here. Please take all the time you require and more. In fact, if you were to take up residence there for two or three years, it might bless me with the opportunity to rid myself of this frightful bout of acne, and the plump, hairy mole on my lower lip.

"There." I set down my embroidery.

"You're finished, Charlotte? So soon?" The headmistress rose from her flowered wing chair.

Fiona and Theodora grinned at me, smug that upon inspection Mrs. Burnhamthorpe would find fault.

The woman lifted her magnifying glass and examined my handiwork. She obviously needed to use spectacles or pince-nez, for she squinted at most things. However, she'd told us that ladies should never be seen in public wearing eyeglasses. I agreed with my father that her excuse was ridiculous, but no matter how much he'd tried, he could never convince her that a need for vision far outweighed vanity. It was a shame, as I'd seen some pretty eyeglasses at the court, dainty and covered in jewels.

"Very nice work, Charlotte," said Mrs. Burnhamthorpe. "Precise. Clean. The knots are invisible. And when I turn your work over to see the underside, it's as clean as the front. Most talented of the group, by far."

I wished she hadn't said that last bit. It wouldn't help me in my battle with the sisters. I didn't bother looking at their expressions as I said good-bye and hastened to the Silver and Glass Spider.

CHAPTER SIXTEEN

I entered the grand foyer of the Engineering Hall and hoped I wouldn't bump into Mr. Snow. He became irritated if I visited too often.

Since it was a workday, the Hall was filled with staff. Two cleaning men mopped the marble floors and another dusted windowsills, while a fourth wiped the tall neo-Gothic windows. Engineers, some talking in pairs, made their way along the corridors. Other craftsmen in oily work clothes carried gadgets and supplies.

The heat and steam power of the Silver and Glass Spider rumbled through me as I took a few steps forward.

"Afternoon, Miss Sycamore." The brown-haired junior engineer who'd been with Mr. Turnbull two days ago, whose name still escaped me, gave me a friendly look as he strode past in jacket and cravat. "What brings you here today?"

"The puppies," I fibbed. "Came to see them."

"Ah," he said, "I'm headed downstairs myself. Shall we?"

I couldn't very well say no, even though I wished to. I didn't need anyone's eyes on me. What was this man's name? Yale? Yuleweather? Yates? I nervously clutched my parasol and grabbed the banister of the curved marble stairs, grateful for the support. My head was swimming again with dizziness.

The nameless engineer took his time, step by step with me. He must've thought me awfully timid—or overly ladylike—to be walking so slowly in my fashionable skirt, white blouse, and tailored jacket.

"Yardley," one of his colleagues called as we got to the bottom landing, "what's the equation on that metal you combined with sulfur?"

Mr. Yardley. That was it.

"I'll be right there."

"Go ahead, Mr. Yardley," I said, relieved he was being called away. "I'll be fine on my own." Before he could object, I turned the corner toward the heat coming from the blast furnaces. The puppies were right there by my skirts.

They squirmed on newspaper bedding.

Smiling at the sight, I sank to my knees. Five wiggling cocker spaniel pups were nestled in a row, like pickled herring in a tin can, next to their mother. They were various colors—white, sandy red, and black, with soft bellies, long tails, and wispy, curled fur.

"Annabelle," I murmured, stroking the golden mother. She nuzzled my hand. "They're adorable."

None of the pups had opened their eyes yet. I stroked the smallest one. He was the only solid black pup, with a white diamond-shaped patch of fur between his eyes. The white diamond made him look regal. He wriggled beneath my touch. I desperately wanted to pick him up and hold him, but didn't wish to scare him by removing him from his mother. I would wait several days, until he opened his eyes.

Still crouched low, I swung my gaze down the corridor to the noisy blast furnaces. Two men in overalls were shoving wood into the blazing fires. I recognized their faces but rarely spoke to them other than in passing. One of them was Mr. Turnbull's younger, dark-haired brother Aiden. Another was a red-haired man from Scotland they'd humorously nicknamed Flame—not because of his hair color, but because he liked to work the fires.

There were more workshops down here, too. I rose to my feet and left the dogs for a moment to discreetly search the area for clues.

Aiden Turnbull noticed me from afar. Damp with perspiration, he set aside his shovel and lifted a hand in friendly greeting.

"You've come to see the pups!" he called. He was much like his brother in setting me at ease here, although I didn't wish to speak with him today. I was on a mission.

"Yes, they're irresistible!" I waved back and quickly slid from view down the corridor.

Most of the space here was used for storing gadgets that either didn't work or that the engineers had set aside. They had plenty of those. Sometimes they used the shops to carry out large and messy projects that couldn't be handled on the main floor. I ducked my head into the main room and nearly stepped in a puddle of oily water.

I jumped back to avoid it.

The room was empty and I didn't notice anything suspicious from the doorway. This was where the engineers were currently working on a series of cast-iron stoves, fitted with timers, that would burn wood for periods of controlled duration. The timer could be set for anywhere from twenty minutes to five hours, and the wood was extinguished by being doused with water from an overhead bucket. Yet thus far the contraptions had been faulty; they had produced only sizzle and large volumes of blackened water spilled on the concrete floor. Such as the puddle in front of me that I'd almost stepped in.

Hence the experiment was being abandoned.

I heard footsteps and turned to see Cameron Turnbull exiting a small office several yards away. And, good Lord, the Prince of Wales was with him!

"Yes, absolutely," His Royal Highness was chuckling as he spoke to Mr. Turnbull. "Send me the specifications and I'll share them with Her Majesty. You're quite right, the Queen may be interested in updating the kitchens with several of your gadgets. I remember when she first consented to using gas stoves at Windsor, but of course that was at my father's prodding. He was always looking to the future; quite a visionary."

The Prince, heavyset and dressed impeccably, finally noticed me. I curtsied deeply, praying I wouldn't topple with dizziness. His eyes flickered but he did not address me, despite the time we'd shared at my engagement party; thus I remained silent. He nodded politely.

"Very well, Sir," Mr. Turnbull said.

The men parted and the Prince took his leave by the stairs. It wasn't uncommon to see him here speaking with Mr. Turnbull and the others, though it always gave me a jolt, as though I'd been caught stealing a sweet from a forbidden jar.

Mr. Turnbull seemed to be in good spirits. "How did your grand celebration fare, Charlotte?" His white shirtsleeves were rolled up to his elbows. His dark vest and cravat matched his dark hair.

"Very well, thank you. Mr. Abercrombie would've been pleased to see such a turnout of his colleagues."

Mr. Turnbull's eyes flickered. "I heard Mr. Darwin was there."

"He was. Complete with fire-spitting cane."

"I wish I'd witnessed it." His face lit up with amusement. "Does the fire come directly from the bottom? How does it work? By a button, or is it triggered when he thrusts it in a certain direction?"

"I looked closely, but couldn't deduce it myself."

"Apparently he's only had it for three days."

Did I detect a bit of friendly rivalry? Mr. Snow was the same way when he spoke of scientific gadgets.

"Do you happen to know where he got it?" I asked. Someone in London had produced it. Who? And did he have the capability to make mechanical dogs?

"I'm not certain."

The Royal Gadget Engineers worked only for the Crown and were forbidden to give away their products or their secrets, so it hadn't come from them.

Mr. Turnbull walked me back to the stairs, and I heard dogs yelping.

"Miss Sycamore? Charlotte? I asked how do you like the pups?"

I snapped back to the present. I'd been daydreaming. How odd that my mind had run off like that. "Sorry . . . I lost myself. What did you say?"

"The pups. Which is your favorite?"

"They're all so . . . I think the one wearing the diamond."

Mr. Turnbull chuckled. "Look at all the folded skin on his forehead. Let's hope he grows into it."

I used the parasol for support as I slid down and stroked him. "It makes him look as though he's frowning, as if he's deep in thought, like a poet."

"Do you think your father would allow you to take him?"

I pivoted so quickly in Mr. Turnbull's direction that my vision blurred for a second and a new pain jabbed my ankle. Still crouched, I quickly rebalanced myself. "What do you mean?"

"You can have one if you'd like."

"For my very own?"

He nodded. "We need to find homes for all of them."

"Mr. Snow won't mind?"

"Why would he mind? Charlotte, I think you . . . you misunderstand him sometimes. He's not that cantankerous."

Slowly, I got to my unsteady feet and brushed off my navy skirt. "I would love to take a puppy. But my father . . . I'm not sure he would allow it."

I would beg and barter and promise anything in the world for a dog of my own.

"Perhaps if you ask."

"Perhaps if I mentioned it to the Queen, and she spoke to my father . . ."

"Ah, yes," he said. A wave of exhaustion rolled over me, and his face went fuzzy. I wasn't sure what I was seeing. Mr. Turnbull continued, "It is useful to be on Her Majesty's good side." His mouth twisted and his voice sounded odd. What was happening to me? "The Queen's opinion would hold a lot more weight than mine."

I tried to stabilize my balance. I inhaled sharply, and my senses came back to me. Thankfully, it had been only a momentary spell of dizziness. "Is Mr. Snow here? I'd like to speak to him about the pup." Maybe this was my chance to ease into a more friendly conversation with the head engineer.

"He's not in this afternoon. Not sure where he went."

"That's a shame. Then I'll broach the subject tomorrow." I was confused. "I'm sorry. Where did you say he went? Parliament?"

Mr. Turnbull gave me an odd look. "I didn't say."

"Hmm. And he'll be back when?"

"Tomorrow morning."

"Ah."

"You look pale. Are you well?"

"Yes, yes. I'm fine. I must have risen off the floor too quickly." I excused myself and made my way toward the stairs. Mr. Turnbull went to speak to Aiden and the other men near the blast furnaces. As soon as I left the heat of the corridor, I felt better.

Another thought occurred to me. If Mr. Snow was absent today, perhaps this might be a good time to snoop through his things.

⚜

To avoid suspicion, I went straight to my worktable on the main floor of the Engineering Hall and pretended to concentrate on my own gadgets while contemplating how best to investigate the area. How would Peter handle this?

I wondered what he was doing and if his ankle was getting worse. He was fighting so hard for all three of us. It was easier for me, being pampered by the Palace staff. I couldn't imagine what he and Jillian were going through. And I hoped like mad that Benjamin's involvement wouldn't end in mortal danger.

Half a dozen men nodded hello. They continued with their business as I sat on my stool by the tall windows that overlooked the lake.

This was where I spent several hours a week, working on my hobby inventions, whenever I was in London. I pulled one of them out, another sword with a rotating blade, and flicked the button on the top. It jammed. With a small screwdriver, I yanked out the button. Wires came undone. Aha, a loose connection. I fixed it and snapped it back into position.

It worked now.

Where had I stored the sister blade to this one? The one I'd used to fight off the dogs. Where had I put it? I had taken Peter's sword and my own into the barn and placed them somewhere safe so others couldn't find them . . .

Where?

I rubbed my temples. It would come to me.

I looked to my right. There were still two men working in the Great Exhibition Room, so I couldn't snoop through Mr. Snow's displays just yet. But to be completely honest, I was scared to go in. Scared to discover that Mr. Snow might be the creator of the monsters.

138

I placed my hand underneath the tabletop and groped about until I found the other experiment I was working on. My set of goggles. I pulled them out and tried them on. Nothing more than magnifying glasses.

I focused on the lake through the window and was amazed at how sharp and clear the water was. A goose flew by. I saw her webbed feet.

I removed the goggles. What else could I add to this? What had I seen Mr. Snow and Mr. Turnbull do to their experiments when they seemed doomed to fail?

There were solutions and potions on one of the side tables three seats down. I rose and read the labels.

SLIME FROM THE INNARDS OF A FROG. DIRT FROM THE PALACE ROOF-TOP. ICE-MELTING SOLUTION. Hmm. I took that one and kept reading. MEMORY TONIC—BEWARE. That one sounded interesting. The next two I picked out solely on the basis of color. One was a lavender liquid, the other the color of a sunny June sky—like today's. I took both.

When I returned to my worktable, I pulled out a little paint-brush and dabbed the tonics on the lenses of my goggles. I should've been writing the names and order of solutions in the journal I kept, but my eyes couldn't focus well enough to write. So I painted, turned, and brushed. I didn't remember if I'd already added the lavender, so I added a bit more. Ah. That was enough. I blew on the glass and it dried quickly. While I was waiting, I limped back to the tables, about to set the potions back on their shelf. But when I pivoted, another knife-jab blasted my ankle.

"Ow!" What was wrong with my foot? Was it getting worse?

Two workers walked by as I rattled the bottles nervously and placed them in position. I looked up, startled at their sudden presence, but they weren't paying close attention.

"Working on something, miss?"

"Another failed experiment," I said.

"Keep trying."

I nodded.

They had just left the Exhibition Room, which meant it was empty now and I could sneak in. I slipped the freshly painted goggles onto my head once more and peered out the window. Nothing. How disappointing. The lake, the birds, the trees—they all looked the same.

I was about to remove the goggles when I glanced at my own hand. I nearly screamed.

It crawled with life. I saw beneath the skin to the pounding arteries carrying vivid red blood, the layer of blue veins beneath it, muscles and tendons strapped to bones. My pulse beat underneath it all like a boiling pot of water.

Shocked, I whipped off my goggles and frantically tucked them under the table.

Hallucinations. Seeing things that weren't there. That was a sign of rabies, wasn't it?

Horrified that I was losing my grip on reality, I rose from the table and looked to the exit, fighting the urge to flee. My heart raced. I wasn't brave enough for this. But then I looked in the other direction, to Mr. Snow's private office. Perhaps the key to overcoming rabies would be found right there.

Leaning on my parasol, I went in. Blueprints were stacked neatly on his desk. Collections of crystals from faraway places. Semiprecious stones.

Nothing out of the ordinary.

I took my parasol and shuffled back into the Exhibition Room.

Mr. Snow was a great admirer of Mother Nature, and his collections mirrored his interest. There was an astoundingly perfect monarch butterfly under glass. I imagined it had inspired the design of the Golden Butterflies for the Palace.

I moved on. African darts. A display of poisonous frogs. And then live tarantulas behind glass.

I shuddered at the gruesome spiders, but there was nothing here I hadn't seen dozens of times before. Something else nagged at me, though, something I wanted to remember but somehow couldn't. Was it the meeting place of Mr. Snow today? Was he meeting at the Houses of Parliament or the Albert Memorial or the Old Bailey criminal courthouse? Had Mr. Turnbull told me where Mr. Snow had gone?

And then I remembered.

The Queen! I was due for checkers with the Queen!

CHAPTER SEVENTEEN

I raced to the Queen's private quarters, past the sentries, out of breath and nervous that someone would notice my limp. Fortunately, it was sunny outside and I entered from the outdoors, so no one would question why I'd brought a parasol. Unfortunately, my blouse was damp with perspiration from my stress and illness.

I wore my thinnest white gloves for presentation to the Queen. When I turned a corner, I nearly bumped into two men wearing turbans encrusted with jewels and long robes that shimmered as though they were spun from real gold. Maharajas—princes—from India, likely here on state business with the Queen, since she had been officially declared their Empress. I murmured apologies to their assistant and hurried on.

Two minutes later Mr. Russett, in his well-pressed livery, greeted me at Her Majesty's inner office. "Miss Sycamore, are you well?"

"Quite fine, thank you. And you?" I swallowed.

His round nose skewed upward, as though not exactly convinced. He nodded and opened the heavy door for me nonetheless.

I swallowed again. There seemed to be a lump in my throat, a scratching that was causing an irritation, and it worried me that my brain couldn't seem to catch up with time. I started wondering what my father's apprentice, Mr. Bloomberg, had been dragging into the medical rooms at five o'clock this morning. Why was I thinking of it only now? It had sounded like a dead body being dragged across the floor, but that idea was preposterous.

More hallucinations on my part?

Was I slowly going insane, perhaps with furious rabies?

Inside the expansive room, two gentle greyhounds came to greet me, then retreated to the fireplace rug.

Her Majesty was seated at her glossy desk, surrounded by a handful of men who seemed to be advising her about the papers she was reading. The Lord Chamberlain of the Household stood at her side. The Private Secretary indicated where she should sign, and two other businessmen, outsiders I didn't recognize, chatted in good spirits. Heads turned at the sound of our footsteps.

"Russett," said the Queen in acknowledgment.

"Your Majesty," he announced, "Miss Sycamore arrives for the game."

I took a deep breath, gave the Queen a deep curtsy, leaning heavily on my parasol, and returned to my feet with a shaky smile.

If these people knew I was tainted with rabies and was now exposing the British monarch to it, there would be no mercy. Public hangings had been abolished, but I would no doubt be taken away and hanged in the privacy of the courts.

Good God, what was I doing here? I hadn't even thought this through until now because I'd been consumed with my own strategy.

I looked at her stern face and the unsmiling features of the others.

But she wasn't in any danger from my illness. My father had unknowingly assured me of that. And I believed with all my heart in my father's brilliance as the Royal Surgeon.

The Queen's expression mellowed. "Good afternoon, Charlotte." She wore her signature black dress, heavily starched, with her hair pinned upward as it always was, and several golden necklaces sitting upon her wide chest.

"Your Majesty."

"Come in, come in." She peered over my shoulder. "Russett, some tea, please."

"Yes, Ma'am," he replied.

I heard his shoes shuffling on the Persian carpet as he backed out of the room. The door clicked closed. The other men exited with their papers, bowing to Her Majesty and bidding her good afternoon as they backed out.

"Do have a seat." She motioned to our favorite arena—two wing chairs by the fireplace. The seating was done in yellow chintz fabrics, flowery and pretty. Priceless paintings adorned the walls. Some of her private collections of sculptures and timepieces surrounded us. The checkerboard was already set up, no doubt by Russett. It always looked deceptively normal, until you peered closer.

"Are you feeling up to losing today?" she asked.

"No, Ma'am," I replied instinctively. "I have a mind to win."

She chuckled.

It always started this way. She asked me if I'd like to lose, and I told her no.

She gazed down at my parasol. "I think there's enough shade in here. You won't be needing that."

I mustered a wide smile and scrambled for an explanation. "I'll be needing it soon enough. I thought perhaps after our game, Your Majesty, I would take a victory stroll in the gardens."

Her chuckle was even deeper. "We are amused."

It was odd when she spoke of herself in the plural. We are this, and we are that.

But who was I to question a monarch? Sometimes, though, as she grew more comfortable with me, she dropped her formal language.

Her jaw was still swollen from her dental surgery.

"Are you feeling better, Ma'am?" I touched my cheek to indicate her tooth.

"Your father recommended strong brandy. It seems to be working."

Had she been drinking? My gaze shot to her desk. A bottle of Cognac sat by the window, along with a brandy snifter containing a few drops of brown liquid. I'd never been with the Queen when she'd had anything other than a glass of wine at dinner. Did alcohol affect her as it did other people?

She was not drunk. She was clear-eyed and aware.

What a shame. For a moment, I'd hoped there was a chance I could outwit her. Leave my gloves on, for example, without her noticing.

"Have a seat, please, my dear. You may remove your gloves."

I groaned inwardly.

When I approached the chairs, I felt as though I was marching to the gallows. All the possible questions she could ask me . . .

I took my chair, my side of the battle arena.

Finger by finger, I removed my gloves and set them down beside me. She, however, tugged hers on. Black silk.

The checkerboard sitting on the tea table in front of us was masterfully crafted.

The board was shaped like a six-pointed star, made of gleaming black marble. The men were made of special pearls found in the Hong Kong seas and shaped into miniature pyramids. There were two colors—white pearl and pink pearl. The object of the game was not to hop over your opponent's checkers and thereby capture them, but to get all of your checkers to the other side before your opponent got hers to this side. There was often a battle in the center, when spaces became so crowded that it was nearly impossible to move.

The pieces radiated magic. They were an invention of Mr. Snow's, developed when he'd visited the British colony ten years ago and collected the pearls, which had been rumored by the locals to be magical. When you touched the pearl pyramids with your bare fingers, they would reveal your emotions. They would turn green or blue or yellow or purple or red or black, depending on your mood. The Queen always wore gloves, which blocked the magic, but her opponents were never allowed to.

So I usually felt as exposed as a lame duck while she bombarded me with questions about my life, then watched how the checkers reacted beneath my touch. Lies didn't work, for the pyramids always revealed the truth.

The Queen took her place across from me. She lifted her great gloved hand and moved her first man.

"So, Charlotte, how did you get on with your engagement party?"

I moved my man. "Very smoothly. Thank you, Your Majesty, for sending the royal photographer." My pyramid turned blue—the color of calm and truth.

"It's a shame your groom wasn't by your side." She made her move.

I deliberated. She wasn't truly asking a question, so I needn't respond verbally, but my touch would nonetheless give me away. I was glad he *wasn't* there. I hopped two spots. My man turned red and I winced. Red meant turmoil.

However, she could interpret that in any fashion she wished. Of course I felt turmoil, didn't I? It was to be expected of any girl in my position, having to carry on without her partner at her side.

The Queen's eyes flashed up at me. "I had a great depth of feeling for my late husband, too."

She'd misinterpreted what I felt—that I was pining in the absence of my fiancé. And she'd dropped her formal "we" in confiding about her husband.

We kept playing. She hopped three spots along the side. "Who wore the prettiest dress?"

I disliked it when she placed me in competition with the others, but answered as truthfully as I could. "With your kind generosity in lending me your dressmaker, Ma'am, the prettiest dress was of course mine."

My pyramid turned blue. She smiled in approval.

"But there were many other beautiful gowns, too," I added.

"Hmm." She concentrated on the board. "Did anyone argue?"

I frowned. "Not that I can think of." I made my move, but my pyramid turned yellow, which indicated nervousness, then progressed to deep brown, which indicated I wasn't being truthful.

Her gray lashes swept up to study my face.

My stomach squeezed with anxiety and my eyes widened in embarrassment. I was lying? I scoured my memory. Who? Who had argued? "Oh! Charles Darwin, Ma'am, arguing with Joseph Lister and the other scientists."

She smiled. "Did he have that incredible cane with him?"

"The fire-throwing one? Yes, indeed. Gives him a lot of amusement, I should think."

We continued playing, my men returning to a calm green, indicating that stress was leaving my body, and then settling to a soothing blue.

"Did any other young men look your way at dinner?"

The heat of embarrassment seeped into my cheeks. She was asking if anyone had flirted with me.

I had to think on it. There had been something about the way men's heads had turned to watch me be seated at dinner. But I had never given them an opportunity to progress further. There'd been Benjamin at the stables . . . what was all that business with dropping his firewood? But that had been outside, and not at dinner, as the question was stated.

"If they did, I didn't notice." I touched my figure. Blue. I relaxed.

"Did anyone speak ill of the Crown?"

I swallowed hard. It was a question she asked me each and every time we played. Maybe I would ask it, too, from the very nature of my isolated existence, if I were the Queen with a magical board in front of me.

"No, Ma'am."

This time she relaxed when my man turned blue. God help me— and the other person—if I ever had to answer yes.

My eyesight blurred. I tried to blink it away. My left foot was throbbing, almost as if it had a life of its own.

We continued playing. Russett brought in her favorite tea, Earl Grey, and we drank it from the finest bone china ever to touch my lips. The cup and saucer swirled in colors of gold, white, pale yellows, and the most mesmerizing turquoise. We had cucumber sandwiches and scones with berries and clotted cream.

I added a lemon slice to my tea and my throat instantly felt better.

Russett sat in a chair by the door, at Her Majesty's call.

Next she asked about my embroidery classes, what good books I was reading, what horses I'd recently ridden and which was my favorite.

"Rapunzel," I responded. "She's very calm and doesn't jitter at the sound of other hooves." There was often much distraction on the Palace grounds, such as the marching of the guards, the unexpected sound of trumpets, and rumbling coaches.

"Ah, yes. Rapunzel comes from good stock."

An hour had passed. My bladder was getting full from the tea. Please, would this end soon?

However, the pain in my foot had subsided, and my vision had cleared. Was it the food? The tea? The lemon?

I saw an opening on the board and made my way toward it. It

would take one more move to place this last man. The Queen, however, had three men left. It was inevitable that I should win again.

She sighed and made her move.

I slid into the final spot but didn't dare look up at Her Majesty to see how she was handling my win.

She was silent. No word of congratulations.

It always ended this way. Her stewing in silence. My hurrying to leave.

"Thank you so very much, Ma'am, for your kindness and generosity in allowing me to sit with you this past hour."

I felt awful not only for winning, which made her feel dreadful, but because I had forgotten to ask if she might put in a good word to my father about my taking a puppy. It would be useless to ask now. I rose to leave, and made the mistake of glancing at her.

"You don't look well, Charlotte. Very pale. Is something wrong?"

A flash of fear came over me. I fumbled for a reply, but couldn't very well tell her the truth. I was so very grateful the checkers game was over, that I didn't have to touch the pieces again. She wouldn't be able to distinguish if I was fibbing or not. So I answered as I had to, pretending all was well.

"I'm fine, Your Majesty."

She watched me for a moment, then asked, "Would you slide those pieces this way?"

"Pardon me, Ma'am?"

"To the side, to help Russett clear the board."

She wanted me to touch the pieces, so she could gauge the truthfulness of my reply!

I backhanded the pieces and shoved them aside as quickly as I could, then rose to leave.

She was staring at the pieces. I couldn't fight their magic. To my horror, they were turning yellow to dark brown to deep, glossy black.

Outright lying! I was outright lying to the Queen!

"Russett," the Queen called with a snap, raising her black-gloved hand in the air as an executioner might hold his ax. Russett jumped up from beside the door.

She pressed her cold, hard gaze on me, and my stomach nearly flipped into the air. What was she going to do to me?

CHAPTER EIGHTEEN

SEATED across from Her Majesty with Mr. Russett darting to her side, I searched for an explanation that would satisfy her and keep me from prison. It had to be truthful enough to fool the checker pieces if I touched them again, yet spoken in code to conceal my condition from the Queen.

"I humbly apologize," I squeaked. Hot perspiration clung to my spine.

"Yes, Your Majesty?" Russett asked. "What may I do?"

Visible above the black collar of her dress, the artery in her throat was pumping as quickly as my own. She parted her lips, about to give him a command.

Frantic to convince her I was not deliberately lying, I picked up one of the playing pieces. It was still black, the color of liars, and burning hot. "I'm not well at all. In fact, I'm heartsick about this whole situation with Mr. Abercrombie." I opened my palm, and the color of the pearl receded from black to dark brown. I continued talking as though my life depended on it. My life *did* depend on it.

"I'm heartsick that I have a fiancé in South America." *That he might come home at any time to ruin my life.*

The pearl piece lightened to brownish yellow. It was getting cooler to hold.

"It's been a stressful few days. I'm exhausted. Recovering from a headache. My shoes were much too tight at the party, and they pinched my toes to distraction."

Yellow faded to green.

"You see, Ma'am, I'm not well at all."

She waited until it turned blue in my palm before she closed her lips. Light from the windows bathed the red, tight swelling on her jaw. The sharpness in her weary eyes softened. With a flick of her plump fingers, she signaled to her footman that he was not needed. He retreated to his corner.

I'd never seen her wrath before, and prayed I never would again. She and her court would do whatever it took to protect the Monarchy.

"You should take more care in the choice of your words," she reprimanded.

"My sincerest apologies, Your Majesty. I didn't wish to trouble you with my problems and thought I could dismiss them."

She nodded, softer now. "Entertainment parties can be very stressful. We don't find . . . we don't find much pleasure in them ourselves."

Back to the plural "we."

I nodded politely, gripped my parasol, and rose on my swollen foot.

"You're off, now, are you? For that victory stroll in the Palace gardens?"

"Yes, Ma'am," I said with a final curtsy, although it no longer felt like victory.

❦

I stepped out of the Queen's chambers catching my breath. Although my time with her had been torturous, I noticed some odd changes in my body. My mind was clearer, my limp almost unnoticeable. I believed the tea and lemon had done me some good.

Perhaps it was only the lemon. The last three times I'd taken some, yesterday and today, I noticed marked improvements in my symptoms. The day before, I'd taken my tea without lemon, and saw no benefit. Was it citrus fruit in general?

Unfortunately, the effects seemed to wear off after a couple of hours. So, since I was feeling better, I thought I'd dash from the

Queen's office to my father's library in hopes that it was empty and I could do some reading.

Luckily, it was.

I poured myself a glass of water, but couldn't seem to drink. I gulped in small sips. Why was I having such problems swallowing?

Sitting down in the far alcove by the windows, I smoothed my skirts. My billowing sleeves floated through the air as I opened the book and read more about the severe symptoms of rabies.

The pupils may enlarge; there may be a harsh reaction to sunlight. . . . During furious rabies, the patient usually has an uncontrollable fear of water.

What?

This fear of water, known as hydrophobia, often begins with difficulty in swallowing.

My eyes bulged at this.

Later, drinking any type of liquid results in throat spasms, and painful spasms beneath the lungs. When hydrophobia intensifies further, the mere sound or presence of water causes extreme fear that these spasms are about to begin. Irrational behavior with thrashing, spitting, or biting may result. It is often during this aggressive phase that rabid animals attack and bite.

The rain, I thought. The mechanical dogs had attacked us in the rain. Was it possible that the creator of the dogs had given them hydrophobia?

The patient may develop acute insanity.

"No!" I lurched back and slammed the book shut. I did not have this. I could not have this. Rabies symptoms didn't usually appear for two to eight weeks. This was only the third day! This was not describing me. I did not have difficulty swallowing, simply a sore throat.

This was some sort of medical gibberish.

But—the logical side of my brain argued—you were not bitten by a regular dog. This was a scientifically developed monster. What if the poison on its teeth was much stronger than normal and its symptoms emerged sooner?

I slowly cracked the book open again and read the rest, skimming because it was too horrid to comprehend.

In place of "furious rabies" the patient may develop "paralytic rabies," so named because the muscles of the entire body slowly become paralyzed. Numbness begins at the wound site and spreads. The victim will lose consciousness, followed by heart and lung failure, then certain death.

I closed my eyes for a moment to absorb it. My father was right. This was gruesome.

I rubbed my injured foot to test it. There was feeling there. Lots of it. It was sore, which meant there was no paralysis. At least I didn't have those symptoms.

Yet.

I read the final paragraph.

If symptoms of rabies should develop, death is inevitable. There is nothing that can be done to save a victim. Aim to comfort the wounded and ensure the victim does not injure himself or attack others, until death.

"But this is not regular rabies!" I shouted at the book.

There was no more to read. I slammed it shut.

I wanted to curl into a ball and sleep for a week, and when I awoke I wanted this to be over. I worried about Jillian and Peter, if they were going through the same things I was. Headaches, muscle weakness, dizziness, blurred vision, and, heaven forbid, difficulty swallowing.

I had to get more lemons.

I rose from my chair and returned the book to its shelf. When I did, I heard my father enter his private office on the other side, close to the fireplace, along with Mr. Bloomberg. I went back to the alcove where I couldn't be seen, just to listen to the comforting sound of my father's voice. It had always soothed me as a little girl.

Sitting down, I placed my head on the desk, lulled by the hum of his words. I couldn't hear everything they were saying, but my father's deep voice, the way he phrased his sentences, the pauses he took, brought me a needed warmth.

"Your oral examinations . . . covering skeletal muscles . . ." And then he added, "Two hours followed by . . ."

I closed my eyes, about to fall asleep.

" . . . those damn dogs have struck again."

Dogs? I lifted my head and turned an ear toward their voices. Surely they couldn't all be mechanical, for London had had occasional problems with real dogs, rabid packs, ever since I could remember.

"Rabies," said my father. "When will the city be rid of these dogs? I've got to press the police captain to catch them. The packs are multiplying."

"What about that brother and sister?" said Mr. Bloomberg. "How could they have had the gumption to attack their guards? And their two accomplices? They'll all be caught, rest assured, now that there's a warrant for their arrest. Attempted murder, for pity's sake."

Attempted murder? No, no, no! It was self-defense. The guards had attacked *us*.

Officially wanted by the police. How low had I fallen? Along with Jillian and Peter and Benjamin. Peter's chances of qualifying for Scotland Yard might be ruined.

I rubbed my mouth and wondered where we could go for help.

No matter how many times I asked this question, I always came up with the same reply. We were on our own.

"I'm going today to see the police surgeon," said my father. "Word has it he's completed his autopsy of the street beggar."

How could this knowledge assist me? How could I turn this to my advantage?

I was still thinking of solutions when my father fell onto another topic. " . . . guard the wagons. Three loaded with cargo, ordered by the team of royal physicians. The ship comes in tomorrow. Medicinal supplies and surgical equipment."

"Perhaps your daughter can clear the cupboards."

"Not you, Bloomberg?"

"I've promised the Prince a soak of Epsom salts for his feet. His new riding boots have given him blisters."

"Very well."

Here was my chance. I sprang up from my seat, patted my skirts, and straightened my hair. I walked past my father's office as if I'd only just arrived. The door to the office was open. They were both seated.

"Good afternoon, Father. Mr. Bloomberg."

"Charlotte, we were just speaking of you." My father leaned onto his grand desk. He looked so full of life. "We need you to clear the cupboards for another shipment of medical supplies."

"Where on earth shall we put it all?"

"Squeeze the bandages and gauzes together. The tonic bottles can be put on the lower shelves. The blankets in there"—he pointed to the right of the door—"can be shifted to the linen closets down the hall. That frees up an entire cupboard."

When he pointed, I noticed a new sack in the corner. Plaster of paris, the label read, for soaking bandages, making splints for broken limbs, and applying poultices. When had that arrived?

My father was still speaking. "Perhaps those cauldrons can be stacked one above the other. Make room in the corner."

"I'll get started tonight." I took a deep breath to gather some courage. "Perhaps we might spend some time together this afternoon, first? Play some cards, sir? Perhaps discuss a book? Last week I was reading *Tales of Robin Hood* and came across a passage I thought you would enjoy—"

"There's no time for that, Charlotte. There's much on my mind. Orders to be given. Meetings with important people."

My shoulders sank with disappointment. Wasn't I important, too? I needed to speak to him. I wanted to question the loyalty of Mr. Bloomberg, without Mr. Bloomberg listening, as he was doing now. I wanted to discuss the rabid dogs and what the police thought, and what my father was doing to track them. I wanted to put in a good word on behalf of Jillian and Peter, that they weren't capable of attempted murder . . . that perhaps the guards were to blame.

"Sorry, Charlotte." He ran a hand through his black hair, and his posture softened. "How about a carriage ride through the city?"

I smiled in surprise. "Lovely."

"Prepare your hat and gloves."

"This instant?"

"Yes. We'll head to the photographer's shop. The one who took our portraits at the party. He told me they'd be ready to view today."

I pursed my lips. This wasn't in my plans, but it was as good an excuse as any to share some time with my father.

"I'm sure you'll want to send Mr. Abercrombie a photo or two."

Weaving my fingers together, I gave my father a guarded smile. "I'll hasten to get ready."

"Very good. But you're to stay in the coach when we reach Scotland Yard."

"Scotland Yard?" I said in a panic.

"While we're out, I'll combine some work with pleasure. You

won't mind, will you, Charlotte? I need to speak to the police surgeon about . . . about some medical matters."

The autopsy results, I thought.

I desperately wanted to know the results myself, whether they showed any signs of metal fragments or mechanical dogs.

But more desperately, I did not wish to go within ten miles of the police station. Wasn't I someone they were looking for? Didn't they want to capture me and my friends for attempted murder?

"Perhaps another time, if—if you're busy, sir." I struggled to slide out of it.

"Nonsense. I insist. Hurry, now, off you go. I'll meet you shortly at the Mews. Carriage waiting."

CHAPTER NINETEEN

IF I stayed inside the coach when we arrived at Scotland Yard, I reasoned, then no one would see me and I would be safe traveling with my father. It might be my only opportunity to hear about the autopsy results, which might lead to clues for a cure. So I hurried to prepare.

I changed into more formal attire, with a fitted bodice and tweed skirt. Polly pinned up my hair and added a hat. We gathered more lemons from the storage room off the kitchens and hid them in a satchel that I would bring to Benjamin, who would hopefully deliver it to Peter. I bit into a slice. My mouth puckered at the sourness, but it gave me a spurt of energy and, within minutes, subdued my limp. I wrote a note to Peter, explaining the power of the lemon fruit and asking him to meet me at ten this evening. Then I dragged the bag to the Mews, along with my parasol, and found Benjamin.

He was cleaning an empty stall next to a work horse. I slid in to pat the mare's soft coat, and discreetly lowered my satchel between us, where Benjamin could reach it. "This is for Jillian and Peter."

"I'll arrange for delivery as quickly as I can."

"And my soiled skirt, please. The one I left behind in your trunk. Could you take the lemons out of this satchel and put the skirt in?"

He waited until two grooms walked by, then leaned his pitchfork against the boards and disappeared round the corner with the satchel. I fed a carrot to the draft horse as I waited. Benjamin returned within minutes. I took the bag, much lighter this time, and whispered my thanks and good-bye.

My father was already in the carriage house, speaking to the men preparing our everyday coach. It wasn't one of the fancy ones the Queen rode in, yet by anyone's standards it was still top-of-the-line.

Two working women sauntered by, staring at my father with flushed faces and mumbling under their breath. He gave them a glance but nothing more. When they disappeared into the leatherworks and harness area, my gaze flickered over him in his frock coat and pressed shirt. To me, he was simply a hardworking man, much too serious most of the time. He wasn't interested in trivial things, as he called them—namely, anything that didn't involve life and death.

With the coachman and a footman riding on the outside of the carriage, we wheeled through the Palace gates and onto the quiet streets. We turned west toward Kensington Gardens, where we would find the photographer's studio.

Inside the coach, I nestled against the blue velvet cushions. Through my veil, I watched my father remove a shiny textbook from his black medical bag.

"Is that a new book?" I hesitated, wondering how to ease into the things I needed to discuss.

He nodded. A curl of black hair dropped onto his high forehead. "One of my colleagues wrote it and wants my opinion. He's suggesting we use it for training. I thought perhaps it might be of use to Mr. Bloomberg, but I'll need to skim it first."

My father used every minute to work.

"The diagrams are nicely detailed."

My father's green eyes flickered at me. He lowered the book to his lap. "That's a rather large hat."

"Do you approve?"

"The blue suits you. I like the grouse feather." He furrowed his brow. "It's a rather formal veil, though, is it not, for early afternoon?"

"It—it protects my face from wind and sun." This much was true, but it also shielded my face from anyone at the police station who might have gotten a description of me at the scene of the crime. I'd also pinned my hair very high—to give me an extra six inches of height, in case they had an estimate of that, too. Not that I planned on leaving the carriage, but in the event that someone peered in.

"Father . . . did you know that Annabelle had her pups?"

He turned his page but didn't look up. "Did she?"

"The engineers are . . . are looking for homes."

His gaze swiveled up. "Charlotte, you know what I think."

We'd discussed the subject repeatedly in the past two years. "But you haven't seen these dogs."

"Why can't you enjoy the ones in the royal kennels? The Queen has plenty running about."

"Because they're not mine. I can't train them to do as I say. I can't select a name. I can't take them into my sitting room and snuggle with a good book. I can't confide my problems to them or talk to them when I need a friend."

"A pup will only cause more toil for your maids."

"I shan't let that happen. I'll do all the work, I promise."

"You already have etiquette classes and riding lessons and French and German and Latin—"

"I'll schedule around my lessons."

"—and you assist in my medical rooms. There are absolutely no animals allowed in there. They harbor germs."

He turned another page, as though the matter was closed.

With a sigh, I pulled the curtain aside and looked out. We rolled past the greenery of the parks, then the Albert Memorial. I gazed up at the Queen's tribute to her late husband, a fourteen-foot bronze statue of Prince Albert. He was seated beneath a very tall neo-Gothic pinnacle, surrounded by columns and marble reliefs. The whole monument was set on a massive platform at the top of stone stairs leading up from all four directions.

Dozens of people sat about in clusters. If the Queen were here, she'd have no privacy to enjoy the statue peacefully. It was no surprise she visited at midnight.

The coach came to a stop. My father ordered the footman to enter the photographer's studio and retrieve our package.

While we waited, I reached for my satchel and removed my oily skirt. I took a deep breath and simply asked him outright. "Father, I've been trying to remove these stains from my riding skirt, and soap doesn't seem to work. Have you any ideas?"

My father took the material and held it up to the light. "Looks like the oil they use on machinery. Perhaps from the undercarriage of the coaches."

"It's rather black, isn't it?"

"Dirt, I'd guess. Metal filings get into most oils and cloud the color. Tell Jolene to try bluing agent, but likely the skirt is ruined. What is it doing in your bag?"

"I had left it in the stables to soap it there. But it didn't work, and I kept forgetting to take it with me." I stuffed it back into the satchel, disappointed with my father's answers. The oil stains didn't appear unusual to him.

The footman returned, put the package on the seat beside my father, and climbed onto the coach. We'd view the photographs later. I wasn't in any rush.

The coach turned and headed back in the direction we'd come, going to Scotland Yard. We jostled over a rut. I grabbed hold of the strap by the window.

"Father, what . . . what did Dr. Kenyon say about the condition of my two friends?"

My father laid his book aside. "They were doing as well as could be expected, but apparently they left the house they were ordered to stay in."

"Did you hear where they might have gone?"

"Some friends of theirs broke in. Smashed one guard over the head very hard. And shot him in the leg." He looked extremely upset. "The other man was nearly beaten by an angry crowd, but luckily a bobby on patrol stopped it."

"I know Peter and Jillian. They don't have it in them to injure anyone. Perhaps the guards were attacking *them*. Perhaps Jillian was weak and unable to defend herself—"

"Charlotte, don't go on about matters you know nothing about."

"I *know* my friends."

"You don't know what they did in this situation."

"Perhaps I do."

"Why would that be?" he snapped.

"I . . . I . . ." My mouth opened but I couldn't think how to respond.

He stared at me. "Charlotte, if your friends ever come round, you're to stay out of this. Understand?"

I nodded, but peered nervously at the blue velvet curtain.

"Scotland Yard is investigating for attempted murder."

The words hit me again like a terrible blow to the chest.

"You don't look well, Charlotte."

My hand flew to my throat. "I don't?"

"Are you feeling unwell?"

The coach rocked. "It's my motion sickness," I fibbed. The jostling did sometimes affect me, but usually on longer journeys.

"Ah, right. Turn your gaze out the window. It'll relieve the nausea."

I did as he asked, watching for a while as we rolled down the streets. Soon we were passing Buckingham Palace, then Clarence House on the Mall. We continued then turned south at Trafalgar Square with its statues.

I had better get to my other topic—my father's apprentice. "How does Mr. Bloomberg feel about the rabies and the dogs?"

"Bloomberg?" My father shrugged. "He's not involved."

"He's been with you only six months. Do you trust him?"

"Why on earth would you ask that?"

"I was only curious, since you mention he's not involved with the rabies investigation."

"He's involved in every step of it that pertains to the staff of the Royal Mews. He's not involved in the direct care of the brother and sister, is what I meant."

"Oh, I see. But . . . sometimes I'm very uncomfortable around him. He never wishes to discuss anything scientific with me. And he's very rude when you're not about."

"Ignore him, Charlotte, as best you can. He's new in his position. His anxiety sometimes shows."

I still did not trust the man. He was capable of anything.

Our conversation came to an abrupt halt as the coach made a sharp turn onto the narrow street called Great Scotland Yard. We rumbled to a stop in front of the entrance to police headquarters. Several stories high, the brick and stone building shadowed our carriage. An officer on horseback clomped by to the police stables across the street.

However, to my shock, several other officers came into view, leading handcuffed drunks and screaming prostitutes into a side entry.

My father, his dark face furrowed in dismay, looked from the spectacle outside to me in my formal dress. "Come inside with me, Charlotte."

I sat up, alarmed. "No, please. I'll be fine here."

"I shall not have my daughter subjected to this—"

"I'll be fine," I pleaded. "I'll wait with the coachman."

"You shall come with me," he commanded. He tapped on the side of the coach. The door opened. The footman unfolded the stairs and my father stepped out first. I was ever so grateful I'd worn a hat and veil, but still trembled that someone might recognize me. Looking for a distraction that I might hide behind in the station house, I slipped my father's medical book beneath my arm. My satchel with the soiled skirt would be fine left here.

I followed my father inside the damp, poorly lit building. We came to a large desk. The police sergeant looked up. His hair was the color of coal. "Dr. Sycamore."

"Please, Sergeant Clark, a private room for my daughter as you and I have a word."

"Yes, sir. This way."

He led us into a quiet corridor. He opened a door for my father and indicated a bench in the hallway for me. "Afraid this is as private as we get here. But she's out of the way of the crowd."

My father looked about. The commotion was all taking place down the hall, at another police desk and the cells beyond that. This was a calmer wing of the building.

"Don't be alarmed, miss. You'll be fine here."

"Thank you, sir," I mumbled with my head lowered.

My father and the police sergeant entered his office. He closed the door, but there might as well have been only a sheet between us, so great was the gap beneath the door. I could hear almost every word.

"Guards say there were at least two accomplices. One of 'em a young woman."

"A young woman?" My father tut-tutted. "What sort of female would involve herself with that bunch?"

Me. I slid out my father's textbook, opened it, and pressed it to my face, wishing to hide.

"Children are raised all sorts of ways these days," said the sergeant. "Tougher and meaner than you'd expect. No parental supervision at all."

"And obviously they planned the escape."

"Claimed the other guard had bubonic plague. He nearly got a good beating, but one of my men stopped it before it got too far."

"Yes, so I heard. Any clues as to who they were, Sergeant?"

"They have to be friends of the Moreley children. The mother and uncle swear they don't know who they could be."

"Any clue to the whereabouts of the brother and sister?"

"They were spotted by the river several hours later. At least we believe an eyewitness sold them sausages and bread."

I was startled at how quickly the police were closing in.

"You're patrolling that area, then?" asked my father. "I'm rather concerned about their disease progressing."

"Can only spare an extra man once a day, from six to midnight. Got other criminals to catch, Dr. Sycamore, worse still."

Oh, no. I had to warn Peter and Jillian to stay indoors from six to midnight. How was I to get word to them? It was almost five o'clock now. By the time we got back to the Mews and I spoke to Benjamin, there was no telling if he could get the message to them in time. And I had just sent a note for Peter to meet me at ten!

My father mumbled something I couldn't decipher.

"Indeed," said the sergeant. "I'll notify you if I hear."

"And the autopsy's complete?"

"Finished yesterday."

"Were the wounds consistent with dog bites?"

"Absolutely."

"Anything unusual?"

"There was something strange, the coroner said. Maybe you can shed some light on it. We found metal fragments embedded in the wounds."

Finally! Solid evidence of the mechanical dogs. I closed my eyes, awash in relief.

"How big?" asked my father.

"Tiny fragments. Metal shavings."

"What sort of metal?"

"Hard to say."

"In all the wounds?"

"No, only the one at the throat. The artery severed was what killed him."

"Well, it's obvious, then, isn't it?" said my father.

Yes, yes, I thought, he's got the answer now. He has to realize the teeth were made of metal. I leaned forward with my book, eager to hear. Eager to hear what plan my father and the sergeant would devise to fight the evil criminal behind this.

"The metal shavings had to be sitting on the surface of the man's throat before the dogs bit into it."

What? *No!* I wanted to shout. *That's not right!*

"They had just broken into the shop to steal the spoons," said the sergeant.

"You said he had a file to break through the lock. So metal shavings, perhaps from the file, got onto his hands. If he rubbed his throat, the shavings transferred."

"Hmm," said the sergeant. "We were thinking along those lines, too."

I banged the book on my lap in quiet frustration. They'd gotten it all wrong!

"Did you conduct autopsies on the other bodies? The ones attacked by the other dogs?"

"Afraid we didn't have the time or manpower. Hopefully the attacks are comin' to an end. We tracked down a pack of rabid dogs this morning. Destroyed 'em all."

"Wonderful news."

Obviously, I thought, the dogs they'd caught and destroyed were real, otherwise the sergeant would've mentioned otherwise. But that did not mean the other deaths had been caused by natural dogs. No autopsies meant no proof.

Chairs scraped in the office. Quickly, I buried my nose in my father's book again. I waited for footsteps, but none came. Perhaps the sergeant was showing my father some papers. All was silent.

I stared at the pages open before me. How odd.

Suddenly interested, I focused on several diagrams of different types of suturing patterns, the most amazing patterns, all neatly sketched in ink. They were very similar stitches to the ones I used in embroidery, except these closed surgical wounds. The diagrams showed how to stitch the lower layers of muscle together, then the fat layers, gradually working to the upper layers of the dermis.

The simple continuous stitch.

The interrupted stitch.

The corner stitch.

All of these I could do, and extremely well. How intriguing that someone could use similar techniques to suture skin together as they could fabrics—

Voices broke my train of thought.

"Good evening to you, too, Dr. Sycamore."

My father was at the door before I had a chance to turn my head. I kept my face lowered to the book and yanked on the edge of the veil.

"Did you get a description of the two who attacked the guards?" my father asked the sergeant. "If they were friends of the Moreley children, perhaps my daughter here had occasion to witness them about the Mews."

The police sergeant bored his dark brown eyes into me and I nearly retched from fright. "The young man is perhaps eighteen or twenty, very tall and thin," he said, mistaking Benjamin for someone older. "The young lady is quick on her feet. About your build, miss. Blond hair, though."

He scrutinized my hair, and I felt as though my insides were burning. I was ever so grateful I had worn a blond wig then.

I rose and turned to leave, gaze to the floor. "I shall ask around the Mews."

The sergeant addressed my father. "Thank you, sir."

With my father's hand pressed to my shoulder, I'd never felt so anxious to leave a place in all my life. I kept my head lowered as we maneuvered through the crowd at the door, and wondered again how and if I would be able to get word to Peter and Jillian to remain indoors at night. The police were on the hunt. They had an eyewitness, an extra officer prowling the streets, and were eager to arrest us for attempted murder.

⬥

Worried about his sister's condition, Peter urged her through the darkened streets close to the wharf. It was nearly ten o'clock, the appointed time for meeting Charlotte. He reached into his pocket, inside a small burlap cloth, and pulled out another lemon slice.

"Take another bite, Jillian. Charlotte says it'll give you strength." The lemons were helping him. His limp had disappeared, and his strength had returned.

Wrapped in a dark cloak, Jillian stumbled. "They're too sour, Peter, and they haven't done a blasted thing for me. I'm tired. Couldn't we go back to the barn?"

"You need fresh air. I dare say you've had ample sleep."

"My shoulder is numb. I can't feel it."

"How long has it been that way?"

"More than an hour. I don't know, perhaps two."

He slowed his pace, staying near the walls of the buildings, allowing other pedestrians to pass by. "Just a bit farther. It's past the corner." He looked above the heads and noticed a bobby in a white helmet strolling their way.

"Stop," Peter whispered. "Police."

Jillian froze. The bobby was coming closer. Peter nudged his sister gently into a café swarming with people, and coaxed her along. They eyed the bobby as he strolled by the glass storefront, and when he passed they exited to the street by another door.

"It smelled so good in there," said Jillian.

"Sorry, we don't have the coin."

"Where's Charlotte meeting us?"

"Here, near the corner." Peter looked at the sign to ensure he had the correct spot. It read CAFÉ FOR ALL SEASONS. It was the appointed place, but they couldn't stand out in the open and wait. Even though they were in the disguises Charlotte had sent, it wasn't safe.

Jillian turned her head in the darkness, leaning against him in her weakness, and gasped. "The bobby's coming back."

164

CHAPTER TWENTY

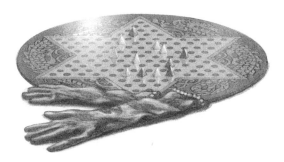

RUSHING to meet my friends at the café, I saw the policeman at the same time I saw Jillian collapse against Peter. Benjamin was sauntering ten paces behind me so we wouldn't be seen together, for we knew the police were on the lookout for a couple. I panicked at how close the bobby was to them, even though the man hadn't noticed them yet.

Stepping out from the night crowd at the wharf, I waved at him. "Officer!"

Up ahead, Peter shuffled to escape with Jillian, but halted in his tracks when I called out. He shook his head, cautiously warning me not to attract the bobby's attention but to keep moving.

But I ran faster toward the man in the uniform and white helmet. He was ten yards away. "Officer!"

Illuminated by a gaslight, he stopped and wheeled toward me. His face was a mask of intimidation. He looked strong enough to stop a charging bull.

My ploy to draw his attention away from my friends succeeded.

Peter pulled Jillian across the street and slipped through the oncoming crowd. I noted with satisfaction that Jillian was wearing the curly blond wig I had sent earlier through Benjamin. Peter was also wearing a blond one. I'd found the wigs in my trunk, left over from my theater classes when I'd had to memorize Shakespeare.

This time, I had changed into a black wig streaked with gray. It was pinned into a chignon at the nape of my neck, and I looked many years older. My dress, laced up to the throat, with a drab brown skirt, made me look older, too. Bless her, Polly hadn't interrogated me when I had asked to borrow some of her clothing in exchange for a large slice of pie.

"Yes, miss?" asked the bobby.

"Which way to the wharf, sir?" I panted, out of breath as I reached him. "I'm to meet my aunt off a ship coming in from America." Surely, I reasoned, he wouldn't think to suspect me as the young woman they were searching for. What person accused of attempted murder would run to a police officer and ask a question?

"That way, miss." He pointed beyond the winding paths. "Take the second street over. It opens to the docks. This one here's a dead end."

"Yes, I've been going round in circles." Past his shoulders, I saw Peter leading Jillian beneath a big sign that read THOMAS COOKSTONE, TOOL AND DIE.

When Peter and Jillian were safely concealed behind the building, I thanked the officer. "You're awfully kind."

I looked where he'd pointed, behind lopsided buildings, toward the Thames. The river roiled in blackness. Dozens of masts bobbed above the rooftops.

His eyes examined me, then he seemed to catch sight of something more interesting over my shoulder. He frowned and blew his whistle. It blasted my ears. I turned to see two ruffians racing alongside a gentleman lugging a suitcase, who'd obviously just landed on the wharf himself.

"Hey, dammit!" the man shouted with an American accent. "You took my wallet! Come back here!"

Off they went, tearing through the crowd—the American traveler, the two pickpockets, and the running bobby. *Welcome to London*, I thought. Poor man.

The bobby's whistle shrieked, penetrating the night air and my bones.

I looked at Benjamin for the first time since speaking to the bobby, careful not to let anyone know we were together. Tall and gangly among the pedestrians, he gave me a scowl, as if disapproving of my approaching the officer. What was I to do? I gave a shrug. The distraction had worked.

I drew my cloak tightly about myself and headed toward the tool and die shop, followed at ten paces by Benjamin. Since the rest of us were wearing disguises, he didn't need to.

When we reached the side street, to my dismay Peter and Jillian had disappeared. Panic seized me again. I spun about, looking for them.

Benjamin, though, rushed in from behind and turned the handle of the shop door. It opened. This late in the evening? How odd.

We ducked inside. Thankfully, our friends were there. The lemon in my pocket bumped against my thigh. I hoped Peter and Jillian had eaten some of the ones I'd sent, but I worried when I saw Jillian seated on a bench by the fireplace, body slumped. Her blond wig dipped forward, slightly askew. I prayed no one else noticed it.

Peter stood rubbing his hands, looking for an opportunity to speak to a man in a leather apron who appeared to be the owner, Thomas Cookstone.

The man was giving instructions to two workmen who were lifting large crates. "Take them to the alley, then return for the rest."

"Aye, Mr. Cookstone."

There wasn't much here. An empty desk, a couple of stools. A few crates. Where were the machines?

I debated whether to acknowledge Peter and Jillian, or pretend we were here as separate patrons. In the end I took my cue from Peter, who stepped forward when the workmen left. Benjamin paced nearby, aggressive in his posture, on the chance we needed protection.

"Good evening, sir. Now that we're all here," said Peter, looking at Benjamin and me, "let's tell Mr. Cookstone what our circus needs."

A circus? Benjamin's face lifted in surprise equal to mine. What was this story Peter had conjured?

I sat beside Jillian on the bench, dipping my shoulder against hers in the event she needed support. I discreetly adjusted her wig. She acknowledged me with a soft hello. Her pale face, almost bloodless, contrasted with the darkness of her cloak.

"Lemons?" I mouthed.

"They don't help," she whispered.

I groaned in disappointment.

Peter stepped forward beside Benjamin, both dressed in black. Peter looked strange with golden hair. The coloring was off compared to his brown eyes. "You come highly recommended," he said to Mr. Cookstone. "I'm told you're able to make a special clock needed for our family business."

"And that's a circus, you say?" The machinist didn't seem at all surprised, as though people of all sorts walked in requesting unusual things. He placed his soiled hands on his hips, peering at each of us. Dirt smeared his forehead and the creases of his knuckles, as though he'd been working for hours.

"Three elephants. Two lions," boasted Peter. "Large trapeze. These ladies here—sisters—work the trapeze. My brother and I," he said, thumbing the air in the direction of Benjamin, "assist with the organization of the show. I'm the ringmaster."

Jillian and I locked gazes, then smiled slightly into our cloaks. Ringmaster, indeed. What a far-fetched tale. I liked the bit about me and Jillian being sisters, though.

The man looked at Benjamin. "And you? What's your position? The lion tamer?"

"No, he's the chief mime," Peter replied, to our further amusement. "A clown. Been at it since he was four. He doesn't speak much, I'm afraid; he was born slow. But he communicates with the audience in other ways."

Benjamin gave Peter a frustrated look.

I supposed Peter robbed him of speech so he couldn't contradict anything Peter said. It would keep the fibs aligned.

The man pulled out a pocketknife from his apron, causing us all to stiffen in alarm, then removed the pencil from behind his ear and used the knife to whittle it sharper. We relaxed.

"Now you've caught my curiosity. What is it you think I can do for you and your elephants?"

"Make us an extraordinary animated clock that lowers into the middle of the ring. Like a cuckoo clock, but with a face and teeth.

The teeth must look real. The whole face has to, preferably with skin or fur."

Now I understood why Peter had made up such a fantastic story. He couldn't very well stroll in and ask for a mechanical dog; he had to ask for something equally detailed and lifelike.

"Aye, I could do that," the man answered. "But I won't."

"Why not?"

The man placed his newly sharpened pencil back behind his ear. "Didn't you see the sign on the door? I'm movin'."

We all swiveled to the door to see what we'd missed. We'd been in such a hurry to enter, so terrified of getting caught by the bobby, that we'd raced in without noticing.

Peter stopped smiling. "Where to?"

"America."

Peter's eyes flickered.

The man explained. "I've been here for seven years, watching the ships pull in and out of harbor, calling out exotic names—Hong Kong, Venice, Cape of Good Hope. Always wishin' I was on one myself. Well, the wife and I have decided to go."

"When are you leaving?" asked Peter.

"Two days."

That would explain why the place was nearly empty. He'd already packed or sold most of his equipment and samples. That's why his shop was open at this late hour. He needed the time to move out.

"I see." Disappointment registered in Peter's voice, and we all felt it. "Best of luck to you and your wife."

"Thank you." Mr. Cookstone heaved a crate filled with metal bolts onto his empty desk as we regrouped to leave. "There's another fella you could see about that clock. Justin Longfellow in Piccadilly. Heard he just made Charles Darwin a fire-breathin' cane. He might help, if you ask him nice."

⁂

"Since he's leaving in two days, he can't be the one," said Benjamin when the four of us left the machinist. We'd stopped in the dark door-way of a closed china shop. "The person who developed the mad dogs did it for gain. For the wicked power, or to prove a point, or to . . . to I

169

don't know what. But he wouldn't be leaving the country. He'd be staying for further glory."

"That was my thought, too," I said.

Peter nodded, standing shoulder to shoulder with Benjamin. "The name Justin Longfellow keeps cropping up. I'll try to visit his shop tomorrow."

"I'd like to be there," I said to Peter's handsome, dark profile. "More eyes might pick up more clues." I selfishly wished, looking at him, that we were here tonight for better reasons. Happier ones.

Jillian stumbled in the darkness. All three of us reached out to steady her.

I turned to Peter again. "Maybe she needs more lemons. Did you give her enough?"

"Twice as many slices as I took. They *are* helping me, so they *should* be working on her."

"I'll be fine," Jillian mumbled.

We lowered her to the stoop. I slid down beside her.

"Careful," whispered Benjamin. He edged us farther into the doorway. "Bobby."

Peter jumped in beside us and we didn't flinch for a solid minute, in fear we'd be discovered.

Benjamin peeked out into the night. "All clear."

We exhaled. I removed the bulky lemon from my pocket and peeled back the burlap cloth to reveal the slices. I offered them to Jillian and Peter, then took one myself.

"There is something else I came to tell you," I said to Peter, biting into sourness. "Unfortunately, when I visited Scotland Yard with my father, he said they're patrolling the area for you. Between six and midnight every night."

"Oh, lovely," said Jillian.

Peter muttered a curse. "It's not twelve yet, is it?"

"More than an hour to go." Benjamin rocked back on his heels, shifting his focus from one end of the nearly empty street to the other. "Where are we going to hide till midnight?"

"Where else?" I looked across the way to a dimly lit tavern. The cracks in two window panes caught the moonlight. Weathered paint peeled off the boards. I rubbed the coins in my pocket. "Let's eat and drink while we can. Perhaps a good meal will set you right, Jillie."

※※

When we were led to a quiet corner of the tavern, Peter and Benjamin both reached for the chair next to mine. Perhaps it was just a coincidence, but my face heated with embarrassment.

I ignored them and concentrated on Jillian, across from me.

"The lemon did nothing?" I leaned over the square table toward her. The candle on our tabletop flickered. Rowdier patrons to our left began singing a drinking song.

Jillian shook her head. The long, golden hair of her wig jiggled on her shoulders. "Still dizzy."

"Drink some water," Benjamin told her. He'd taken the chair next to mine. As I took in how his dark hair and silhouette cut a strong outline in the candlelight, I noticed again that he was quite handsome. Peter, too. My gaze lingered on the depth of emotion I saw in his face.

Just then Jillian tried to lift her glass but nearly knocked it over. Luckily her brother, seated beside her, reached out to help before it spilled.

"What is it?" he asked with concern.

"I still can't feel my shoulder," she answered. "Now my arm is numb as well."

It was so much worse than I thought! Everything frivolous flew out of my mind as I was struck by this news.

Paralytic rabies. Numbness begins at the wound site and spreads.

I stared at Jillian, wondering how else I could help my friend. I tried to swallow from a cup of water but felt as though I was swallowing bits of glass. Was I developing hydrophobia?

While Jillian was fighting paralysis, were Peter and I fighting the other kind of rabies? The one that might lead us to mental distress, fear of water, humans biting humans, hallucinations, and lunacy?

Should I tell them about my worries?

A surly barmaid delivered two of our platters, setting them before me and Jillian. The cottage pie smelled delicious, a combination of minced lamb and potatoes. "Ale?"

Peter looked at Benjamin. Anyone over the age of nine was

allowed to drink. If we were here as a group of friends enjoying the evening, the boys would order ale, but we needed to keep our thoughts clear and thus declined.

Another barmaid appeared with platters for the boys. We ate.

"What is it, Charlotte?" Peter took a forkful of mutton and potato crust. The hair on his blond wig fell stiff and straight, not wavy and rich like his own coffee-bean color. "You haven't said a word for ten minutes."

I gasped. "Oh, it's awful."

Then it all poured out of me, every bit of what I knew about rabies. "There are different kinds. Paralytic, where your body grows numb and you can't move. Then the one like ours." I nodded at Peter, describing the harsh symptoms I'd been having. Dizziness, sore throat, muscle weakness, fuzzy thinking.

They were silent for a moment.

"I don't think my symptoms are that rough just yet," said Peter. "Mild headaches. A bit of trouble remembering. But I'm still fast on my feet."

"Good," I said with relief.

"I'll fight on behalf of everyone. But, Charlotte, please don't tell me your symptoms are that severe. . . ." Peter looked so sorrowful, I didn't have the heart to tell him how awful I felt at times.

Jillian turned to me. "You can't give up, Charlotte."

"I won't," I promised them all.

Benjamin stared at me as if desperately searching for answers. "I wonder why the three of you have such different symptoms."

"Different dogs bit us," I replied, leaning back against my wooden chair.

"We're different sizes, too." Peter scooped some peas onto his fork, apparently deciding that we should keep eating. We followed his lead. "Jillian is the smallest. Not by much, but maybe that's why she suffers the most exhaustion."

We nodded, then ate and drank and talked for more than an hour. It was comforting.

When it was time to go, we hesitated to leave the sanctuary. The clock above the door read fifteen minutes past midnight. The bobby was no longer looking for us.

Outside the tavern windows, the night had grown ominously quiet. The eerie silence and yellow haze from the gaslights loomed over the streets. I remembered the ghastly feel of three nights ago.

"Do you think it's safe to leave?" Jillian peered through the windows. She'd eaten most of her meal, and color had returned to her lips.

"Hard to say," Peter told her. He looked across at me, then back at his sister. "Take another slice of lemon, and let's find out."

CHAPTER TWENTY-ONE

THE four of us walked together, Jillian and I concealed in our cloaks and hoods, Peter and Benjamin scanning the alleyway for trouble. A fog had rolled in. The night was quieter. Gone were the voices of the crowds, the shop doors opening and closing, travelers carrying suitcases, and bobbies blowing whistles. Instead, barges on the Thames rumbled their mournful horns, a tomcat howled in the distance, and two men, neighbors, argued above us from their windows.

"Direct your bleedin' smoke away from my bedroom!"

"I can't control which way the wind blows! Close your window!"

"That'll make it hot as Hades!"

"Then open the window on the other wall!"

And on it went.

I didn't mind the distractions; the attention wasn't upon us. We would be walking together for three more blocks, then Peter and Jillian would go in one direction to their makeshift home, Benjamin and I in another. I tried not to worry about how we'd maneuver past the sentries at the Palace gates this time of night.

We were walking quietly past a narrow door when Jillian suddenly tripped. Peter caught her. He accidentally touched her injured shoulder, and I winced, waiting for her moan of pain. When it didn't come,

I grew more frightened for her because it meant her wound was still numb.

Why hadn't the lemons offered her some remedy, as they had me and Peter?

But the effect of the citrus was fading even on us. The lemons used to work for two hours. Less than an hour had passed since I'd had my last slice, yet the swelling in my left boot pressed against my ankle bone, and my eyesight was beginning to blur again. Peter's limp had returned.

We walked up the slope, away from the wharf, and turned a corner, passing a grocer's shop long closed for the night. All was dark.

"Shh," said Peter, abruptly stopping ahead of us.

We halted behind him and listened. The creak of wheels and whinny of horses echoed from the main street a block ahead of us.

We hid in the shadows as the ground shook slightly beneath our boots. Horses' hooves echoed closer. The houses remained dark. Likely the residents were accustomed to ships loading and unloading all night long.

Jillian's breathing grew easier. I urged her to rest on the stoop of the grocer's shop, in the darkness where she couldn't be seen. She seemed more energetic after the meal she'd consumed, but I wanted her to save this newfound strength.

My ears picked up another sound. A horribly frightening one.

Dogs.

Peter and Benjamin must've heard the growling, too, for their shoulders flexed in the dim light of the moon. While we listened, the clouds rolled over again and blackness pervaded everything. Between the lack of natural lighting and the fog, I could barely see six inches in front of me.

Which made the dogs all the more terrifying.

Where were they?

With gloved hands, I grabbed onto Benjamin's cloak. He turned his body toward me but moved as silently as a ship slicing through calm waters.

The wagons were coming our way. I rose on tiptoe and bobbed around Peter's wide shoulders to get a better look. The outline of three wagons appeared through the fog. They were hitched together one behind the other, pulled by a team of six horses. The two drivers in front didn't look in our direction, but turned right, past a red-brick factory. Then the clouds parted and moonlight shone on the overflowing cargo, and I recognized familiar but unlabled packaging of bandages and surgical supplies.

These must be the medical wagons my father had spoken of to Mr. Bloomberg. The wagons themselves had no markings to indicate that they belonged to the Crown, yet I felt sure they were headed to the Palace gates. Or perhaps this time of night they were headed to the Royal College of Surgeons, where they would be inspected and sorted in the morning, then delivered to the Queen. But if they were headed directly to the Palace now, perhaps Benjamin and I could sneak aboard and pass through the gates undetected.

A sudden burst of growling rippled through the air. *Dogs!* Jillian whimpered, and Peter, Benjamin, and I shuffled protectively near to her in the fog. Where were the animals? Were they mechanical?

We didn't budge.

I had no sword for defense this time, but Peter and Benjamin removed daggers from beneath their trouser legs.

The dogs growled again, closer now, to our left side. Jillian gasped and rose to her feet with my heart-thumping support. Peter and Benjamin squeezed in tight around us, wielding their weapons.

"Follow the wagons," Peter whispered. "The men are armed with pistols to be sure, ready to blast any sick dogs."

We rushed onto the road, following the Queen's cargo.

A herding dog with shaggy, speckled fur bolted ahead of us, darting among the wagons. I saw more tails and legs—sinews of powerful mastiffs and hunched shoulders of crazed canines.

The drivers hollered, "Get the hell out of here!"

"Good God, they've got rabies!"

"Get away from the horses! You blasted devils!"

The fog and darkness still limited visibility, but in a flash of moonlight I could make out dogs racing at the horses, trying to attack.

The wagons careened to a stop, slightly skewed in their positions. Horses snorted and reared. A whip cracked the air.

The first wagon jolted forward to the right, dragging the other two at bizarre angles. Just then, one of the dogs turned round and stared directly at us, teeth bared. I shivered.

"Move away," Benjamin called to me. "Take Jillian and run for cover!" He tossed me a blade.

"Where to?" asked Jillian.

"Someplace high, out of reach," I said.

"Who's there?" shouted one of the men in the fog. "Anyone there?" Silently I led Jillian by the elbow toward some trees, where the path widened between factories. The wagon jarred again and the men spewed curses, causing the menacing dog in the road to prick up its ears. It left us to slink toward the cursing men.

Benjamin and Peter, knives out, proceeded forward to help. But knives were useless against the dogs, unless they were close enough to reach.

From my vantage point, I could see one of the drivers jump to the ground. He grabbed hold of the lines, trying to calm the horses.

"Easy there, easy."

But when a dog lunged, the man on the seat fired a pistol. The bang ripped the air and the mare bucked. The driver holding the lines crashed backward to the ground, while the man on the seat plunged forward and fell six feet to the dirt. One of the dogs leaped at him as he rolled under cover of the wagons. Benjamin jumped in with his knife, slashing and plunging. I wasn't sure if he'd nicked the dog, but he did manage to scare it off.

"You evil beast!" the man beneath the wagon shouted. I wasn't sure whether he could even see Benjamin helping, but I waited, breathless that my friend might be injured.

Another dog lunged at a horse, which bucked and kicked but missed. Meanwhile, the wagons were becoming unstable. The rear wagon suddenly teetered on two wheels, dangerously close to where Peter and Benjamin were slashing at another diseased animal that was about to strike. Terror seized me.

I rushed to Jillian. "I have to unhitch the wagon before it crushes them!"

"I'll run with you!"

I dashed to the hitch and heaved, but it wouldn't move. Fighting panic, I tried to align the holes to yank the pin, but the wagons kept shifting, making it impossible. In a sweat, I looked behind me to where Jillian was wrenching with all her might.

I tried again to pull the pin and missed. My shoulders ached. I dropped my dagger, and the next time the hitch squeezed together, I seized the pin with my gloved fist and pulled it as hard as I could.

The pin came shooting out and hit the dirt behind me. I let the hitch fall to the ground.

As the two remaining wagons straightened out, the demented dogs seemed distracted by something to our left. I scooped up my blade again and saw two huge cats running atop a fence. The crazed dogs tore after them, but the cats raced along, too high for the dogs to reach. It drove the canines wild; they were hungry for a kill. Their barking receded into the blackness as the animals faded away.

The horses settled, the fallen man jumped back to his seat. The second man grabbed his reins and shouted, "He-yah, He-yah!"

They didn't realize they'd left the third wagon behind.

"Wait!" I shouted. "You forgot one!"

They didn't hear me. My voice was drowned by the sound of hooves and the panic of the men. Blackness and fog engulfed their fleeing forms.

The two drivers barely got a glimpse of the boys, and I felt certain they didn't know Jillian and I existed.

"Is everyone all right?" I asked.

We all nodded and glanced at each other.

"Let's get out of here before the dogs return," said Benjamin.

"Are you able to walk?" Peter asked his sister.

Jillian, filled with the heat of battle, seemed to find new strength. "Yes, let's go."

"What about this wagon?" Benjamin panted, catching his breath as he looked at the abandoned crates.

Peter lowered his knife. "They'll come back for it in the morning."

"Unless . . ." A new plan struck me.

"What?" asked Peter.

"Maybe there's something better we can do with it." I handed Benjamin the knife he'd lent me. "Let's push it out to the lower streets."

"But it'll get robbed blind."

"Precisely," I said. "I know where these wagons are headed. They're intended for the Queen. Medical supplies for the monarchy.

I've been cleaning cupboards all day to make room, and there's still not enough space for it."

"I say we leave it put," said Benjamin.

The idea was well-formed in my mind. "The people here can make better use of it."

Judging by their silence, they knew I was right.

"You realize the consequences?" Benjamin asked. "Stealing from the Queen is punishable by death."

"No one saw our faces. They couldn't have. If I can't identify the men—and I was watching them closely—they couldn't possibly identify us." I marched toward the wagon. "What will the Queen do with more bandages and salve and painkillers? She already has enough to care for herself and her family, fifty times over."

The Queen's advisors would accuse me of treason if they heard me speak in such a manner. Yet Peter and Jillian lived in these slums. They knew how difficult it was to get medical help, especially after having been imprisoned for rabies.

Peter took a few steps to the wagon hitch and lifted it, about to steer. "You're right."

"Yes," said Jillian, moving to help him.

But Benjamin worked in the royal stables, and he stood his ground. "The consequences for you—and therefore your father—are grave."

His concern for me rather than himself was touching.

"This is more important than I am," I said.

We looked at each other for a moment. Finally he nodded his dark head, his profile swathed in moonlight. "You know I shall always say yes."

"Hurry," said Jillian, already out of breath, putting her hands to the wagon. "Hurry before the mechanical dogs come racing back."

"How do you know they're mechanical?" I asked.

"Just a blind guess," she replied.

⫘

After we delivered the wagon, I said good-bye to Peter and Jillian, wishing we could remain together but knowing we had to go our separate ways. "Take care of yourselves," Peter whispered, more to me than Benjamin. I thought I detected a look of longing in Peter's smoldering eyes, but then he turned away from me to bravely lead his sister out of danger, his shoulders squared and his long stride resolute.

Benjamin took me home as quickly as we could manage—by closed carriage. He hailed one in the street and we climbed in, hoods and all.

"Piccadilly Circus," he told the driver. To me he added quietly, "We'll walk to the Palace from there."

The coach was so different from the one I'd taken with my father to Scotland Yard. This one was old and smelled musty. The velvet on the bench was ripped and puckered and stained. The curtain on my side didn't hang properly.

Yet it felt safe.

Being with Benjamin—and Peter—always felt safe.

I thought about what Benjamin had said to me earlier. If the Palace guards discovered it was my idea to take the stolen goods, then my father, as my guardian, would be held accountable. I shuddered to think what might happen to him. On the other hand, I had to believe that we would never be caught.

I'd been frightened tonight of so many things. Terrified for Jillian and Peter and of our possible rabies. Then I'd been petrified to see the wagon leaning over Benjamin and Peter when they were fighting off the dogs.

Now I felt only the gentle rocking of the carriage as the wheels rolled through the darker side of London, headed for home.

Benjamin sat quietly to my right. There wasn't much room inside, or perhaps it was because he had such a large frame, but he seemed to be sitting terribly close.

He'd been such a good friend to me tonight. They all had.

Perhaps Benjamin was thinking about the same thing, for when we turned onto the second street, he reached out and touched my gloved hand with his bare fingers.

I was startled by the gesture. When I realized he wasn't removing his hand, I looked out my window at the dark, foggy street, embarrassed by my inability to know how to react.

I liked the warmth of his hand. I liked the size of it, covering mine.

But I was perplexed. How did he feel toward *me*?

Why else, you silly girl, would a boy hold your hand?

Why would a boy embrace you, either, as tightly as Peter had?

But I'm engaged.

Peter was right. I wasn't allowed to hold anyone's hand but my future husband's. I couldn't explore any feelings toward other boys, and they certainly were not allowed to touch me. When the coach jostled over a bump, Benjamin's hand slipped off mine.

Relieved, I quickly pretended that I needed to adjust my crooked curtain, then placed my hands firmly in my lap.

Benjamin didn't seem bothered that the awkward moment had ended. He wasn't scowling, nor was he trying to sit closer. The touch hadn't lasted more than a minute, so perhaps it had been only a gesture of friendship.

"The fog's lifting," he said cheerfully, peering out the coach window when we crossed the bridge.

We turned along the embankment. "How on earth will we get past the guards at the Palace gates?" I asked.

"I've got a friend who's on duty tonight. Let me do the talking."

When we reached Piccadilly Circus, the coach stopped and we slid out.

Neither of us said another word as we marched through the quiet streets and slipped in through the back gates. I was bouncing with nervousness that we wouldn't be allowed in, but his friend, a night guard, gave him a wink, likely thinking from my disguise that perhaps I was a kitchen maid. I believe he thought the two of us had gone out for a rendezvous.

Which was fine with me, because it got us inside.

"Good night, Charlotte," Benjamin said. He said it as he always did, matter-of-factly, as though there was nothing between us. Perhaps there wasn't.

I was probably reading more into the hand-holding—and Peter's hug—than either of them had intended. Sometimes it was so hard to know what a boy was thinking.

It was a restless night filled with nightmares of Benjamin and Peter pulling pranks on me, then laughing when I was caught by the Queen's guards and marched up to the hangman's noose.

CHAPTER TWENTY-TWO

I didn't wish to be with my father, nor the Queen, but I was stuck with both the next morning. My father was with me in the medical library, reviewing an article he was writing for publication. I was skimming through *The Lancet*, hoping some genius somewhere had just discovered a cure for rabies, when someone knocked.

My father adjusted his cravat and opened the door.

On the other side of it, Mr. Russett nodded. His gray hair was combed back neatly, but his face was damp with concern. "Sir, Her Majesty would like to see you in her private chambers. Straightaway, please. She asked me to send for Miss Sycamore, too."

Alarmed, I felt my face flush. "Me? Whatever for?"

My father turned in my direction. His color rose. "You don't question the Queen."

I bowed my head, embarrassed that I'd embarrassed him, and tucked away the journal. Going to see the Queen so soon after our encounter with the dogs and the medical cargo last night had me worried. Did she suspect something?

My father dismissed Russett, then went to retrieve his medical bag in the event it might be needed. I took a lemon slice from my pocket. I sucked on it and discarded the peel in the trash as we left the room.

Luckily, I had my parasol with me. I didn't need it, for my limp wasn't present when I used the lemons, but it offered me a sense of protection. This morning when I inspected my injured foot in the bath, the red streaks along my veins were still there, including the swelling and redness at the puncture wounds, but the throbbing would fade as long as I had lemon juice in my system.

It wasn't a cure, but I was stalling the disease. At least until we found the madman behind the mechanical dogs and discovered a treatment.

"James."

"Your Majesty," my father greeted the Queen moments later.

I curtsied.

Two of her senior legal advisors were present, along with a fellow in a working man's suit who stood ill at ease, not quite sure, it seemed, where to look. The presence of legal advisors meant serious news. The only time they were included in conversations was on formal business.

What legal business did the Queen have with my father and me?

This was not going to be good.

"Do have a seat." Her Majesty indicated the settee near the large windows that overlooked the grounds. She didn't smile. Ironed creases ran along the sleeves of her black dress. Sitting in a firm chair made her bosom slump forward and her waistline widen.

I was thankful to take my place on the settee. When my father took the other end, his weight jostled our shared cushion.

The taller of the Queen's counselors spoke first. She had so many advisors that when I was younger, I could never keep their names straight. So I had called these two Mr. A and Mr. B. I had named her advisors in the order I'd met them. Mr. C and Mr. D usually traveled to Windsor Castle with us.

Mr. A, the taller man with the thicker gray hair and larger nose, addressed my father. "Allow me to introduce to you Detective Plumb, from Scotland Yard."

My breathing, my heartbeat, my life froze.

I swiveled my gaze to the working man. Perhaps he'd meant to nod, but he actually grimaced in my father's direction.

Mr. A cleared his throat. "We received word early this morning from the special branch of the police. The coachmen delivering three wagons of medical supplies were robbed en route from the docks, late last night. One wagon was stolen."

Oh, sweet Lord.

Alarmed, my father sprang up on the cushion, rocking me again. "Robbed? By whom?"

"We don't know as of yet. The coachmen didn't get an accurate view of the two young men."

They knew about Benjamin and Peter.

"One wagon? Why did they take only one?"

Detective Plumb finally spoke. "That's what we intend to uncover." He had a raspy voice. It was rather alarming, as though his throat had once been burned by fire.

Mr. A's baggy eyelids quivered. "It seems these two men distracted the drivers using rabid dogs."

"No!" gasped my father.

But we didn't inflict any dogs on anyone! We were trying to *save* the drivers from the dogs. Had the beasts gotten away unharmed? Had no one found any trace of injured animals to examine?

I turned and gaped at the Queen. She didn't flinch, but her gray lashes flickered, the only indication she found the situation distressing.

"How could anyone escape with an entire wagon?" My father turned to Detective Plumb. "Surely there were tracks left behind."

"Indeed," the detective answered. "The tracks indicate they separated the wagons on the factory road where they attacked the coachmen. Then they backed one out three streets over and two blocks down to the slums. There the wagon tracks abruptly disappeared."

"Did it rain last night? Were the tracks washed away?"

"No rain. The tracks simply disappeared."

Now I was confused. I leaned forward, clasping the smooth wooden stem of my parasol, to hear from the detective how this could happen. Surely no one owned any magic that could make an entire wagon disappear.

"The soil about the wagon was surrounded by footprints. Dozens of them. People were hauling off everything they could carry. Barrels, boxes, pills, tonics, bandages."

"Everything lost," said the Queen.

Her voice and her words silenced us for a moment.

"And what of the tracks?" asked my father.

Mr. B, the shorter advisor with the thinning gray hair and a huge red lump on his chin that never seemed to fade, added his comments. "Whoever dragged the wagon there knew very well that the poor would take every last medical supply they could carry. I wonder if they realized that the poor would also break apart the wagon and carry off every board. The wheels, sprockets, frame—gone."

His companion, Mr. A, ran his hand along the lapel of his gray frock coat. "It's almost as if the people agreed to wipe out all evidence that a wagon had even been stolen."

"They were covering for the thieves," said my father, understanding.

A slight smile crept across my lips. The people had protected us.

Her Majesty shifted her weight. Sunlight coming from the windows grazed her downy cheeks. "But someone must've seen something."

"Rest assured, Your Majesty, we will find them," Detective Plumb declared in his gravelly tone. "Mark my words."

He looked capable of it, I thought. I nervously skimmed his features. Beneath his working man's suit was a figure used to walking great distances, exercising horses, and never sitting idle.

Mr. A for the first time turned his pale blue eyes to me. I leaned back, startled. What did he want from me?

"Your friends," he said. "I've been informed you know the Moreley twins. I'm sure you've heard they escaped from their confinement. What have you heard about their whereabouts?"

All eyes were upon me. I winced.

"I haven't—haven't been following the gossip."

"I shall ask that you open your ears to it," he said. "Immediately inform your father—or one of us—if you hear of them."

My fingers trembled on the parasol. "I understand." My voice quivered. "But what about the dogs from last night? Did anyone capture the rabid dogs?"

Detective Plumb answered, somewhat pleased. "Two have been spotted within the hour, in a deserted section of the wharf. They're vicious and aggressive. When they're caught, they'll be destroyed."

That would be fortunate, I thought. If they examined the diseased bodies, they would likely find the dogs were mechanical. And then Scotland Yard would be working *with* me and my friends, not against us, to find the real criminal.

My father exhaled in relief. "They've been tormenting London for weeks. God knows how many there are. They're multiplying."

"Capturing the dogs might provide more clues to the robbery," said the detective. "We'll examine the carcasses. We're hoping to piece together who sent the dogs to attack the drivers."

Mr. A nodded in agreement. "The criminals were working from inside the Palace. Or very close to it. For who else would know where and when the medical cargo was being unloaded? The wagons were unmarked. Yet there are spies among us, it seems, who would steal from the Crown. Who knows what country they work for. Spying is high treason, and high treason is punishable by hanging."

Hanging, I thought, with a crushing ache in my chest.

I should feel awful about this. I was taught never to take things that didn't belong to me. But the needy poor were no longer faceless. Matilda was raising a baby girl in a tin shack. How could anyone say that giving her a blanket and Vaseline from the Queen's excess was wrong?

Of course they could say it, and if I were caught, they would.

I would assume all the blame. It had been my idea to divert the medicines. But despite these terrifying gray men in their gray suits, I knew that if faced with the same choice, I would make the same decision again.

Would my father be horribly sad if he knew this? I was simply doing what he'd always told me: *Charlotte, you must always be truthful to yourself and your beliefs.*

He, too, faced hanging. I had inadvertently dragged him in with me.

Peter, Jillie, Benjamin, and I could defend ourselves against the charge of attempted murder of the guards, for it wasn't true. But the charge of theft and treason against the Crown was indefensible.

⊰⊱

I hurried alongside my father after leaving the Queen, but he had more bad news for me. "Let's head to the Mews. I'll ask the staff if

186

anyone's heard more about any rabid dogs, and you'll ask about Peter and Jillian's whereabouts."

"Now? Couldn't it possibly wait until after luncheon?" I searched the pocket of my long skirt, but I was out of lemons. My symptoms would overcome me soon if I didn't acquire more. Already I had to lean heavily on my parasol and was winded trying to keep up with my father's stride. I desperately wanted to return to my chambers.

"I'm occupied this afternoon. Let's not argue about this, Charlotte."

I could separate from my father once we got to the Mews, I thought. Rush back to my room for more lemons without him knowing.

"Fine, sir."

His jaw was taut, his mouth a thin line of tension. I knew the look. He was outraged by this theft. "I will leave no stone unturned," he said with frightening calm. "No one does this to me and gets away unscathed."

"I don't think they meant it as a slight against you, sir."

"No? And what do you think they meant it as?"

He gave me a glare so cold it gave me goose bumps. I tried to explain. "It sounds as though they only wished to provide the needy with medicines."

"And made me look like an incompetent fool who can't protect the Queen's supplies."

"I don't believe anyone said that."

"It's called reading between the lines."

This had nothing to do with him. I wished he would believe me. The remaining two wagons would still provide more than enough supplies for the royal family. I saw how much they used. At the end of every year, we sorted the cupboards and donated the excess—perfectly good items—to the Royal College of Surgeons, and they dispersed it among their members.

We exited the Palace to the grounds. Clouds gathered above us as we made the long walk down the tree-lined path. My father slowed his pace. His angry expression faded. "You seem sluggish today."

The morning air on my face felt as warm as steam. He didn't seem to be affected by any heat, so why was my hairline drenched in perspiration? "Didn't get enough sleep," I mumbled. "Bad dreams. I'll be fine." My boots crunched on gravel as we neared the stables. "Now, about my two friends . . . they never would've attacked their jailers unprovoked. They're innocent of those charges."

"I'm not concerned about the charges. I'm concerned about their illness. Rabies is a painful disease. I'd like to ease their transition."

"You mean you'd send Dr. Kenyon."

"Yes, of course. I thought I had explained that."

"As their condition worsens, and they go through transition, what . . . what exactly might Dr. Kenyon do for them?"

"Keep them comfortable. Give them morphine. Ensure they have enough to eat and drink."

I was hoping he might give me new things to try. These were things we were already doing for ourselves.

When we entered the stables, my father noticed the veterinary surgeon in high rubber boots and working jacket, and went to join him.

I breathed a sigh of relief, ready to return immediately to the Palace in search of more lemons the moment my father turned his back.

The sound of water sloshing into a trough made me turn. Benjamin. He'd purposely been noisy to catch my attention. An Arabian mare dipped her mouth to the water and slurped.

"Did you hear if they made it home all right?" I asked, referring to Peter and Jillian.

"They did."

I relaxed at that, but had to warn him. "The Queen's discovered her wagon's missing. Scotland Yard's investigating."

"So soon . . ." Benjamin looked at me, but his stance didn't waver. "Are we still on for later?" He rubbed his wet hands on his work pants.

I nodded. We had agreed to meet Peter near Piccadilly, at Justin Longfellow's engineering shop. Peter was to send the man a note this morning, to make an appointment at five. Fortunately, his shop was fairly close. Perhaps we'd discover once and for all that he was the madman behind the dogs.

"I'll see you by four," I whispered, taking notice that my father had disappeared and I was free to do the same. "I have to leave now."

Benjamin stepped out of the stall, discreetly sliding past me as though we hadn't even been talking. Empty buckets dangled from his long arms.

I turned to the open doors, my head spinning a bit too fast, and spotted Fiona and Theodora breezing in, wearing bright blouses with lacy sleeves. I darted to the side of the Arabian, trying to shield myself from the sisters, but they saw me. I must've stepped awkwardly on my left foot, because pain seared my ankle. I stumbled against the boards.

"Charlotte!" Fiona hailed. "Charlotte, I say! Do come and look at my pretty new riding boots!"

I stepped out and pretended I was interested. "They're lovely."

"I got them on the Strand. Marvelous new shop."

"And *I* bought a new crop," said Theodora. "With the most amazing red leather strap."

She continued bragging as nausea overtook me. The lemons were wearing off, but surely I had more time available. When had I taken my last piece? I rubbed my pounding temple, trying to remember.

"Charlotte?" asked Fiona.

"Lovely scarf, too," I mumbled. My knees weakened. I reached for the stall boards, and to my surprise someone's hand shot out to my lower back to support me. I turned my head and saw Benjamin's look of concern. I grabbed the post in front of me, and he backed away before anyone could see that he'd assisted.

I tried to focus my blurry vision while he kept the girls occupied.

"Ladies, good morning."

"Morning, Benji," cooed Theodora. "Are you here for your riding lessons?"

The sound of the Arabian trampling on her straw drove me to distraction. Did she have to be that loud? Why didn't she stop? And the sound of her slurping and slurping . . . The thought of all that water repulsed me.

My father came round the corner with Fiona and Theodora's father, Dr. Hill—the veterinary surgeon.

"We should like to invite you and the girls to dinner one evening," my father told him, looking at me for approval.

"Perhaps at the end of the month," I said, trying to postpone it.

"We're free tomorrow," Fiona interjected.

"I'm unable tomorrow night, I'm afraid," said my father, and I could've kissed him in gratitude. "I'm conducting an oral examination."

Ah, I thought, Mr. Bloomberg's.

The men continued speaking. "Thank you for the information on the dogs," my father said.

I swallowed my nausea, spun about, and squinted. Which of the tall figures was my father? "They caught the rabid dogs?" I asked weakly.

"Yes," my father said with great cheer. "Just happened."

"At the wharf?"

My father nodded. So he was the blurry figure to my left.

"That's wonderful," I said. "Now the detective . . . in fact all of you . . . know of the mechanics."

"Charlotte?" asked my father. His fuzzy face moved in closer to mine.

"The mechanical dogs," I explained. "Rabies."

"What mechanical dogs?" asked Dr. Hill.

"Of last night," I declared. Why had the girls grown silent and withdrawn? I wished I could see them better. They were a blur of plaited hair and colorful fabrics. "Do they indeed have rabies, father? Or was it some trick of engineering?"

"Charlotte, what are you talking about? The dogs they caught and destroyed were normal canines, infected with rabies."

"Normal?"

"What's all this talk of engineered dogs? Where did you get such ideas?"

My eyes strained, in and out of focus. My head ached. My mouth was so dry my upper lip caught on my teeth as I spoke.

"Where's my parasol?" I asked in a panic. I twirled about but didn't see it. "Where is it? I need it."

Benjamin, standing somewhat away from us all, delivered it in a flash. I grabbed the wooden handle and groped to find firm footing.

"Charlotte?" The concern in my father's voice topped everything.

"There's something wrong with her," said Fiona.

"I'm fine," I insisted.

"Her eyes are bloodshot," Theodora added.

"James," said Dr. Hill, "she's unsteady."

"I must bid you . . . all a good . . ." I wavered, turned, and took a few shaky steps forward. My eyesight had cleared enough that I could see the door.

"Are you limping?" My father caught up to me.

"My new shoes are tie–tight," I explained.

"She's pale. Look at her hands tremble." Fiona hovered at my other side.

"Charlotte," my father repeated. "You are not well. Would you sit with me, please? Over here?"

I tried, I honestly tried, but my feet wouldn't move.

I couldn't be caught like this. Not with so many witnesses. They would lock me up. My father would be the first. I strained to lift my toes off the ground. The muscles in my stomach wobbled. My throat tightened in despair. My legs wouldn't work.

When I collapsed, it was my father who caught me.

CHAPTER TWENTY-THREE

MY father's face wouldn't come into focus as he carried me out the doors of the royal stables. He looked like a twisted painting ... one dark shadow of a shaven jaw ... brown eyebrow lifting ... his jaw clenched in concentration on the path ahead ...

"Do you know what's wrong, Charlotte?" His voice sounded far-away, as if spoken through a tunnel.

"I'm hoping nothing."

"Why didn't you tell me you were ill?"

"I didn't think ..."

My eyes closed. The June breeze lifted my hair. Birds chirped much too loudly. I winced at the sounds.

"Get the bird away from my ear," I mumbled.

"There is no bird, Charlotte. It's high in the tree."

"Then the carriage ... don't drop me in front of the carriage."

"No carriage, either." His voice grew muffled. My body sagged against him and he walked rhythmically; he must be climbing stairs. "She's imagining things."

To whom was he talking? I struggled to open my eyes, but failed. Chaos and voices carried with us along the hallways.

"I'll get a damp cloth." Was it Polly speaking?

Then the feel of cool sheets as I settled onto a soft bed.

Tick-tick-tick.

"The clock, the clock is too loud."

The sound disappeared. I felt a slap of cool water on my forehead. Heavenly.

"I'll get Mr. Bloomberg to examine her," said my father.

No, I wanted to shout, but my voice box seemed to close. *Not him!*

"Not yourself, sir?" Polly again.

"She's family and I'm ... too close ... need an objective consultation."

I heard the heavy emotion in his voice, and wondered if my father, in all these years, had stayed away from giving me medical advice— even performing the simplest check of my ears or throat—for fear he might lose me as he did my mother. That he might be blamed, or blame himself, if I never recovered.

"Not Bloomberg," I squeaked, but no one heard me.

"Charlotte," Polly said with desperation, grabbing my arm. "Open your eyes. Your father is gone. Open your eyes and tell me what I'm to do. He'll be back any minute with Mr. Bloomberg. *Open your eyes.*"

I strained to lift the concrete bricks holding down my eyelids. My body arched. My eyes fluttered open, pushing against the light pouring in from my bedroom window.

"Lemon."

She frowned, glancing at my nightstand. A pot of cold tea sat there along with a plate of lemon slices. "One of these?"

"Hmm."

She held it to my mouth and I bit it. The juice seeped into my throat. I reached up and took it from her, then ate everything but the rind. I was hit by a burst of energy. The air in my lungs seemed to expand. Polly gasped. She stepped back.

"You can't catch what I have, Polly."

She hadn't asked, and I suspected she never would, but she visibly relaxed when I told her.

"He's not to see my foot. Please, Polly ... he'll lock me away."

"Which foot?" She moved to the end of the bed, staring at the covers. "Which one?"

"Left ..."

"But maybe he can help you." Her whisper was hoarse.

"Yes, but he's not to see my left foot. The Queen's advisors will imprison me." My strength was returning. I reached over and took another lemon slice. I was still unsure how much to tell her about my possible rabies.

Polly put her hands on her hips. Her apron was draped around her. "They'll send you away. Like they did my mother."

"Your mother?"

"She was ill with diphtheria. A maid in the Queen's court, no less. They sent her away, they did, said they'd bring her back soon as she got better. Well, she did but they didn't. When you work in the Palace, they've got the power to give you the world, and to take it right back away."

I sympathized.

"Let me take the stockin' off your right foot," said Polly. "Quick now."

My mind was still too weak to comprehend why, but I trusted her. I knew she would stay with me. In the past, I had always had a personal maid present during medical examinations.

The door burst open and she never had the opportunity to do what she wished. In cantered Mr. Bloomberg, knees first, medical bag in hand.

"Good afternoon, Charlotte." He nodded to Polly as well.

I mumbled hello.

When he turned his thin back toward me, arranging his equipment, Polly took the moment to yank the stocking off my good foot. She thrust the stocking under the mattress and yanked on the hem of my skirts to cover my left foot but expose my right.

Mr. Bloomberg spun to face me. "What seems to be the problem?"

"I'm dizzy . . . haven't eaten much since breakfast."

"Your father seems to think it's more than that. Said your pupils are dilated. Breathing irregular. Cyanotic nails and lips. Hallucinations perhaps."

His words left me speechless. What a terrible bedside manner he had, frightening his patient!

Polly seemed to have more sense than he did. "It's not all that bad, sir. She's speaking right and regular now, ain't she?" Her cap bobbed on her head.

Mr. Bloomberg ignored her. He took out his stethoscope, pulled up a chair beside the bed, and placed the bell above my heart.

"A bit fast. Nice and steady, though."

He listened to my lungs. "Clear enough."

He pulled up my eyelids and examined my eyes. "Still dilated. Have you had anything strange to eat or drink lately?"

"No."

"You have access to your father's medical supplies. Have you taken it upon yourself to consume any opiates?"

"I *beg* your pardon," I snapped.

"I apologize, but I must ask. I believe some tablets have gone astray."

So he'd discovered the missing morphine. "Of course I don't take opiates." *You idiot*, I wanted to add.

He asked me to open my mouth and say ah, which I did. He muttered something, then examined my ears and the skin of my face and neck. He picked up one hand, then the other, and turned them over, examining my fingers. His skin was cold and scaly, like a cobra's, I imagined, though I had never touched a snake.

He poked and prodded at my abdomen, through the fabric of my clothing. My stomach gurgled while he pressed a stethoscope to it.

When he was finished, he took a deep breath and glanced at my feet.

Now I understood why Polly had removed the stocking on my good foot. Beneath his gaze, I wiggled my right toes, nice and pink and healthy, while I hid my injured ones.

"If you ask me to lift my skirts to examine any other part of me, I shall report you to my father."

"Your father expects a thorough examination."

"Her father," said Polly, looking him square in the eye, "perhaps don't realize the young miss is having her monthly course. No doctor should be inspectin' that area at a time like this. If'n you'll forgive my frankness."

Well done, Polly. A perfect lie.

Mr. Bloomberg's face flushed a deep crimson, right to the base of his hair roots.

He would never make a good surgeon. Ever.

"Well," he said, tucking away his stethoscope, "your feet look fine. We can finish the examination, if you don't get better, at a later date."

Luck was with me. Mr. Bloomberg didn't like me, and I knew he didn't really care whether I lived or died, which made it all the more easy for him to pack up his things and leave.

I wondered if he was capable of being cruel enough to create the dogs. He certainly had access to scientific minds. He had the wealth, too, coming from his family's shipping background, to buy the silence of those who helped him. Knowing how petty he was with me and envious of my proximity to my father and the Queen, I judged him to be quite ruthless.

Interesting, I thought. I was feeling much better.

⋇

Since I was forced to lie in bed after lunch even though I had energy to spare, I decided to make the most of my time and thus began another letter to Mr. Abercrombie. My engagement photographs were strewn about my bed. They were decent enough, but I would not include one in my letter. The gesture would be much too intimate, and I was trying to keep an ocean between us. How could I make it apparent that we were not a suitable match? That marrying me would be nothing but a headache for him? Perhaps if I meddled in his work . . .

> *Dear Esteemed Sir,*
>
> *You were so generous in sending me an engagement gift, and finally I think I have found the perfect one for you.*
>
> *I shall hire you an assistant in London, while you are away at sea!*
>
> *My search will start tomorrow for the best low-priced person to scrutinize your research papers at the academy and organize them in some clever fashion. Similar to how my maids recently shelved my collection of animal books and puzzles. Perhaps we shall box up and discard some of your older papers to make way for the new!*

A knock on the outer door interrupted my flow. I quickly gathered the photographs and slid them into my nightstand. "Come in!"

196

Polly entered. "I'm here to tell you the verdict. Your father thinks you're sufferin' from stress and fatigue. From engagement preparations, and the fact that Mr. Abercrombie is away." She straightened the empty platters on my tray. "You're to remain on bed rest for the next few days."

I rose from the pillows. At my father's insistence, Polly had helped me change into a nightgown, although I had wanted to stay in proper clothing to be ready for escape. "I can't remain in bed for days. I have things to do." One of them was meeting Peter and Benjamin by five o'clock, close to Piccadilly.

"Your father told me you would say that. Jolene and I promised to keep you quiet and rested."

I heard Jolene's footsteps. She carried in a tray of hot tea and biscuits. I frantically wished to talk to Polly alone, to explain that I might have rabies and that Benjamin knew. That the doctors—including my father—believed nothing medical could be done. I also wanted to confide that we were looking for mechanical dogs. She'd proved herself to be trustworthy, and I needed all the allies I could find in this household.

However, Polly had to defer to Jolene, her senior. Jolene was already perturbed that she hadn't been with me when I'd fainted and that Polly had stepped in during the medical examination.

Jolene perched her tiny frame on the edge of a nearby chair. She poured the tea.

"Please, where is the lemon?" I asked.

"Sorry, there are none left in the kitchens," said Jolene.

I shot Polly a terrified look.

"We'll check again," said Polly.

"Please," I said.

"I've already looked," Jolene insisted, clearly irritated that Polly was again overstepping her bounds. "There's a shortage, for some reason. Cook says he's saving a couple for the Queen, but more will come in by the end of the week."

It was only Tuesday!

"Yes, ma'am," said Polly, lowering her gaze. But she gave me a private nod and left the room, which told me she would do as I asked and check again.

Jolene settled me in, being sure to leave the embroidery that Mrs. Burnhamthorpe had sent within reach, then left. She'd been gone for twenty minutes when Polly returned. I was feeling lightheaded again and was losing some clarity of thought.

"No lemons," said Polly. "Jolene was right. Cook says they're all gone except the ones he's storin' someplace for Her Majesty. He doesn't understand where they all disappeared to. But I found one slice"—she held out her hand, revealing a lemon slice wrapped in a kerchief—"on the Queen's tray."

"Oh, Polly, you didn't."

"Afraid I did."

"Bless you." I bit into the slice.

Polly adjusted my bedcovers. I sipped at the lemon as my head cleared and I thought about what to do.

I was anxious to see my friends. I wondered if Peter had discovered any more clues about the mechanical dogs. I was certain that wherever he was, he was trying hard. He'd always been honorable that way, and quick-thinking. And terribly handsome and exciting. Just thinking of him made my pulse rush. I wondered if he had heard I'd fainted and if he was worried about me in any particularly special way. It was selfish of me, but I hoped he was bothered more than a little bit that I was cooped up in bed.

I didn't wish to acknowledge it, but a small part of me also wondered what Benjamin had thought when he'd seen me fall in the stables. He'd been awfully attentive standing close by, trying to help me mask my symptoms in front of Fiona and Theodora, reaching out to touch me when he saw me stumble. I had always noticed Peter, but Benjamin had somehow shot out of the dark to surprise me. How could I not swoon over Benjamin's tall, handsome looks and his unwavering, quiet loyalty? He took such risks on my behalf. My feelings for him were growing beyond my control. The trouble was, I liked both boys, and they were so very different. . . . Oh, for goodness' sake! How could I be thinking about boys at a time like this?

Snapping out of my self-concern, I thought of poor Jillian and her health, and what I could do to help her. "Polly, I can't possibly wait until Friday to leave my room. I promised to meet with Benjamin later this afternoon."

"I just got word." Polly adjusted my pillow. "Benjamin sends two messages. The first is that he says you should wait till you feel better. I'm not quite sure what he's referrin' to."

"I can't wait. We have to meet the engineer today."

"Who?"

"A mechanical engineer. He may hold the key to this entire situation."

"Why is it lemons make you feel better?" Polly looked at me timidly, as though she knew she might be overstepping her role as a maid. Here was my opportunity.

"I believe what I'm fighting is . . . rabies."

Polly's face went pale. "Mother Mary." Slowly, she sank onto the chair by my bed. She looked to the lower portion of my sheets. "That's why you were hidin' your left foot. Bite marks." She moved her gaze back to my face. "Please go on. I won't spill any secrets."

It was what I was hoping to hear. "Thank you."

"How d'you know it's rabies?"

I took a deep breath and explained it all. She was flabbergasted to hear I was with the Moreley twins when they were bitten.

"But can't your father help you?"

"I questioned him about the disease, without him knowing I was asking for myself. He said there was nothing he could do to help Jillian and Peter. When Dr. Kenyon examined them, he confirmed it."

"So your hope is to find the person who developed the blasted dogs, and pray it ain't true rabies. That there's a cure."

I nodded in agreement.

"The lemons help," she said.

"Yes, I'm not sure why. They're not listed as a cure or a treatment in the medical books. Which tells me that this rabies, or whatever I have, is not the same type of rabies spread by regular dogs."

"Who d'you think could . . . could be so evil?" Polly's expression was sincere and trusting, and it was a relief to confide in a friend. I wanted her to know who the suspects were in case something happened to me.

I drew the sheets up to my chin. "So far, I think it's between three men. This mechanical engineer, Justin Longfellow. The Royal Gadget Engineer, Mr. Snow."

She gasped at that one.

"And Mr. Bloomberg."

Polly didn't seem so surprised at the third name.

I rubbed my cheek as a new thought occurred to me. "Could you send someone to the market, Polly, for lemons?"

"Heavens, I forgot to tell you the second message. Benjamin said he already sent someone. They're racing to help you!"

CHAPTER TWENTY-FOUR

PINEAPPLES didn't alleviate my symptoms. Nor did oranges, bananas, mangos from India, apples, nor any other fruit Polly brought to my bedchamber in the next hour. I was perspiring now, as though drenched with rain. My eyelids were so heavy I fought to keep them open.

"Polly, could you please post this letter to Mr. Abercrombie?" I had managed to finish it, after adding a wee anecdote about my uncontrollable temper.

"As soon as I arrive downstairs." She tucked it into her apron. "Benjamin says to remain strong. The person he sent to the market should be here soon." Her pink cheeks dimpled in concern. She fluffed up my blanket. "He sends other bad news, I'm afraid."

"What is it?"

"Says Jillian isn't gettin' any better. The numbness is still in her arm."

I sank against the feathers. How long were we to last?

"And the lemons are becomin' less and less effective for Peter, too. Down to eighty minutes at most."

"Mine only last an hour. Oh, Polly, I've got to get out of here. I have a feeling this man Longfellow is somehow the missing link."

I closed my eyes for only a moment. My limbs went heavy.

I fell in and out of sleep, but it was a fitful one. I wrestled with a headache, dizziness, groggy brain, blurry eyesight. Someone brought tea to my lips and I tried to sip, but it seared my throat. I couldn't swallow. "Sorry, Polly," I mumbled. "Maybe later."

"It's not Polly," said my father.

Startled, I attempted to sit up. I clutched the sheets to my nightgown and wondered why the sun was still in the sky. How long had I slept? Was it hours or days?

"Can I make you more comfortable?" he asked.

I mumbled. He fussed about and straightened my covers.

"May I read to you?"

"Umm-hmm." I forced my eyes open a crack and spotted a newspaper on his lap. "The paper."

"Wouldn't you prefer Shakespeare?"

"Not today." My mind drifted.

He glossed over the headlines. He cut himself short as he tried to find something appropriate. "War in Africa Creates—no, not that one. Two More Drowned—perhaps not that one, either. Bats Found with Rabies—"

He swore softly and mumbled to himself, "Bats now, too?" The loud crinkling of the paper made me wince in my stupor. "Here's one that's not offensive."

He went on and on, reading details about horse riding in Hyde Park. I captured only a few words. " . . . rentable by the hour or half day . . . carriages through Kensington Gardens . . . visitors to the Albert Memorial . . ."

When I awoke again, it was dark. He was seated underneath the lantern at my bedside, reading from my books. He clutched *Tales of Robin Hood*.

I recalled how enthused I was whenever he'd read to me about the good-hearted outlaw of English folklore who lived in Sherwood Forest . . . who robbed from the rich to give to the poor. Little John, Robin Hood, and his true love, Maid Marian. How good their cause, how thrilling their escapes . . . but my thoughts all mixed together.

I murmured, "Clockwork dogs . . . bats . . . keep them away from me. . . ."

"Charlotte, you're dreaming."

There was someone else in the room. I heard him cough. Mr. Bloomberg.

"I'm worried," my father confided, "about her sanity." When he rose and the other man followed, I thought for certain they'd locked the door behind them, and for a minute envisioned myself in prison.

I screamed and screamed.

I heard Polly's voice: "I've brought some tea and lemons."

"She can't drink now, she's too distraught." My father filled a syringe and injected my arm with it. It made my muscles grow weak and my breathing deep.

When I opened my eyes a crack to say good night, it wasn't my father's face I saw, but the pinched mouth and protruding nose of Mr. Bloomberg as he held up a large, empty syringe and dripping needle.

I screamed again from the depths of my being.

⊰⊱

Nothing made sense to James about his daughter's delirious ramblings, but when he awoke the next morning, something was bothering him. Charlotte kept mentioning mechanical dogs, even in her sleep. She'd heard it in the royal stables that very first morning after the attacks.

It was time he asked more questions. Within an hour of rising, he checked on her—thankfully she was still sleeping—rushed through breakfast, and once again stepped through the doors of Scotland Yard.

Minutes later, he was seated in Sergeant Clark's office.

James pulled out the newspaper he'd been reading to Charlotte. "Do you know anything more about this bat attack?"

The sergeant glanced at the headline and skimmed the article with his big finger as he read. He shook his head. "Nothing more than what it says here. My men found no trace of the bats, night before last. Someone was almost bitten, but without a specimen to examine, there's no way of tellin' for sure if the bats were rabid. The reporter exaggerated the problem. Dislike these type o' reporters. Cause nothin' but panic."

James dug his wide back into the chair. "I know you're short-handed, but were you able to perform any more autopsies?"

"There was an attack last night at a jeweler's."

"Dogs?"

"Aye. One jewel case was broken, but the thief didn't have enough time to abscond with anything. Coroner's just finished the autopsy. Writin' up the report as we speak."

Another attack? Dear God. And another robbery. What did it mean? "May I discuss it with the coroner? It's a matter of dire business for the Crown."

"Of course. Follow me to Dr. Hamilton."

Sergeant Clark rose from his desk and led James down a private corridor to the rear. They stepped out of the way as two policemen carried a wooden casket out from the autopsy room. James and the sergeant entered.

The coroner—sometimes called the crowner because he was appointed by the Crown to perform autopsies in murder cases and accidental deaths—was a short fellow no taller than four and a half feet. There was a height minimum required for the police force, but James knew the man personally and that he was quite brilliant, so the rules had been bypassed.

Dr. Hamilton was wiping down a metal autopsy table. His long blond hair was pulled back and banded together into a tail. He wore a white laboratory coat over his specially tailored police uniform. Behind him, windows overlooked a small garden and alleyway, where the bobbies with the casket loaded it onto a horse cart.

"Ah, James. Forgive me if I don't shake your hand." Dr. Hamilton hopped off the wooden box on which he was standing, tipped a brown bottle of carbolic acid onto his cloth, hopped back onto the box, and continued wiping.

"Please, carry on, Abe," James told him. "Good to see you."

"How is the Queen's favorite doctor?"

Sergeant Clark seemed amused by the question.

James had no time for harmless ribbing today. "Very well, thank you. But I'm troubled by the recent dog attacks. May I ask about the autopsy you just performed?"

"Certainly."

"Cause of death?"

"Massive bleeding from a throat wound. Caused his heart to fail."

"Were there any other wounds?"

Dr. Hamilton stretched as far as he could to wipe a corner. "His hands were badly bitten. Lacerations on his right ankle."

"How did the wounds appear?"

"Consistent with dog bites. Large dogs. Seventy to eighty pounds in size." He tossed the cloth into a bucket on the opposite side of the room. It made a loud splash.

"Ha!" said the sergeant, visibly impressed.

"Great throw, indeed," said James. "Were the wounds made by several dogs or only one?"

"At least two. Possibly three."

"How do you know for certain?"

Dr. Hamilton climbed off his wooden box. He walked to the far end of the room and stepped onto another crate to soap his hands at the basins. "Some of the bite marks indicate one of the dogs was missing a top tooth. The gap is quite prominent. On other bite marks, the teeth are all there."

Very nicely done, thought James. "Did he die at the site where he was found?"

"Lividity indicates the body was not moved."

Dr. Hamilton noticed the look of confusion on the sergeant's face, and thus explained. "As rigor mortis sets in, blood in the body will drain in the direction of gravity, and settle in the lowest parts, permanently. If a person dies facedown, such as this unfortunate bloke, blood gathers in the chest, face, front of the thighs, and so on. So if the body had been moved, say turned over to the back, the blood pooling—lividity—would be inconsistent with the position found."

"Ah, yes," said Sergeant Clark. "We simply call it blood pooling."

"Time of death?" asked James.

"Middle of the night, consistent with the story of the street cleaners who found him."

"And what about the bite marks, Abe?" James leaned in closer and studied the various bottles on the countertop. "Can you tell if the dogs were rabid?"

"I can't tell from the body itself. There wasn't enough time to manifest rabies, from the moment he was bitten to when he died. However, I would say the dogs were rabid, from the viciousness of their attack. Excess saliva found in the wounds. And . . ."

James looked up from the bottles.

"... something strange showed up."

"May I hazard a guess?"

Dr. Hamilton raised an eyebrow. Still standing at the basins, he dried his hands, unrolled his cuffs, and did up a button. "By all means."

"You found metal shavings in the wounds. Similar to the ones found in the autopsy of the other man attacked by the dogs."

"How on earth would you know something like that? I've only pulled the shavings out an hour ago." He took several golden rings off the counter and put them on his fingers, then hopped off his box and walked to the counter beside James. He lifted a glass jar. "And told no one."

James bent down to the man's level to have a look. Metal filings, no more than an eighth of a teaspoon, were soaking in a clear liquid. "I had my suspicions," said James. "The rumor is these dogs aren't normal. That someone is creating a team of mechanical monsters."

For the first time since they'd gone to medical college together, Abe looked shaken.

"What's that?" James peered closer into the bottle at a flat, rectangular piece of black metal no bigger than the nail bed of his little finger. One edge was as sharp as a knife, the other jagged, with a tiny protruding piece of wire.

"I haven't identified it yet."

Their eyes met as it dawned on them both. James whistled. "The dog's missing tooth."

⁂

The Queen's dogs barked outside my bedchamber windows on their morning run. I opened my eyes. Polly was here. In apron and cap, she set down a tray of food on my nightstand. "The lemons." The freckles on her nose stood out. "They're working again."

I turned to the other tray near my head and saw a pile of lemon rinds. "Did I chew all those?"

Polly nodded. Her apricot-colored hair was pinned high beneath her cap. "Benjamin got them to me yesterday afternoon, but your father wouldn't let me near you. Last night, I tried again but couldn't rouse you. I put them to your mouth but you did nothing. This morning, it took one and a half lemons to get you out of your stupor."

"Thank you for trying so hard." Then I exclaimed in a panic, "I slept through yesterday?"

She nodded.

"What about Longfellow?"

"No one went. Peter and Benjamin are headed there shortly, Benjamin said, with or without you."

"Then I've got to rush." My mouth tasted like the scrapings off a dungeon floor. I sat up, weakly, and looked for my dental brush.

"It's here." Polly helped me stand. My legs shook, but I made it into the bathing room and brushed my teeth. I examined my injured foot. Red streaks still there. No pus. No change. I washed the tender skin with tonic, wincing at the soreness, and bandaged it.

When I returned to the bedroom, my friend helped me to the tray of sandwiches she'd brought. When I finished eating and drinking, I felt better. Steady enough to walk.

"Your father is bound to come lookin' for you. How can you excuse yourself?"

"Find Russett. Tell him you can't find my father to tell him directly, but leave word that I'm feeling better. That I'm taking you and going to the market."

⎯⧮⧭⎯

I was happy to be with my friends again as we walked through Piccadilly. But Jillian was too weak to join us, which dampened everyone's spirits. Peter kept asking how I was doing, and Benjamin wouldn't let me out of his sight. Polly, too, had come along and would be helpful if I needed her. She also knew Jillian from the Mews and was saddened by her illness.

We entered Justin Longfellow's shop. It was located in a much wealthier section of the city and was far more crowded than the last two tool and die shops we'd visited. He had a staff of three to contend with: two men who worked the forge in the far corner, and an older woman behind the counter who was following Benjamin round the aisles as though he might be a pickpocket. As I studied the shiny metals, the colorful Venetian glass bottles, and the steam that gushed out of a large cylinder, I realized these gadgets were every bit as good as the ones in the Royal Gadget Engineering Hall.

Peter brushed my sleeve as he stopped beside me to gaze at the same gadgets. He was dressed in fine clothing. He'd told us outside that he'd gone to a secondhand shop for a proper wool jacket and finely pressed shirt, to look the part of a baron's son. He needed a disguise for his questioning, he'd said.

He leaned in to my right. "Amazing work, isn't it?"

"Incredible," murmured Polly to my left. She'd removed her apron and cap and looked pretty in a blue day blouse and matching skirts. Peter was still wary that I'd brought a stranger into our midst, but after I'd listed all the things she'd done to help me these last few days, he'd begun to soften.

Benjamin, though, was watching me from the corner. He'd had a scare in the stables yesterday seeing me collapse.

Unsteady on my feet, I reached for the wall to support myself.

"What's wrong?" Polly whispered as two nearby customers, men in top hats, browsed the shelves.

"I'm a bit shaky, but I'll be fine." Perhaps I had underestimated the recovery time I needed. The last lemon I'd bitten into was half an hour ago, yet I could feel my energy already waning. "I'll need another lemon soon."

"You've taken three more than we thought you'd need. Only two pieces remain."

"I brought more in my pocket," Peter offered. "Since Jillian doesn't use any . . ."

Every time he mentioned her name, my throat quivered. "We're here for her, too," I said. "This has to lead somewhere."

"I'm afraid if we don't find a cure soon, we might . . . we might lose her." Peter, for the first time since this ordeal had started, looked undone. He rubbed the spot on his forehead where his dark hair fell. My heart went out to him. I simply touched his shoulder.

"God, you mustn't ever say that," Polly told him.

"Good afternoon," said a man behind us in a loud voice. It snapped us to attention.

"Mr. Longfellow, some people to see you." The female shop worker stepped forward to introduce us by the false name Peter had given her. "Mr. Simon, sir. The youngest son of Lord Waycastle. And friends."

Peter, quickly regaining his composure, stepped forward in his dapper clothes. Polly and I shifted nervously. Benjamin watched from a nearby aisle.

Mr. Longfellow, intimidating at six and a half feet tall and three hundred pounds, stared at our group. His presence gave me the jitters. His huge handlebar mustache wiggled as he talked, and I was speechless for a moment.

Peter stood his ground, tall, muscled, and in control. "We're here to order a fire-spitting cane for my father, fashioned in the likeness of Mr. Darwin's."

"Are you?" Longfellow was a daunting man with a daunting voice.

"Yes, sir. I'm afraid we don't have time for a long wait. My father sent me to view the engineering gadgets in your portfolio. I'm to order the greatest and most unique among them."

I admired Peter for his tactics. He'd dropped the pretense of being circus performers, to pursue the opening that the last tool and die maker had given us about Darwin's fire-spitting cane. It was a stroke of brilliance, asking to see all the best items this man had available. We'd see in a flash whether he was capable of clockwork creatures.

A thick artery pounded in the man's temple. One of his hairy eyebrows twitched. His nose turned red. Then his mustache wiggled, as if his lips were quivering with tension.

"Tell me who you really are."

Polly gasped. Peter's self-assurance looked strained. Benjamin took a few steps toward me and Polly in a gesture of protection. My hands shook. The shop was suddenly empty. When had the other customers left? Where was his lady assistant?

Peter found his bearing. He crossed his arms in that haughty way titled men often do. "Shall I tell my father you refuse his gold coins?"

"Bring him here. I'll tell him myself."

Peter blinked. I sensed danger.

The giant leered at us as though we were fish he wanted to spear.

Peter changed his tactics. "You've caught us red-handed, sir. This is intended to be a surprise for my father. On the occasion of his meeting with the Queen later this month. He desires to give Her Majesty a great gift, and we thought of Mr. Darwin's cane. But our apologies if we've disturbed you."

While Peter finished, Benjamin signaled us to move to the door, to leave *this instant* before the giant exploded. We all four turned on our heels, murmuring apologies, when the giant's great hairy hand clamped over mine. He spun me toward him. He hurt my wrist. He seemed to sense I was the weakest.

His mustache quivered again. "Is it Harold Snow? Did he send you?"

It was a desperate plea rather than a question. His black gaze seared mine, and the walls around me spun. I replied, "I'm s-sorry, perhaps we shouldn't have come."

"Harold Snow," he roared, clutching my arm and yanking it so hard I nearly toppled toward him. "Or Cameron Turnbull. *Which one sent you?*"

Hairs on my neck stood on end. His wide nose grew blurry. I wobbled, but then three sets of hands shot out and extricated me from the giant.

"Sorry, sir."

"Our apologies."

"Fine shop you have here."

Then we burst down the aisle and out the door as if running from a monster.

"The man's unstable," I said, leaning against the boys as they lifted me along the cobbles. "Clearly insane!"

CHAPTER TWENTY-FIVE

HOURS later, I stepped into the Engineering Hall past the spitting Silver and Glass Spider to look for my father. I would inform him that I had heard a rumor that the sinister Mr. Longfellow had some sort of hatred toward our engineers, Mr. Snow and Mr. Turnbull. I was still recovering from my encounter with him. For now, the lemons had worked their magic, but I worried how long they would remain effective.

The oral examination my father was giving to Mr. Bloomberg was well under way. I heard my father's voice coming from the oratory theater and headed toward it. The orals were always public events, held before an audience of like-minded scientists, engineers, and surgeons. I slid inside. When I found a seat among the dozen men in the bleachers overlooking the floor below, I wondered how long I'd have to wait.

I placed my parasol beside me and leaned over for a better look. Both men were dressed in formal attire. My father sat comfortably on a large oak desk, while Mr. Bloomberg stood stiffly beside him, as a soldier might stand by his commander.

Mr. Snow and Mr. Turnbull were not present.

"Give us three circumstances under which you would attempt a Caesarean section."

Mr. Bloomberg slowly listed his points. "If the water sac has broken and labor hasn't progressed in three days. If the mother is close to death. If the delivery is breech."

"What?" exclaimed my father. "Breech is not necessarily a cause for surgery. Why, my own daughter was a breech presentation, and she was safely delivered down the birth canal."

I was a breech delivery? I didn't come out headfirst in the normal way, perhaps feet or buttocks first? How could my father tell a roomful of strangers this before he'd told me?

A few faces glanced my way. My skin prickled with discomfort.

Did my positioning have anything to do with my mother's death?

"I didn't—didn't mean all breech presentations." Mr. Bloomberg fumbled to correct himself. "Only those circumstances in which the surgeon suspects the baby may get lodged in the birth canal, and thus needs to be delivered by another method."

My father nodded to indicate the answer was acceptable. On to another topic. "How would a thirty-two-year-old man present to you, if he had fish poisoning?"

"Fish poisoning, sir? I didn't—didn't think that topic was included tonight."

"I asked you to read pages sixty-two to sixty-eight last night, did I not?"

"Yes, but sir, it was late and I didn't think you meant it to be included. . . ."

"Shall we tell the man with fish poisoning his surgeon was too tired to study that bit?"

A chuckle from the scientists around me made Mr. Bloomberg's cheeks color.

"My profuse apologies, sir. I imagine the fish poisoning would present similarly to any other foodstuff poisoning. May I list the general symptoms, then, for partial marks?"

My father nodded. He leaned forward, sitting on the desk, and listened.

"Vomiting. Extreme abdominal pain. Diarrhea. Rapid pulse. Dizziness."

"Go on."

Mr. Bloomberg grappled for more symptoms. "High fever . . . perspiration . . ."

When it was obvious he couldn't think of any more, my father prodded. "What is it you should be most concerned about, with eating contaminated fish?"

Mr. Bloomberg's mouth opened. A little gasp came out, then nothing.

"The patient's breathing," I whispered to myself. "Swelling of the tongue. Choking. Page sixty-six."

The man took out a handkerchief and dabbed at his sweaty forehead. My father took his pocket watch from his vest, looked at the time, slid it back, then looked up at the gallery. He froze for a moment when he noticed me, then focused back on Mr. Bloomberg.

"I'm sorry, sir . . ."

"Some people are highly susceptible to fish," my father answered for him. "It's breathing you must be concerned about. Eating certain fish, those with shells especially, may cause the tongue and throat to swell, obstructing the air passages. Page sixty-six."

"Thank you, sir."

"The rules of examination require me to give you half marks for your answer. Which is being rather kind, for I'm afraid the choking patient would give you zero."

Those around me chuckled again. Mr. Bloomberg glanced up sheepishly at the gallery of men. He noticed me and glared. His jaw clenched and his eyes blazed.

"Sir," he asked my father, "since when do we allow women in here, to witness the business of men?"

My father didn't need to look at me to understand the reference. Instead, he posed a question of his own. "If you should graduate, do you intend to practice medicine only on men?"

"No, sir. I intend to practice on everyone, including women and children."

"Then I suggest you learn to gain their trust."

Mr. Bloomberg's nostrils flared. "Yes, sir."

His embarrassment gave me little joy. Peter and Benjamin were always receptive to my opinions. It didn't matter that I was a girl.

I didn't like this man and he didn't much care for me. Everything he did seemed highly suspicious. When he got very angry and was alone behind closed doors, was he capable of creating deadly monsters?

Yes. I grew dizzy and my stomach clenched at the realization. What could I do? I left the room. Half an hour had passed and my body was shaking. I needed a lemon.

Alone in the corridor, I removed a slice from my pocket, ate it, and returned the rind to my kerchief. In an emergency, perhaps the skin of the lemon would also work as medicine.

I decided to wait outside the theater for my father. The doors remained open, so his voice followed me as I walked through the empty marble hall. It faded as I passed my work station. Out of curiosity, I sat down on my stool and glanced over my things. All seemed to be untouched from the last time I'd been here, when I was working on my goggles. What had happened then? Had I really developed magical goggles, or had it been a delusion? A rabies hallucination?

I slid my hand into the cubbyhole and pulled out the goggles at the same time a male voice behind me asked, "Working on something?"

I jammed the goggles into my skirt pocket and spun to face him. "Mr. Turnbull. Good evening. You're—you're not listening to the oral exam?"

Circles rimmed his lower lids and his dark hair was rumpled. "No time tonight." He held some papers. I gathered he'd been working. "What's in your pocket?"

"Pardon me?" My stomach tensed. Did he mean the lemons or the goggles?

"I saw you. What interesting thing are you taking from the Engineering Hall?"

My throat went dry. "I wasn't taking anything, sir. It's simply an experiment I've been working on." I slid out the goggles to show him briefly, then slid them back in.

"Ah, forgive me. I forgot what it's like to be young and excited about new discoveries. When I was your age, I used to hoard batteries. Buckets of them, left over from my father's scientific studies. My brother and I had a rivalry to devise ways to recharge them. Quite surpassing my father's expectations of us both, I might add."

"It was well worth your interest. Here you are, assistant to one of the greatest minds in Her Majesty's service."

He turned away and nodded. "Yes. The Queen tells me every time she sees me what a great assistant I make." He said it with restraint; perhaps he didn't wish to brag, and I admired him for that. Footsteps clicked down the hall, distracting us.

"That's wonderful," I said to Mr. Turnbull. He had definite reason to be proud of his position. I knew how it felt to be *un*appreciated.

The footsteps grew louder. We turned and spotted the new engineer with the beard, Mr. Yardley, hurrying toward the Silver and Glass Spider, papers in hand. He disappeared down the staircase. It seemed everyone was working tonight.

A fresh idea came to me; I would appreciate having another look through Mr. Snow's things. I turned to Mr. Turnbull. "Do you think Mr. Snow would mind if I took a stroll in the Exhibition Room?"

"Why would he mind? You're with me." He pretended he was put off by the suggestion that I might need permission. "Did you know the puppies opened their eyes?"

"They did?" I smiled, envisioning the faces. "I'll have to visit them."

His friendly manner disarmed me. Surely he couldn't be connected in any diabolical way with Longfellow. Not that I completely trusted Mr. Turnbull—my eyes and ears had to be open to the possibility that anyone here could be involved. Yet he always put me at ease.

Perhaps I could extract some answers from him.

"Why is it Mr. Snow seems so unapproachable?"

"He's not, really, once you get to know him."

"I've known him for two years already."

"As a scientist, if you don't mind my saying, Miss Sycamore, you need to develop more patience in order to see results."

That's what I liked about Mr. Turnbull. He treated me as if I could be a scientist one day. As if any girl could, if she put her mind to it. When we entered the exhibition space, he was drawn to a new railroad mechanism. I noticed an aquarium labeled SEAWATER AND OCEAN FISH.

"Another invention," I said with delight, peering at an assembly of pipes and wires underwater. "Someone's added bubbles so the fish can breathe."

They swam in schools—pretty gold colors, fuchsias, and big green eyes.´

When I straightened up again, I was standing near the darts created by African tribesmen. Three tarantulas squirmed behind glass. I shuddered at their hairy size. In a cupboard below them were various potions and mixtures. Perhaps there'd be something else I could coat the lenses of my goggles with.

I read labels—TINCTURE OF AMAZON BELLFLOWER, ANTIDOTE TO POISONOUS DARTS, and COPPER POWDER. The last was in a glass vial, a pretty shade I could add to the rims of the eyewear to make them attractive. My vision blurred at the finer print, though squinting helped. The poisonous darts were made with the venom of frogs, so it seemed possible the antidote to repel the venom might repel insects, too. The Amazon bellflower was of the Venus flytrap family, a plant that captured and digested insects, which might also be useful.

I slid all three vials into my pocket. I wasn't taking them for good; Mr. Snow let me borrow whatever I pleased, as long as I kept it all at my work station and returned it when I was finished for the day. I would leave the vessels at my work station before I left.

I was getting nervous. How long should I wait for my father to finish? I could feel my legs jittering already. Could I sneak another lemon slice without Mr. Turnbull noticing? I turned to see where he was, and standing right behind me, peering down at my face, was Mr. Snow.

"Ah," I yelped, and stepped away.

He seemed amused to have frightened me.

"Sorry, lass."

"Don't you ever say hello, Mr. Snow?"

He shook his head, his unruly white hair slipping about his ears. "If I don't say hello, I won't have to say good-bye."

Sometimes he spoke in riddles.

I looked about for Mr. Turnbull, but he'd vanished. Suddenly I got the eerie feeling that perhaps these two men were working together. If mechanical dogs were involved, there would be an awful lot of work to do, and . . . and . . . two men could accomplish more than one.

My skirts brushed against the lower shelves as I sought to distance myself from Mr. Snow. Then across the room, Mr. Turnbull popped up from the mechanism he was studying. My heart jumped again. He hadn't left; he'd just been tinkering with a gadget.

I couldn't take being alone with these two. When I approached the door, I heard no footsteps racing after me. My breathing calmed. Turning, I decided to try one last tactic before I left them. "Do either of you kind sirs by chance know Justin Longfellow? He was asking about you the other day, when I . . . when I bumped into him with my father."

Mr. Turnbull blinked.

Mr. Snow's neck turned red, then a strange glimmer crept into his eyes.

I'd hit a nerve with Mr. Snow. He lunged toward me. "How did you—"

I dashed out, terrified he would grab me. I raced down the hall, clutching my parasol like a weapon. All was silent. The voices from the theater had stopped. I kept going, dashing past the hiss of the great spider.

"If yer lookin' for yer father," said a cleaning man sweeping the floor, "he just left by that door."

"Father!" I burst outside into the evening light. He turned on the path. The tails of his coat blew up in the light wind.

"Charlotte, there you are. Why aren't you in bed resting? How many times do I have to tell you?" His black hair lifted about his temples.

I stopped when I reached him. "I wished to speak with you."

"You're not to go back to the Engineering Hall on your own."

"Ever?"

"For a while. You're to stay away from Mr. Snow in particular."

"Why, may I ask?"

"I don't wish to alarm you, but . . . the police are handling a matter. Until it's settled, you need to stay away from Mr. Snow."

"But why?"

"Mechanical dogs." He tilted his head. "We've found proof."

"You believe me?" I whispered.

"Yes."

Finally, finally, finally.

So they suspected Mr. Snow. I always knew he was a strange man. I shuddered that he could be so evil. What would Peter think? He'd want to get his hands around the man's throat. But it wasn't proven yet; he'd have to be patient.

My mind and my mouth worked at light speed. "Why do you think he made them? He frightens me. Did he work alone, or with Longfellow? For the last few hours, I was suspecting everyone. Including Bloomberg and Turnbull. Now that I think of it, even that Yardley man is odd. How do the dogs work? Every time they appear, there seems to be a robbery." I gulped some air. "Please tell me there is a cure for artificial rabies."

My father stepped back, mouth agape. "Charlotte, my dear, you're still unwell. Your thinking is jumbled. Look at your eyes. You're feverish. The police don't know any of it. That's what they're trying to uncover."

"If mechanical dogs did bite Peter and Jillian, you can lift their quarantine."

"It makes no difference, artificial rabies or natural. People still wouldn't allow them to walk about freely." His mouth turned down with displeasure. "And they're still wanted for attempted murder."

So nothing had changed.

Nothing.

I shuffled my feet, the soreness pumping through my left ankle. I was right back where I started; desperate to tell my father of my injury, but more desperate to keep my freedom until they proved Mr. Snow was guilty and we found a cure.

My father grabbed hold of my wrist. "Come. I'm taking you to your room. Since you refused to obey me on bed rest earlier, I will put you there myself. Mrs. Burnhamthorpe will sit outside your door."

Panic shot through me. I tried to wiggle out of his hold but it was rock solid. "I'll obey. I'll do it on my own. I promise."

"I want you to get better, Charlotte." He dropped his hand, but his firm stance told me this was a battle I had lost. His deep voice rumbled. "You're to stay put in your room for the next three days. That's an order. Now come with me."

CHAPTER TWENTY-SIX

"MRS. BURNHAMTHORPE?" Much later that night, past the hour of eleven, I pressed my face against the door that led from my chambers to the main hall. "I truly do apologize for your having to sit there. I promise you'll find me here at eight o'clock in the morning, if you'd like to rest in your own bed tonight."

There was a pause behind the door.

"How thoughtful of you to be concerned for my comfort." Her voice rippled with sarcasm. The implication was that I should have thought of her comfort *before* I disobeyed my father's order on bed rest earlier, so she wouldn't be in this position now. "I'll summon Russett to bring you some chamomile tea."

I sighed. "All right. Thank you." At least I had a plentiful supply of lemons in my room, the ones Benjamin had delivered from the market. I helped myself to several slices. My lips puckered and swelled from the quantity I was eating.

While I waited for the tea, I soaked my left foot in Epsom salts. I stared at my plump red toes, horrified. I barely felt them anymore when I walked. They'd gone from being extremely painful to numb, like Jillian's wound. The red streaks along the veins of my left leg now reached my hip. If the streaks made it to my heart, would my heart explode?

I wondered what more my friends and I could do.

Someone rapped on my outer door.

Still dressed in my day skirts and blouse, I shoved my bare feet into plush slippers and opened it. Mr. Russett came into my sitting room and set the tea on the low table between the two settees. Mrs. Burnhamthorpe followed behind to pour.

"Won't you stay and have a cup with me?" I asked her as the footman left. As much as she was loath to admit it, Mrs. Burnhamthorpe enjoyed chitchat, and perhaps I could coax some gossip from her. Even one clue might prove helpful.

She nodded in agreement, her dark bun neatly pinned despite the late hour. She tucked her pleated skirts beneath her and took a seat. She squinted at the teapot, but managed to pour herself a steaming cup unscathed. "Why is it that young girls choose to disobey their fathers?"

"It's not that I try, it's that his ideas are old-fashioned." I sipped the hot brew. I swallowed, but seemed to have too much saliva.

"What did you do to upset him this evening?"

"I went to the Engineering Hall on my own. Instead of staying in bed."

She surveyed me over her cup and saucer. "How did Mr. Snow seem to you?"

How much did she know about the situation? Had my father told her anything? Likely not, until the police could prove the accusations. I swallowed again. This time my mouthful went down, but in a painful gulp.

"Grumpy as usual."

"Probably extra so, considering the time of year."

"Time of year?"

"His granddaughter, Violet, about your age, passed away two years ago. Right before you moved here. Accidental drowning."

Shocked by the news, I set my teacup onto its saucer with a clatter. "I didn't know that."

"He had a church service for her a few days ago."

That's where he'd gone that afternoon.

"It hit him hard. Changed him. He used to be quite jovial."

Jovial? Mr. Snow? Oh, the poor man.

"He once told me," Mrs. Burnhamthorpe said, peering closer and squinting at my face, "that you remind him of her."

I tried to comprehend this. So that's why he was so cold to me. That's why he withdrew and preferred to frighten me rather than get to know me. I reminded him of what he'd lost. I remembered his words to me tonight. *If I don't say hello, I won't have to say good-bye.*

My mind reeled as I struggled to put together the timeline. "Violet passed away. I moved in. Shortly afterward, he accidentally blew up the engineering lab."

"What a disastrous year that was for him. Some say he was so distraught by Violet that he lost his concentration." Mrs. Burnhamthorpe refreshed our cups, but I had lost my appetite for tea. The thought of swallowing any liquid . . . I shoved my cup and saucer away with a rattle.

"He had a lot of competition to head the new Engineering Hall when it was being built," she added.

I'd never heard this before, either. "Competition? From whom?"

A streak of saliva dripped from the side of my mouth. I swiped it with my napkin, extremely embarrassed in front of my etiquette teacher. She frowned at my behavior, but I couldn't help the stumble in my manners. I swallowed twice more to clear my mouth.

"Two other men wanted his position. One you don't know—Mr. Justin Longfellow, a blustering man well known in the engineering circles. Plus the overly confident, much-too-young Mr. Turnbull."

The information left me speechless. How did this tie together? They'd been competitors, the three of them. Mr. Snow had ultimately won back his position, but it must've bruised his pride that he'd had to reapply for it after the explosion.

"Well, I must be going," she said abruptly, perhaps regretting that she'd divulged any information. "Russett and I are to take turns manning your door, so please do be a good girl and sleep as much as you can."

She rose to leave. When I stood, the settees seemed to spin around me. I closed my eyes for balance, then followed her the few steps to the door.

This was all wrong. I was trapped inside when I should be discussing this new information with Benjamin and Peter and Jillian, trying to decipher who the madman was.

When Mrs. Burnhamthorpe opened the outer door, Polly was rushing down the hall toward us. She was hastily pinning her cap to her fallen hair, obviously just roused from bed.

"What is it?" asked the headmistress.

"Mr. Snow," Polly panted. Her gaze shifted to me. "He's been arrested."

"Good God," Mrs. Burnhamthorpe exclaimed, "what on earth for?"

"Murder charges. Developing mechanical dogs."

I clutched the door, too shocked and confused to speak.

"Scotland Yard took him away, ma'am." Polly spoke to her, but was watching me for my reaction.

Then a commotion broke loose in the hall. My father flew out of his medical offices in a formal shirt and loose cravat, a darkness to his face I'd never seen before.

"Is it true, Dr. Sycamore?" called Mrs. Burnhamthorpe. "Harold Snow charged with murder?"

"I'm heading to Scotland Yard myself, to confirm." He shoved an arm into the sleeve of his frock coat. "You're to stay here, Charlotte. Bed rest."

"He's not the guilty one," I whispered.

"What's that?"

"It's not Mr. Snow. I thought it was, but it's not."

"Do you know something about him the police don't?"

"It's simply a feeling. I can't give you any proof, but he's a sentimental man who's misunderstood."

"You're to keep her here," he instructed Mrs. Burnhamthorpe.

"Yes, sir."

He was dismissing me again. "Father, please." I stepped out. "It's not Mr. Snow. Ask them to check into Justin Longfellow. Cameron Turnbull. Even Mr. Bloomberg. I don't trust any of them. And where did that Yardley fellow come from?"

"Mr. Yardley came personally recommended by *me*. As the son of a dear friend."

"Oh."

"I've known Yardley all his life."

"But . . . but then what about the other three?"

"I'll mention it, Charlotte," he said without an ounce of conviction, "but you're to get some rest."

He didn't believe me. He strode down the hall, heavy boots pounding the carpet runner.

Mr. Russett suddenly dashed out from around the other corner to speak to Mrs. Burnhamthorpe. His movement disturbed a Golden Butterfly on the wall that was swooping in on a crawling beetle. The butterfly flew away.

Mr. Russett and the headmistress spoke to each other as I turned frantically to Polly. "You've got to"—I was woozy—"get me out of here."

"Charlotte," she pleaded, "what happens when you need a lemon every five minutes, then four, then three?"

"It's not at that point yet."

Her eyes welled with moisture. "Benjamin sends word about Jillian."

I stumbled back. Warm saliva overflowed from my mouth. "How bad?"

Polly gulped back emotion. "Near death. A day or two at most."

⚜

Some of the answers came to me when I awoke halfway through the night.

"Mr. Bloomberg and Mr. Snow are both innocent," I mumbled aloud.

Moonlight streamed in through my windows as my eyes blinked open. I pulled myself from my restless dreams as I deciphered my thoughts. The weight I'd heard Mr. Bloomberg dragging into the medical offices was not a dead body, as I'd imagined. It was a sack filled with the plaster of Paris I'd seen with my own eyes. Used for medical splints and procedures. Harmless.

I rose from my pillow, but didn't feel well. My muscles were heavy. Someone had partially drawn the curtains. Silence roared in my ears as I swallowed gobs of spit. How long had I slept? I recalled someone coming in with warm milk and honey. Had my father given me a sleeping potion?

I rubbed my forehead, trying to remember. No . . . if he'd returned from Scotland Yard, I hadn't seen him. Mr. Russett had planted himself on a chair outside my door. Unfortunately, he had ignored Polly's pleas to replace him.

Knots at the base of my neck crackled as I turned my head to the clock. Thirty-one minutes past the hour of three. My experimental goggles sat there on my nightstand, too, along with the three potions I'd brought from the Engineering Hall, which I'd forgotten in my pocket and discovered only when preparing for bed.

"Mr. Bloomberg didn't do it," I repeated. Besides being innocent of dragging dead bodies about, the man was too much of a coward to attempt anything so daring.

So if neither Mr. Snow nor Mr. Bloomberg was guilty, who was?

I tried to reach my goggles but clumsily hit the clock instead. It pinged and fell with a thud to the carpet. Trying again, I grabbed hold, pulled the goggles to my chest, and with a deep breath, strapped them to my head.

Were their wondrous powers real? Or had I imagined them, the first time I'd donned them in the Engineering Hall?

I glanced down at my hands, streaked by moonlight. *Oh!* My arteries pounded like deep, red rivers. My veins swooshed in the opposite direction with blue blood headed to my heart and lungs. The goggles were real!

Goodness!

I could see the prints on my fingers, the skin wrinkled at my knuckles, the fingernails growing in size as I stared. Gathering what little strength I had remaining, I tugged off the bedcovers and examined the bite marks on my foot. Great deep gashes. Blockages of blood flow, a bubbling of germs deep within the wounds. It all pounded with life, almost unbearable to watch.

I yanked off the eyewear, swung my legs over the edge of the mattress, and took a step forward. My vision spun and I toppled to the carpet.

Flat on my stomach with my face embedded in the knotted silks of Persia, I knew I didn't have much time. If they didn't arrest me for attempted murder of the guards, they would hang me for high treason. Even if I escaped that, rabies would kill me.

Jillian was near death, Peter not far behind. The wrong man imprisoned, the guilty one free.

I watched, fascinated, as a Golden Butterfly swooped down beside my face. It must've entered my room in the chaos of last night. Its mechanical beauty mesmerized me. Fluttering wings, painted in real gold, glinted in the moon's rays. I focused on the blur and watched its pincers grab hold of a spider that had been creeping toward my face.

"Ugh," I mumbled in disgust at the spider.

It took a moment for my heartbeat to subside.

"What is my problem?" I asked the silent butterfly. "Do you know how to fix it?"

It merely fluttered its wings and flew away.

Mr. Snow, the man who gave the butterfly life, was not the one responsible for my rabies. Not Mr. Snow. Not Mr. Bloomberg.

As for Justin Longfellow . . . he was openly angry at having lost the head engineering position to Mr. Snow. He wasn't even sly enough to conceal his fury from me and my friends. In the shop when we'd asked about Charles Darwin's incredible cane, Longfellow had exploded because he'd thought his rivals, Snow and Turnbull, were trying to steal his scientific secrets. He was angry as a scientist, not as a killer.

So it wasn't Longfellow, either. I simply knew it.

That left Cameron Turnbull.

The friendly man who'd always been kind to me. I moaned.

I had no proof, only the overwhelming sense that the man who had done this to me and my friends was the same man who was so eager to give away a healthy puppy. It was his own cruel joke. Why? To prove that his mind was even more brilliant than Mr. Snow's?

When Mr. Snow had held the church service for Violet and left the Engineering Hall for the afternoon, he hadn't even confided his whereabouts to Mr. Turnbull. That's how little regard he had for him. They might be forced to work alongside each other, but Mr. Snow kept his personal life to himself.

Good Lord, they must despise each other.

Turnbull had tried to cover up his hatred, even defending Snow to me, telling me the man was not unapproachable and to give him more time. But if Turnbull wanted revenge, why not order the dogs to attack Snow, then? Or . . . was he simply trying to frame Mr. Snow, so that when he was hanged, Turnbull would be awarded the head engineering position?

Could my deductions be correct? Or was I jumping to ridiculous conclusions?

My mind was swimming. I felt weaker, but I recalled something else Turnbull had said last night. He'd mentioned his brother Aiden . . . that they'd surpassed their father's expectations in experimenting with batteries.

Why would someone with a brilliant mind like Aiden's be satisfied working the blast furnaces? It was a laborer's occupation, not for someone with scientific skills . . . unless . . . unless he was using it as cover to hide what they were truly up to in the Engineering Hall.

I *wasn't* jumping to conclusions. Aiden's skills were a concrete truth. Turnbull had told me so himself.

I had to . . . had to tell someone.

"Help," I called weakly from the floor. "Mr. Russ . . ."

I crawled to the nightstand in order to pull myself higher. As I reached partway up the wooden leg, I spotted the potions lined up in a pretty row on the top. What good were they to me now? I might never finish perfecting my special goggles.

My gaze fell on the middle bottle, the antidote for poisonous darts made by African tribesmen. They dipped the dart tips in liquids extracted from . . . from venomous frogs. And when those tips punctured the skin of their enemies, those men would die. Unless the victims . . . received the antidote.

Why hadn't I thought of it earlier?

If this antidote counteracted the venom of frogs, could it counteract the venom of mechanical dogs? Artificial rabies?

Perhaps Cameron Turnbull had also stumbled upon the poisonous darts in the Engineering Hall, and they had inspired him to create his monsters.

There was only one way to find out. With shaky fingers and dripping sweat, I reached for the slender bottle.

CHAPTER TWENTY-SEVEN

SOMEONE nudged me. My left cheek was flattened and numb, and my right shoulder socket felt ready to explode.

"Rise, Charlotte. Get up off the rug. *Please.*"

I heard Polly's voice as though my head was underwater and she was murmuring from the surface above. Another yank, this time on my right arm, made me realize I was sleeping with it over my head. The hard surface beneath me had bruised my hip. I lifted my head off a cushion of woven threads.

"How long is it you've been down there?" Polly gave me another tug. "Charlotte, it makes no sense goin' on like this. You must tell your father about the rabies and how weak you are."

"No, please. They'll lock me up."

The hem of her skirts and petticoats brushed my shoulder. She peered at me strangely, like a doctor studying a sore. "You seem awfully clear for someone who's collapsed. Talkin' in straight sentences."

I turned over and slowly sat up. I smacked my dry lips together. "I'm not quite sure what happened."

"You must've fallen. Oh, Charlotte, I do apologize. When you didn't respond to my knock for breakfast, we all thought you were sleepin'. Your father insisted we leave you alone to rest. You slept through lunch, too. Heavens above! You must've been lyin' here this whole time!"

She stood up and pulled the drapes open. Light gushed over me. I squinted and rubbed my head. I tried to recall the course of events that had gotten me here.

"This is too much for you to handle alone," Polly insisted. "Dear Lord, he's a physician. There's got to be somethin' he can do."

"What did you bring on the tray? It smells good."

"You have an appetite?"

She helped me to the chair, then watched me eat the entire bowl of rabbit stew in less than two minutes.

"Blimey! That's the most you've eaten in three days."

Feeling stronger, I set down my spoon. I glimpsed the carpet. A vial of liquid had rolled beside the bed. My eyes widened. I leaped for the antidote to poisonous darts and held up the glass vial, three-quarters filled with liquid.

"Oh, my, I think it worked!"

I straightened my elbows. Fine.

I twisted my neck and shoulders. Good.

I rubbed my temples. No headache.

I bounced on my feet as she shot out in a whisper, "Careful!"

I walked to my desk. No weakness in my legs.

I dashed to the entry of my private bath, touched the wall as though I was playing tag, then raced back, grabbed Polly by the hands, twirled her about the room, and with a bubble of laughter flung her onto the far chair.

"What's gotten into you? Did you"—she stopped and looked at the plate of untouched lemon slices—"did you consume more lemons?"

"No."

"Then how . . ." She looked at my smiling face.

"I drank this potion before I passed out."

"It accomplished all this?"

"Yes, yes. It's something I took from the Engineering Hall. An antidote they use in Africa against venomous frogs."

"Good God," she said with horror, *they have venomous frogs in Africa?*"

My mind raced. "Yes, and thank God they do or we wouldn't have this. In everything I've read about rabies, there was never any mention of using lemons or antidotes to venom to help with the disease. Therefore I couldn't have contracted real rabies ... I must've been poisoned by something that imitates its symptoms. I must get this antidote to Jillian and Peter." I rushed to look at the fallen clock beneath my nightstand. "Nineteen minutes past five! In the afternoon? All that time gone!"

"You needed the sleep. How long'll the effects last?" asked Polly.

"I haven't a clue. But I feel even better than I did eating lemons."

Polly whooped with delight, then cupped her hands over her mouth. "Mrs. B's out there."

"Maybe I'm cured," I whispered.

"Ah," she said in wonder.

"Or maybe," I mused, "maybe the artificial rabies simply faded on its own. Perhaps I would have gotten better with or without this potion."

"The only way you'll know for sure is if Peter and Jillian get better, too."

"I was thinking the same."

She rubbed her hands against her apron in a nervous gesture. "You can't go runnin' off just when you're startin' to feel better. What if it's not the potion? What if it only works for an hour? What if the next time you fall flat on your face it'll be in the center of London somewhere, under the hooves of a horse?"

"I have no more to lose than what's already at risk."

"But your life."

"Can anyone guarantee I'll live longer, sitting here in my bedchamber?"

Polly gave a sharp sigh.

I looked at my sore foot. The bite marks were still there, but the punctures had closed over. When I lifted my nightgown, the red streaks along my veins had faded to pink.

Oh, hallelujah!

I raced to my wardrobe and withdrew stockings, an everyday skirt, and a loose corset, blouse, and jacket.

"Mr. Snow has obtained legal counsel," Polly informed me. "They're still keepin' him in the jailhouse, though."

"It's not Mr. Snow. It's Cameron Turnbull."

"Him?" Polly puckered her face in protest. "But how can . . . he's so terribly nice."

"Terrible, yes. Not so nice." I shuddered at the gruesomeness of his crimes.

"You've got proof?"

"Not yet. But I must tell my father. Do you have an inkling where he is?"

"I'll check on the sly. And I'll see if I can't make some excuse to Mrs. B that she's needed elsewhere. We need to pry her from the door if you mean to slip out. I'll go with you."

Polly left and I quickly slid into day clothes. I tucked my special goggles into my desk, then changed my mind and slipped them into a satchel I would bring with me. I packed a few other things—the potion, fresh bandages, medical supplies for my friends, lemon slices, and an extra cloak.

There was a gentle knock on the door again. Polly's familiar rap. When I called, "Enter," she burst in.

"Your father's not here. He's gone to Scotland Yard again. To discuss more evidence of whatever they found at the Engineerin' Hall. Lo and behold, when Mr. Turnbull came to work this mornin' and was informed what happened, he told everyone that Mr. Snow's arrest has shaken him and he needs a few days of rest. So he left!"

"He's trying to escape. Do you know if his brother remains?"

Polly frowned. "Not specifically, but police have closed the doors of the Engineerin' Hall for investigation. The Queen—oh, Lord, the Queen—is *royally* upset! "

"They're all getting away."

"Where to?"

"I'm not certain. But I have to send word to my father." I flew to my desk and scribbled a few sentences on a piece of paper, then tossed the note and pencil into my satchel.

"Charlotte," said Polly, "Mrs. B is at the door and she jolly well won't budge. We'll have to bide our time and try to leave later. When she goes for tea, perhaps."

"I can't wait. This potion has to get to Jillian and Peter. I don't dare send another messenger."

She frowned at me. "By what other means . . ."

"I'll need you to do me a tall favor, Polly. I'll have to go alone. Quickly, please, change your clothing with mine."

"How will that help?"

"Throw me your cap." I opened my trunk and withdrew the black wig that looked similar in color to my natural hair. "Here, put this on." When I tossed the wig, she caught it.

I found the other wig, the blond one that came close to her hair color, and yanked it over my scalp. While I added Polly's apron, she braided my blond wig and pinned the tails over my crown so it looked like her hair.

"Finished?"

Polly nodded and pointed at the bed. "You want me to slide under the covers and pretend I'm you?"

"Precisely. I doubt my father will return this evening before my bedtime. He's preoccupied. If he does return, simply groan and roll over. Mumble that you'd like to rest. He'll leave you be." One more instruction. "If I'm not back by morning, you're to sneak out and be yourself inside the Palace. You mustn't get dismissed because of me."

Polly rubbed her cheek. "But I can't stay behind."

"And why not?"

"What if the effects come back? You'll need assistance."

"I don't believe I will. I feel fine."

"Then what if, God forbid, you're stopped in the streets? What if they bring you back here? Who's going to deliver the vial then to Peter and Jillian? Huh? Who?"

I blinked at her. I thought and blinked some more, but couldn't respond with a reasonable reply. "But how can we both get out of this room?"

"As soon as you leave your chambers—pretendin' to be me—I bet Mrs. B has Mr. Russett take over so she can go for dinner. She likes to take it at six. Then I'll slip out—as myself—and he won't even think it's unusual to see me. If he questions me, I'll say I forgot to give you somethin'. Then I'll leave. He'll assume you're still inside the room."

I nodded; that could work. "Brilliant."

"I'll say he's not to disturb you till the morning, 'cause you're slee-pin'. Then I'll put the disguise back on and meet you outside the gates."

Disguises were important so no one could possibly recognize us and report us to the Palace. My father would be furious at my improper behavior, sneaking out and walking the streets at night wherever I pleased. Polly would be dismissed for aiding me, and she would never get a letter of reference for another decent position of employment.

"We've got to be back by six in the morning, when my father rises," I said.

Agreed, we hugged briefly and walked to the outer door. I picked up the empty food tray and hid my small satchel underneath the silver domed cover. I yanked my cap into position. I was depending on Mrs. B's poor eyesight and refusal to wear spectacles to help me escape undetected.

Polly called, "I'm ready to come out, Mrs. Burnhamthorpe, if you could please open the door. My hands are full."

"Yes, yes. Here I am."

We heard the squeak of a moving chair.

"Miss Sycamore is feeling better," Polly added loudly. "She's fallen into a deep sleep and has asked not to be disturbed unless she calls."

"Fine, then, I can take my dinner. I'll get Russett to sit here."

"Well done, ma'am."

We watched the knob as it turned.

Polly slid behind the door to hide, and mouthed silently to me, *Good luck.*

"Meet on Birdcage Walk. Twenty minutes," I whispered, holding the tray steady.

She nodded.

The door opened. Before I revealed myself from the shadows, in disguise, I thrust the tray at Mrs. Burnhamthorpe unexpectedly so her natural instinct was to look down at it, rather than at me. Then I made a sharp right turn and carried it down the hall toward the kitchens. She could see me only from the back.

I was perspiring as though someone had lit my blouse on fire. I blew a few loose strands of hair from my eyes, took the servants' stairs, and left the tray outside the kitchen doors.

Escaping through the servants' entry at the Palace, I made my way toward the Royal Mews, where the staff was sweeping up.

Benjamin, with broom in hand, spotted me. He spun in surprise, and when I signaled for him to follow me out through the gates along with the rest of the evening staff, he nodded and disappeared behind the stalls so we wouldn't be spotted together.

He met me ten minutes later on Birdcage Walk. We turned and searched the darkness for a young maid to appear.

⁂

The River Thames rippled underneath us as Benjamin, Polly, and I raced over the stone bridge toward Waterloo Station, all of us thrilled at how fast I could walk.

"I can hardly believe it," Benjamin said with a wide grin, towering over us in his dark work clothes. "I can hardly believe you found an antidote."

"Let's hope it works for the others."

"Don't walk so bleedin' fast." Polly raced along in her dark cloak and wig. "We're bringin' attention to ourselves."

It was difficult to slow down when we were so excited, but we managed. When we reached the transportation depot, we hired a hansom cab and ordered the driver to the Tower of London. I had plenty of coins in my pocket. The horse clomped among other horses and their riders, behind double-deck buses crowded with middle-class men returning from work, past three bicycles and one bobby on horseback patrol. The three of us turned our faces away when we passed the officer.

One more turn, and we were safely at the grassy slopes of the Tower. By the time we hopped out, Benjamin had been caught up on what had happened to me in the last twenty-four hours.

I removed the folded notepaper from my satchel, tore off the part addressed to my father, and handed it to the driver with a generous payment. "Could you please deliver this to Scotland Yard? To Dr. James Sycamore. If he's not there, please give it to Sergeant Clark."

"Yes, miss." He pocketed the coins, flicked his reins and tore off through traffic. I crossed my fingers that he would be true to his word.

"What was that note?" Benjamin led me through the pedestrians along the outer walkway of the Tower. It was nice to know he was here, by my side. But I had no time now to decipher my feelings for him compared to Peter.

"It says not to let Cameron Turnbull escape. To check the employment records of his brother Aiden. They will likely find he was working as an engineer before he came to work for the Queen. That his position working the furnaces doesn't make sense."

"Did you sign your name?"

"I thought it might hold more weight if I left it anonymous." Unfortunately, I wasn't certain my father—or the police—were ready to take my word.

A horse's hooves pounded the ground beside us as one of the Tower guards made his rounds of the outer perimeter. Every noise startled me; I felt as though everyone in the city was looking for us. When we made it past the Tower and entered the narrow, crooked streets to the east, I stopped to don my black hooded cloak. Polly was already wearing hers, and I still had one extra in my satchel.

We arrived at The Bull and Tale in the warehouse district within a quarter hour.

We were about to step into the lane behind the tavern, toward the goat barn, when a bobby crossed our path. He purposely blocked our way.

My heart clamped beneath my ribs. Benjamin's shocked intake of breath was audible.

The bobby, as tall as Benjamin but twice as meaty, glanced at my cloak. "Evenin', all. Now where might you young people be headed?"

He seemed to be staring down at Benjamin's ankle.

"Just a walk, sir." Benjamin remained calm. "To the livery stables. There's a fine horse there I'd like to see."

The bobby's white helmet flashed in the setting sun when he turned to Polly. "How's your shoulder, miss?"

Polly mumbled. "My shoulder?"

She didn't understand immediately, but I did. He was looking for Jillian and Peter. Polly's wig was black, close enough to Jillian's dark auburn color when viewed in the shadows as we were.

Polly shrugged, turning out both hands as she did so. "Both shoulders fine, sir."

Being perplexed at the question added to her appearance of innocence. Wouldn't any innocent girl wonder why an officer was asking her about her shoulder?

"And yours?" he said to me.

Although my hair was currently blond, unlike Jillian's, he was being thorough.

I pulled the string at my throat. My cloak opened to reveal both shoulders draped in my linen blouse. The fabric was so thin, it couldn't possibly be concealing bandages. I pretended I didn't know which shoulder he was referring to, and turned the right one toward him, knowing that Jillian's left was the one injured.

"Fine, thank you." He moved through the crowd.

We kept our heads down, and I pulled up my cloak. Benjamin guided us to the goat barn. With a quick glance about, he knocked, then entered without waiting for an answer.

CHAPTER TWENTY-EIGHT

I braced myself for the worst. Jillian was sprawled on the straw, eyes closed, mouth open. Were we too late? The left sleeve of her blouse was torn off, revealing brown, bloody bandages in desperate need of a change. Peter hadn't been able to do it because he was lying in the other corner, damp with sweat, also with his eyes closed. I hadn't realized he was so weak. It made my heart turn.

A mouse skittered past my feet, dragging a scrap of bread. Polly gave a little gasp.

The shack smelled of stale air and rotting food. Benjamin rushed to open the little window, and a fresh breeze whistled in as I raced to Jillian.

She *was* breathing, though they were shallow breaths. She was getting little oxygen, for her lips were blue, but there was hope.

Polly and I lowered our hoods and settled down on the straw beside her.

I patted her soft cheek. "Jillie? Can you hear me? It's Charlotte." She didn't respond. I unbuckled my satchel, took out a glass jar filled with fresh water, and brought it to her lips. She didn't move. I dribbled a little into her mouth, and she swallowed.

"That's it," said Polly. "Drink."

Straw crunched behind me. Benjamin was checking on Peter.
"Peter, good news. Wake up. Charlotte has a cure."

I took the precious elixir, uncapped it, and dropped some onto
Jillian's lips. She smacked them together. I did it a second time, then
a third. Each time she responded by swallowing. But I didn't see any
improvement in her color.

"Jillian," I said, "breathe deeper."

No response. I scooted to Peter's side. He opened his eyes, but
there was no recognition in them, as if he wasn't seeing me. Benjamin,
beside me on his knees, watched as I gave Peter fresh water, the antidote, fresh water, more drops.

To my dismay, he had a violent reaction to the antidote on the
fourth round. His head jerked off the straw. He sputtered and gagged,
then rolled over and coughed.

"Bloody rubbish," he wheezed, "what the hell was that?"

We were stunned by his reaction. Then Benjamin softly laughed.
Polly and I giggled.

"What in God's name—are you trying to kill me?" Peter swiped at
his mouth.

I didn't know if it was the relief of seeing our friend come to life,
or the way his reaction was so very much the Peter we knew, but his
words made us laugh more.

I let Benjamin and Polly tend to him while I slid back to Jillian.
Her eyes were still closed, lips blue. I gave her more water, more antidote. I was afraid to administer too much; she might react as violently
as her brother had, which might arrest her breathing.

"She's not responding," I said.

"Give her more time," Benjamin replied. He helped Peter lean
back against the wall. "Don't move too fast. Charlotte just gave you an
antidote for the rabies."

Peter turned his sweaty head toward me. His dark hair was glued
to his temples. He was present again, behind his eyes, aware of me.
"Where'd you get it?"

"Engineering Hall. It's used against frog venom. I was lucky to
find it."

"It's not luck that saved us . . . it's your brains."

My pleasure in seeing Peter, in hearing the charm in his voice, and in watching the color return to his dashing face was muted by the fact that my dearest friend was still unconscious. What if it never worked for Jillian?

She hadn't combed her hair in days. The glossy auburn sheen had dulled, and it was tangled about her shoulders. Dirt was embedded in the lines of her forehead and beneath her fingernails. Yet there was nothing I would love more than to spend the rest of the afternoon with her, just like this, if only she would awaken and talk to me.

"How long did it take?" Peter started to rise from his spot. "Before you felt better?"

"It leveled me for fifteen hours."

Peter whistled softly in response, then appeared next to me, wobbly on his feet. It was an incredible joy to see him up.

"I'm glad you wore disguises," he said to us, staring at my wig.

"How is your ankle?" I asked.

He lifted his trouser leg to reveal loose bandages caked with dried blood. "Feels a lot better than it did. But it doesn't look terribly healthy beneath the bandages."

"I brought more supplies. I'll rewrap yours first, then we'll do Jillian's."

Polly removed her cloak, preparing to help.

Peter went to the wooden washstand in the corner. He'd found a basin somewhere, and poured water from a pitcher. He soaped his face and head and toweled off. He changed into a clean shirt as I turned away, heat rising to my face at having witnessed a boy—a nicely muscled one—bare from the waist up. He was deeply tanned, I imagined from his tour with the Royal Navy in the Caribbean.

I gave Jillian another dose of potion, with no response. "I don't think I better give her more." I peered up at Polly's freckled face. "She's already had twice as much as I took. It may cause an overdose."

Peter sat beside us. He leaned back and I unwrapped his ankle. The bite marks had healed over, and the red streaks similar to mine were already fading. It took some time to cleanse the area and gently wrap fresh gauze to support his ankle. It took even longer for Jillian's injury. Benjamin and Polly assisted as I soaked away her crusty bandages with the saline water I'd left behind earlier. We unwound the cloth and winced at the sight of her gaping wounds. I was now working in semidarkness, by the light of the moon coming in through the small window. It was unsafe to light a candle, for we'd be seen from the alley.

"Sorry, I don't have the stomach for this." Polly turned away.

Benjamin and Peter watched as I rinsed Jillian's injuries. The muscles at the top of her shoulder had been chewed off, but judging by her movements, the bones, thank heaven, seemed untouched. I rinsed the area and applied fresh bandages.

"Why doesn't she flinch when I handle her shoulder?" I whispered. "It must be painful."

"I wonder," Peter said glumly.

I barreled on. "Harold Snow's been arrested as the creator of the dogs."

Peter pulled back in surprise. "The Royal Gadget Engineer?"

Benjamin offered a sip from his canteen. "He's not the one behind the dogs, though."

"What makes you think not?" said Peter.

"Some things we've discovered," I said. "You remember when we visited Justin Longfellow? Apparently he was in competition for Mr. Snow's position when the new Engineering Hall opened. He and Mr. Turnbull."

"Turnbull? Isn't he a bit young to head the engineers?"

"Quite. But very aggressive for his station. I believe he's the one behind all this."

Polly joined the conversation. "Why would he create somethin' so evil?"

"I have no proof of anything, no motive." I finished with Jillian, sank back onto the straw, and disclosed the details of Turnbull's behavior and what he'd said about his brother Aiden's scientific skills. I added that Turnbull had taken a leave of absence.

"What did your father say when you told him all this?" asked Peter.

"Generally, he doesn't believe me."

Benjamin ran his fingers over the crisscrossed leather straps he wore across his shirt. I had noticed on the night we took the Queen's medical wagon that he used the straps to anchor daggers and weapons. "Is there anything we might do," said Benjamin, "to investigate Turnbull or his brother?"

"Yes. We could find out where he lives," said Peter. "Who his friends are."

"Why do you think there's always been a robbery whenever the mechanical dogs appear?" I asked.

"It's as if the dogs are used as decoys while the true crime occurs," said Peter.

"Maybe you're readin' too much into it," said Polly. "Some people are plain greedy. There's a lotta crime about, and if thieves see a fallen man, they simply ransack his pockets. Happens every day, I should imagine."

I pondered that as I opened my satchel and offered apples to the group.

Polly shook her head and declined, as did Benjamin.

"When was the last time you ate something, Peter?" I asked.

"I can't eat while my sister's down."

"You have to eat, for that very reason. So you'll have the strength to help her when she awakens."

He hesitated, then reached for an apple.

I continued along my train of thought. "It looks to me as if Turnbull's after revenge against Mr. Snow. He lost the head engineering position, and he's trying to prove a point."

"Who made the final decision on who received the appointment?" Peter asked between bites. Goodness, he was recovering quickly.

Polly wrapped her hands round her knees and thought about it.

"Likely the Queen," I guessed.

"Precisely," said Peter. His gaze snapped to mine and a heated look passed between the two of us, as a new realization dawned.

"What is it?" asked Polly, looking from one to the other. "What're you thinkin'?"

"That perhaps," I said uneasily, "Cameron Turnbull is out for revenge against the Queen."

Polly stared in horror. "He wouldn't dare."

My throat tightened in growing alarm. "He's mentioned it on a few occasions when he's been with me, but I didn't understand. How bitter he is about her. It's not so much the words; it's his expression and tone of voice. I was distracted last night in the Engineering Hall because Mr. Yardley walked by, but . . ."

"Charlotte," said Benjamin. "Slow down. Tell us what he said."

"He said, 'The Queen tells me every time she sees me what a great assistant I make.' I thought he was proud of the position, but he sneers at it. I assumed he was restraining himself from bragging, but it was *disgust* he was holding back. He can't stomach Queen Victoria."

We were all flabbergasted by the very idea.

"What sort of revenge do you think he—he wants against our Queen?" Polly plucked at her skirts.

I rubbed my forehead. "He's created deadly weapons that have already murdered people. He knew Jillian and Peter were badly injured, yet did nothing to help. He stood by as Mr. Snow was arrested. He covers for his brother Aiden, and who knows how many more monster dogs they've created. The revenge Turnbull wants can only be the worst kind."

"Oh, Lord," Polly gasped. "Is he aimin' to kill her?"

"It sounds far-fetched," said Benjamin. "But it holds logic. If Turnbull does away with the Queen, the Prince is next in line to the throne. I've seen him interact with Turnbull. They get on well. There's a good chance the Prince would select Turnbull as Snow's successor."

Peter exhaled. "Then Turnbull would get his revenge against Mr. Snow and the Queen in one fell swoop."

"He could bring in his brother Aiden," I added. "They'd rule the entire division."

Peter continued. "The country depends on its royal engineers, more and more, and will into the future. Who knows how far they'd go in their quest for vengeance and power." He shook his head, then slowly finished his apple.

While everyone thought about that, I noticed Peter's physical transformation. It was remarkable. His energy had returned and there was strength in his movements.

I looked at his sister: still sleeping, lips and nail beds tinged blue. Terror gripped me again. *Why does she not move?*

"So you think he's made an army of mechanical dogs?" Benjamin asked. "And he and his brother intend to sic the dogs on the Queen?"

"Go on. That seems ridiculous," said Polly. "A few dogs can't slip past the guards to get to the Queen."

Peter rubbed his jaw. "Then Turnbull needs to get to her when she's alone."

"God's sake! When is Her Majesty ever alone?" asked Polly.

Benjamin and I glanced at each other, because we both knew the answer.

"The Albert Memorial," I said with increasing dread. "She often visits. My father once told me that when Prince Albert was alive, he used to be her advisor. Even now that he's passed, if she's trying to assess a problem, or when loneliness strikes her, she goes there to talk to his spirit. She climbs out of her coach and sits on the steps. Alone. Well, with very few guards."

"How could Turnbull possibly know when she's about to visit?" asked Peter.

"It's almost every Sunday night," said Benjamin. "Everyone at the Mews knows. It's an open secret."

"And," I added, "if Turnbull is out to harm the Queen, then he's been watching her movements very carefully, at least for many months. He would certainly be aware of her visits."

"Today is Friday," Benjamin calculated, "and she'll be there Sunday. We only have two days to stop it."

"But she also goes when something is bothering her." I continued with a feeling of looming danger. "She's upset now. Didn't you tell me that, Polly? How distressed Her Majesty is at Snow's arrest?"

Polly nodded,

"Which means she may go tonight," I said with a gulp. "At midnight."

"There's something else quite troublin'," Polly exclaimed. "I heard that when Turnbull learned of Mr. Snow's arrest, he kept askin' about the Queen, 'specially how distressed she was about it all."

"So Turnbull could very easily predict her visit to the Memorial tonight, too," said Peter.

We were speechless. How could we possibly halt this?

"Tonight," Jillian said softly behind us.

Astounded that she had spoken, I turned to look at her. "Jillie?"

We crowded about. She was blinking and struggling to focus on our faces.

"It's good to see you talking." Peter, ever so gently, gave her a bit of water but it dribbled from her mouth. Polly dabbed her chin with a handkerchief.

Jillian took a deep breath. Her voice was ever so weak. "What are you all doing?"

"You're not well," I said. "Can you move? Walk?"

"But there's police roaming outside," Polly whispered. "One of them stopped us on the way here."

Peter cursed. Jillie moaned. Benjamin sliced an apple for her. She sat up to take a bite and still seemed to be in no pain, which troubled me a great deal.

She ran her hand along her injured arm. "Still numb." Her lips were as blue as ever, but at least she was talking.

Peter looked at me. I saw the concern in his dark eyes, but we couldn't spend too much time tending to her here. We had to find another safe place to hide.

"What do we do?" asked Polly.

"Go to the police," Peter answered.

"They'll arrest us," Benjamin declared. "All five of us. The four of us for attempted murder of those two guards, and Polly for aiding."

I kneeled at Jillian's side, gently trying to nudge her up.

"What are you . . . talking about?" she said.

"The Queen," I answered, and explained about Turnbull and our theory of revenge.

"Oh, no," she mumbled.

"I'll write a note," said Peter. "Similar to the one Charlotte wrote to her father at Scotland Yard, except I'm going to sign my name. I'll tell them not to let the Queen go to the Albert Memorial. I'll tell them I'll be there. If nothing else, the police will arrive to arrest *me* and contain my rabies."

Benjamin hopped to his feet, looming over us. "The Queen doesn't always go precisely at midnight. Sometimes she arrives earlier and stays longer. It must be close to ten o'clock now. We might already be too late to stop her."

"We're taking a risk," I said. "If the dogs do not attack tonight, then her men—or Scotland Yard—will surely apprehend us if we show up. Turnbull will still get away."

"It's a chance we take together," said Peter, looking at us.

Our eyes blazed in agreement, even Polly's.

"If we're headed in that direction," Benjamin said with concentration, "there are shacks and stalls in Kensington Gardens. For the flower sellers. No one will be there this time of night. If we can find one that's unused, we could let Jillian rest inside. Only until we find something more permanent tomorrow."

"Agreed," said Peter.

Jillian nodded, too.

I rummaged through my bag and found my pencil and another bit of paper. Peter sat beneath the window and read aloud as he quickly wrote the words.

"Dear Dr. Sycamore, I require your help to clear my name, and to save the Queen from assassination. I believe there's a battle planned for tonight at the Albert Memorial. The same criminal—Cameron Turnbull—who has created the rabid dogs intends to use them to overthrow the Crown. I would appreciate your assistance, and that of the Queen's men and Scotland Yard. Sincerely, Peter Moreley."

I reached for Jillian's cloak and draped it over her. "Shouldn't we send a note to the Palace, too," I asked, "to warn the guards to keep the Queen away?"

The boys agreed and Peter wrote another hasty note. Polly reached for her cloak and I took out the extra one from my satchel for Benjamin.

"I'll slip outside and pay someone to run the message," said Benjamin. "I have coins."

"Be careful to watch for the police. And we need to retrieve our swords from the barn," I said to him. Then I looked from Jillian to Peter. "Remember? When we were attacked that first night, I hid them in the floorboards of the barn. We'll need them to fight the dogs."

"*We?* I plan on going to the Albert Memorial to fight this man and his creatures," Peter said to me. "But I don't expect you to fight, Charlotte."

"I'm going, too," Benjamin vowed.

"This is my battle as much or more than yours," I told them. "And I'm good with a sword."

They shuffled their feet. They couldn't deny it.

"Someone needs to stay with Jillian until we return with the swords," I said.

"I can do that." Polly slid beside her on the straw. Jillian looked barely alive. I wondered how far she could walk. It was quite a distance to Kensington Gardens and the Memorial.

I turned to Benjamin and Peter. "Meet me here in a few minutes. I need to find my friend Matilda and inform her we're leaving. It's the least I can do, to give her some warning if the police should begin knocking on doors."

We looked out, saw no bobbies, then the boys left to find a messenger to deliver the notes, and I went to the tin shack where Matilda lived. When I tapped lightly on the door with my fingertips, it took a moment for anyone to reply.

"We seek no visitors," Matilda warned through the door. "Leave us be, or my employer shall be forced to deal with you."

"Sorry to disturb you," I whispered. "It's me, Charlotte."

"We are tryin' to sleep."

"Please, only a moment."

There was a rustling behind the door, then it creaked open. Her curly dark hair framed her face. Moonlight streamed over her sturdy features and her flannel nightgown. There was an open crate behind her on the dirt floor filled with bandages, ointments, cleansing tonics, and cotton batting. So she'd gotten some of the medical supplies from the Queen's wagon! I was delighted. She looked from my gaze to the crate, as if sensing some connection.

"I wanted to let you know we're leaving now," I said softly. "For good. Thank you for all you've done."

Matilda glanced from the medicines to me. "You brought these supplies 'ere, didn't you?"

"The less you know, the better."

"Followin' rules and followin' orders never got me anyplace." Her voice was quiet. "I waited patiently in line with my husband, exactly as they asked. Nice and orderly. That's what I did, but he still died. You've given me more in a week than anyone's given me in a lifetime," she whispered. "Bless you, Charlotte. Fare well."

I nodded and hastened away, refusing to put her in any more jeopardy.

CHAPTER TWENTY-NINE

FIVE minutes later, we escaped to the streets. We took my satchel, crammed with the precious medical supplies I'd brought from the Palace, and left the other less useful items scattered behind. Polly and Peter braced Jillian on either side as she stumbled along. Benjamin and I walked ahead a few paces.

"We'll be quick about this," I said, peering round the narrow streets. "We'll reclaim our swords. Then off to find shelter for Jillian, and then the Albert Memorial."

When we turned the corner, I took the lead through the warehouse district. I heard the clatter of hooves and signaled everyone to hide in the shadows of a crumbling building. A bobby on patrol rode past. When he faded away, I motioned again and we dashed through the night.

It had to be close to eleven by now. We needed to hurry. I couldn't look back too often at Jillian or my sympathy might slow me. I knew that Peter or Benjamin would carry her if need be.

When I passed a stone factory that looked familiar, I paused.

Jillian sank onto a stoop to catch her breath and Polly sat beside her.

"Ah," said Peter, looking about. He likely recalled the place where our ordeal had begun.

"What is it?" Benjamin saw me glance down at the gutter, where I remembered the black oil seeping from the dogs. A gaslight lit up his tall, dark figure. The wind snatched at our long cloaks.

"This is where the dogs attacked us." I looked about, searching for the barn. "There it is." After all these days of fatigue and memory loss, I had finally remembered what I'd been trying so desperately to picture in my mind—the place where I'd hidden our swords. The five of us entered the barn. Jillian sat on a pile of straw with Polly.

When the boys and I ventured to the stalls, the awful memories flooded back to me. I must've frozen, for Benjamin rocked me by the shoulder. "You saved Peter and Jillian. Don't forget that. Be rid of the rest."

Benjamin was such a good friend. I took a deep breath and scoured the interior, half-expecting the fisherman's raincoat to be hanging on the hook, but of course it wasn't. It was in my wardrobe within the safety of the Palace walls. Where I'd be safe, too, were I there now.

I walked across the floorboards and thumped each one with the back of my boot heel.

Peter watched me. "Charlotte, we don't have much time. Can I help?"

A hollow thud rewarded my search. "Here." I dropped to my knees and pried up the loose board, the boys coming to my aid. We peered inside, three eager faces, and I groaned in relief at the treasure. My sword and Peter's, both there!

We removed our weapons, fencing masks and vests. "We only have two sets," said Peter. "You take mine, Benjamin." He held out his gear.

"Won't do me much good, since I prefer to fight with my daggers. Besides, you've still got an injured ankle. You take it."

"My ankle's almost one hundred percent. You, Charlotte?"

"My foot is fine."

"Let's split the equipment, then," Peter said to Benjamin. "Mask or vest?"

"Take them both."

"No," Peter insisted. "I'll take the mask. I can wrap these around my chest for protection." He held up a handful of burlap sacks. "Look how many they've got here. You take the vest."

"All right," said Benjamin quickly. "Let's bring a few of those sacks with us. I can slice one and slip it over my head to protect my face, like a mask, when we get there."

They agreed and we moved with haste. I slid on my vest but would leave my mask until we got to the Memorial. We didn't wish to bring attention to ourselves in the streets. I removed the antidote from my skirt pocket and sipped it for extra strength. "Here, take a drink," I said to Peter, who was standing very near my side. His proximity was comforting.

When he finished, he passed it to his sister. Polly helped Jillian drink, but her color was still pale. In fact she looked a bit green but I prayed it would pass. I went to her side and offered her the water canteen.

"Jillie? Take a sip." I tried to sound reassuring.

The others dashed to collect things we might need.

Peter found a fisherman's net hanging in the back of the barn. "This might trap a few dogs." He rolled it up and shoved it beneath his arm.

Polly found a rope. Benjamin took the extra burlap bags.

"How many dogs d'you think there'll be?" asked Polly with a shiver.

"Even one is too many," Peter said quietly. "It's best not to think about the numbers. You'll stay with Jillian, and we'll do the fighting."

Polly shuddered again.

"Everyone ready?" I looked at the faces. All nodded, and I was ever so grateful to have such a group of friends beside me. "Let's be on our way."

We left the stalls for the clear night air and the battle that might await us. As we drew up the hoods of our long cloaks, I suspected that from afar, the five of us could pass as men.

As we headed for the Tower of London, Jillian stumbled. Benjamin was closest and braced her as we walked.

"We'll need a coach," I said to the others. "To speed up the trip and allow Jillian to rest. I can pay; we simply need to find one."

We walked along the Thames in the general direction of the Memorial—toward Hyde Park and Kensington Gardens. Five minutes later, a rickety coach pulled by two shabby horses rolled past. We concealed ourselves in our cloaks.

"Cab!" Peter swung his arm in the air.

He gave the coachman directions and asked him to hurry. We climbed in, nearly sitting on top of each other, the benches were so narrow. The coach jostled on its way, the axles beneath us shifting and squeaking.

"An apple, Jillie?" I asked.

She shook her head.

"Hold on a little longer, all right?" Benjamin said to her. "We'll find a safe spot for you."

She nodded.

"If this fight . . . if this fight doesn't happen tonight . . ." I turned. Peter was pressed against me on the left. His body was warm and gentle beside mine. Polly was on my other side. Across from me, Benjamin met my eyes in the dim light. I could feel the unasked questions hovering in the air as they waited for the rest of my words. "If anything goes amiss tonight, I think it's vital you should all leave London."

"Leave?" Jillian mumbled. "How could we possibly?"

"Charlotte is absolutely right," said Benjamin, looking directly at Polly. "The Albert Memorial is halfway out of London. You'd best continue going to the end and disappear. You can't return to working in the Palace. They'll find you out."

"What about you?" Polly asked him.

"No one would suspect me in the Mews. I believe I'd . . . be all right."

"Peter?" Jillian looked at her brother.

"Charlotte's right . . . we must have a second plan if this one doesn't work." Peter's dark profile nodded in the shadows. "If any of this blows up in our faces, I'll lead you all out of London. Including you, Charlotte."

I was touched by Peter's bravery and his thoughts of my safety. Yet I had to make myself clear. "But if they catch me—and detain only me—I need the rest of you to promise you'll leave London without me. Including you, Benjamin."

He wouldn't promise. He simply stared at me from across the coach, his tall figure inches higher than Jillian beside him.

"Remember?" I prodded gently. "You shall always say yes?"

He sighed and finally nodded his agreement.

As did Polly, Jillian, and after a great pause, Peter.

But when the coach lurched and my leg bumped against Peter's, he whispered tenderly in my ear, making me flush at the intimacy. "When I get the others to safety, Charlotte, I'll return for you. I'll find you and take you with me. I promise. Wherever you may be, from whoever might be holding you. I'll take you back at gunpoint if necessary."

My throat quivered and swelled. I was incredibly moved by his simple declaration. He was telling me I wouldn't be alone; I would never be, because I had him.

No boy had ever made such a moving promise to me. I could hardly speak for the next little while. I had never realized the depth of Peter's comittment to me, or the depth of my feelings for him until this moment, when I might lose him.

I tried to bury the ache in my heart as the coach continued along the road. Suddenly the axle beneath my bench gave another loud groan.

"Hold tight," Peter warned us as we teetered.

When things settled again, I peered through the smeared glass window. We'd reached the grassy fields of Hyde Park, where everything was still and quiet. On the other side of the wide road, houses and buildings sat equally motionless. Candlelight shone through some windows, but for the most part, this affluent section of London had gone to bed. A clock hanging above a tavern read twenty minutes to the midnight hour.

My heart began to thump as we rolled past the wooded areas of Hyde Park and reached the grassy stretches and trees of Kensington Gardens. Peter whistled for the driver to pull in along a tree-lined lane. The coach shook as it turned.

"D'you think anyone received our notes?" asked Polly.

"I wonder," said Peter. "The messenger was traveling on foot. We're in a coach, so we're likely ahead of any others."

"Hopefully the authorities have read the notes," said Benjamin. "And hopefully they'll keep the Queen at home." He took a deep breath and peered out at the silhouetted gardens just as the axle gave one loud, shuddering snap. Suddenly the rear end of the coach crashed to the ground. We all bounced upward, smacked the roof, then fell back down again as the coach slid to a dead stop.

"Bloody hell!" Polly yelped.

Others groaned.

"You all right, Jillian?" I leaned over to check, since she'd fallen right over my lap. She sat up slowly and we looked about.

Outside, the driver was cursing up a storm. "Bleedin' bad luck! Damn awful equipment!"

"Collect your things," said Peter, swinging open the door and leaning forward to help Jillian climb from her seat.

"Everyone all right?" asked Benjamin.

We nodded and stepped out very close to the ground, in a grassy patch rimmed by trees. I clutched my satchel full of medicines. We hurried to hide the fisherman's net, rope, burlap sacks, masks, daggers, and swords in our cloaks.

The driver, a tiny man in a greasy cap, inspected the damage. The rear axle and wheels had sheared completely off the coach.

"That'll be two bob," he growled at us. "I gotcha far enough, didn't I?"

Peter paid him. "What're you going to do?"

He muttered, spit out a mouthful of chewing tobacco, and swiped his mouth. "Take the horses home, I suppose. I'll come back in the mornin' to fix the coach."

I couldn't stop wondering and worrying if the police or the guards or my father had received our notes. Had they warned the Queen?

I turned westward, to my left, but couldn't see the Albert Memorial. We were standing among the trails of Kensington Gardens, and the statue sat beyond the wooded area. When I squinted, I could make out the top of the magnificent spire silhouetted by the moon, perhaps two or three hundred yards ahead. To the other side in the far distance, I thought I saw the faint shape of cantering horses. Did they belong to the Palace? Several dozen guards were always sent to secure the area before the Queen's second troop of men and the Queen herself arrived. I imagined the guards cut through the private lanes of the park to keep their presence quiet, rather than taking the main road beside us.

The boys helped the driver unhitch his team and we watched him ride off into blackness. I glanced round, breathless, for a sign that dogs might be coming.

Nothing moved. Nothing of living flesh or clockwork.

"Maybe there are no mechanical dogs," said Peter.

I wasn't certain what I hoped for: dogs that would prove we were right, that we were innocent and Turnbull guilty, or no dogs so we wouldn't need to wage a war.

"Whether anyone's coming or not," said Benjamin, "let's get Jillian and Polly someplace safe."

"Anyone see a shack?" Peter put his arm underneath his sister's good shoulder. She was dragging her feet, exhausted. I went to her other side.

"Some shanties over there." Benjamin pointed east.

"Gently now," Polly said to Jillian. "Let's be followin'—"

But her words were cut short by the shimmer of something dark about her shoulders. She screamed and jumped away in alarm.

Something black fluttered by my neck. I screeched and slapped the air.

"Bloody hell!" Benjamin cursed. "Bats!"

"Damn creatures!" Peter hollered.

We twisted and whacked at the shadows.

Frantic, I tried to make sense of it. With a sickening jolt, I recalled the newspaper headlines my father had read to me when I was trapped in bed. "Bats can carry rabies, too! Good God! Did they make mechanical *bats*?"

"Black devils!" Polly shouted.

"Put the net over your heads!" Peter tossed the net, but it twisted.

With my heart pounding triple-time against my ribs, I scrambled to untangle the mesh. Then came another flutter and another. We watched in repulsed fascination as dozens and dozens and dozens, then hundreds, swooped down at us, an army of flying black soldiers with bulging red eyes, sent to kill.

CHAPTER THIRTY

"MOVE under the net!" I shouted to Jillian and Polly.

On her way down, Polly found a stone and hurled it through the air. She hit a bat. It made a squealing sound and plopped to the grass, oozing oil. Jillian tossed another stone but missed in her weakness.

I threw the netting over my two friends, and they continued pelting rocks from beneath it. Two more bats fell, squealing bloody murder as they went down. Peter slashed the air with his sword, keeping the bats at bay until he and I donned our fencing masks.

Benjamin pulled a burlap sack over his head, slashed so his eyes were visible. He ripped another burlap sack into strips with his daggers.

"Wrap these about your throats!" he hollered.

We caught them but had no time to secure them round our necks. The three of us ducked and sliced the darkness with our weapons, then slowly rose to full height again in bewilderment as the cloud of blackness swooped past us toward the Memorial.

"Why have they stopped attacking us?" Benjamin's hood fell to his cloaked shoulders.

"They *must* be mechanical." I nearly hyperventilated at what horror was about to descend on the guards, if indeed they were in place already. "A normal bat wouldn't differentiate between humans. It wouldn't bypass one victim in preference for another."

"They've been mechanically instructed," said Benjamin, peering through the trees. "Coded internally in some way, for the guards and their location."

"Perhaps by latitude and longitude," Peter added with a gulp.

If we stepped across the grass to the Albert Memorial, within that same latitude and longitude, we would also be targeted.

Polly helped Jillian to her feet, both still protected by their netting.

"I ain't seen nothin' like it." Polly's black wig flattened over her shoulders.

"Sickening." Jillian pulled her cloak tighter. She clutched stones in her hands, staring after the flock. A few stragglers flew behind. We swatted the air, but they weren't after us. They headed to the Memorial.

"How can anyone fight off this many?" I shuddered at the almost serene sound of hundreds of fluttering wings in the distance.

"Metal bloodsuckers!" Peter took out his sword and brandished it in the air. He swung and nicked one of the black things. It made a high-pitched wail and its eyes popped out like cherry pits. Black oil spurted everywhere, then the thing fell at his feet. Dead.

"When I was ill, my father read me the newspaper," I told them. "There was an article about bat attacks in the city. I was slow to think of it, but rabies affects all types of mammals, not only dogs. Foxes, bats, and even cats."

"Mechanicals bats with artificial rabies. What a horrifying plan." Benjamin's face was aghast in the moonlight. "Turnbull and his brother made enough of them to kill every last guard. Not to mention the Queen herself."

Peter's spine was rigid in the shadows. "No guard can whip out a pistol and accurately shoot at a bat."

"Or hit it with a billy club," agreed Benjamin. "One bite on the neck and the guard is a goner."

Polly let out a sob. "What'll happen to us all?"

I turned to the girls. "Go to the carriage. Close the doors."

Peter added, "Don't open them again till you know it's safe."

Jillian nodded, and she and Polly moved toward it.

"You should go inside, too," Peter said to me, then was distracted by new sounds.

Across the grass, hundreds of yards away, gunshots and screams echoed from the stone courtyard and stairs of the Memorial. In the darkness, two of the Queen's guards came running in our direction, clawing at their necks as a dozen parasites descended.

I shuddered at the gore. So the guards were here. The Queen was on her way, apparently unaware of any danger.

Wasn't anyone else coming? Where were the police? The other guards? For God's sake, her entire army?

I quickly bandaged my neck with burlap. The boys did the same. I looked frantically down the wooded trails as I helped Jillian and Polly into the coach, but saw no one.

Benjamin shouted at me, "Stay there!"

"Stay where it's safe, Charlotte!" Peter repeated, and both raced across the field.

They didn't wait for me. The darkness gobbled up their shapes.

I turned to Polly, now seated inside. We helped Jillian lie down.

"Don't leave until you know it's safe," I told them again. I tossed in the net.

Though my heart went out to Jillian, there was nothing I could do for her that Polly couldn't. But I was good with a sword.

I gripped my weapon with its rotating blade and ran to follow the boys. I hadn't gotten too far when I was stopped by the sound of oncoming troops. But why was the sound coming from the north? The Palace was to the east.

Thundering hooves shook the ground beneath my feet. I backed into the trees and waited for them to arrive, then thought perhaps I should warn them about the bats.

However, instead of the dark uniforms of the Queen's guard or the white helmets of the Metropolitan Police, these men—two dozen of them—were cloaked in black robes, and each held the strangest thing in his black-gloved hand.

Blue rays shone out from their clenched fists, some rays soaring through the trees, others zigzagging across the sky. The sources were some sort of crystalline rocks. I wondered what their purpose was, but my thoughts were distracted by two men who rode at the rear of the pack. Though their faces were not visible beneath their hoods, they stood out among the rest; instead of blue crystals, they gripped red stones. Crimson beams, twice as thick as the blue, shot out from between their gloved fingers.

They were the commanders.

And then the mechanical dogs came: two dozen vicious, snarling creatures scurrying alongside the horses. I gasped and stood terrified, wondering if they were going to lunge at me. But as the men and horses and rabid dogs raced across the fields, a flock of bats swooped over the group in the moonlight. Undaunted, the men on horseback raised their fists and the blue rays lit up the dull sky. The bats instantly retreated.

The crystals signaled the bats—and the dogs—to maintain their distance from the men.

Swallowing my fear, I raced behind them, believing they wouldn't attack me unless I approached the longitude and latitude of the Memorial.

Peter and Benjamin were there somewhere, though, unprotected.

I kept running. The spire came into view ahead, the bronze statue of Prince Albert glinting in the moonlight. Dozens of the Queen's guards were fighting and fending off bats. Guns and clubs didn't seem to be working, as they were slow and difficult to aim. Knives and swords worked to a degree. Two men managed to stab two dogs before the bats descended, while another took out a pistol and shot a leaping canine. To the left of that awful scene, a sleek coach had arrived, pulled by two Windsor Greys.

Oh, God, the Queen!

The coach was surrounded by mounted guards doing their utmost to fight the bats, but body after body plunged to the pavement. More dogs went down in gunfire.

Where were the two commanders and their men?

I whirled about, searching for them. They had gathered to my left, behind the woods. I dived to the grass and crawled on my belly to the safety of the trees. Sitting up with my back pressed into hard bark, I overheard snatches of conversation.

"What a glorious sight," said one of them, still cloaked. "And to think, the Queen does not see my genius as an engineer." I recognized the voice. Cameron Turnbull's.

He was sickening.

"Soon she'll see our brilliance up close," said the other one, clutching his red stone. He sounded like Aiden. "When we slash her throat."

I moaned and sagged against the tree.

"The Prince eats out of my hand," said Cameron Turnbull. "It's a pity his foolish old mother prefers Snow."

"I wonder how much she'll fancy him when he's hanging from the gallows, blamed for this treacherous night."

Savage laughter crackled through the air.

Swallowing my disgust, I peered past the tree trunk to the men on horseback. In the shafts of light I tried to see their faces, but the two commanders had their backs to me. Among the other assassins facing my direction, I was alarmed to recognize a few laborers from the blast furnaces. One was the red-haired Scotsman named Flame. Another two of the underlings, perhaps from India, wore turbans beneath their hooded cloaks. Why were they here?

The ground drummed beneath my boots again. Turning, I watched as more horses stormed in. Relief and joy tumbled to my throat at the splendid sight of the Queen's army—dozens and dozens of men—and police from Scotland Yard. They had received our note after all!

I froze beside the tree trunk, certain that the assailants behind me were also watching the Queen's men ride in. If I dared to move, they'd spot me and I'd receive a blade through my spine.

To my utter surprise, I recognized my father riding near the rear of the troops, medical bag hanging from his saddle. He was flanked by two men in police uniform. All three carried medical supplies. The men were here to help the wounded, my father to save the Queen.

But they wore no protection!

I no longer worried about being seen, and lunged into the lane, shrieking after them. "You carry no crystals! You need crystals to fight the bats!" My voice was drowned out by the fury of hooves behind me.

"Charge!" Cameron Turnbull commanded.

I heard the galloping rush of assassins as they stormed toward the Memorial and the Queen's men. I leaped from their path, tumbling to the ground.

But why charge when they were outnumbered?

Oh, I thought in dismay, jumping to my feet. Turnbull's numbers wouldn't matter if they could reach the Memorial. Their stones would keep them safe from the creatures there, but the bats and dogs would do their cruel work on the Queen's men, and the numbers would be whittled in Turnbull's favor.

"Stop! Father!" No one heard my cry.

Turnbull's troops turned left to attack some of the Queen's guards, while my father's turned right.

I ran behind my father's men and watched as they raced toward the Memorial to chase away the others who were poised to kill her Majesty.

My father jumped from his horse to have a look at the fallen guards near the Queen's coach. He yelled orders to his assistants. One of them opened a wooden box. I recognized it. It held the instruments and medicines of a battlefield surgeon.

Still running, I gazed at the sky over the pointed spire above Prince Albert's statue as a streak of black swelled higher, growing like a thundercloud, dotted with twitching red eyes. Blood was about to be spilled in great quantities. My father did not stand a chance.

The bat cloud hovered and then, in a sudden swoop, descended.

"No!" I shrieked. Sword raised, I raced across the field, my vision framed by the rails of my fencing mask. *"No!"* My cloak was well tied beneath my chin to secure my hood and mask my identity. As I neared my father, he and his assistant cursed at the oncoming storm of bats.

A policeman shouted, "You bloody devils! Get away! Away!" He pulled out a pistol and shot, but missed. A swarm of bats went for his throat. They lifted him from the ground with their bites. The man crumpled, likely to his death.

"Percy!" my father yelled.

Twenty paces away, one of the Queen's guards raced at an assailant on horseback, and in the skirmish the man dropped his blue crystal.

I dived for it, my black cloak billowing, and tossed it to my father, who caught it midair. He held it up and the bats recoiled. A crazed dog also turned away.

They all came after *me*.

I stabbed the dog first, holding my sword steady with all my strength, then, one by one, severed the heads of a dozen bats.

"Who are you?" my father shouted. "With the police or army?"

I said nothing and continued battling the black creatures. When I spotted another blue crystal on the grass, I jumped for it just as the bats dived for my throat. They clawed the strips of burlap at my neck, squealing in a frantic high pitch as some tried to rip through my fencing mask.

Clutching the crystal, I held it, trembling, to my face. In a blink, the bats swooped away.

I looked at the other medical assistant, but he'd already secured a blue crystal of his own. He continued to help the wounded.

Peter. Benjamin. Where were they?

Panting, I ran into the fray. Dozens of human bodies lay strewn on the grass. Some were ours, some theirs. Fallen blue crystals shimmered everywhere.

Finally, I spotted Benjamin in his makeshift mask. He was defending himself from an assassin on horseback trying to run him down. Not wanting to maim the mare, Benjamin hesitated to use his daggers. But thankfully he held a blue crystal.

Peter was sword fighting. While he was occupied with one man, another assailant appeared behind him, sword raised. Just as the unseen attacker was about to thrust his blade into Peter's back, I leaped in and smacked it to the ground, knocking his blue crystal from his hand. He turned in fury toward me, but bats rushed in and plunged at his exposed neck. He screamed and tried to run, but quickly dropped, stone-cold silent, to the ground.

I grimaced at the sight.

"The red stones!" hollered Peter. "The red stones are fleeing!" The brute he was still fighting lunged at him, but Peter was faster and struck his blade into the man's chest. The man doubled over and Peter raced up the stone steps with Benjamin and me at his heels. It was difficult to determine which men belonged to which side. As for the bats, we'd barely made a dent in their numbers.

I noticed with alarm that two frothing black dogs were circling us.

Peter watched carefully, and when one creature lunged, so did he. "That's for my sister!" The other mad dog leaped and he impaled it as well. "And that's for me!"

Those seemed to be the last of the mechanical dogs. We raced round the steps, only to come upon the two commanders with red stones.

One of them was sword fighting with my father.

I stood in awe at his skill.

I hadn't seen my father fight since I was a girl of seven, when he'd first showed me how to handle a blade. My training went on for five years, until one of my governesses announced it at a dinner party before his friends. My father had been shamed into admitting that he was showing his daughter what only a young man should be trained to do.

From that day on, he'd discouraged me from ever picking up a sword again.

Now I raised my sword alongside his, ready for battle.

Benjamin, with his daggers, leaped in to help my father.

Peter and I pursued the second commander, dueling along the steps until we were all in front of the Memorial, near the Queen's carriage. Not one of her guards remained. The coach doors were closed.

I prayed Her Majesty was safe inside.

As we kept our opponent occupied, the man my father and Benjamin were fighting sprang toward the coach. When the man turned the handle and opened the door, my father smacked the man's sword to the ground then whacked off his hood.

"Cameron Turnbull." My father's voice wavered.

With a distorted smile, Turnbull first tilted his dark head at my father, then looked inside the coach at the Queen. She sat there, cloaked in a black shawl, huddled in the corner.

I'd never seen Queen Victoria look so small. Or so human.

Peter, from behind, knocked the sword and the hood off of *our* opponent.

It was indeed Turnbull's brother Aiden. His brown hair was drenched in sweat.

"Leave me be!" Aiden shrieked as his weapon clanged on the pavement.

Another cloaked man raced in from the shadows, but Benjamin ran after him and gave chase round the statue.

While we were distracted, bats swarmed toward the Queen's carriage, ready to attack her. I dashed toward Cameron Turnbull and thumped my sword over his fist. Peter did the same to Aiden. Their red stones fell to the hard pavement and shattered.

"No!" shouted Cameron Turnbull. "My lovely creatures!"

I braced myself for the bats that were sure to attack, praying that the black monsters would be diverted from the Queen's throat to the Turnbulls'.

To my amazement, bats began to fall from the sky like heavy black hail. Some splattered. Some cracked. Eyeballs popped. Mechanical brains oozed.

All dead.

We spun round in disbelief. The red stones had controlled them completely.

"Turnbull." My father lowered his sword and stepped to within an inch of the man's face. "You will hang for this."

Cameron Turnbull, the man who'd so quietly befriended me two years ago, twisted his dark face into that of a cornered animal's. "You know nothing of my life. You, the Queen's surgeon," he scoffed in disgust, "think you know anything of survival and competition, and getting what's due?"

"I know what's due for you."

"Your Majesty." Confidently, Cameron Turnbull turned his gaze to the Queen and tried another tactic. "I was here in order to protect you from the bats. To save you from Snow. That is why I brought the red stones."

She sat up straighter, her spine as rigid as a post. All eyes turned to Benjamin, returning from his chase with a seized prisoner who wore a turban. The Queen's gaze fell upon the foreigner. "Did your allegiance to Cameron Turnbull cost much?"

"You shall never be Empress of my land," the man said with scorn.

"No!" Turnbull shouted at him. He turned and groveled to the Queen. "I know nothing of what he speaks."

"Your Majesty"—Aiden rushed in with a frantic plea of his own—"I had no inkling my brother was developing these creatures!"

"Liar!" The brothers turned on each other.

"You did this!" Aiden shouted. "You led me here with deception and false promises!"

"Your Majesty"—Cameron turned and pointed at his brother—"he released the other dogs and headed the robberies!"

"You foul-mouthed swine! You said we needed the money to fund the plan! You said we needed to test the strength of the artificial rabies! It was you! Not me!"

I listened to the screaming with pity and revulsion. So the mechanized dogs had been released in order for the robberies to occur, to fund their criminal cause, and to test how the artificial dogs and rabies would function in a true setting. As for the other men, the followers, it seemed they all had their own reasons for aligning with the Turnbulls. Some likely followed orders because they were well paid, others were no doubt promised great positions in the new order of the Engineering Hall, while a few from faraway lands were disturbed by the Queen's rule and simply wanted her gone.

The Queen didn't give the Turnbulls the satisfaction of looking at them further. She spoke to an officer from Scotland Yard. "Arrest these treasonous leeches."

"It'll be my pleasure, Your Majesty." The officer handcuffed the outraged Cameron Turnbull. "I hereby arrest you in the name of Her Majesty the Queen."

Turnbull spit in his face and attempted to punch him. The officer flinched and struggled to restrain him while Aiden Turnbull kicked another policeman who approached him with handcuffs. More of the Queen's men rushed in to subdue them.

"You should've promised your daughter to me!" Cameron Turnbull shouted at my father.

Benjamin, Peter, and I, still in our cloaks, faces obscured by masks and burlap, turned to watch in dismay as Turnbull screamed at the top of his frantic voice. "Not Abercrombie! Not some pathetic naturalist!"

"That's enough!" ordered my father.

"Sanctimonious bastards! All of you!" screamed Turnbull.

Turning away from the firestorm, I whispered to my two friends, "I don't wish to hear any more." Trying to recover from the onslaught of emotions, I strode a few steps away and nearly tripped over a fallen assailant who'd had his neck chewed. In the moonlight, metal shavings from the bats glimmered in his wounds.

"*Oh*," I said with my heart thumping, suddenly understanding so much more. I took a deep breath to regain my composure.

"What is it?" asked Benjamin.

"I know why Jillian doesn't grow stronger." I pivoted to face him. The hem of my cloak spun about my boots. We were no longer needed here. "Come!" I called, eager to find Jillian.

Benjamin and Peter sprinted behind me.

"We need my father's supplies."

"But he'll need them, Charlotte. He and his assistants to help the wounded," said Peter.

"They've brought plenty more." I knew my father would focus on calming the Queen if she required it, and would call for Dr. Kenyon to help organize medical attention for the fallen men.

When we reached the outer field and the horses that carried the medical supplies, I lifted my father's surgical bag. We raced across the grass, through the lanes and trees, and back to the carriage where we'd left Jillian.

"Hurry!" I shouted to my friends. "Before it's too late!"

CHAPTER THIRTY-ONE

"I think Jillian has poisoned metal lodged inside her shoulder," I explained, panting from the run. "Similar to the fallen man I just witnessed." Peter and Benjamin knocked on the dilapidated coach, hidden among the trees.

Polly opened the door. "You all right?" she asked hesitantly, then peered out to look at us and the night sky. When she saw no bats, she relaxed.

"We're fine," I said. "And you, Polly?"

She nodded to indicate she was unharmed.

Benjamin tore off his burlap mask and cloak. "The Queen is secure, too."

Peter removed his fencing mask. "How is Jillian?"

Polly sighed. "Not well, I'm afraid."

She opened the door further to reveal Jillian lying motionless on the bench. I stepped in, slid off my mask, and knelt on the floor. Polly moved my satchel of medical supplies off the bench behind me and sat down to help.

"The metal fragments inside her shoulder are seeping poison," I said. "The antidote that worked for me and Peter isn't strong enough to overcome it."

"So that's it." Standing outside the door, Peter stripped off his black cloak to reveal a dark shirt and trousers. "We never had any leftover metal."

Benjamin came forward and opened the other door. It gave me far more light, for the moon shone in and there was a gaslight on that side. He leaned over, his tall body overshadowing Jillian's frail one, to get a better look. Her lips were still a purplish hue, her face greenish, her breathing even shallower than it had been. I noticed someone had left a washcloth and canteen beside her tangled hair. Polly must've tried to comfort her using what she could find in my satchel.

Peter brought my father's medical bag to my side. "You plan to surgically remove the metal?"

I tried to overcome my sudden bout of nerves. Could I possibly do this? "I thought I'd approach from the back of her shoulder to make a clean incision."

Peter ran a hand through his wavy brown hair. He rubbed his neck then looked at me, his brown eyes pleading. "You'll take good care, won't you?"

I nodded, my blond wig shifting about my face. I tugged it off and set it on the bench. "My best. But I don't believe you should watch."

"I'd like to assist if I may."

"Your presence will only make me nervous," I said. "You're her brother and I know how much she means to you. Please don't stay."

"I will," said Benjamin. "To assist."

Peter rubbed his neck again. "All right, then. I'll be over by those trees. Benjamin, call if you need me." He sauntered off into the shadows.

"I'll wait with Peter." Polly eased her way out. "My apologies, but I don't have a stomach for this."

I removed my cloak, opened my satchel, and used the cake of soap and canteen of water to wash my hands. Then I opened my father's medical bag. It had his name stitched into the inner folds of the leather: DR. JAMES SYCAMORE. I had to look past it or I'd never be able to overcome my anxiousness.

Charlotte, you must always be truthful to yourself and your beliefs.

"This is what I believe in," I whispered.

"What's that you say?" Benjamin stood on the grass by the open door.

"It's nothing." I removed a cloth drape, tucked it beneath Jillian's shoulder, and placed the surgical instruments on it. Scalpels, scissors, retractors, sutures, needles. I knew the instruments well, for I routinely boiled and disinfected them.

I studied Jillian's face. "I mustn't give her any pain medicine for the incision. Or chloroform to render her unconscious. Either one could slow her breathing so much that it would stop."

"Sounds reasonable," said Benjamin.

"You'll need to help me roll her toward the rear cushion so I can view the back of her shoulder."

He did as I asked. It took a few moments to position ourselves.

"There, that's it. Benjamin, please watch her face. If she turns bluer or seems in distress, tell me straightaway."

"Right."

I swabbed the back of her shoulder with cleansing tonic. She hadn't yet moved.

"Here I go."

The incision was easy to make. Easier than I thought. What I hadn't predicted was the amount of blood it would produce. I wiped it with gauze, but couldn't find any metal shavings.

"Benjamin, I can't see. There's a pair of magnifying goggles in my satchel." I nodded at the bag. "Can you put them on me?"

He rushed to secure the goggles to my face. My vision swam for a few seconds, then Jillian's wound magnified a hundred times. Arteries pounded, flesh throbbed, blue veins carried blood back to the heart, and blockages became apparent.

I went for the blockages, where I believed I'd find the fragments. My hands moved with speed and precision. Within seconds I was holding in my tweezers what appeared to be a metal dog's tooth. "One."

I pulled out another. "Two."

Three more smaller shavings. I took another long look. All the blockages were gone; only clean, healthy flesh remained.

"Put some antidote to her lips."

He did as I ordered, and Jillian jolted out of position. He softly swore.

"Hold her arms down," I said. "She can feel this. Thank God, she can finally feel this!"

I threaded the surgical needle, knotted the end, and closed her incision. She moaned and twisted, but Benjamin held her arms to her waist to keep her still while I stitched in layers. They were stitches I'd done a thousand times in my embroidery classes, the same ones I'd seen in my father's textbook.

When the suturing was completed, Benjamin helped me remove my goggles.

Jillian took one loud, deep breath. I quickly bandaged her shoulder with fresh supplies and repositioned her blouse as best I could. Her breathing had become much easier and the bluish tinge was leaving her face. I wrapped the bloody instruments in the cloth drape, then slid outside and quickly rinsed the blood from my hands.

"Are you done?" Polly called from a distance in the bright moonlight.

"Yes!"

"Would Mrs. B be proud of your stitchin'?"

Teary-eyed and emotional that the surgery had gone well, I nodded at her and smiled.

Peter, perhaps alarmed at the amount of blood I'd washed away, shouted as he paced beyond another tree. "Is she all right?"

"Yes, but I need to check on her once more!"

When I reentered the coach, I knelt beside Jillian. "Her lips are pinker," I said to Benjamin, watching her face come to life.

I looked at him, and we shared a glorious moment of achievement. The dark hair on his forehead was tipped with perspiration. The deep lines of concern in his face eased.

"You've been a true friend in all of this," I whispered to him. I didn't know exactly what to say, but I did need to tell him something, to explain the things I'd discovered in the past several hours. "You're the most loyal friend I could ever have." It sounded like such a childish thing to say.

After a slight hesitation, he placed a rough hand on my shoulder. Although the warmth seeped into my skin, his touch felt awkward, just as awkward as it had when he'd held my hand in the coach that night and I was so uncertain about what it meant. This time, perhaps we both knew his hand didn't truly belong on my shoulder.

He let his fingers slide away, and nodded at me as if he perceived what I was trying to communicate, even if it hurt for me to express it and for him to hear it: that there was nothing burning between us. Or at least that there wasn't anymore.

In that quiet way of his, he simply said, "I wasn't sure. But now I know."

If God granted me a wish to choose my own brother, I would surely choose Benjamin.

He tilted his head and added, "You were brilliant tonight, Charlotte."

Jillian took a loud breath beside us, and the sound captured my attention. Her eyes fluttered open. Those clear, wonderful brown eyes flashed up at the roof. She saw Benjamin's face first. He murmured in delight.

She turned her head toward me. She frowned as she searched my face, then the vial in my hands and my father's surgical bag.

"Did I pass out or something?" she asked weakly.

"Something," said Benjamin with a gentle smile.

"You're going to be fine, Jillian. We removed metal fragments from your shoulder." I wiped her forehead with a cool cloth. "Are you in tremendous pain? As soon as we see your breathing is fine, we can offer a morphine tablet. Another few minutes, all right?" For the moment, the antidote was likely keeping her discomfort at bay, for her color was healthy and she moved with ease.

"Where's Peter?" she asked softly.

I looked out through the open door to the wall of trees. "I'll get him."

꧁꧂

I stepped away from the coach into moonlight and found Peter staring at me from across the grass. Polly turned and rushed to the coach to see Jillian, but Peter stayed where he was. I made my way over to talk to him. A row of swaying branches shielded us from the view of the others.

"Your sister's fine," I said. "Awake and talking."

Peter exhaled with such pleasure that it buoyed me. His firm jaw unclenched, his broad shoulders relaxed, and his warm brown eyes sparkled.

"You found metal?"

"Two big slugs. Dog's teeth. And a few smaller pieces."

"That was the problem! You were right."

I smiled. "Not a problem anymore."

"It's all fixed, then, isn't it? My sister. Turnbull's capture. Maybe now your father and Scotland Yard will believe that we didn't attack the guards at the house, that they attacked us."

I nodded, basking in the favorable turn of events. The night breeze lifted the edge of my skirts, strained the cloth of my blouse, and wafted through my hair.

My hair ties had come undone, and the warm wind captured the loose black strands. They danced across my face. Peter moved to brush them away.

I held my breath at his closeness.

"Charlotte, I thought of you," he murmured.

"When?"

"When I was away, fighting pirates."

He'd thought of me? And how I'd often thought of him—what he might be doing. Were they making him work hard. Did he know how to hoist the sails and run the anchor. What interesting people had he met along the way, and would I ever see him again.

But I didn't admit it. Instead, I whispered a soft "Oh?"

"Umm-hmm. I wondered how it might feel to touch your hair. It's silky."

My lips opened slightly. My heart drummed in warning.

"And then I came home and discovered you were engaged."

I frowned. "My father's doing."

"Not yours?"

"I've never even met the man."

Peter dipped nearer.

I tried to pull away, I truly did. But my body would not obey my command. His sleeve brushed mine, and the skin on my arms quivered in response. I felt so very different with Peter than I ever had with anyone else.

I looked up at him in the moon's soft rays, his hair windswept, his shoulders straining at the corners of his shirt, his jaw so straight and true.

When he stepped closer, I could barely breathe.

When he reached out and tucked his fingers around the nape of my neck, I could barely think.

When he lowered his lips to my own, I could barely imagine anything this exhilarating.

My first kiss.

His mouth was warm and tender and evoked such a surge of reaction that it made my blood pound and my muscles throb.

It hadn't lasted but a moment when Polly's voice called from the coach. "Where's Peter?"

He pulled away from me, but ran his thumb along my chin. Every inch of my skin that he touched caught fire.

It had been an unexpected kiss, unplanned, yet perfect.

Tonight in the coach, when he'd declared that he would come back to London to find me and save me if I were imprisoned, was when I truly knew how I felt about him. I wanted to be with him every minute of every day.

Yet sadly . . . I was engaged to someone else. Even though I didn't wish to be, I still felt loyal to . . . loyal to the bonds of possible marriage. I would never do anything to taint my engagement until I was able to sever it completely. That was how a decent girl behaved. She didn't dally with one boy while engaged to another.

"The kiss was my fault," Peter whispered. He dropped his hand and stepped back into darkness. "I shouldn't have done it."

"I'm glad you did," I murmured, and somehow I think he understood.

CHAPTER THIRTY-TWO

I was still reeling from the incredible kiss when the others joined us. I turned beneath the rustling trees to see Benjamin and Jillian approaching, he supporting her by the elbow. I was relieved to see her take a few steps, however halting. Polly walked beside them, proudly watching.

Benjamin looked from my face to Peter's, and I wondered if he suspected anything. He didn't appear to be troubled; in fact he had a ready smile for Jillian and Polly, and seemed to be enjoying their company. Could he tell I'd just been kissed? Could anyone?

My face felt hot and flushed.

"Jillian, you do look wonderful." I took a few steps closer and smoothed her messy reddish hair. The fresh morning wind cooled my blistering cheeks.

"It's nice to be standing . . . but I'm in need of that morphine."

"Of course!" I swooped past her into the carriage and returned with it. She took the tablet as I continued to tidy my equipment, packing things into my satchel and my father's surgical bag. I repositioned the blond wig on my head. If anyone from the Palace recognized me or Polly now, coming home in the early morning, we'd be harshly punished.

Polly scrambled with her disguise. "Dawn is breakin'. I'm scheduled for duty at six!"

"I have to get back, too." Benjamin bundled up his cloak.

"If my father discovers I've been out against his wishes," I said, "he'll pack my things and send me away to a convent." I turned to Peter, who'd grown unusually quiet. "What are your plans?"

His dark eyes shimmered with emotion, then he turned to his sister beside him. "It's time we go home, Jillian. What do you say?"

Jillian sighed and leaned her head against his arm. "I think Mother's been through enough."

Benjamin shoved his daggers into his boots, lifted my father's medical bag, and draped it with his cloak. "Aren't you fearful of what the authorities might do when they discover you're home?" Benjamin asked Peter.

"They have Turnbull and his brother in custody," Peter replied. "They'll see that Jillian and I no longer have rabies—not that I'll tell them about the antidote. I'll let them assume the artificial rabies wore off. As for the attempted-murder charge, I'll speak the truth. One of the guards assaulted Jillian, and I protected her in self-defense."

"They know Benjamin and I were there," I reminded him.

"I'll say you were two helpful people off the street," Peter said with a great deal of thought, "also targeted by the guards. That I don't know who you are."

It seemed a reasonable plan.

Polly and I were the only ones who donned our cloaks and wigs; the others thought they'd be less noticeable this time of day in their normal attire.

I disliked leaving them, but we parted with warm good-byes. I couldn't very well embrace Peter or kiss him again with everyone watching, though I wished to. He gave me a private smile and his gaze lingered, making my skin ripple with gooseflesh. Then he and Jillian were off.

Polly rushed to my side. Benjamin, carrying my father's bag, led the way for us in the opposite direction to Jillian and Peter and hailed a hansom cab. We stopped two streets before the gates of the Royal Mews, where Polly and I parted with Benjamin. I took the bag. Polly and I wedged ourselves among dozens of gardeners and laborers. Once we were on the grounds, we removed our wigs, though we remained cloaked so as not to attract attention. If someone spotted us, we would claim I couldn't sleep and we were out for an early morning stroll.

No one stopped us.

We raced up the servants' stairs, nodding at two footmen who came charging round the corner. "Mornin', Miss Sycamore," said one. "Mornin', Polly."

"Sir," she mumbled.

We reached the upper floor where my chambers were located. I removed my cloak, using it to conceal my father's medical bag, hoping no one would notice the dirt and oil streaks on the bottom of my skirts. Polly carried my satchel.

I peeked past the corner. Mrs. Burnhamthorpe was seated outside my door, reading the morning paper, holding it two inches from her face. What was I to do? It had to be past six. I heard the rumble of voices at the other end of the hall. It was one of the chambermaids. "The Turnbulls were workin' right outta the Engineerin' Hall!"

"The audacity," replied Russett, rubbing his large, vested belly. "Has Snow been released?"

Mrs. Burnhamthorpe shot up from her seat. "I heard he was." She placed the newspaper on her chair and slid away to join the conversation, which was now taking place outside my father's medical rooms.

"Now," Polly whispered in my ear. "While their backs are turned."

I lunged down the hall toward my chambers, Polly at my heels. I turned the handle, slipped inside alone, and took a deep breath.

"Polly!" Mrs. Burnhamthorpe called from the hallway.

"Yes, ma'am?" she replied, outside the door.

"Is Miss Sycamore awake? Would she like to take her breakfast?"

"I was about to check with her this minute, ma'am."

"Where's your cap, girl?"

"S-sorry, ma'am. I believe I left it in her sittin' room last night."

"Well, put it on, for heaven's sake."

"Yes, ma'am."

There was a light tap on the door, and I swung it open to let Polly enter.

Once inside, we collapsed on the settees. We were both dressed in dowdy skirts and blouses. We both needed to wash. More banging on the door startled us.

"Charlotte!" My father's voice.

"Just a minute, sir," I hollered back, glued to the floor in a panic.

"Quickly, beneath the covers." Polly took her apron from my satchel. I tossed my father's medical bag into my traveling trunk, then dived into the bed as she tucked the duvet up to my chin. I decided I would keep my father's medical bag, perhaps for future use. I would need to rinse and disinfect the equipment when he wasn't looking. He had plenty more bags to replace the missing one.

Polly tidied her apron over her skirts and walked calmly to the door. When she opened it, my father strode in. He looked at her head. Her face flamed a deep red as she realized she still wasn't wearing her cap.

He turned to me. He had shaved since last night, and wore a fresh shirt and cravat. "How're you feeling, Charlotte?"

"Quite better, thank you."

"The color's returned to your face."

"You look well, too." I leaned back on my pillows, grateful to see him alive.

"It's been a mad night. Have you heard?"

"Polly's been filling me in."

"Ah, I see." He lowered himself onto the edge of my bed. My mattress rocked. He patted my hand, and I inhaled the calming scent of his shaving soap. "I'm pleased you slept through it. Thank you for listening to me and staying put."

⚹

"Where are you taking me, sir?" Later that afternoon, my father walked me through the Palace gardens. Flowers bloomed and butterflies swirled past my braided hair. The sun moved behind a fluffy cloud. I'd gotten a solid six hours of uninterrupted sleep and felt bright-eyed. The swelling in my leg had subsided to nearly normal.

"Mr. Snow wishes to speak with you."

I halted in my tracks. My navy skirt swayed at my heels. I wasn't sure I was prepared to face him yet.

"Come along, Charlotte. There's something . . . else I must tell you."

His voice dropped and I panicked. The pressure in my chest instantly soared. "What is it?" What did my father know about me and my friends?

"It's about Mr. Abercrombie, I'm afraid."

Oh, *that*. I sighed. "Yes?"

"He sends word through his parents that his ship has been delayed."

"Why, may I ask?"

"For business reasons, apparently."

"But he manages that ship. He's the one who decides if it's delayed on business, does he not?"

"Yes, I'm afraid so. I'm sorry, Charlotte."

My mind raced to comprehend this. He was postponing his arrival. It was up to him to direct the ship and its business, and he was delaying it.

This could mean only one thing.

My plan had worked! He'd taken a good look at my dim-witted, childish letters, and he no longer desired to marry me!

I tried not to sound too delighted. I attempted to mask the cheer in my voice. "Well, I see." I kept my facial muscles flat. "Did he give another date of arrival?" *No, please no.*

"Well, that's—that's the point." My father stumbled over the words, which wasn't like him. "He hasn't given another date."

Oh, joy!

I fluttered my lashes. "I don't see how I'm supposed to take this. It's quite rude, is it not, for him to treat you this way, sir? You've arranged this marriage. And to think, he sent the message to his parents and not to you."

My father sputtered. His dark eyes flickered with anger. His shoulders reared back. He adjusted his cravat as though it was a tight noose. I rarely saw him this upset. "I think I may have been too hasty with this man. Perhaps he's unprepared to be your husband."

Oh, sweet heaven above!

Don't gloat. Don't gloat.

"As you wish, sir."

We turned and continued to stroll along the beautiful sunny path, with its sunny flowers and the sunny sun beaming on my face. This was most excellent news! Mr. Abercrombie thought I was dull and boring, and everything else I hoped to convey!

What would this mean for Peter? My life and future had been returned to me.

I wondered which of my letters had caused Mr. Abercrombie to turn sour. It was too soon for him to have received my last one, so it had to be one of the others. Perhaps even the first.

Dear Esteemed Sir,

It was truly an honor to hear of our engagement. I was in the gardens at the time, playing Ring Around the Rosy with the four- and five-year-old children, when I was informed we would be married, and that this meant you would buy me my own pony.

How happy I am!

My heart races to think of those soft fluffy ears, and how those lips tickle when they eat carrots out of my hand.

Now that we are an engaged couple, I hope you understand that this might be the very last trip you ever take for your employment. I look forward to the day you might take over my maid's duties to teach me French and German—she hates it so when I cry—and to sit with me while I practice my cross-stitching, night after night. I know you will have much more patience with me than—well, let's only say I would be grateful for a husband who will have patience.

It's late evening now, and I shall set out for a walk. Have you ever squinted up at the night sky to watch the stars, only to find yourself getting the most awful headache?

Well, I hope someday to meet you.

"Charlotte?" My father nudged me as we walked through the Palace gardens. "Charlotte, are you listening?"

"Yes, absolutely." *Peter. Peter. Peter.*

"Charlotte, please don't fret over this debacle. Rest assured, you will one day marry well."

I nodded gently. My father could still try to ruin everything by choosing another stranger for me to wed . . . but I didn't see that in the gracious smile he offered now, and I wouldn't allow myself to be pessimistic.

"Come along," he said. "We must speak to Mr. Snow, and I have a two o'clock appointment with Her Majesty."

We entered the Engineering Hall, and the power of the glass spider rumbled through me. I took in the wondrous sight of gushing water against polished steel. Such brilliance took place beneath these vaulted ceilings, yet it was odd being here, knowing that it had housed such evil minds.

I had heard from Polly, who had heard it from a footman, who had heard it from a gardener, who had heard it from an Engineering Hall cleaning servant, that the bats had been made right here in this building. The large underground room where the Turnbulls supposedly had been working on the self-dousing stoves was a decoy for the true experiment. The two brothers had access to all the steam power they needed while creating the mechanical devices. They'd ordered materials on the Queen's purse and had hidden everything here. No one ever went into that sloppy room. The last time I'd tried, I'd nearly stepped into a puddle of oil at the door. The brothers had likely put the puddle there on purpose to keep others out.

I had heard more specifics about the night robberies, too—that their purpose had been to pay the other fighters who'd gone into battle with the Turnbulls. Some of the robbers had been promised enough money that they would never have to work for the Crown again.

"What will happen to the Turnbulls, sir?"

"They're headed to trial. There is plentiful evidence to convict them and their six remaining men who weren't killed in the battle. They've caused such a waste of life. It will end in death sentences for all. But that's not something you should concern yourself with."

I shuddered and rubbed my arms through the white linen of my blouse.

"Miss!" The shout made me turn.

Mr. Snow approached in his usual gruff manner, head of white hair billowing about his wide shoulders. He indicated that we were to follow him into the gardens. My father strode beside me, completely silent.

We entered the peaceful gardens with the lake well in view, lined by sweeping willow trees. When we turned a corner, I saw Annabelle sitting in the shade. She rose, golden tail wagging, and nudged my calf in greeting. Five pups leaped alongside her, pulling and nipping at each other. My, how they'd changed in only a few days. Gone were the limp ragamuffins, replaced by jumping brothers and sisters. All with eyes open!

Mr. Snow nodded at the pups. "As soon as they're old enough, I'd like you to have your pick."

"But my father—" I turned to gaze at him.

My father shrugged his shoulders, his gray jacket shaded by the branches of the willow. "Mr. Snow has convinced me a pup would do you good. That a dog builds character and responsibility. The staff of the Queen's kennels could walk him for you, if on occassion you should be occupied. He needn't sleep in your room, so the germs could be contained."

"Thank you, thank you," I told them both, so unexpectedly cheered by all the wonderful news that I could have bounced from the sky. I swept my little black cocker spaniel into my arms. His forehead, marked with the white diamond, was still a mass of folded silky fur, which made him look as though he was concentrating intensely, as a writer might.

"Poet. That's what I shall name you. Poet."

My father smiled, said his good-byes, and left.

I nestled Poet beneath my chin and sat down on the plush grass.

Mr. Snow eased down beside us. "I'm told that you defended me when no one else would."

"I didn't think you could possibly be so mean."

He chuckled. Mr. Snow and I continued to play with the dogs beneath the willow tree. From a distance, I imagined, we looked a lot like relations, he the grandfather I never had and always longed for, spending time with his granddaughter and her new pup on a beautiful London day.

❧

Summoned to the Royal Mews later that afternoon by my father, I rushed along the path, taking Polly with me.

"What, pray tell, is the hurry?" Polly pinned a loose strand of apricot hair to her cap.

"I'm not certain. My father said Peter and Jillian are meeting him, and that he must make some decisions." I prayed it wouldn't be bad news. I was too concerned to think about anything but their safety.

When we stepped into the breezy air of the stables, Fiona and Theodora, some of their untamed blond hair flying about their ears, were selecting horses. They were outfitted in new riding boots and crops. "If you ride with us, Charlotte," said Fiona, "I promise to show you how to maneuver a new jump. I know how weak a rider you are."

I wasn't weak at all and had a mind to tell her so, but strode past her instead. "Another time."

I heard Theodora nudge her sister. "Look, there's Benji."

Two stalls over, Benjamin was expertly brushing the coat of a draft horse. It was no wonder girls were entranced by him. When he spotted me and Polly, he waved a friendly hello. Always charming, he gave me no more attention than he gave Polly now, or Jillian last night, and I wondered how deeply he'd been infatuated with me. Perhaps not as deeply as I'd fancied. In any case, I was pleased that he didn't seem to be dwelling on the feelings.

As Polly and I walked through the stables, Benjamin lifted a bucket of oats, then tripped and nearly dropped it. Polly giggled, mesmerized by everything he did. He followed behind us, pretending he was delivering the oats somewhere, but I suspected he actually lingered in order to hear what this meeting was about. His concern for Jillian's health had been obvious last night, the same concern we all shared.

When we entered the carriage house connected to the stables, I spotted not only Peter and Jillian, but their mother standing with them. Her uniform was freshly pressed. She was shorter than Jillian and twice as wide, but her dark eyes were just as friendly and her hair was the same rich auburn.

Jillian and Peter's faces brightened at the sight of me, but I looked away in case my approaching father noticed the glances between us. I especially looked away from Peter's gaze.

Detective Plumb, the same man I'd met in the Queen's presence when he had told us about the stolen medical wagon, stood beside Mrs. Moreley with his arms behind his back. His posture lacked the strain I'd seen before.

"Mrs. Moreley," said my father, stepping closer. "Good morning."

"Sir," she said. "How are you this fine day?"

"Never better. And your children?" My father searched their faces.

"Healing nicely, sir. Thank you for sending Dr. Kenyon earlier today."

"Any word on who the surgeon was?"

My heart fluttered in dismay. Peter and Jillian looked alarmed. Beside me, Polly stopped shuffling her feet. My father knew. That's why he'd called me here.

"Still haven't found him," said Peter.

"Let me understand this. It was a dark night. You'd left your sister's side to obtain something to eat. At that little goat barn, where your things were found. Two men in dark clothing apparently entered, you were told, and patched your sister's shoulder."

"Fixed it up good, sir." Peter stood with his arms at his sides, unwavering.

"If I may, Dr. Sycamore—" In the surrounding stalls, one of the other carriage cleaners, a thin, hunched man, rubbed an oily rag over a coach wheel. "People are callin' him the Robin Hood Surgeon."

My father frowned at the man and shook his head with indignation. "Because he's the one who also stole the Queen's wagon filled with medical supplies?"

"Stealing from the rich to give to the poor. Like Robin Hood, sir."

I was stunned that they'd given me a name. A smattering of soft cheers arose from the back of the stalls. My father whirled round in anger, but whoever was there dipped from our view.

"These are *my* things he stole, as representative of the Queen. Perhaps he also took my medical bag. He's a spy. A traitor to the country. When he's caught, he'll hang for high treason!"

The thin man shook his head, Adam's apple bobbing. "Shame he did it to you, sir."

"The Queen's put a price on this thief's head. A thousand pounds!" my father declared.

The thin man whistled. The carriage house fell silent. I estimated this was several years' salary for an average working man.

Heat scorched my face. My stomach clenched. This was a dangerous game I was playing. Not only was I jeopardizing my neck, but my father's, too. Who would believe he had no inkling that his own daughter was Robin Hood?

"There's no need to think about that today. We're here for better news." My father turned his dark head toward Mrs. Moreley and smiled. "I'm told you'll be working for us again, madam. Assisting the carriage cleaners?"

"Yes, sir. I'm very fond of my job."

"Very good. Now, I'm told you have something else to tell me?"

"Sir, as I explained to the police, the guard—the one my children are accused of attacking—well, sir, last night that same guard drank to oblivion. He tried to . . . tried to assault my neighbor. She broke her arm runnin' from him."

The police detective nodded to confirm it. The gray hair at his temples matched the gray of his drab suit. "Seems her children were telling the truth," he said in that deep, rattling voice. "He's a lecherous man. I've had a word with him. We're dropping the charges against these two. And whoever it was who helped them flee that night."

"Well," said my father. "That is a lot of news."

I exhaled at the amazing turn. Jillian and I exchanged glances. I looked across at Benjamin, who was nodding in relief at Peter.

"So I was wonderin', Dr. Sycamore," said Mrs. Moreley, "if you wouldn't mind, sir, giving my daughter the all-clear—I mean her shoulder and all—to come back here so she can work with me cleanin' the carriages."

My father softened at the sight of Jillian. Her shoulder would never be the same. No one said it, but everyone knew.

"I believe that can be arranged."

Jillian beamed in my direction. Benjamin glanced at her, very pleased, and I knew he'd help her in whatever way he could when she returned to the workplace.

My father would never know what happened that awful night a week ago; but then, fathers don't need to know everything.

Finally I looked at Peter, as I'd been avoiding doing for the last twenty minutes. When his dark, warm eyes met mine, his smile was riveting. My stomach jumped and my throat went dry. He was more muscled than the men around him. His short brown hair ruffled in the breeze that filtered through the open bays. His tanned skin gave him a look of brawn and strength. Gazing at him, I could well imagine him sword fighting with pirates at sea, then one day fending off a slew of young ladies awaiting him onshore. I wagered that day had come.

I couldn't wait to tell him about my new freedom—that I was no longer engaged.

I knew, I just knew, we were opening a whole new world.

"Welcome back," my father said to Jillian, then Peter.

There were handshakes all around. I moved closer, close enough that Peter brushed my fingers with his own. His touch rippled through me. It was only a fleeting graze, unseen by anyone else, but it meant everything. As laughter and warmth filled the carriage house, I peered at my circle of friends, Polly and Benjamin and Jillian and Peter, and realized I'd found my place among them. There was no place I'd rather be than here, with them. They had showed me that I wasn't so odd that no one could ever like me. That my interest and ability in medicine, which came naturally to me, wasn't strange. That they would always stand beside me, and that I should always do what I believed was right.

When I was with them, I liked who I was.

Looking at their bright faces, I wondered what my friends were doing later this evening . . . say, around midnight.